The Fall and Rise of Lucy Charlton

Elizabeth Gill

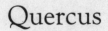

Quercus

First published in Great Britain in 2014 by

Quercus
55 Baker Street
7th Floor, South Block
London
W1U 8EW

A CIP catalogue record for this book is available
from the British Library

ISBN 978 1 78087 849 2 (PB)
ISBN 978 1 78087 850 8 (EBOOK)

10 9 8 7 6 5 4 3 2 1

Typeset by Ellipsis Digital Limited, Glasgow

Printed and bound in Great Britain by
Clays Ltd, St Ives plc

In memory of all the wonderful moggies we had over the years. Among them were Dickens and Spider, Thomas, Dogtanian, Lucky Randolph and Little Miss Tabbytoes, who for obvious reasons went by the slick name of Kitty.

ONE

Durham City, 1919

Lucy Charlton went home to Newcastle for her sister's wedding. The preparations for the wedding were all that her mother and Gemma had talked about for months. The wedding dress was the most important thing of all. Gemma and her mother had chosen the dress in a shop in Grainger Street and Gemma wanted her sister to see it. She was going for her final fitting the first afternoon that Lucy was at home.

The inside of the shop was hushed. As they entered it a fair-haired woman came out from an inner door and ushered Gemma away. Lucy sat down on a big sofa. Another woman appeared and offered Lucy tea. After a few minutes Gemma came out of the fitting room. Lucy couldn't help but stare.

The dress made her sister look like a doll. Her cheeks were flushed, her eyes were bright and her hair was so shiny that it looked like a wig. Her fluttering hands and the cream satin material set her beyond reality. Lucy was astonished. The dress ended just above the ankle with wide skirts, like a three-tiered cake. It didn't suit her. In the cap with a trailing veil, Gemma looked tiny and scared, but Lucy knew what she must say – the anxious eyes of her sister told her so.

'It's beautiful,' she said. 'It's so lovely . . . and you look just right in it.'

'Do I?' Gemma said, hesitating. She needed Lucy to say more, to say that she had never seen another bride who looked better, so she did. She could hear the echo of her voice afterwards; she hoped it did not sound as hollow as she thought it did. Was that envy? She could never look that way. Gemma turned and turned like the figure in a musical jewellery box when you lifted the lid and some plaintive air came forth to jangle at your nerves.

Round and round she went and Lucy sat there, admiring and anxious, yet when Gemma had gone back in the room to change Lucy found that she was shaking, and it was not the kind of problem a cup of tea would solve.

Finally, when the seamstress was happy with the dress, they left. Lucy was glad of the air and suggested they should go to Pumphreys in the Cloth Market and have coffee. Pumphreys always smelled so good with the coffee roasting. The windows there were intricate green glass and the sofas red velvet.

They sat down at a table near the back of the room and she said to her sister, 'Are you feeling all right?'

Gemma looked offended. 'What do you mean?' But Gemma didn't let Lucy get any more words out. She looked down at the table and she said, 'I know you don't want me to marry. You've made it perfectly obvious and I wish now that I hadn't asked you to be my bridesmaid even though you are my sister. You pretend that you like Guy but it's so obvious that you don't. You hardly ever come home and you never answer my letters and you don't seem to want to be associated with us as if we are beneath you somehow now that you're at university with all your clever friends in Durham.'

'Gemma, that's not true!' Lucy exclaimed, horrified.

Gemma turned to her, eyes glassy with tears. 'Guy is a perfectly nice man and I'm sorry that you're jealous of him but really you know we cannot go on as we are. Don't you understand anything?'

'I don't know what you mean.'

'Of course you don't. You never think about anybody but yourself. Father isn't well and we have no money. All I have is that I can marry a respectable man who will help us, but you . . . you . . .' Gemma got up and ran out of the coffee house.

Lucy stared, astonished, as the customers watched; some of them had turned around, teacups or cake in hand. Then she got up and ran after her sister, but it was not easy. Gemma set a good pace and they were most of the way home when Lucy, panting, caught up with her.

Gemma had stopped, by then, out of breath.

Lucy could not help saying, 'What happened to the money? Daddy is a wonderful lawyer. He makes lots of money.'

Gemma looked at her from pitying and rather glassy eyes. 'He isn't making enough any more. He gets very tired. He isn't well and he has to pay for my wedding and for your stupid university course or whatever you call it. You were never happy with how things were, always wanting to change everything. Nothing was good enough for you and now look.'

'What is wrong with Daddy?'

Gemma shook her head and took her handkerchief from her pocket. She spent a long time wiping her eyes and blowing her nose, turned half away from Lucy. Finally she screwed the handkerchief into a soggy ball and returned it to her pocket, her cheeks still wet with tears.

'Nobody seems to know and you mustn't say anything because we aren't supposed to be aware of it. Mother kept it from me until I found Daddy wandering around the living room, confused. He doesn't remember things as well as he did. But Mother is happy now I'm marrying Guy. She won't have to worry about anything any more because Guy has money.'

Lucy could not imagine that her father was ill and she did not know it. She had always been closer to him than Gemma. In a way Gemma was her mother's child and she was her father's. Lucy had always been very much aware that her father had dearly wanted a son and she had tried to be that son. She had thought she was doing the right thing; her father was proud of her for being so academically clever and one of the first women ever to go to Durham University to study law.

Lucy had seen the light in his eyes and even though it had been very hard to leave when she wanted to be here with him, in his office and by his side, she had left because it was the only way she could study law and make him happy. Now she felt as if she had done the wrong thing.

She looked again at her sister. Gemma had always been beautiful – red-haired, creamy-skinned, eyes like emeralds

– and she was a pale imitation – tall and rangy rather than neat and slim, her eyes darker, her hair not quite blonde and not quite red and frizzy. It didn't matter what she did with it, it could not be tamed. Now Gemma was thin and pale and sad about their father and Lucy wanted to put an arm around her except that Gemma would have shrugged it off.

'But you do want to marry Guy?' She immediately wished she could take back the words, but they needed to be said.

Gemma's face was flushed with tears. 'I like him very well.'

It was a sentence that Lucy did not forget.

'It's easy for you,' Gemma said and she walked away.

Lucy couldn't imagine how her sister thought that things were easier in Durham except that she had been able to leave home other than to marry, but she knew that was not something Gemma had ever wanted. She caught up with her sister and they walked slowly home and didn't speak at all.

Lucy had dreaded Gemma's wedding day and now she knew why. Gemma was obliged to marry well and Lucy no longer wondered why she did not care for the sound of Guy's voice in the hall. She wished he had done something which would pinpoint him as the enemy so she could say to Gemma that she must not marry him, but she could see things so much more clearly now than she ever had before. Her parents had nothing but the damp house beside the river. Her grandfather had died young and her father had had to keep his mother and his sisters and all of his family too. Their house beside the Tyne was very slowly sinking into the sand, into the silt, into the very river itself. She felt it was sinking beneath her expectations.

It was the night before the wedding and the house was full of presents. Gemma had been keen to open them and couldn't wait for Guy to arrive. When he did, he laughed and said it would be all table napkins and that he had no interest in such things. There were velvet canteens of cutlery and tall vases in red and purple which Gemma grimaced at.

Gemma exclaimed afresh at each opened gift. Lucy had no more interest than Guy in silver and crockery, but she had to admit that the dinner service would look good upon the oak table which Guy's parents had given them as a wedding present, along with a dozen chairs. They were buying a modest house in Jesmond, which Gemma had not offered to take her sister to visit.

Lucy's bridesmaid dress had flounces. Guy's sister and his three cousins were to wear the same peach-coloured outfits with little bonnets with orange ribbons tied under their chins. They would carry small baskets from which they would strew the aisle with rose petals, the last from Guy's mother's garden. She had kept them aside for this very occasion; they were cream and yellow and orange to suit. Lucy was silently appalled. She thought she looked like Little Bo Peep.

Lucy had become aware that her parents were paying for everything; her mother was always with lists about her – how many people were attending and what flowers would adorn the church, the pews, the altar. The reception could not be at their home, to her mother's chagrin, as it was not big enough to accommodate all Guy's relatives and friends. Instead it was to be at a huge hotel in Newcastle, not a usual idea, but her mother was proud that they had managed to afford it.

After Gemma had opened the presents, Guy had taken her to visit some relatives. It was usual for the groom to drink deeply on the eve of the wedding and for the bride to stay at home, but he had so much wanted Gemma to meet his mother's family from Kent that she had gone there for the evening.

They were late. Lucy lay awake, listening for her sister coming home, thinking that Gemma would not be there again, that their childhood and her place in her sister's life was set back and altered forever.

Lucy heard Gemma say something as they returned to the house. It was sharply uttered and Guy said something also. She heard her sister's footsteps come up the stairs and the door was closed quietly. She thought she heard something more downstairs. She put on a robe. She almost didn't go, but in the end she could not rest; she thought that perhaps Gemma had left her purse and Guy had discovered it in his motor, so she went down in the darkness and opened the front door. There was no light outside. She was about to go back when she saw Guy and she moved forward, beyond the house.

'Has Gemma forgotten something?' she said.

'Nothing.'

Lucy was about to go back inside when he came quickly to her and put his arms around her. Lucy pushed back from him.

'What on earth are you doing?' she said. She could smell the alcohol on him.

He gathered her against him and kissed her, and through

7

the material of his clothes and her nightwear she felt his body, warm and urgent, and her own senses screaming at her to move away. He was drunk; young men did such things. Perhaps that was what the raised voices had been before Gemma came inside. She pushed at him with both hands, thinking this would be the last of it and they would smile at it tomorrow when he had a sore head on his wedding day, but he did not let her go. His mouth became cruel, his tongue probing her teeth. She had not reasoned that a man was so strong. She had never had to think about how strength might be used against her.

He got hold of her arms, held her hands behind her back and opened the dressing gown she wore. He slid one hand inside her nightgown and onto first one breast and then the other. Her body went into shock, she was so repulsed. She screamed but he had his mouth on hers so that she was silenced. He put his tongue deep into her mouth. Panicking, her legs working against him, Lucy fought.

Out there in the street, in the black of night, he lifted her to him. She was so slight from university food, she found herself panting with the frantic attempt to break free. He held her up, pushed his cruel fingers between her flailing legs and then he went into her. Lucy wanted to scream with pain and shock, but he placed his hard hand over her mouth so that there was no sound.

She did not know how long this invasion went on. Under the strong hand she cried and sobbed as he hurt her. The water fell from her eyes, the snot from her nose, the spit brimmed from her lips and ran down her chin. Inwardly she begged him to stop the pain, the burning, the way that he seemed to eat her body, but he kept on and on until she grew weaker and the defeat turned her body limp. Soon he was holding her to stop her from falling.

Some vile eternity later he came out of her. She moaned with pain again under his hand, his body relaxed and then he let her loose. She couldn't stand, she was shivering, shaking and there was a disgusting sticky moisture between her legs. She was so sore that she thought it would never go away. Her body lurched and bent double and then she began to throw up.

'That serves you right. You nasty little tease. You thought you were so clever,' Guy said, and then he walked away.

She wanted to run after him, to strike him, but the cold air was piercing her body and she could barely stand. She drew down her nightdress and shivered. When she had finished being sick her mouth felt as vile as the rest of her and she sobbed against the wall of the house while the river flowed on regardless.

The crying went on and on until she thought it would never stop, so it was just as well that nobody else was there, that nobody but the night could hear her. She pulled the dressing gown around her. Her face was bitter and stinging with tears and the wind on the river pulled at her to come to it, to come and not to think about anything ever again. The water looked so dark and comforting; she loved the rhythm of how it moved, how it swelled and went on in its relentless quest towards the North Sea. She was sure that it would be warm once you grew used to it.

The house was behind her. When she turned, the door stood ajar, beckoning. She managed to reach the sanctuary of it. Once inside she essayed the stairs, crawling on all fours in order to get further up. She saw the entrance to her room. She made her way across the floor and went inside. She lay there until she was so chilled that she knew she must get up and when she did she reached the bed and it was all she could do. She lay down and slept, but it was not for long. The hurt between her legs brought her back to consciousness again and again.

She lit a candle by the small light that came through the window. She never drew the curtains; she didn't like to shut out the night and the river. She poured water into a bowl and found the soft sponge she liked so much and she put it between her thighs. It came away red and she sobbed again. The water was cool rather than cold and of some comfort. She took the towel and held it there and then she went back to the bed. She was exhausted now, and so shocked that she knew she would sleep. She was grateful to reach the comfort of mattress and pillows. She pulled the blankets over her and though she cried she could feel herself heading down the long passage towards sleep.

She awoke in the grey light and remembered. At first she thought it had been a dream, but she was still in pain so she was obliged to dismiss this thought with huge regret. It had happened. She lay there, trying to take in the fact that Guy had forced her the day before he married her sister. It couldn't have happened – but it had.

It must have been later than Lucy had imagined because the next moment she heard Gemma bounce into the room, talking of how pretty the day was – the sun was shining, had she seen it? That was a good omen.

She came over to the bed. Lucy couldn't move, she ached so much. Gemma stared down at her.

'You're very pale. You aren't ill? Not on my wedding day, surely.'

'I was sick in the night,' Lucy said. She didn't open her eyes; she didn't want to see her sister.

'You look awful.' Gemma sat down on the bed. Lucy moved as far away as she could. Her mind was racing. What could she do, what could she say, could she get somehow away from her without making obvious what had happened? She must. She could not ruin her sister's wedding day with such stupid things. And then all the horrors of the night came back in detail and she squeezed her eyes tighter against sudden tears.

An overwhelming desire to be sick came upon Lucy at that point. When she began to heave Gemma ran for the ewer which held the water for washing. Her sister stared into it. Lucy knew that it was bloody.

'Oh my God,' her sister said, and then Lucy was sick on the bed, over the bedclothes and everywhere. She retched when there was nothing left to come up. Gemma looked accusingly at her.

'How can you be ill today?' she said.

'It's nothing, really,' Lucy managed.

'Is it your monthlies?' Gemma said hopefully. 'No wonder you feel bad. I'll get Mother to make ginger tea. That always makes me feel better.'

'I'm fine, really. I'll get up in a minute.'

Gemma went out. For a few moments there was peace and then Lucy heard heavy footsteps on the stairs and her mother's breathing. She came briskly into the room.

11

'I've brought you some hot water and ginger. Sit up.'

Lucy couldn't somehow. Her mother deposited the jug of water on the marble-topped washstand and came over, clicking her tongue at the mess on the bed.

'You'd better get out and I'll strip it,' she said. 'You can't be comfortable like that.' Her mother swept aside the bed-clothes, saw the towel and the blood and the sticky moisture which Lucy had thought was washed away and was silent for a few moments. She studied her daughter carefully, she looked at her for a long time, and then she said in a strange stilted tone, 'What is this, Lucy?'

'Nothing.'

'It's not nothing.' Her mother sat down heavily on the bed and said, 'Have you had a man in here? Is there some lad you haven't told us of and you and him have been sinful together last night – is that it?'

Lucy didn't answer. She kept her eyes closed; somehow she thought that would help.

'Tell me,' her mother insisted. When Lucy had said nothing for what seemed like a long time she said, 'Do you want me to get your father up here so that you can tell him instead?'

Lucy thought of her father not being well, of how he hesi-tated over getting up from the table, how he could not think of what he was trying to say and how hard he laboured to appear as he should, and she couldn't think of the words to allay her mother's fears.

'Who is it?' her mother said. 'You've been hiding things from us. I knew no good would come from letting you go like that to be educated beyond your expectations. Is it some shiftless lad from Durham, or some educated fool who knows no better?'

Lucy found her voice. 'No,' she said.

'Then who is it?'

'Nothing happened except what always happens.' Lucy tried for normality in her voice but it didn't deceive her mother.

'Nothing of the sort,' her mother said and for the first time that Lucy could remember her mother slapped her face. She did it in a hard determined way as though it would send the words out of her daughter. Lucy's head swung back and her head, neck and cheek hurt. She was so shocked that she complied.

'It was Guy,' she said.

She heard her mother's intake of breath. 'What?' she said.

Lucy didn't think her mother wanted to hear it again. Her mother needed time and space to recover, as though anything would be the same again, or right. How could everything be fine one day and the next the whole wretched sky had fallen and everything was ruined? She couldn't believe it, even now.

Her mother towered over her, bigger than she had been before, blotting out the sun.

'Why would you say such a thing,' her mother said, 'when Gemma is all set to be happy? Do you want to ruin everything because she has landed such a man and you have not? He is a real gentleman, not some stupid student who doesn't know his backside from his elbow. Not that you managed to find anyone who would suit; not that you ever would. It must have been some daft lad with glasses and no more sense. Who was it, Lucy? You tell me now. Who is the lad you haven't mentioned? Somebody unsuitable? Somebody clever from a poor background? I wouldn't put it past you.'

When Lucy didn't respond her mother began to hit her around the head and face and neck and shoulders such as she never had before and as though she would never stop. Lucy sobbed as the blows came.

'How could you be so disrespectful and so unloving towards your sister as to say such a thing – and now, of all days?'

'He made me do it,' Lucy said, 'he forced me!'

She tried to burrow beneath the covers as her mother went on hitting her. She was not prepared for the door opening again and Gemma coming in. 'What on earth is wrong?' Gemma shouted. 'Stop hitting her.'

'She's been with some man and she hasn't even the decency to tell me who he was—' Her mother stopped short and then she said in a wavering voice, 'She says it's Guy, that he made her do it. She is a liar – she is no daughter of mine. She let somebody have her.'

'She what?' Gemma said. Her mother pushed aside the bedclothes completely and most of Lucy's ragged nightwear, and Gemma stared.

'Mother, she's covered in bruises—'

'Some women like it that way. Some stupid lad from Durham University has been sinful here in our own house with her. I knew she would get things wrong. I knew we should never have let her go. It's disgusting, that's what it is.'

Her mother flung from the room, sobbing and wailing, crying at such a rate that Lucy was astounded. There was a lawyer part of Lucy that said her mother should not have told Gemma. It could not help now.

'Is this true?' Gemma said, voice quavering.

A slight hope rose in Lucy. Was Gemma ready to believe her? At last, sanity of a kind, and yet what would their future be?

'I heard noise and I went outside—'

'What were you doing outside when I had said goodnight?' Gemma asked her. 'What could you possibly be doing out there at such a time?'

'I was just finding out what was happening—'

'You miserable liar,' her sister said. 'Guy would never have done such a thing. You have made this up and there has been another man, perhaps anybody that you could find on the street – with your looks you might be that desperate – and you were so jealous that you wanted to make me unhappy. How could you do it? Didn't you see that I had to marry, that one of us had to, and that you never would? You begrudge me a decent man because you are so skinny and plain and all you've got is your stupid ideas. You are jealous. You don't want me to leave here and yet how can I stay when my parents need me to marry well because it's all they'll ever have.'

Gemma was crying. Lucy started to think that the river could not have so much water as had been spilt here in the past few hours.

'Because I'm so much bonnier than you,' her sister said.

She sat up. She must convince Gemma that she could not marry such a man.

'You can't do this, Gem.' The use of the old childhood name would surely help, but it made Gemma dry-eyed and furious, Lucy could soon see. 'He's not who you think he is,' she continued. 'Not if he would do such a thing to your sister.'

'You so obviously thought he might,' Gemma said, with terrible calm, 'that you went out and offered yourself to him so openly in your nightwear. But he didn't. I know him well and, whoever you had here, you should not say such dreadful things. Don't you see what you have done to us?'

'Gemma—'

'I will not listen to it a moment longer. Guy is a gentleman and he loves me, and you have no one to love you because you are a horrible person, ugly and skinny and stupid. I'm sorry that you have not the ability to bring a man to you except by disgusting means. I'm so sorry for you, I really am.' Gemma turned and ran from the room.

Soon afterwards her father came in. He shuffled as though he didn't want to be there and she didn't blame him for that. She wanted to be back in Durham, or anywhere rather than here, rather than now. He coughed as he always did when he was worried, embarrassed or upset and she remembered how she had watched him struggling the previous day to appear as normal when he was not well. He appeared much older than he had looked the last time she had seen him. He had put on ten years.

'Oh, Lucy,' he said. 'What have you done?'

'Nothing. Nothing, really.'

She had to make him believe her. The tears ran freely down her face and somehow she was ashamed as though it were her fault. She had gone over and over it. Was it her fault? Had she really gone out there because she wanted him, because she was jealous he was marrying her sister? It was true that he was rich and handsome and charming and all the things that a man should be when you were marrying him, and she had envied Gemma in some ways, but it had not in a long time been something she wanted for herself. It was not her road, not her fate.

What she wanted was to be there with her father in the office and for him to admire her and for them to go forward together – so that if he really was ill then she could help, she could aid all her family and they would be proud of her and all be together as they were meant to be. When she finished in Durham she would come back in triumph as a junior solicitor and her father would introduce her to his most valued clients with pride in his voice, saying, 'And this my daughter, Lucy, who is to become a solicitor – and it will be Charlton and Charlton.' She dreamed of it, in gold, on the windows of the office. She had dreamed of it for so long.

His eyes were full of sorrow. She would not forget the way that he looked at her then. He did not believe her. She had never thought her father would do such a thing.

'I did nothing.' Her voice broke. 'You have to believe me; it wasn't my fault, really it wasn't. I just—'

'Your mother wants you gone from the house before Gemma is married. Your sister is crying and she too wishes you gone. There's nothing more you can do, as far as I can judge. Gemma is about to be married to a fine young man and I know you must wish it were you . . .'

She stared at him. He wasn't listening to her. He assumed her guilt. Why did he do that? She was his daughter; she was important to him and he loved her. Why did he imagine she had done such a thing?

'Daddy, I didn't—'

'Don't say any more. You must go.'

He wasn't even looking at her. His figure seemed so much smaller, so much more crouched down, as if the blow was too much – and it would be were it true, but it wasn't, it wasn't.

She tried to protest, but couldn't get the words out. She hated to disappoint her father more than anything, but it seemed that he did not believe her, that he did not even want to. *Did* she resent Gemma's success in finding a young man of wealth to marry her, somebody she liked? Was that what it was? Had she imagined the hurt, the blood? Was it her fault? Perhaps it was. Guy would not have done such a thing. Why had she gone outside? It was entirely her own doing.

'I'm so sorry,' she said.

Her father did not respond and she could tell that he assumed her guilt. He was not against Guy, he was not against any man, and she realized that he could not be. Guy brought with him respectability, the future, children, and in the end those things mattered most of all. He was a man her father knew, and he cared for these matters, and therefore it must have been her fault.

He shifted and then he said, 'You must go from here. Gemma is being married in two hours. Gather your things and leave, and don't ever come back.'

He turned. Lucy got up and ran to him.

'Oh, please don't,' she said. 'I didn't do anything wrong. I really didn't. I didn't. I didn't.'

She didn't know how many times she denied it. He stopped and shook her off. She followed him across the landing, crying and pleading. And finally he turned back.

'You have disappointed me more than you can imagine. I don't ever want to see you again. Get out of my house. Get out and don't come back.'

TWO

London, 1919

Joe had dreamed of going home so often, had wanted to get out of France directly the conflict was over, but he was asked to stay and he did not feel that he could refuse. So many of his men, the older ones, had wives and children to go home to, and the young ones had parents. He had a parent too, his father, and a fiancée, Angela, but it was part of his nature to offer first to do everything, to be there for everybody. He had brought his men through danger so often that he had become a bit of a legend. They would have gone anywhere with him because they felt safe.

It was an illusion, Joe thought, and then uncomfortably reminded himself how he had seen what would happen and so managed to avoid it. He had kept his men close to him, so that they joked and called him Lucky Joe. Not to his face of course, to his face they called him sir.

He allowed himself to feel that yearning for England so that he could barely wait to reach it. He wanted to run, to push the ship and then to hurry the train, and when he finally arrived in London he was so grateful he could have

20

cried. He took a cab to his father's house in Belgravia. He didn't notice until he got outside into a bitter cold winter wind that the house was in darkness.

He told the cabbie to wait and rushed to hammer on the front door, but there were no lights at all. He had never seen such a thing. If his father had gone out for the evening there were always servants at home, always somebody waiting. He felt frustrated. He had written and said that he was coming home; he had expected not quite a party but certainly something of a reception. He was anxious to see Angela, but his father was on his mind first of all.

He stood about. He couldn't stay here, he decided, so he told the cabbie to take him the few streets to Wilton Crescent where one of his dearest friends lived. Toddy would know what was going on, and Joe cheered himself with this and climbed back into the cab, but he was unable to ignore the instinct which told him this was going to be nothing like the homecoming he'd expected. By the time he reached Wilton Crescent he was feeling very low.

The cabbie took down his luggage, and Joe paid him. Here at least lights winked out from heavily curtained windows and Joe found admittance when he banged on the door.

The man who greeted him was not the same one who had been with the family before the war, Joe realized sadly. Everything was changed.

However, it seemed there was a party going on. It lifted his spirits immediately. He was left standing in the hall, listening to merriment from somewhere beyond. He waited impatiently; whatever was Toddy doing to make him keep his friend standing about like this? After some minutes he was ushered into the library. A fire blazed in the enormous grate, but even so the room was cool, as though not often used, and he could hear nothing through the closed double oak doors.

And then his friend appeared between them. Joe was about to greet him lightly and eagerly, but he didn't. Even before Toddy came into the room Joe felt himself step back. He watched Toddy hesitate in the hall, as though he were taking several deep breaths before he made himself come in. Joe had been right; Toddy was not about to greet him with joy.

They had not seen one another since Toddy had come back from France a year ago. Now as he entered the room there was not even a smile on his young face. He was wearing evening dress, the day being well advanced by now and darkness having fallen hours since. Joe managed to greet him affably.

'Toddy,' he said, coming forward with his hand outstretched to shake. 'Sorry to call at this time. I'm sure you're about to eat but I thought you might know what is going on.'

He half expected Toddy's smile to widen and that he would know everything that Joe needed to, that he might ask him to dinner and even to stay, but all Toddy did was to stare at him for longer in society than would have been deemed polite. Toddy had still not said anything and his face had gone pale as though he were suffering from a bad shock, his features drawn, spaced. He looked to Joe as though he would gladly have run from the room.

'The house is all locked up,' Joe said. 'Has my father gone

to the country? Nobody there at all, you see. I don't understand it. Thought you might be able to enlighten me since
you're so obviously still in London.' Joe could hear himself
talking on and on because he had the feeling that once he
stopped the world would crash and he was not certain he
could bear any more conflict. 'Has my father buggered off
to Northumberland for Christmas? It seems unlikely – the
damned place is always bloody freezing at this time of year.'

Joe thought with slight hope that perhaps his father had
planned a surprise there, that friends had gathered for his
return, but if he had then what was Toddy doing here and
anyhow, it was a stupid idea: why would his father plan a
homecoming two hundred and seventy miles away?

Toddy looked down as though something interesting had
just landed at his feet and Joe began to wish that he hadn't
come here. There were other friends he could have gone to,
it was just that Toddy and Sarah were close to him. Angela,
Toddy's sister, was the love of Joe's life. He longed to see her.
He had thought of her each day, dreamed of her nightly, of
how lovely she was, his blonde, beautiful, clever girl; they
would be married now that he was at home, and everything
would be fine. He hadn't heard from her for several months
since he went back to France. There was nothing in that;
letters were unreliable and he was moving around a great
deal, but the ache to see her, to hold her, to spend the rest of
his life, to be happy now – he could hardly contain it. They
must be married as soon as possible. He didn't see how he
could stand another day without her. Home for good. He
was home for good after five impossible years. What had
kept him going in that time had been falling in love with

her and how she had waited, been there for him, met him at the station, seen him off from there so many times.

'Is everything all right?' Joe said, beginning to wonder and then forcing himself to shut up to give Toddy the space to say something. Anything would do but this lengthening silence.

Toddy glanced with a desperate look at the closed doors, as though he wanted to escape.

'I didn't realize you were back,' he said.

'I have just got here,' Joe said, indicating his uniform.

Joe waited again.

'You didn't get my letter?' Toddy said.

'Obviously not.' Joe was becoming impatient now and a little angry. 'The house is locked up, the lights are out; something is going on. Do you know what it is? Where my father has gone?'

After a huge breath Toddy said very quickly, 'Your father's dead. I assumed you knew,' and then he looked away as though there were something shameful about the whole thing. His head went down until Joe could not see his face.

'Dead?' Joe, although having gone through five years of killing, didn't understand the word at all.

Toddy let go of his breath and a little colour returned to his face. He even glanced at Joe before moving his gaze again.

'I thought you would have been told. Other people knew.'

'Apparently they thought as you did – that somebody else would tell me. What happened?'

'He killed himself.'

Joe wanted to laugh. Was Toddy having some horrible

game with him? Were his family about to break in and greet him, his father with them? Joe's father had always been a hopeless shot. It was a joke between them. He couldn't hit a house end, never mind a pheasant that was flying towards him. It did happen of course, more often people shot other people, but his father had always impressed upon him that you did not move with an unbroken gun, that was what the crook of your arm was for.

'On a shoot?'

Toddy didn't say anything for a few moments, pursed his lips together and then shook his head.

'It was deliberate,' he said.

Joe stared into Toddy's pale face. Every nerve of him was denying it. His father could not have done such a thing, he was a strong-willed, strong-minded man – some people might have thought too much so.

'He had lost everything,' Toddy said.

Joe was getting tired of surprises. 'I don't understand what you mean.'

'My mother knows more about it than I do.'

'Really?' Joe said.

'She's . . . she's in Norfolk.'

'Oh right,' Joe said, dazed at the irrelevance of this.

'Visiting friends,' Toddy said, as though it mattered.

Joe was looking so hard at Toddy that his friend moved nervously. The whole thing was perfectly ridiculous; it could not be true.

'He hated being without you, that was what she said.'

'So he killed himself when I was due back?'

'That wasn't what I meant.'

25

'I wish to God you would say something you do mean, instead of standing there like a tailor's dummy.'

'You've been away for a very long time and your father hid how things were, that's what my mother says. He was drinking a great deal and playing cards.'

Joe knew this. He had been worried too, but he had had other things to think about and had dismissed it time and again from his mind. He knew that his father hated being alone. His mother had died when he was a small boy and he was the only child of the marriage. Right from the beginning his father had begged him not to go to war, so unlike other men who wanted to be proud of their sons and sent them off to war with barely a thought.

His father had wanted him at home, had begged him to try to find a job here in London. Joe had explained over and over that it was not possible. His father would never see him to the station or even say goodbye and things had gone further downhill, Joe remembered – many paintings were sold to meet his father's debts and had left smudged oblong shadows on the walls. His father had sold off the Yorkshire estate and spent his summers in Northumberland, where most of the servants had long since gone to the war and some of the buildings were falling down.

Toddy seemed to have found his voice.

'He lost everything that was meant to be yours and afterwards put a pistol to his head.'

The last time that Joe had been home the house in London was so bare; his father drank or slept or went out and barely seemed to notice his presence. If he was able to be truthful to himself, Joe thought now, he had not wanted to come home because he knew that things were sliding away so very fast. He had told himself that everything would be different when he came home for good. He would take care of it all, look after his father.

'His friends were worried about him and he worried about you. He thought you would be killed. My mother says that after your mother died your father was heartbroken, that you were all he had left.'

Joe wished he could go back a couple of hours, when the world had been a better place for him. But then he thought the world didn't treat anybody decently, so why should it start with him?

'Yes, well, I can't say anything about my mother – she died when I was small. I don't remember anything about her.'

This was not true. He remembered her funeral, his father had insisted on taking him, and he had not forgotten watching his mother's coffin being lowered into the ground. It had been one of those grim wet winter days which never got light, the fog thicker than shadows.

His whole body had tightened up by now, the way it did when confronted by any crisis. He had grown used to it, it would first do that and then he would go cold and see the situation with such precision and foresight that he could have led his men anywhere and they would have followed him.

'My mother always says your mother's death was quite sudden, your father wouldn't talk about it, he was devastated. He had lots of friends and they tried to help him many times over the years but he didn't listen. He just went on grieving. There's nothing left, don't you see, because of the way that he behaved. Is that clear enough for you?' Toddy coughed and stuttered and said, 'I didn't mean it to sound like that, Joe. I don't know how else to put it, I'm sorry. I was dreading you coming home even though I thought you would have known long since. After all, France isn't so very far away.'

Joe supposed that depended on how you looked at it; now it seemed like the end of the earth.

From somewhere beyond the library doors Joe could hear laughter, as though the people who were staying for dinner were moving through the hall into another room, probably the dining room. Doors opened and closed, the conversation loud one moment and subdued the next. Toddy looked in the direction of the noise as though he longed to be there.

Things had been bad all his life really, Joe admitted to himself now. His father, unlike most men, had never got over his wife's death. His father had had plenty of women since, Joe thought cynically, but they were not the kind of women one married.

At that moment the library doors opened and a lovely young woman stepped inside. She was pretty, dark-haired and brown-eyed, with generous lips and a soft, sweet face. She had a slender figure and was wearing a cream dress that accentuated her shape. She was smiling with pleasure and then she saw him and the smile went.

Joe would have gone forward, but she stepped back when she recognized him. He greeted her, but his lips were as stiff as wood. She didn't reply and turned her gaze to her husband.

'Are you coming back to the party, darling? Everyone is

going in to dinner.' She went out without another word. Joe kept his eyes on the door, thinking she would come back in and somehow make things better, but nothing happened.

'Where's Angela?' The one thing which would save his day from total ruin. He looked eagerly at the door as though she might suddenly appear. Even if she couldn't tell him that everything was all right, she would help, she would comfort him, be there for him, and after they were married he would feel better than he had ever felt in his life. He would have someone all to himself, somebody to come home to, and he would somehow manage to live with his father's death, awful though it was; he would learn to come to terms with it just as many thousands upon thousands of people had had to do in this dreadful war. If she was there, by him, if they could be together, then he could manage anything.

'She's not here,' Toddy said.

Joe didn't understand that. She must be here; this was her home. Her parents lived here, it was the family London base, and during bad weather she would not have been any-where else, especially at this time of the year. And besides, he thought, she would have been waiting for him to come home, she would want to know that he was here. He couldn't wait another moment to see her.

Toddy sighed and then looked straight at Joe and said, 'My father has sent her away. You must understand, Joe, that you and Angela can't be married.'

Joe stared at him. What on earth was he talking about?

'She couldn't possibly marry you now. My father would never allow it.'

'But – we're engaged,' Joe said, idiotically.

He was still searching the door as though it would open at any second and she would come into the room and fling herself into his arms, as she had a habit of doing, not caring who was there. Her mother had reproved her often for her open manners, for her adulation of Joe. From the second they had met at a party she had told him that she adored him. He had loved how she had cared nothing for the stuffy manners which other people thought were right. Her eyes, her whole beautiful face with its perfect features, had shone for him. She was his life.

Toddy wandered around the room, finally stopping in front of the fire and giving one of the logs a huge kick.

'I'm sorry, but you really can't expect it, you know. Not after what has happened.'

Joe frowned. 'It's not the first time a man has blown his brains out!' He was almost shouting.

'You have no money and no consequence. A title like yours is nothing without those.'

'Angela never cared for such things.'

Toddy finally turned around. 'But she would in time and you could hardly think her family would allow her to marry into poverty – because that's what you are now. I daresay you have nothing to your name other than your army pay, and the way that you behave probably not much left of that.'

Joe had been well known for treating his men to whatever he could come across to make their lives easier amidst the hell of war. Some of the meaner officers thought him stupid. Some followed his example.

'Where is she?'

'My father arranged for her to go abroad. She understands

that she cannot marry you, so there is no point in trying to do anything about it. I don't know where she is. And since you should behave honourably, it would be best left alone. You cannot think to ask her to marry you in the circumstances in which you find yourself.'

'I could work.'

Toddy didn't quite laugh. 'Really?' he said. 'And what on earth are you equipped for other than a reputation for shooting people accurately and getting common soldiers to go over the top? Now I really must go – I have dinner guests to attend to. Trevors will see you out.'

'No!'

Toddy hadn't moved, but his look was full of pity. 'I'm sorry, Joe,' he said, 'but there's nothing anybody can do. You wouldn't want her to be miserable, would you? She's used to the best of everything: you know that. If you're honest with yourself you know you couldn't make her happy.'

Joe couldn't bear it. 'I'm not going anywhere,' he said. 'She must be here. You're lying to me.' He hauled open the door and strode through into the dining room where he and Angela had dined so often with her parents. A dozen pairs of eyes turned as people took in the uniform, the face, who it was, and a frost came over the room so hard that Joe could have sworn he was still in France when things had been at their worst, men dying and horses sinking in mud and confusion and blood. He felt the same numbness he'd had before he led his men out to face the impossible.

He tried to breathe. He saw Sarah, Toddy's wife, and their guests, all of them supposed to be his friends. Toddy's parents weren't there and neither were Sarah's. He thought back to the last time he had been home when they had had a dinner like this. Nobody held his gaze, nobody spoke; they turned away or looked down.

He spun around and Toddy, just behind him, stepped back. 'Where is she?'

'I've already told you. There's nothing you can do.'

'You must know where she is.'

'I don't know anything about it. I've told you what happened.' Toddy gazed around at the dining room behind Joe, obviously embarrassed for his guests and himself and maybe even for Joe. All Joe could think was he wanted to get hold of him and slam him up against the wall. So he did.

'You bastard!' he said.

The men in the dining room got to their feet and two of them pulled Joe off. He turned around and hit them, he downed them both; they had come back from war and had gone soft, falling before him so easily. Some woman began to cry, though he didn't even care who it was, and then another shrieked. The others, four of them now, held him and dragged him to the door. They threw him out, in spite of his struggling, and the front door was slammed. Joe lay in the gutter, in the bitter night air, which had never been quite as bad as it was now.

He tried to remember what had happened, but he couldn't put his thoughts into any kind of order so he hailed a cab and sat down, wondering how things could have got so much worse after his five years of soldiering, and surviving. Wondering how he could come back to his father dead and the love of his life apparently gone and with nobody knowing where.

Angela was at the front of his mind, but he was in shock, he couldn't think clearly, and so he tried to think about his father first because he was dead and hopefully Angela was nothing of the sort. How awful must his father have felt to be so alone, to feel so bad that he didn't want to be here any more, even though he had a grown-up child. The trouble was that Joe had never made him proud. His father hated soldiering, everything about it. He had wanted Joe to be different. Joe had won medals and done well, but his father had never mentioned it.

Joe could not stop thinking of his father in that bloody great house all alone. He had always been alone, Joe had not been able to stem that loneliness, and by God he had tried as he was growing up. It was no wonder he was no good at school; he was always trying to get home to save his father from the person he had become. He had spent all his childhood thinking that his father would die. His mother had died, so why not?

He had been a coward. He had gone willingly to France because he no longer wanted to face the man his father had become. Every time he left he thought they would not meet again, that his father was fated to meet such an end. France had been his retreat, his cover. It was almost amusing. Other men were terrified to die, scared of having limbs blown off, of being in pain they could not bear. Joe hadn't understood until now that he was not afraid because somehow in his heart he had known that he would come back to this. And now he had. And the one person who could have saved him from total despair was gone from him.

His first instinct was to run after her, to go wherever she might have gone, to bring her home, to hold her safe, but he knew in an awful way that Toddy was right. She was not there and by God they had made sure he would not find her. What had they done with her?

He tried to see how she would feel about him now that he was nobody and had nothing. He could not reconcile Toddy's view of his sister with the woman he loved. She would not have deserted him, ever. She would not have let them send her away. She adored him. She had loved him so very much, almost as much as he had loved her.

He tried to think otherwise, that she was young and beautiful and used to the best of everything. Her family was old and respected and she was well loved and cared for and he could not take her down with him to wherever he was going now. It would have been the most awful thing of all to do to her. His lovely golden girl. She would have gone with him and he could have managed something – surely people would have helped? – but what would have been her fate? Her family would never have allowed it. They had talked her round, they had held out something beyond him, they had made sure that she was not there for when he came back. He admitted that much to himself at least.

It seemed strange that the war had not defeated him, yet the homecoming had. What an odd end to it. Worse still, he now remembered the weekend he and Angela had stolen.

He had come back a few months ago, not told anyone, and she had lied to her family because they had wanted to be together so very much. They met at a hotel on the south coast, used his name, and Joe had the best time of his life. It seemed to him now that he was paying for it hugely. He wondered if she felt the same.

It had been a big place, in grounds which fell to the sea. A gentle summer breeze wafted through the open doors which led to a balcony and they had spent the whole time in bed, calling for room service and going nowhere. She had said there was nowhere else on earth to go and that they would always be like this, always feel like this.

The cabbie dropped him at the house. The street was deserted. Joe pushed at the first window he reached, but it was either stuck or locked and now he could see the shutters behind it, closed and with the lock across them to keep out wind, rain and, doubtlessly, intruders. He left it and tried again at the next and then a third. It moved, he pushed it up and here the shutters were slightly ajar so he shoved at these until they parted and then he heaved himself and his belongings inside and dropped to the floor. The sounds of the floorboards were like cannon blasts to his ears. It wanted to make him run and hide. He pushed down the window, but left the shutters so that he could see through the shadows, though the echo of his feet had already told him that there was little to be seen.

It was his father's library. It smelled of old books. His father had been no reader, Joe thought, but he had gone in there to smoke and drink brandy by the fire for as long as Joe could remember. The room was so cold that Joe shivered. There had been no fire lit in here for many days.

The oak bookcases which lined the walls were almost empty. What kind of person bought books? Perhaps they had been valuable. Joe had never been interested in books so he had no idea, but it seemed to him that if his father had been forced to get rid of whatever collections there were he must have been desperate indeed.

His father's old leather chair stood to one side of the fire. Joe ran his hands over the top of it, remembering his father's thick dark hair and the quick turn of his head when he was being funny and how his eyes warmed and his mouth curved up before he laughed. Joe made his way into the hall and into the other downstairs rooms. Now not just some but all of the paintings were gone, and so was the furniture in the dining and drawing rooms, as though it had been a house clearance, as though the master of the house had been already dead.

Which room had his father chosen for dying? It made him shiver. There was no blood anywhere and for a few stupid moments he thought there had been a mistake: his father was not dead at all, he would be there in a second, just as Angela would be. Everything would be all right, except that it wouldn't and he knew it now.

He paused in the hall. The sweeping staircase disappeared into the heights of the house and he sat down on the third step, unable to go further.

In the end sheer tiredness forced him to go upstairs, automatically to his own bedroom. That too had been stripped, even his bed was gone. He went next door to the bathroom and beyond it to the linen cupboards and there, opening big doors, he discovered two blankets and a pillow in the recesses and he took them downstairs. He sat down in his father's chair, pushed the pillow at the back of his neck and pulled the blankets over him. He thought of his father and of Angela and that he must find out what had happened. In the morning he would go and see his father's banker, Reginald Barrington. He would know what to do.

He didn't even hope for sleep, he knew it wouldn't come anywhere near; he just sat there as the night blacked and then greyed itself into morning. He didn't expect any more, he had been awake for so many nights before this, but he was not used to it here in London where he had lived, where he had grown, where he had fallen in love, where his father had been for him. He waited the night through.

THREE

Ever since she was a small child, Lucy had always known that she wanted to do what her father did. Somehow, even before she understood, it was her whole life. She remembered being very small and the smell of his office and the industry there. She couldn't even think why at a very young age she had been tolerated. Before she could see over his secretary's desk she had loved the whole atmosphere of that place.

Her father's place of work was further along the river's edge. They lived in Sandgate in Newcastle, right on the River Tyne. Her father's family had been there for three hundred years. The house was Tudor, timbered, black and white, and it followed the curve of the street, clinging to the bankside as though it must hang on for its life. It was, her mother claimed, insanitary, inconvenient, cold in winter, stifling in summer, too small, in a bad area and sinking into the river, but the family loved it.

Her father walked from there to work every morning and Lucy very often went with him. The building was all brass and mahogany, and the rooms had marble fireplaces.

When she first went to school she would run away and turn up at her father's office. He had to explain to her that she must go to school so that she would be useful later in the office.

'You can be like Miss Shuttleworth.'

'I don't want to be like her, I want to be like you,' she told him.

'Just don't tell her that,' her father would say.

She went there every day after school, whereas Gemma went home to be with her mother. Her father did not seem to mind her presence and she spent her school holidays there; indeed he took her with him to court when he could and she would hover in the corridors where people grew used to her. She knew all the local police and her father's clients and even though she was not allowed into his office while he spoke to people he would tell her all about it. By the time she was ten she had a fair idea of what it was he did and that it was exactly what she wanted to do.

Her mother complained that there was never any money because her father gave it all away, and her mother was right. Her father helped poor people, he turned nobody from his door; those who needed legal help were always seen. The offices therefore were different from those of other solicitors' places of work, as Lucy came to understand when she went to various others to take letters or parcels or messages of whatever kind. They didn't smell of people and sweat, and they had Turkish rugs on the floors. The people she saw there wore suits and the women had large hats and long winter coats.

Miss Shuttleworth was forever giving out tea and biscuits to the people who came to the office. It had an openness about it which Lucy did not experience anywhere else.

Lucy worked hard at school, but it was only because her father said so. She was good at it. Her mother complained.

'I don't hold with too much education for girls, it just gives them daft ideas,' she had said.

Her father ignored her, and though she grumbled she did not try to persuade Lucy not to spend her time at the office. Meanwhile Gemma liked being at home. Her mother taught her to bake and cook and embroider and knit and sew and make clothes and all the other things which Lucy hated. There was, however, one thing the girls agreed on.

They loved their home. They were convinced that nowhere in the whole world could better it. Their bedroom looked out across the river and as small children they lay with the windows open listening to the cursing of the men who came in with the ships and the cries of the gulls high above. These cries were Lucy's favourite sound; she thought of the gulls as lost souls weaving and circling above the earth.

She loved the sounds of the street traders and she and Gemma would lie in the comfort of the big double bed, listening to their singing, drunken and lewd, which Lucy preferred to the Sunday hymns in the cathedral. Then there were the smells – of fish and dirty water and the general odour of people.

Their mother would come into the bedroom when she thought her children were sleeping and close the windows because she feared the night air unsavoury, but the moment she was gone one of them would get up and open the window wide again. They loved the winter best, huddled beneath their blankets, the curtains pushed well back against the walls. They would watch the snow fall on the river and the icy moon rise and move across the sky above the water. In spring the yellow flowers danced upon the bankside in Gateshead and the air grew softer, though it was not often hot for more than a few days at a time.

In high summer, June or July, the light barely left the sky and the sailors would hump the prostitutes in the shadows down by the quayside. She and Gemma would snigger over it – though they knew little and made up what they weren't sure of – and the cries of the women, either true or not, echoed across the water. In autumn the river was awash with leaves and the wind threw handfuls of them into their backyard where clothes were hung out to dry.

Lucy and Gemma fell asleep to the sounds of the Tyne like a lullaby, breathing in the smells from the houses of easterners who had come to Newcastle selling silks and spices. The food smelled strange and wonderful – apples, raisins, sultanas, and rice as white as snowflakes. On the windowledges they grew green and red chillies, which looked odd to Lucy upon the bushes, like new moons. In their gardens grew tarragon, parsley and mint.

She and Gemma knew the names of all these things, how they smelled and tasted. They had a nursemaid when they were small who lived among the people from eastern countries and so they learned much about them. They did not tell their mother, or the girl would have been dismissed, especially since she sometimes took them away to eat with her family. The food was so much better than the fish with parsley sauce they had at home on Fridays, the tough liver with onions which needed a sharp knife, or the overdone, leather-like beef on Sundays accompanied by limp vegetables which lacked butter.

They had a cook in those days and her cooking was not the best. She made a decent cup of tea and her cakes were light and tasty, but that was the best you could say for it.

In season they would catch the stink of the herring boats, watch the girls with their pinnies and bonnets, and hear their indecipherable Scottish twang which hung on the air like music. They followed the boats. When she was eight Lucy longed to be one of them; she envied the brazen way they moved with a sway of their hips, as though they knew exactly who they were. That was how she wanted to feel, only she would do it another way, through being her father's partner and helping to run his office.

As she got older Lucy began to notice how beautiful her sister was. Gemma had bright red hair, you might have warmed your hands upon it, her skin was smooth and white and she had her mother's eyes, so blue they could have graced the skies. She was slender, each limb perfect, so lovely that every time she went out men watched her, women envied her. She was not so tall that she looked straight into men's eyes, nor so short that other women were above her. She moved like a dancer her father always said. Her voice was sweet and soft and she was kind and loving.

Lucy looked, she thought, as though her parents had run out of energy or ideas by the time they reached her. She was tall and skinny, her hair the colour of rust, her eyes as dark as the seaweed on the shore. She was so pale that people were inclined to ask if she was ill.

She was, however, very excited when her mother bought her first dress for her first dance. It was in the Assembly Rooms, and she went there with her parents and Gemma amid lots of people. The music began and Lucy spent the whole evening waiting for somebody to ask her to dance. She watched the young men going past again and again. She waited and waited until finally her lips turned to cardboard and her legs to wood. The evening grew yet as she watched her sister and other pretty small girls being turned about the room with smiles and elegance and conversation.

The following morning, a Sunday, Lucy told her parents she was going for a walk. She had the address of the head-mistress at her school and she had decided to go and see her. It was not an area she had ever been in before and she walked a long way in rain which turned into sleet. She was astonished that it lay in so poor a part of town. The streets were dark and narrow. The window frames of the back-to-back houses were rotten, and in some cases the space was boarded up. The yards contained coal houses and lavatories. Grubby children played in the streets.

She walked up to the front door of No. 3 Percy Row and rapped her gloved knuckles hard against it. There was no answer; Lucy was half assured Miss Sheane had not come back from church yet, or that perhaps she had got it wrong and the schoolmistress did not live in such a place.

She almost didn't try again, but she had come a long way; she was glad she did, for she soon heard footsteps beyond the door. The bolts went back, the big key turned in the lock. The door was not often opened; Lucy could tell by the way that it stuck for several seconds. No doubt it was almost permanently swollen because of the damp, in spite of Miss Sheane's attempts to prise it open.

When she did so Lucy saw a woman she had feared and respected brought down. She was dressed in a shapeless nightgown of a colour Lucy would have called dirty if she had thought that far. Miss Sheane's lank grey hair fell to her shoulders. She wore a shawl.

'Lucy,' she said in dismay.

'I'm sorry, Miss Sheane, but I had to talk to you. I do hope you don't mind.'

Miss Sheane opened the door wider. Sleet was falling almost sideways by then. Lucy was glad to be invited in.

The front room was the colour of sludge. The fire wasn't lit and the whole place gave off a smell of mould.

Miss Sheane sneezed into her handkerchief, holding it before her red face while waving a hand to indicate that Lucy could sit down.

'I cannot offer you tea, I'm afraid – the fire in the kitchen has not been lit since last weekend.'

The very idea made Lucy shiver. She took a chair, though she was not sure it would hold her; it was an armchair of sorts, but felt lumpy and old. She tried not to move around. She did not want the schoolmistress to see how shocked she was at the poverty of the way she lived. It was not at all how she had thought such women got by. Miss Sheane regarded her with a little humour.

'Not much of a recommendation for the single life, is it?' she said.

Lucy didn't know what to say.

'That is what you're here for, isn't it?' Miss Sheane sat down across from Lucy as though the fire burned between them. 'You've been thinking about university.'

Lucy tried to smile. 'I don't know,' she said. 'I thought I knew what I wanted when I was a little girl. I wanted to work with my father and help people. I'm not much good in houses, but then I went to a dance last night and . . .' She didn't know she was going to look at the other woman and tell her, but she did. 'It was so awful. Nobody asked me to dance and I just hated the whole idea of being so disadvantaged that I had to wait to be asked. I know that sounds silly, but all the boys wanted to dance with my sister. She's very beautiful, you see. I was so excited at the music and the crowd and . . . and all the evening I stood there and I wasn't the only one. I felt so sorry for the other girls too – those who were tall didn't get asked and those who were . . . were rather plain neither, and it all seemed so very stupid somehow. I thought it was what I wanted.'

Miss Sheane nodded. 'You could study law and be like your father.'

'But women don't. It's what I want to do beyond anything and I know it's what my father wants for me, but now I'm hesitating. Can I really do such a thing?'

'Somebody always has to be first. It wouldn't be like this for you. I was a poor Irish girl with a brain. Two of my sisters went into a convent. They were the lucky ones. There were fifteen of us. My mother died. My money has always gone back to Derry, you see. I have nothing. Would you like me to talk to your father?'

45

'It seems such a lot to ask though I think – I know that he will support me against my mother.'

'It isn't really so bad here,' Miss Sheane said. 'I have all this space to myself. I can sit by my fire and I usually make one every evening when I come in but I haven't been well enough to do anything but go to bed when I return from school. I'm luckier than many women.'

Lucy could hear shouting through the hall, loud cursing and then a crash.

'They're always fighting,' Miss Sheane said. 'Do the things you want with your life, Lucy. Don't let other people tell you what to do. They will try but you mustn't give in. Don't let this scare you.'

The following day Miss Sheane came to the house in the early evening. She was back to her usual scary self, tall and imposing and wearing a tweed suit, her grey hair twisted into an intricate bun. Lucy had never before wished that the rooms did not have thick wooden doors.

When Miss Sheane had gone Lucy's father called her into the study and his eyes were lit.

'Your headmistress thinks you could go to university and do well. Is this what you want?'

'I want to be a lawyer like you.'

She had never seen her father so pleased. Her mother had heard Miss Sheane leave and she came in now from the sitting room. When Lucy's father said that Miss Sheane thought she should go to university her mother shook her head.

'No good will come of it,' she said. It was not what Lucy had expected. There were tears in her mother's eyes and her mouth trembled. 'I don't want you to go,' she said, looking

46

at Lucy in such a way that the tears sprang into Lucy's eyes too. 'I don't want to lose you to all those clever people. You won't be same afterwards; you'll have so much book learning that you won't ever want to come home.'

'I will always want to come home,' Lucy said.

'I want both my girls to marry Newcastle gentlemen and be here and have children so that we can always be a family together.'

'Lucy will only be going to Durham if they will have her, Miss Sheane says.'

'Durham is an awful place,' her mother said. 'It's not on a good river like the Tyne.' Though Lucy couldn't have explained what her mother meant, she did understand it. 'We'll never be a family the same again, and just for her to do what men do – sitting in offices all day and dealing with the scum of the earth and . . . and with policemen and laws, it's awful,' she said. 'I don't want that for one of my girls.'

When her mother had gone back to the kitchen her father held Lucy in a close embrace and said, 'I will miss my little lawyer.'

'I'm not going far and I will be back when the terms end – and I will come to the office just as I've always done and one day maybe you'll let me be your partner.'

He laughed, but not in scorn: in admiration, she thought. He had taught her so much already and now she would have other teachers. She would come home and they would stay late in his office which looked out over the river and talk about what she had learned and discuss what more there was to know. She was so happy she thought she would burst.

*

Lucy had a tiny room to herself when she reached university. She had thought she might share and make friends and that it would be like she and Gemma had been when they were children, talking late at night, gazing up at the stars which twinkled beyond the windows, making plans about who and what they would be when they were older.

The tiny room had a single bed and past the window there was nothing but a wall which shut out most of the natural daylight. It was rather as she had imagined prison cells to be.

The women students lived together in a big building on Palace Green. The sight of the castle and the cathedral and the green, as well as the various university departments close by, excited Lucy.

Her first meal in the big hall where they sat with their eyes lowered, whispering to their immediate neighbours, didn't boost Lucy's spirits. The food was grey, the vegetables were unrecognizable, the custard had lumps and whatever fruit there was with it had been dried long since and was tough.

There was nothing to drink but water, or tea so bad that her mother would have called it 'sweepings up'. She tried to talk to the girls at either side of her, but they seemed entranced with their neighbours and ignored Lucy's remarks.

It was rumoured that one young woman had been sent down because she spoke to a young man on the green, although he was her brother. The lecturers might have been interesting – and she wanted to enjoy them – but they were all men and ignored their female students. One of them, finding no male student at his lecture, turned and walked back out, saying, 'There is no one here.'

Lucy made herself not go home that term. She had escaped. She could not now go back and admit that she had been wrong, but she began to wish that it was Christmas, to long for Mrs Moon's cooking, despite her previous opinion of it, and most especially for Gemma's company.

When it finally approached, she thought Christmas in Durham so pretty, but that was because she was leaving the place. Students sang carols in the cathedral and in groups in the busy streets. It snowed and she watched how the big fat flakes fell into the grey river and she longed for the Tyne, 'an honest river', as her mother called it. She could not keep warm; her room was so bitter with frost that she could not sleep. She would have given a great deal for a fire. She counted down the days.

Nobody came to meet her at the station. Her father was busy at work and her mother getting the house ready for the festivities.

When she reached home Mrs Moon made tea and Lucy told her mother all about her new life. 'I thought you might have got over it by now,' her mother said, as though it were a bad cold. 'Gemma has new friends and among them a very nice man called Guy Brown.'

FOUR

Barrington's Bank had looked after Joe's family since the bank had begun and Joe had known the head of it, Reginald, all his life. He knew that Mr Barrington was proud to be the family banker and that when other landowners scorned such people because they were in business his father reckoned some of his best friends among business people. Joe had always been very pleased at that.

Mr Barrington saw him at Joe's convenience and when Joe walked into the huge office, all marble and mahogany, he felt almost at home.

'My dear Joe,' Mr Barrington said, coming forward and taking Joe's hand between both of his, 'I am so very sorry to hear about your father. What a homecoming for you. I tried to contact you but I didn't know where you were; I knew that nothing would reach you but that you would come here. Anything I can do . . .' He stopped there.

Joe shook his head. 'I know things are really bad. I just want to know if there is anything at all left.'

'Of course you do. Sit down.'

He pointed Joe to a deep leather chair then sat down himself across the desk. 'I did my best to stop this. I wouldn't like you to think that I didn't try.'

'I don't think anyone could have stopped it.' Joe was relieved he could talk about it as though he were still a rational human being. He felt nothing of the kind, amazed to hear himself being polite. My God, he had had a decent upbringing. Manners maketh the man. They certainly bloody did, he thought, smiling as though his very existence depended upon it.

'My father would not have accepted help, I imagine.'

Mr Barrington looked down and shook his head. 'I did what I could, but—'

'I understand.' Joe didn't understand, but there was no point in saying such things. 'Are there still debts?'

Mr Barrington paused, but only from sympathy, Joe could see.

'I'm afraid so. If everything is sold they will be discharged,' Mr Barrington said neatly.

'I should have done something well before now,' Joe said, but he was very glad when Mr Barrington looked shocked and surprised.

'What on earth could you have done?' he replied.

'I tried not to think about it. Quite wrong.'

'And the war?' Mr Barrington said, practically. Joe realized that this was what he had always liked best about the man. He said what you wanted to hear and Joe needed to hear that he was not to blame. 'The war was another tragedy; the men who should have known better did not as they never do and you did your duty. That is as much as any young man can manage. You couldn't have been here, so disabuse yourself of any such idea.'

Mr Barrington let this sink in and then he continued, 'You know if it hadn't been for your great-grandfather, Barrington's would not have survived.'

Joe looked at him. He hadn't heard about this. Anything new which might distract him from his problems was a relief.

'There was a run on the bank when times were desperate and your great-grandfather announced to everyone he knew that he would back the bank, that he would put everything he had into it – and so he did.'

'He was the last sensible one of us,' Joe said, finding a little humour.

'He was a great man. You know, I'd be glad to make you a loan until the houses are sold—'

'No, no.' Joe put up both hands. 'I don't believe I could ever pay it back and I would hate to think I had put you into such a position when I know, though you don't say it, that you were good to my father beyond anything. The house is not entailed and must of course be sold, I understand that. What about the Northumberland estate?'

He loved that best, he thought now, the getting away, the lovely wild winds up there, the unrelenting snow and the way the puddles were frosted sometimes even in April. He liked it best in June when the sky was barely dark and everything looked so friendly when you went to bed in the almost-light. Other people went there only when the weather should have been soft but never was, and Joe loved that and so did his father. He was sorry indeed when Mr Barrington shook his head.

'That too. I have already had some interest on both houses and will put the business into operation.'

Joe could not believe he would not take Angela there again. She had loved the long wide beaches and the old ruined castles and how you could walk for miles and miles and watch the tide crashing hard against the wet sand. She had loved the farms and the people and the burr in the accents and she had said to him, 'When we're married let's go there a lot – I feel it's where we should be.'

'The Yorkshire estate is of course long gone,' Mr Barrington said. 'Your father dealt with that.'

'Will there be anything left?'

'A little, I think, depending on the sales of course. I will do my best to make a profit for you.'

'You always do,' Joe said.

Mr Barrington cleared his throat and shook his head. 'I did manage to secure your belongings, your clothes and books and your guns. I didn't like to leave anything valuable in the house; I was afraid someone might try to break in. I will have these sent to you – though I do think you should come and stay with us for the time being.'

Joe could think of nothing worse than Mr Barrington's house, full with half a dozen children and his still-young second wife, so he thanked him and refused.

The first thing that Joe did was to travel to Yorkshire. He wasn't sure there was any sense in it, but Angela had loved both the country properties and Joe thought he must go everywhere. In time he would travel to Northumberland also. It must have been three years since he was briefly in

Yorkshire on some business for his father; then it had still been a fairly prosperous place.

It was neglected now, and Joe understood that. His father had never liked the estate, said it was a continual drain on his pockets. The house itself was eighteenth-century, but it was the enormous water gardens which cost so much. His father called it 'prissy' and it was indeed very formal except that the gardens were now very much overgrown and the water features full of pondweed. As Joe approached the house too seemed to have a vacant air as though nobody lived there. He didn't know who had bought it, it didn't seem to matter, though Mr Barrington undoubtedly did. It was almost derelict. Someone had bought it and had either left it uncared for, which seemed unlikely, or they had not had the money to keep the house going. You could fall in love with such a house, Joe thought, and only then discover how it ate at your resources.

There had been a manor house on the site at one time, belonging to Joe's ancestors, so he was told. The main house which had been built and rebuilt was vast, mostly Georgian, and covered a huge amount of land. Joe had liked the place when he was little, partly because his father had taken friends there and they'd had parties in the summer. His father never went in the winter.

As Joe got nearer he realized that the problem with the house was worse than he had anticipated. The windows were blackened and the outside stone was dark. When he got closer he could see that there had been some kind of fire. The windows were all gone. He pushed open the front door and saw the ceilings had come down on that level and on the floor above. He could see as high as the outside, beyond the roof. The place was all but ruined.

He heard footsteps behind him and glanced around. An old man stood there.

'Why, Mr Joe,' he said, 'it's you.'

Joe remembered him instantly. 'Ben.'

Ben Harrison had taught him to ride a horse shortly after he could walk. Ben had taught him how to shoot. As soon as he could hold a shotgun Ben had put only one cartridge into the gun, knelt in front of him with the barrel across his shoulder and Joe pulled the trigger, squeezed it carefully, as Ben had told him. The gun went off, though God knows what it had done to Ben's ears. The recoil sent Joe clean back over and Ben had to rescue both the gun and the boy.

Joe had gone and stayed with Ben and his wife when he was small. They had no children of their own and idolized him. Ben had been a huge part of Joe's childhood. He had been proud to introduce Angela to the old man and see that he approved.

'Didn't know you were back,' the old man said, 'and what a sorrowful time for you to come home. Your father . . .'

He stopped there. Joe nodded.

'And for you to see this place in such a way.'

'What happened?'

'Your father sold it to a man who had made a lot of money in some industry or other. It was to be for his son.' Ben looked down. 'The poor boy, like so many others, didn't come back from France and his father was so grief-stricken that he set the place on fire, as though it was responsible for everything. How could he do such a thing when millions of other people lost their sons and had to learn to get on with it? How could he take it out on such a beautiful place as this? Nature is never the cause of the problem and yet it gets blamed for so many things.'

Joe shook his head. 'Do you hear anything of Miss Toddington?' he asked. 'You do know what happened?'

'We heard and I'm sorry. I just wish she had come to me; I would have helped her, done anything for her. This war has ruined people's lives without killing them – you and Miss Toddington and your father. Nobody around here knows anything or I would have made it my business to help her and you. If I learn of anything I will be sure to let you know.'

Joe left him Mr Barrington's bank address and went home, explaining that he would not be living at the house in London for much longer.

Joe awoke when it was dark. For no reason at all he suddenly knew that Toddy had told him a pack of lies. Angela had not gone off anywhere. It was a stupid idea. He didn't know why he had believed it. He sat up in the chair. Angela had done nothing of the sort. She would never have done so.

He couldn't sleep after that. He lay there for as long as he could make himself do so and then he got up and prowled the house.

Later in the morning he turned up at Toddy's. He knocked on the door and was admitted by the same man. He acknowledged him without a smile. Joe waited in the hall for quite some time before the man came back and told him that Mr and Mrs Toddington were not at home.

Joe pushed past him and walked into the second room on the right from which the man had come.

There Sarah sat, her eyes wide in horror at his intrusion.
'You can't do this,' she said.

The man had followed him. He was fifty, Joe reckoned, short and fat; he had not just fought in a war. Joe glared at him while Sarah said in wavering tones, 'It's all right, Trevors, you can go.'

Joe could see the panic in her eyes. She glanced at the door, hoping no doubt that Toddy would walk, as he did, seconds later. This time his face was set and angry.

'What on earth are you doing here?'

'Is that the best you can do?' Joe said.

Toddy tried to maintain his pose and failed. His body slouched.

'We don't want you here, Joe. You must know that people who regarded you and your father as good honourable people don't any more.'

'You lied to me,' Joe accused him.

Toddy looked back and the anger was there again. 'I did nothing of the kind.'

'Yes, you did – you and Sarah here and everybody else. Angela didn't leave here because she didn't care about me, or she cared that my . . . what, that my title was worthless without money and estates. All right, some stupid bitches might think so—' He heard Sarah draw in her breath at his language, but he didn't care. 'Where is she?'

'I don't know.'

'You goddamned bloody liar. You know exactly where she is.'

'I don't,' Toddy said. Now his eyes were clear, but he turned them swiftly to his wife; her face was so pale Joe thought she might pass out.

'Sarah?' Joe prompted her. He thought it was the first time he'd seen hate on a woman's face.

'You did it,' she said.

'Don't,' Toddy said.

She glared at him. 'Why shouldn't he hear it? Our friends know what kind of man he is, what happened to Angela.'

'Tell me,' Joe insisted.

He looked at her, trying to soften his insistence with his eyes.

She looked suddenly sorrowful and the words were almost whispered.

'She was expecting a child.'

What was left of Joe's world crashed down around him.

'Have you any idea what that's like in our society? A young girl of high birth who has been . . . been so stupid as to give herself to a man like you? By then your father had shown how low he was – he tried to take money from his friends, he stole, he begged, he went to people's houses drunk and spoiled their family times and he lay on the streets and was sick in the gutters—'

'Sarah, stop it—' Toddy said.

'Let him hear it. He wanted to know. Your father was horrified by what you had done and her father was so ashamed that he tried to make her go to some dreadful place where stupid girls go when they have disgraced themselves – but she wouldn't. He told her—' Sarah stopped and swallowed hard and then she went on. 'He told her that you were dead.'

Joe thought he would never be able to take his eyes off her

white narrow face and gleaming dark eyes. She was crying now; the tears rushed her face as though they had been held back for a very long time and it was only now that she was grieving.

'The day before she was to be sent to such a place she . . . she ran away.'

Joe stood. It was all he could do. He had been so busy sorting things out in France, envisaging how they would be together, and all that time she was going through something which a single woman should never have to.

'Didn't it ever occur to you that that might happen?' she asked, her eyes like hard jewels.

She held his gaze while Joe fought to comprehend the gravity of what he had done, the results of his folly.

'It was one weekend,' he said finally as the waves of horror threw themselves over him.

She was glaring at him now. Joe felt smaller, as if he had shrivelled. He found his breathing all over the place. The room was turning black around him. He fought it, won, and the room slowly righted itself.

'Why don't you get out?' she said.

'But where is she? Where would she go?'

'None of us knows. What Toddy told you was a fabrication. She ran. We have done everything we could to find her; we were so concerned, so worried about her. She thought you were dead and then she disappeared. She couldn't stand the idea that you cared more for indulging yourself in her body than you cared for her reputation, her happiness or her well-being. Toddy went to all our friends and relatives but nobody has seen or heard anything of her and now we don't even know if she is alive. You caused this. So now you know what it has been like for all of us and most especially for her – having a child in some awful kind of poverty because you risked everything, and for what? Perhaps she's even dying. Is that love?'

At that moment – it couldn't have been worse timed, Joe thought – the doors opened and Toddy's parents were ushered into the room. They had obviously been alerted that he was here. sir Felix Toddington glared at Joe. He was a big man; when they had been children Toddy and Angela had both been afraid of him. Joe's father had put up with him because their families were friends. Lady Toddington was tall and stately and always reminded Joe of a ship in full sail. She adored her children and now when she saw Joe her blue eyes were the brighter for the tears in them.

'So she ran away from you?' Joe accused sir Felix.

'It was your doing,' the man roared back, his thin face mottled.

'Couldn't you have helped her?'

'We did everything we could. We wanted to do the right thing but she wouldn't have it. You had poisoned her mind against her family.'

Joe shook his head. 'The right thing? To send her to such a place where they would make her give up our baby? Couldn't you have forgiven us and looked after her? You knew I was coming home.'

'Thousands of better men than you died in France. We didn't know that you would come back.'

'The war was over,' Joe said, and his voice broke. 'Couldn't you have written to me, couldn't you have helped?'

'I didn't want my daughter married to you after you treated her so badly and after the way your father was behaving,' her father said. 'I would rather she had died than marry into such a family.'

There wasn't a lot left to say after that, Joe thought. Lady Toddington stood as if she were stuffed. She didn't cry or turn away or say anything which might have helped, and Joe was a little surprised at that. She had always liked him, had supported them, had been glad that they were engaged. She had even liked Joe's father, had tried to help him during the years after Joe's mother had died. He could remember her very often being there for him, but she offered him nothing now and he understood. She blamed him for everything; they all did.

Joe felt scorched, worthless and, even worse than that, he imagined Angela lost and alone and in despair. Perhaps like his father, she had even taken her own life because she could bear no more. Did she hate him now? If she didn't then she would surely have followed him to France, found him there – but then she was bearing a child.

He somehow got himself out of the house and back to where his chair waited. There was nothing else.

FIVE

Lucy came to, out of the arms of wonderful sleep. She tried to get back to where she had been, to some pleasant dream which included her parents and Gemma, but she couldn't. She had awoken in the dim light and remembered where she was. It took several moments to focus and even that was difficult because the room was in darkness, though fingers of light were trying to reach around the curtains. Then she realized that someone was knocking hesitantly on her door and from out there came the sound of a worried voice speaking her name. She lay for a few moments longer until the voice saying her name for the third time became recognizable. It was Gemma.

She had been forgiven. Gemma had not married Guy, for she knew now that her sister had been right. Her father and mother saw that she had been speaking the truth. All her best dreams had come true – she was going home. She almost fell out of bed, stumbled the short distance to the door, unlocked it, hauled it open and there stood her sister.

'Gemma!' she exclaimed and threw herself into her sister's arms, rapturous with relief.

Only she didn't. There were a few moments before she

could make herself believe that no one stood outside her door. There was nothing but empty air. She had wanted it so badly that she had imagined it.

She thought she had grown used to the sickening feeling, that what had happened could not be put aside as some kind of nightmare. The nightmare was real and went on and on. She tried to breathe and not to cry as disappointment swept over her, overwhelming her with desire to go back into the room, to close and lock the door and get thankfully into bed, staying there forever in the darkness.

She turned over but already couldn't recall more than the shadows of her dream. The family drifted further and further away the more she tried to bring them back until she could barely remember what they looked like.

Thankfully, once again, sleep took over. The next time she awoke it was dark and she was thirsty. She waited until her eyes adjusted themselves, until she could make out the jug on the dressing table which would still have water in it. She got carefully out of bed, went over and put the jug to her lips. The water tasted slightly stale, but there was enough to quench her thirst. She went back to bed. Then she needed the lavatory. By the time she had returned she was wide awake and so afraid.

The cathedral clock was striking eleven. She lay there for hours, shutting her eyes and wishing for oblivion. But she had slept enough; her body was demanding food. She hadn't eaten in days and every time she thought of normal things it brought back being at home. She wished now that she had told her mother she had slept with a college boy. She should have done that. Even though they would have been ashamed of her they would have accepted it and she would not be here like this. She would have been at Gemma and Guy's wedding. The idea of seeing him ever again made her change her mind abruptly.

She thought of Gemma marrying that man and she knew that she had been right to tell them, even though they had not believed her. Even though they had taken no notice no matter what she said, she had still been right. She would have blamed herself when anything had gone wrong in Gemma's marriage if she had kept silent. It was a gamble of course, like most important things were. There was no reason that she knew of why a man who did such a thing would not make as good as husband as any other man, though to her it didn't seem sensible.

Even though it had cost her so very much she could not have done that to her sister. She questioned her own motives. Part of her was still a woman and tried to blame her for what had happened. But it didn't matter how often she went through the scene again – and she made herself do it, thinking that perhaps she had gone outside on purpose to bring him to her – no, she had not. She went over and over it, though it wounded her every time. The lingering physical pain reminded her of another problem. What if she were to have a child?

The panic was enough to send her back under the covers, to exhaust her so that she went to sleep again. She thought if she could just do this every time she woke up then everything would be all right.

She didn't know how many days it was before her body

demanded food again and when it wasn't supplied she began to feel sick until she was sick every time she drank water. It was strange to discover that she didn't want to die after all. If she lay there much longer, she reasoned, she would be too weak to get up and move.

She felt herself going into some deep black place which made her try to claw her way free. If she did not get out of bed now, something told her, she never would – and although she had thought that was what she wanted, it turned out that it wasn't. There was some force which would not let her lie there and then she felt the blood between her legs. At least she was not pregnant. How strange when it was something to be glad of; she had always thought that when it happened she would be married to a decent man and that somehow she would have fitted into her father's business. It made her laugh now to have had such innocent dreams.

She managed to stand up and found the clothes which she had left on the floor for however many days it had been since she had shut herself in here as though it were a tomb. She found her purse. There wasn't much in it, but it wasn't empty. She took up the key and unlocked the door. The corridor beyond would not stay still; it seemed endless. Other people flitted in and out and some of them spoke.

One girl even said, 'Are you all right, Miss Charlton?'

Lucy almost remembered her name and smiled and said that she had had the flu but was much better. But the girl did not seem to care because she did not enquire any further. The corridor disappeared into the distance and Lucy followed it, trying to make sense of the place.

Eventually she came outside. There was sunshine. How

odd. She screwed up her eyes against it. She moved into the shadows and from there walked around Palace Green and down into Saddler Street. She stepped back out into the sunshine in the marketplace, walking further over the cobbles of Silver Street until she reached the café from which wafted the smell of bacon.

She sat down at the nearest table inside and ordered a pot of tea and a bacon sandwich. She ate swiftly because she was so hungry, drank all the tea, paid and got herself outside again. She staggered back to her room. She had not thought about how she felt until now, but she felt worse, hot and cold. Luckily she did not throw up the bacon sandwich and tea as she had begun to think she might. She managed to get the key into the lock and herself back into the room, falling thankfully on to the bed. After that she was oblivious to everything.

Again her sleep was happy, full of dreams of being at home when everything was well. Her stomach was satisfied, and it was strange that something so basic could lift her mood. She had not known the difference it would make. She slept as she had done as a child, which made it all the more difficult when she awoke – because this time she wanted to get up.

The room had become her cell; she felt like a nun or a monk. It was home to her now. She only went back to sleep after promising herself that the following day she would find some work. Her sensible side said that if she didn't have work she would never graduate, that she would not go on to be a solicitor. Considering everything which had happened to her she had to manage that. The money which she had left from her post office savings account must last; she must eke it out until she graduated and then she must find better work.

SIX

Joe didn't have visitors. He only went out for food and into the yard at the back of the house – where the carriage houses and stables were – to replenish the fire. So he was astonished one day in February to hear a banging on the front door. He had fallen asleep some time in the middle of the night in his father's chair. He almost didn't answer it but then he thought of Angela – it could be news from some unexpected source – so as the banging went on he trod through the freezing hall and jerked open the door.

'Major Hardy?'

The man had a slight north-eastern accent, Joe recognized; he had met many men from Durham and Newcastle when he was in France, though they had flatter vowels than this man, he must have been educated, middle-class. He was about Joe's height, in his thirties, and well dressed, with a coat and scarf and hat and leather gloves. And he had been a soldier, Joe could tell; he had about him that rigid, tired air that they all had, those who had come through, as though he had seen too much too young and everything was dulled.

'My name is Edgar Bainbridge. I'm a solicitor. I would like to talk to you. May we go inside?'

Joe ushered him along the hall and into the library. There was still nothing but one chair; it was obvious from the pillow and blankets that Joe was using the room to sleep in.

Joe could see Mr Bainbridge trying not to stare. The fire was dead in the grate – other than his blankets and pillow there were no signs of habitation. Joe tried to look at it objectively, but it defeated him; this was his whole world now.

'You see, Major Hardy—'

'It's "mister",' Joe said.

'I'm sorry?'

'Mr Hardy. I'm not in the army any more.'

'People usually . . .'

Joe waved at the armchair, tired of the whole thing and hoping this wouldn't take long since there was only one chair.

'Do have a seat,' he said.

Edgar Bainbridge nodded and sat down among the cushions and the blankets as though he did it most days. Joe admired that.

Mr Bainbridge hesitated and then said, 'I don't know much about your circumstances, Mr Hardy, so you will have to forgive me if I'm indelicate here. You have been left a house in Durham City, in County Durham.'

'I have been left what?' Joe said.

'A house,' the man said, as though neither he nor Joe had ever heard anything of the kind.

'I think you've made a mistake,' Joe said. 'I had a house in Northumberland where I used to spend a lot of time, but everything's gone now. I know nothing about Durham and nobody of my family or my close friends ever lived in the

68

county. I've never even been there.' He had heard there was a cathedral, surrounded by coalmines. He had never had any inclination to go there.

Mr Bainbridge frowned. 'The will reads simply. It is yours.'

'Is it something I can sell?'

'The will states that you must go and live in it for a year. It's quite a substantial building,' he said, 'a tower house. What we call a pele tower, a fortification. They are often situated in the borders, from the disputed lands in the days of the reivers – many of them have survived, only this is in the city.'

Having an estate in Northumberland Joe knew something of this but hadn't considered it before.

'Is there any money?'

Mr Bainbridge looked patiently at him. 'No.'

Joe smiled in tolerance. 'I don't understand then. Which side of the family is it?'

'I have no idea who it is in relation to you.'

'What is the name of the person?'

'Miss Priscilla Lee.'

'It doesn't mean anything,' Joe said.

Perhaps, he thought, it was some dotty old aunt. Both his grandfathers had apparently been landowners so their families must have been rich at some time, before gambling, drinking and debts took care of it.

'After a year you own it and may do what you please.'

'So this Lee family – who are they and how did they come by such a place?'

'I don't know anything about it. When Miss Lee's will was made I was a small child – my father is dead now and I have no information on the subject. What you do is up to you.' He handed Joe a card. 'When you come north I will give you the key.'

Joe was dazed. After Mr Bainbridge had gone he thought how peculiar the whole thing was. His life was nothing like he had imagined it would be. All he had thought of was reaching home, seeing his father and holding Angela in his arms. He didn't know how to go on looking for her any more. As for his staying here, the house would be sold and he would be homeless. He didn't make a decision, only went back to his chair and fell asleep. It had become his one refuge.

The weather turned bitterly cold and even after what he had been through in France, Joe felt it. He thought that he could only put up with so much for so long and his limits had been reached in every direction. He didn't know what to do, whom to contact – he couldn't think how he might find Angela now. Even this house had become an alien place and yet he could not make himself leave, he felt as though he were clinging to the wreckage of his life.

One morning in January he had a letter from Mr Barrington to say that there were several interested parties for the London house and that he would employ someone to show them around. Joe took that as a hint that he could no longer stay.

He felt like holding doors, hiding in the attic. He even went upstairs – it was darker and colder than he remembered, and daylight, such as it was at this time of the year, peeped in where the roof should have been repaired. It had been left as everything else: neglected.

There were various discarded pieces of furniture, none of them worth anything, some of them broken, and a few of his toys, small painted soldiers in red and blue, and an old rocking horse whose mane had gone and whose eyes were wild. There were books, their pages mottled brown with damp. There was his old school trunk. He opened it; inside was a cricket bat he had once used and a rugby ball and, to his surprise, some papers at the bottom. They didn't look as if they had been casually set aside but deliberately put there – folded thick pieces of paper.

They were letters, he saw in the dim light, dozens of them. He couldn't help but be curious so he took them with him back downstairs and into the chair. He untied the ribbons they were bound with and soon realized they were the letters he had written to his father, each one folded carefully and kept together with blue ribbons.

His father had not written him one letter in five years, but he had kept every one that Joe had written him. It brought tears to Joe's eyes. There were a great many of the letters. Under the ribboned ones he found another whole set, unbound. He opened the first one of these, dated right at the beginning of the war – it was a letter from his father to him.

Why had it not been posted? What was it doing here? Was it a draft of something his father had intended him to receive? Then why had he not received the final thing? He opened a second, then a third and that was when he saw in huge dismay that his father had written to him over and over again during the war, but he had not sent any of these things. Was it because he thought Joe did not deserve them?

Was it because he hated the idea of Joe being so far away that he couldn't send them? Then why keep them?

There were so many. Joe didn't want to read them. He wanted to put them on a fire. His father was dead; what did any of it matter now? He gazed at the black grate, then he got up and went into the back of the house and beyond into the great big courtyard. Here were the stables and the carriages and other outhouses – the washhouse and the hen house and the buildings where the outside servants had lived.

He found coal and wood and he shoved these into a bucket. He hauled them inside and set them down by the library fire. He took some of the letters which he had sent to his father and scrunched them into balls in his hands. He threw them onto the back of the big grate, doing the same with the letters his father had written and when he was happy with that he made a fire. He watched it flicker into life and then sat down until it should be big enough so that he could burn away the only things which were left.

He awoke some time later with a stiff neck. The fire had gone out. There was still a pile letters from his father. They seemed to mock him. He didn't want to try to light the fire again, it was all too much effort. He had dreamed of being with his father in Northumberland; they had been riding into the wide open fields and it had been spring. The buttercups rose tall and bright yellow in the fields, the riverbanks were green and white with garlic, smelling like dinner, and the sky was blue with white scudding clouds, thick like fluff. He thought back to this pleasant dream.

Joe didn't know whether it was that which made him decide to go north, that and the idea that he would at least be able to take a look around the old estate. There just didn't seem to be any point in staying here longer. He put together the things he had with the remaining letters which his father had not sent him and he left the house as the morning arrived, for the last time. He didn't look back. There was nothing to look back for.

On the train he read the first of his father's letters. Even taking the paper from the envelope and seeing his father's distinctive looped handwriting hurt Joe so much that he wanted to fold it back up again and throw it out of the window, but he didn't.

It was on thick quality cream paper and written in black ink. Joe could feel the love that his father had for him even before he read it and that made him feel just a little bit better as the train made its way northward. It was written in the first weeks after he had left home.

My dear Joe,

I cannot bear the idea that you will not come back to me and nightly I tell myself that you will, but at four in the morning when I awake alone I see you dead in France along with hundreds of thousands of other young men. I have seen war and I know what it is like. There is nothing glorious about it. I have seen my friends killed and my comrades badly injured, dying for lack of food, water and care. How can they send all the young men away like this and why should I give up my son for such carelessness?

I want to understand why you went. Youth has never minded age or thought their fathers knew anything. I suppose everyone must learn for themselves how to live, but not how to die. I don't want you to learn about dying when you are so young.

I wish there was something I could do to bring you home. I want to send you impassioned messages to say that I am ill. Can you be ill with loneliness? I miss the boy you were and the enjoyment we had and the time we spent together before you saw me as something in your way. I miss your growing up. You are so different now, not at all as I envisaged you would be. I want to be proud of you because you take your challenges before you, meet each one as yet another part of life, but all I see now is the soldier, my last memories of you going away and Angela going bravely to the station to see you off while I stood there at home, ashamed of myself, wishing you back with us. At the worst times I wish I didn't love you so very much; I have everything to lose.

Angela is my only comfort.

SEVEN

Lucy was glad when she left the university. She was pleased that it was over. But she had nowhere to live and needed to find some kind of work; though she would not be able to pay for articles until she made a great deal of money and that was impossible to think about now. She went to shops where they had 'Help Wanted' in the window, but she was dismissed mostly by a shake of the head. After four such experiences she began enquiring at various public houses and hotels, but it was just the same. After a long day she sat in the Silver Street café because it was so familiar. She said to the woman who was on the desk at the door, 'Do you need any help?'

The woman looked at her in surprise and smiled a little. 'We do, but not from lasses like yourself.' It wasn't said to offend, but Lucy knew that the woman recognized her; she had been in there so many times.

She felt bolder and asked, 'What do you mean, like me?'

'You talk different.'

'I'm from Newcastle.'

The woman shook her head. 'It's not that. You sound like you've had a lot of schooling – you don't belong in a place like this.'

'But I need work.'

'You'd frighten the customers. Sorry, love, but you're above all this; it wouldn't go down well.'

Lucy drank her tea and after it, since the day wasn't over yet, she called at various offices which belonged to the businesses in the town.

Every time it was the same question: 'Do you type?'

It seemed stupid that with all her qualifications the one thing which eluded her was something so small, and yet she didn't know how to use a typewriter. She thought of all those days spent with Miss Shuttleworth at her father's office. Why hadn't it seemed important? She had only two more days to get her things out of her room.

She went to several boarding houses to find somewhere cheap to stay, but single women were not given to doing such things and she was turned away at the door. One woman made her cheeks burn saying that she 'wanted no hoors'. In the cheaper parts of the town she was uncomfortable. Dirty children played in the street. Two of them threw stones at her so that she shouted at them – then they minded her and ran away.

She ended up by the river, which felt better, though the street here was dirty and the smells made Lucy wrinkle her nose. To her surprise a notice sat in one of the windows: 'Typewriting Lessons'. She banged on the door and a middle-aged woman answered. She was large and wore much more expensive clothes than Lucy had imagined anyone wore in such places, though they were rather shabby. She smiled affably and spoke in an educated, cultured voice.

When Lucy said that she needed to take lessons the woman, who'd introduced herself as Miss Slater, invited her in, calling as she did so down the hall, 'Bethany! We have company,' and at that point another middle-aged woman appeared. 'This is Miss Charlton. She wishes to learn to use a typewriter.'

'Oh, my dear, do come in,' Miss Bethany said. She was taller and slimmer than the first woman, whom Lucy supposed to be her sister, and she too wore an almost benign expression as though she could cope with most things.

There was poor and then there was *poor*, Lucy decided. These women had done what was called 'coming down in the world', she guessed. They had some lovely furniture, huge and old-fashioned and quite unsuited for such a dismal place. They even had a piano.

'Sadly out of tune because of the damp,' Miss Slater told her cheerfully.

In the sitting room a large, ragged-eared brown-and-white-haired springer spaniel lay, smelly and snoring.

'Frederick, do get off the furniture,' Miss Slater told him. The dog opened one eye, closed it and began to snore again.

In the back room, what other people would have termed the kitchen and Miss Slater called the 'morning room', there was a table with a large black typewriter upon it. There was also a range though no sign of a sink, and a little pantry beyond that no doubt hid other things.

'How much do you charge?' was Lucy's first question.

'Oh, my dear,' said Miss Bethany, going pale at the indelicacy, 'do sit down and take some tea.'

The biscuits were moist and stale. Lucy ate one with gusto. The tea tasted musty as though it had been in a cupboard for a long time, brought out only on special occasions. The fire was small in there, though rain had fallen for a week without stopping. Lucy's shoes had let in every drop she stood on. They couldn't afford much coal, she realized, even in a place like this where it was cheap.

The sisters asked tentatively about Lucy's background and were clearly pleased to discover that she was a solicitor's daughter from Newcastle and that she had taken a law degree.

'So few girls take responsibility for themselves and so many have to,' said Miss Slater with a sigh.

She told Lucy that before they had moved here their father had been a vicar in a pit village not far outside Durham. When he had died they had come here with their mother because they must allow the next incumbent to have the vicarage. Their mother had died two years later. Miss Slater taught children to play the piano and Miss Bethany typewriting.

'I am also looking for somewhere to stay, somewhere which doesn't cost much,' Lucy said.

The two sisters looked at one another and nodded. Miss Slater said, 'You must stay here with us. I can move into Bethany's room and you may have mine, cheaply. My dear, do come to stay; it would help us a great deal and you are such a charming girl.'

She showed Lucy the little back room which looked onto an unmade street. It was tiny, with a single bed and a shelf above it, cluttered almost to the ceiling with clothes and linen and books. She could not have said no. She liked the two ladies, and felt safe for the first time since her father had thrown her out.

'Are you planning to become a secretary? Such a good job for a girl,' Miss Slater said.

'I want to become a solicitor, but I can't afford to go to any law firm that might take me on – and I don't suppose there are many of them anyway.'

'No, indeed,' Miss Slater said.

For a few moments Lucy was irritated that the woman agreed with her until she continued shrewdly, 'You might join a law firm as a secretary, if you could find anything. It wouldn't be what you really want of course, but it would be one way in. You might learn a great deal, and if you save as much as you can then one day you *will* be a lawyer.' The woman beamed at her.

Lucy admitted to herself that this was a realistic way to look at it and she could not stop the little frisson of hope that dawned within her. She was even better pleased when Miss Bethany told her that she might have the typewriting lessons free if she would help them with other things.

'What other things?' she asked cautiously.

'Do you cook?' They both looked eagerly at her.

'No.'

'Oh dear,' Miss Bethany said, 'that would have been a joy. Neither of us ever learned. Mother didn't think ladies ought to be in the kitchen. She had married beneath her and was obliged to make the best of things, but really we eat so badly. We always have.'

And so it was that Lucy said that she would try. They found her a cookery book which had for some reason been in their father's library. It was written by Eliza Acton and Lucy sat reading it that first evening as they sat around the fire. She discovered that cooking appeared to be mostly about putting the right ingredients together – something that this clever person had found an affinity for.

Miss Acton had a decidedly confident approach, observing the results of different recipes, and depending on things like time of year, kind of fruit and the day it was picked. Her accuracy and enthusiasm made Lucy want to go into the kitchen and take it for hers. How odd when she had never felt so before. Perhaps a woman needed a kitchen of her own, and since the two Misses Slaters were at a loss in there she felt that she could do that. She discovered pots and pans which they had not used. It looked as if they had lived on sandwiches for a very long time – not only not good for them but very dull.

When she dared mention this they acknowledged it with nods of their heads.

'Every time one of us goes in there we have a disaster and we waste food,' said Miss Slater, 'whereas sandwiches are anything one can place between two slices of bread.'

Lucy suggested to Miss Bethany that if she hired a room in the city she might hold classes and make more money than at present. Lucy didn't like to tell the two ladies that it was a rare person who came to such a place as Rachel Lane for lessons of any kind. The people around them were very poor and could never have afforded such things.

'Would it not cost a great deal of money?' Miss Bethany asked. Lucy said she would find out.

The next day Lucy moved the few things she owned into the little house by the river and went shopping for the ladies. She discovered that a great many people in Durham had vegetable gardens attached to their houses and some had allotments where things were ripening, some ready for picking, and if they had a glut they would sell or even give the fruit and vegetables to her. She began making preserves, such as she remembered her mother doing, strawberries and raspberries first, then rhubarb, gooseberries and plums. With Miss Acton's help she was able to look along the jars on the shelf with some satisfaction.

The first time she made fresh pea soup both ladies talked about it for so long afterwards that Lucy was embarrassed. She made cakes. She liked the miracle of it, how she could put the raw mixture into the oven and an hour or more later it emerged, smelling warm and sweet and transformed into substantial rounds.

She made leek and potato soup, and she bought bits of bacon leftovers from when it was cut, or she cooked ham in the same way. With cabbage and potatoes it was a good meal. With onions and potatoes baked in a white sauce in the oven it was even better. When the weather grew colder she baked apples with butter, from the local farmers who brought fruits from their orchards to market along with various cheeses they had made. She went off to the riverbank to see if the fishermen had caught anything. Sometimes it cost nothing and others just a few pennies. They ate a lot of fish.

She found learning to type quite easy; it was nothing more than an act of memory and she was adept at such things. Miss Bethany was a good teacher, encouraging and delighted with all Lucy did. Lucy went to the Miners' Institute to enquire about a room for typewriting lessons. She knew there were rooms there, including a reading room for men to read books and newspapers.

But at the door the man told her that women didn't go in.

'Why not?' she asked.

'Well, I don't really know, love.' He scratched his head. 'We do have beer on the premises and a billiard room – women don't want such things.'

'But you must have other rooms which aren't in use all the time. Miss Slater would be prepared to negotiate terms.'

'Would she indeed?' he said, looking at her with fresh eyes. 'In that case I'll see what I can do.'

Lucy returned with Miss Bethany with her, and although she was certain her papa would have thought badly of her for going into such a place, Lucy wasn't having any indecision. They discovered that the cost of a medium-sized room would be very little. They could put up advertisements outside, as well as in the windows of the various shops nearby.

'If you had just two pupils an hour you could pay for a whole morning here.'

'Yes, but why would they come?'

Lucy began to despair. 'Look,' she said gently, 'I will make certain that people know. What's more, when you make enough money we could go to the newspapers to advertise. That's something we can do cheaply. We might even get them to do an article about it. Do you see?'

Miss Bethany did see and became enthusiastic. That evening all three of them sat at the kitchen table and devised words to encourage women to come forward and have lessons and increase their chances of being able to do office work. It was something Lucy felt sure a great many mothers would be glad of and proud that their daughters could achieve such things.

Lucy printed it all in big letters on paper she had bought from the stationer's, which was part of the newspaper premises. Miss Slater soon decided to do the same for music, only she would give concerts.

Lucy was at first astonished at this, but when they went to see one of the local vicars, the one in the marketplace, St Nicholas's, he liked the idea of holding a concert in the church hall. Miss Slater had privately said to Lucy that she played the organ too, often playing for her father's church services. The vicar was inclined to think Miss Slater should do this free of charge, for God and his worshippers, but Lucy wasn't having that.

'Miss Slater has her living to make,' she told him. 'When their father died these women lost almost everything.'

That settled it. The vicar coughed politely and said that he understood of course. Lucy decided she would make cakes – she could charge for tea and cake in the interval.

Rachel's Lane was not the ideal place for two elderly ladies to live, Lucy had decided as soon as she moved in. It showed how bad things were that they could afford no better, but they regarded it as part of their Christian duty. The people next door, the Formbys, were a family of man, wife and four children. Mr Formby was fond of drink; Lucy often heard him come home singing, whenever the windows were left open, shouting at his wife and children as he entered and leading to crying next door.

This happened one night in Lucy's first week. Soon there came a banging on the back door. Lucy put a cardigan over her nightdress and went onto the landing, only to find Miss Slater there with a lamp, already descending the narrow stairs, followed closely by her sister. Lucy wanted to tell her not to open it, but it was so obviously not the first time because the moment the door was opened three children ran inside.

'Where's Tilda?' Miss Slater enquired.

'She ran off, missus,' the elder boy said, breathing hard.

'And your mother?'

His breathing was ragged and he did not reply. Miss Slater took them into the kitchen and began to bring the banked-down fire back to life. Lucy listened hard. There was no sound from next door.

'What about Mrs Formby?' Lucy asked.

'As long as there's no shouting I think she's safe,' Miss Bethany said. 'She can run upstairs and leave him because he will fall asleep, but when it's cold sometimes they sleep downstairs and he must have come and disturbed them. Go back to bed, my dear, there's no need to distress yourself.'

But Lucy stayed with them. The children wore thin clothes and were skinny. Miss Bethany went into the pantry and gave them the biscuits Lucy had made earlier that day. The children devoured them quickly. They all sat round the fire until the kettle boiled and Lucy made tea. They drank the tea and then the children piled onto the sofa, set back by

84

the kitchen wall. They swiftly fell asleep, falling against one another like a pack of cards.

'Does Mr Formby come here?' she asked.

Miss Slater shook her head.

Lucy soon realized that part of the reason the Misses Slaters had little money was because they fed these children, though the older child, Tilda, who didn't talk to them, was too proud, she thought. Their mother was ashamed and would come to the door, begging their pardon, but she would not come in, telling them only how grateful she was for their kindness to her and her bairns.

The Misses Slaters were not afraid. Lucy thought it must be their upbringing, their father having been the vicar in various pit villages in the area. She assumed that they went to the cathedral on Sundays, but they were quite shocked at the idea. Instead they went loyally to St Nicholas's church in the marketplace where Miss Slater's concerts were beginning to become well known.

Miss Bethany knitted balaclavas for the boys who lived in the street and socks and woolly hats and gloves for the girls, as well as jumpers and cardigans for all the children in the area. They were not always a success – sometimes the sleeves or the bodies were too long – but nobody complained. At least they were warm.

The Formby children began to spend more and more time next door. Lucy came home early one afternoon and when she knew the children were with Miss Slater. Miss Bethany was out most of the day teaching typewriting. Lucy went up the Formbys' backyard and banged on the back door. After a short while the girl came to the door. She was tall, dark-haired and grave-faced, and she didn't look at Lucy even when Lucy explained who she was. A few moments later her mother came to the door. She could not have been any thinner – her bones stuck out in every direction, the skin was pulled over her face and she was pale, as though she had never had enough to eat.

'You're Miss Charlton from next door, I know you,' she said.

'Would you mind very much, Mrs Formby, if I came inside and had a word?'

Mrs Formby opened wide the door. The girl disappeared into the depths of the house. Lucy went in. She had never been into a house that was so poor, though every inch of it was clean. There was hardly any furniture. There was a broken chair in the front room which Mrs Formby insisted she should sit in, since it was all she had to offer. Lucy refused Mrs Formby's offer of tea; she didn't want to cost her hostess a penny and was already thinking to herself that she would make cake and biscuits for the family. Lucy wished they could have sat in the kitchen as there was no fire in here nor ever had been judging by the blackness of the grate, though since Mrs Formby was intent on having everything so clean Lucy couldn't be sure.

She looked straight at the woman and she thought how skinny her whole body was. Her face had dropped from lack of good food, and there was in the house the most awful atmosphere. She thought it was despair.

'Mrs Formby, I don't know that I should be here. You will be quite right to tell me that I should mind my own business and I would go immediately and not bother you again—'

Mrs Formby interrupted her here, even smiling to show several of her teeth were missing. 'The Misses Slaters have been that kind to my bairns, why would I mind you coming here?'

'I'm going to say something very particular to you and I don't think you're going to be pleased, but the moment you want me to leave I will, I promise.' Lucy hesitated. 'I cannot be ignorant, living next door, of the fact that Mr Formby is unkind to you. I know you are trying to keep it from your neighbours and I understand your pride, but if you went to the law you would be granted a separation order and money from him. I know this because my father is a solicitor in Newcastle and he instructed me. If he was here he would help you, and I want to help you too.'

Mrs Formby's eyes filled with tears. 'I just wish it was that easy,' she said. 'He doesn't work, he isn't well, that was the problem in the first place, you see. He drinks the little he has because he cannot stand the man he's become. He hasn't got any money to give us.'

'Then how are you managing?'

Mrs Formby looked proud for the first time and nodded at the ceiling.

'My Tilda has got a job with the store. She's working in the shoe department. Can you imagine that, Miss Charlton? She's a grand lass.'

'Do you want to live with Mr Formby?'

Mrs Formby looked at her as though she were mad. 'He's my husband,' she said.

This was not easy, Lucy thought. 'All I'm saying to you is that if you wanted you could live apart from him.'

Mrs Formby frowned. 'I married him for better or worse, Miss Charlton.'

'But if the worse becomes too much there are other ways. The law would be on your side.'

Mrs Formby looked at her with gratitude, yet as though there were a hundred years between them. She touched Lucy's cheek with her knuckles as no doubt she did with her children and looked on her with pride as though Lucy were her daughter.

'What a lovely lass you are,' she said. 'I bet your mam is proud of you.'

It was only another day or two when Mr Formby came home drunk again, mid-evening. Lucy could hear him shouting, but it was not just at Mrs Formby, for she heard the girl scream. Lucy ran out of the house and burst into the kitchen next door. Mr Formby was a very big man and he had hold of his daughter, her wrist caught in one of his big square hands. She had turned away as though he were about to hit her. His wife was crying and the children were huddled against her.

'Let her go!' Lucy yelled. She hadn't raised her voice for a long time, but it responded well. He didn't take any notice – perhaps he didn't hear her, perhaps he had drunk so much that he was unaware she had entered his house – but when she shouted again, 'I will get the police if you don't let her go!' he did.

And then he turned around. It didn't occur to Lucy to be afraid of him, no matter how big he was. In some awful way she had learned from Guy what men could do to women.

She knew that this man could kill her with a single blow if he chose and if she didn't get out of the way, but she didn't care. The anger had been boiling up in her for a very long time. She stood there, glad of her height and of the way that men had taught her such awful lessons. She held her ground and kept him still with her eyes. She glared at him. He considered her and then to her surprise and horror he started to laugh. Lucy felt all her emotion drain away.

'Why,' he sneered, 'it's the skinny plain lass from next door with the ginger-coloured hair,' and he spat on the floor and began to lumber from the room.

In the silence Lucy heard him making his drunken way up the stairs, banging into either side and swearing until at last he staggered against the bedroom door and cursed again. After that there was silence. Lucy felt deflated and then she saw that this was what some men did to women, they tried to make them feel stupid and insignificant.

Tilda stood in the middle of the room with her hand to her mouth. She was shaking with sobs, yet no sound came out. Mrs Formby took the girl into her arms and the children, who had run off when Lucy shouted at their father, came out of the shadows, unsure. Lucy badly wanted to cry herself, but she felt that she couldn't. She turned to go and Mrs Formby came to her.

'What a brave bairn you are,' she said, reaching up to kiss Lucy on the cheek, something Lucy's mother had never done.

The following morning Lucy left early and went to the police station in Elvet. It was not a welcoming place, gloomy, with a big desk running the full length of the room as though people were desperate to get in – or out, she corrected herself. A big fat man in uniform was writing. He didn't look up.

'Good morning,' Lucy said. He glanced at her in surprise and she thought he hadn't heard.

And then he smiled and said, 'Why, Miss Lucy Charlton. What are you doing here?'

'Constable Keane?'

This was not so very different to when Lucy's father had taken her to the various police stations in Newcastle. The change was that she had done this alone and she felt relief that the policeman knew her. And this man had been one of the best; he would be her friend, she was sure.

'I live here now,' she said. 'What about you?'

He hesitated.

'My lady wife died,' he said, straightening up as he obviously felt he should, 'so I came back to Durham. It's my home. Where would I go but here? I've got no family left. We have no bairns you know and I wanted a change.'

'I'm so sorry,' Lucy said, 'but it's lovely to see you.'

'So what can we do for you, Miss Lucy?'

'I just wish there could be a man on the beat in Rachel Lane where I live, someone to look in occasionally at number four, because Mr Formby is behaving very badly to his family. I think it might make a difference if you were to become involved. I lodge next door with the Misses Slaters at number three. Mrs Formby could apply for a separation order, but Mr Formby doesn't work and she has nowhere to go.'

Constable Keane shook his head and pressed his lips carefully together. 'I'll do what I can, Miss Lucy, but you know we are awfully overstretched and there are a lot of such like incidents. I wish I didn't have to deal with them. It's very bad. We don't have enough men or sufficient money – unless you can give me a crime there isn't a great deal I can do about it.'

'All I want is a policeman in Rachel Lane during the evening. Surely every street is on some policeman's beat,' Lucy said.

He looked again, sighed again.

'I tell you what,' he said, 'I will make sure that one of my lads is seen there at some time late each evening and that from time to time he knocks on their door. Will that do?'

She smiled at him, nodded, thanked him and left.

When Lucy became good at typing Miss Bethany encouraged her to find a job.

'Try the solicitors' offices first.' Lucy didn't want to say that she was afraid she would not get anywhere because it was what she wanted more than anything.

'It doesn't matter if they don't look as though they need help,' Miss Bethany said. 'I'm not sure they would be able to put notices in their windows – I think it's more a case of knowing people, and since you don't know anybody you must go and ask. Give it your best, go to everyone.'

Encouraged, she did, but it was a very hard thing to do. She was dismissed just inside the door by one man, and another let her get as far as the front desk but there told her they did not employ women, which was ridiculous, she thought, as many women worked in different kinds of offices.

Finally, when she was about to slink back to Rachel Lane and admit defeat, she made her way into Bainbridge and

Featherstone, the only solicitors' office she had not been to, as far as she could tell.

It was empty, the front desk unattended. She thought this most unusual, but there was nobody waiting to see Mr Bainbridge or Mr Featherstone, so perhaps they had things to do in the back and were unaware that anyone was inside. There was no bell to press or anything else to summon the clerk or whatever person dealt with such things. Lucy coughed politely and waited for a few moments. She heard the sound of raised voices from the passage beyond.

She nearly left, as it seemed rude to stand there listening, but then gave herself a mental push. She had no job – she had nothing to go back to but to tell the Misses Slaters that she had not got anywhere, and she didn't feel as if she could do that. She called out, not very loudly, just a 'hello', and waited. But it was clear they couldn't hear because they were shouting at one another and the door, which she presumed they supposed was shut in the darkness of the passage, stood open sufficiently for Lucy to detect exactly what they said. It was a man and a woman and they were arguing, as only members of a family would argue, without care.

'You have no right to expect me to come here day after day when I already have so much to do.'

'You have nothing to do. Norah runs the house. She does the cooking, the cleaning, the ordering of the groceries, she sorts out the woman who comes to do the washing – if it wasn't for Hindmarch bringing in the coal and looking after the garden and giving her a hand generally, she could be called a housekeeper. She keeps the whole damned place right. What on earth you do all day I have no idea.'

The girl's voice rose and trembled. 'I don't know how you can say this to me when Mother hasn't been dead ten minutes.'

'She's been dead two years, Em. And he's been gone almost four. I can't do everything by myself, I really cannot. You're about as much use as a snowball in hell.'

There was a sob and a scuffled noise and then a tall, elegant-looking young woman came out of the gloom, pushed through the office and slammed the door hard so that the windows shook. The young man who came out after her wore a good suit. He stopped when he saw Lucy and she thought he had kind eyes. They were blue like summer hills in the distance, but tired, dulled.

'Oh,' he said.

'I did call out.'

'Do you have an appointment? Mr Clarence usually deals with these things but he has the flu.'

'No—'

'Well, even if you did it probably hasn't been written down,' he said. 'Come through to the back and I'll see what I can do,' and he went off again.

Lucy followed him. The hall floor had mosaic tiles in a pretty patterned black and white that made her wonder whether the building had been a house at one time. It certainly seemed it, with this as the side way in, she thought. He ushered her into a large room which looked out across gardens. The view of the river was lovely.

'Do sit down, Miss . . .'

'Charlton. Lucy.'

'I'm Edgar Bainbridge. How can I help?'

'I'm looking for work.'

His gaze lightened on her. 'You do office work?' he said hopefully.

'I can type and . . .' she hesitated, not knowing whether to tell him and then plunged, 'I have a law degree.'

He stared. 'You're going to be a solicitor?'

'I can't afford to become an articled clerk so I thought I would look for work in this kind of office as a secretary if there was any.'

Mr Bainbridge sat back in his chair. 'Did you say your name was Charlton? Is your father a solicitor in Newcastle?'

Lucy admitted reluctantly that he was, and then knew that she must make up a story so she told him half the tale.

'My father isn't well and the business isn't doing anything – he cannot afford to take me on. I need to try for other things for myself and since I was at university here I thought I might stay.'

'My father did business with yours for years,' Mr Bainbridge said, enthusiastically, 'sending people to one another when they needed help in certain circumstances. I'm sorry your father is having such a difficult time, Miss Charlton. Your sense of timing is admirable. Mr Clarence who runs the front office has been ill and I have no one to do anything. I will give you a week to prove that you are a better secretary than my sister. Can you start on Monday?'

Eight

Joe's journey north was long. The views from the window were of fields, mile after mile. Other people came into the carriage and eventually got off, but by the time the train had reached Darlington he was the only one left. Joe did not think this was a good sign. Darlington did not appear to be prosperous, but since the daylight had long since receded all he could see were smudged tops of long terraced houses and narrow streets and what he thought might be industrial buildings beyond them, with chimneys and strange towers of some kind.

His stop was next. When he got off it was like falling from the ends of the earth somehow. The tiny station was on the top of a steep hill and he could see nothing beyond in the darkness with thick fog that swirled like fingers. He found a cab to take him into town, asking the man for a decent inexpensive hotel. He was soon let down among glowing lights and the cabbie got out to help him with his luggage.

'You'll be all right here, sir,' he said. 'If you need another cab just let us know. Paddy's Cabs these are, the best in town.'

*

The next morning Joe went to get the keys for the house. He had no difficulty in finding Mr Bainbridge's office. A passer-by assured him that most things to do with the law were in Old Elvet where the courts were, and beyond there was the prison. The man even told him where hangings had been when they were public spectacles. Joe wasn't sure he needed this information, but he went out of the marketplace and down the cobbled street which led to the bridge. He crossed it and just up there on the right he found a neat plaque which read 'Bainbridge and Featherstone'.

Inside he found himself in a front office where a big fire burned bravely.

There were several seats which looked comfortable enough and three people sat. At the nearest desk was a small, bald-headed man, a few wisps of hair clinging to the tops of his ears. Joe approached the desk. The man looked up and was affable enough, even though his thick accent made Joe lean nearer. He had to decipher as he went along as though he were in another country. And in some ways, Joe thought, he was. It was no closer than that he had met at first in Italy and a good deal more alien than France.

'I have come to pick up some keys,' Joe told him when they got to that stage. 'For Tower House, I think it's called.'

The man shuffled away behind the desks and filing cabinets and opened various drawers. After he had gone through what seemed to be everything that might possibly hold a set of keys he disappeared into the back.

Joe could hear him say, 'Miss Charlton, I can't find the keys for Tower House and the owner's just turned up.'

There was a short wait and then a tall skinny young woman with outrageous hair – the nearest colour he had ever seen to carrots, and completely out of control, although she had obviously tried hard to contain it with grips and pins which were clearly visible, holding it forcibly away from the cream complexion of her freckled face – came to him, smiling from generous lips.

In an educated and understandable though northern-toned voice she said, 'I'm so sorry, we can only find one key. Perhaps it will do for now and I will make sure that you have the others within days. Will that be all right, sir?'

She was somehow not what he had been expecting and it made him want to attempt frivolous conversation for the first time in years. He didn't know what to say to her. He had never seen eyes that looked like that. They were so dark green that they were almost black. He had heard that the best emeralds were the same.

He never looked at young women. Angela had been his only love and for him other women did not exist, but there was something special about this girl. She looked so frankly, so openly at him that they might have met before, but they hadn't – he would have remembered.

It was as though the moment he met her some kind of door opened and let daylight inside and it turned her hair to fire. He knew it was stupid, but that was how it felt, as though the corners of his mind were being gently touched, eased away from the old hurts. It was a very odd feeling. He felt also as though he were betraying Angela, even thinking that some other woman was interesting, though he knew now how stupid that was. Angela was the love of his life and no other woman would ever compete.

He smiled and was polite, taking the key which was large and old and hung on a big rusted ring, like something from a fairy story. He turned away and then back to her, remembering that he had not asked for directions.

'Do you know where this is?'

'If you go down to Framwellgate Bridge—'

'Which one is that?' Joe said.

'You go back across this bridge which is Elvet and up into the marketplace, down Silver Street on the left and across the next bridge. At the end of it you go left down the steps onto the towpath and take the left and it's along there, just before you get as far as where the cathedral stands on the opposite side. There is another way but I don't wish to confuse you.'

Joe thanked her and left. It was sleeting. Joe wished that it would stop because it was getting harder and harder to see anything. The towpath led off into the greyness of the day and even though the buildings across the river stood way up into the sky he could barely make them out. Various buildings at this side of the river were set back, almost into the town, but they had gardens which led down steeply to the river, as far as he could tell.

There was not another building anywhere near the place that he had inherited. He wasn't sure he liked that. The building itself was tall and square and so much bigger than he had imagined it might be. He had lived in huge houses all his life and this one should have seemed tiny to him but they had not the downright gravity of this. It scared him. It sat there as if it were trying to be an insult to the other houses or buildings within the city. It was tall enough to fill the sky and angular enough to make you feel dizzy and wide enough so that you couldn't see what might be behind it. Its stones were huge – some amazingly clever mason must have chipped at them until they were an exact fit.

It seemed to him to lean at all sides, though it didn't. It dominated its area, held the very air around it. The river itself might even have hesitated as it made its way to the sea. Such a strange building it was, tall and slim, as if it were reaching for the sky and yet would hold off any opponents that were necessary, he thought. It was proud.

There were stairs up the outside to the first storey and then a stout wooden door and huge shutters which would have locked over the windows. At the top were turrets and, he discovered later, a ladder going up to a trapdoor which opened to the sky, giving you a view from all sides if you needed to see the enemy coming.

The path wound up to the huge arched front door. The sleet was beginning to clear and a pale lemon sun lit the edges of the scene. The key turned and he took hold of the loop of iron which opened the door and went inside.

There was a kind of yell and something shot past his arm and disappeared into the distance. It took him a few moments to recover. It was only a cat.

He closed the door. It was the oddest building that he could recall having been in. It reminded him rather of a lighthouse in the way that it disappeared as it went up, except that there were several rooms leading off the hallway and the winding stairs showed more doors, all closed. God might have known where the cat had been, but he did not. There was no stink of urine, no furballs, no obvious bed on the chairs.

They were in fairly good order, no rips in the velvet, raspberry-coloured fabric to indicate mice – but then with a cat around there wouldn't have been. They were big chairs but it was a big room, with a stone fireplace that came to a large V at the top. The walls were partly plastered and partly not, and he couldn't decide why he liked the contrast of the white walls and the grey stone.

He went into the nearest room and it was furnished, though not well. The furniture was old and though some of it had been good it was suffering from cold and damp. There were books on the shelves, as if someone had just stepped out, but many of them were mildewed, which he thought was a shame.

Joe was beginning to wish that he had asked more about the house, but he had not been curious. Now he was. In that room there was also a bureau that was locked, but he saw a tiny key in a niche just behind it – no doubt that would open it. He went back into the hall and to the room opposite – a dining room. The table showed large white patches on its top and there was only one chair tucked under, although another way back against the wall, as though unused.

This room had glass doors to the outside, the like of which Joe had not often seen except in big houses with conservatories, with some stained glass in triangles and slender oblongs which Joe thought would make coloured lights upon the floor should the sun ever shine there. As he went across the room he could see the cathedral over the river.

It stood there, grey and so imposing that Joe didn't feel inclined to look at it. First there was the weir and on it stood birds, black with outstretched wings, and herons, grey and white, almost like statues. The river somehow gave off the impression of being wide, a mill on the other side and to the left the castle, with straight walls, and the cathedral –one of the most impressive buildings in the world, he felt sure, to be raised to God's glory.

Between the house and the river lay a large front garden with a stone wall around it and a gate. There were trees around the sides of the house with various bushes and grass and flowers – small clusters of red and purple and blue. He went back into the hall, and entered the next room, a sitting room. Rather disappointingly it had no furniture, but it had the same kind of glass doors. This time they led out to the side of the premises, the view angled back towards the bridge. If anyone had wanted to get inside the house it would have been simple to break the glass with a decent-sized stone, but nothing showed that any tramp or thief had been near.

There was also a kitchen at the back, stretched right across the building, a huge vegetable garden behind it and beyond greenhouses and an orchard. He could imagine it thick with pink and white blossom in the spring and covered with pears and apples in the early autumn.

What a pleasure it would be to live here when nature had given up all her fruits, the sweet autumn breezes coming off the river and the leaves floating away downstream like tiny boats towards the sea. Joe had to stop himself; he was not usually given to flights of fancy like that. It was stupid, he thought.

The stairs to the upper storey were dark and went off at an angle, as though drunk, so that he thought the house must be lopsided in some way.

A hall met him and four doors. There were beds in every room, but they were bare, not a mattress or a pillow left to carry vermin, nothing but the sturdiness of bedframes and then some wardrobes, empty. There were also chairs and a dressing table in one room, but the drawers were empty, including the middle drawer which had a lock but was not locked and revealed no contents.

Above was a third storey with another four rooms, all completely empty. The views on every side stretched far away beyond the small city, here and there showing a light at some remote house or tiny farm.

He went back downstairs after that, and outside. At the far end of the garden was a building containing coal and sticks stacked almost to the ceiling. A goodly amount of logs revealed itself outside under a huge tarpaulin. He picked up a log; it was light and dry, and smelled sweet, like apples or pears. The wood must have been there for years.

Later that day Joe went shopping. He ordered a large mattress, and pillows, sheets, pillowcases, blankets and a quilt of duck feathers. And towels, when he remembered these.

Joe told the shop exactly how to deliver, that they could get close to Prebends Bridge which he had discovered was the nearest to the house. They agreed that they would carry what he wanted from there to the house. Once he paid he then bought foodstuffs, carrying those himself, just enough for a day or two – it was not so far that he could not go into town the next day, and he thought it was all so much easier than France had been, and somehow a relief from London as he had found it. He was still not sure he wanted to be there, but he told himself if he didn't want to stay he didn't have to. He could go back to London and continue the search for

Angela. This was just a distraction for the time being and probably meant very little.

He unlocked the door. There was the squeal again as a cat shot past him, a different cat this time, Joe thought, a tabby or a tortoiseshell.

Joe knew nothing of cats, beautiful or otherwise, and he certainly didn't want them anywhere near the house. As far as he knew cats always lived in stables, where they disposed of mice and whatever else came their way. Though he had found no evidence of cats living inside the house, no food, no leavings – nothing to suggest that a cat had been there. He couldn't understand it.

He brought in sticks and wood from the outbuilding and quite enjoyed laying the fire. When he put a match to it Joe felt more at home than he had done in years.

He sat over the kitchen fire for a few minutes, watching it, and when the cart came with the ordered goods he carried it all himself because they wouldn't help despite their promises. He made up the bed and carried wood and sticks and coal up to the bedroom, though at first he didn't think he would light the fire there tonight. But the sun set so soon he found himself putting a match to it, thinking for the first time how far north he was.

He went back outside in the complete darkness of the late afternoon, standing and looking at how huge the cathedral was. It scared him.

It had been there for seven hundred years. He thought about how even when men and women and children had lived in hovels the cathedral had been built here. He knew from the northern soldiers he had met in France that here the men and their families had suffered from poverty and neglect. They had coughed up blood from their lungs from bringing coal, silver and lead out of the earth for other men's gain and other women's jewels, and they had died and their women had suffered and their children had gone hungry while the church had been rich and had supported slavery and stripped the lead mines of their silver for its own gain.

Joe wanted to fire things at the huge building then, but he didn't have any objects to hand and he could not have reached nearly that far. He hated the worship of fear which had inspired it and the idea of deifying anybody or anything as the Church had done. He hated the way that men bowed down to something they did not understand. He hated it all. Millions had died of war and flu and still the cathedral stood.

As he watched, the sky cleared and the stars came out and that was something he recognized. In France the stars had seemed so much nearer to the ground than they did here and now they gathered around the cathedral like worshippers. He half expected them to shoot off in every direction in order to give the cathedral more majesty than it had – although Joe wasn't sure that would be possible.

He locked the door and went upstairs. The fire was still on in his room. He read the second letter from his father, by lamplight.

Dear Joe,

I wish to God this bloody war was ended. They said it would be over by Christmas and here we are months later and things are getting worse. All the decent servants have left to do war work, the lads have gone to be killed and the women have gone to factories to make bloody bombs and such, for God's sake. Can't you come back? We could leave this hell and go to America where nobody gives a damn. It has nothing to do with us. We could make a new life there, you and me and Angela. Her father would have a fit of course. He was always a useless bastard, I never liked him, and Barbara must be the most overpowering woman on earth. She doesn't know when to be quiet.

I'm going to Yorkshire as I am thinking that I might sell the place. You know I never liked it – it looks like a box of chocolates with all those mini gardens, as though any man worth his salt could prat about with such things. Give me Northumberland any time. I shall go there too when the weather allows it. The air's better up there and I love the sea. Damn it, I wish you were here to go with me – you always loved the place so much and the sea there too, which to me seems to take your very life back and forward somehow.

Joe did love the sea; the estate in Northumberland was his favourite place. One thing now, he was not that far away. He could go there for comfort, even though it was up for sale. That might make it difficult. He didn't know about going back. Could you ever do so and think of the future? He didn't think so.

He didn't know what hour it was that he became aware of a strange noise. He kept rigid, his soldier's training still in him, but it was quite a small noise and it was not aggressive in any way. He turned over carefully in bed. The curtains were not closed and the moon cast its beams across the sky.

There on the table beside his bed, next to his glass of water, he could see a large ginger-and-white tomcat, lapping the drink from his glass. It didn't seem at all disconcerted and was aware of him watching. It turned its green–gold eyes upon him for a brief moment and then carried on.

Joe was entranced. He watched until it had drunk its fill and then it yawned and touched a white-tipped paw upon the bedclothes and, as though it happened every night, delicately moved down towards him. The cat looked at him as though they had known one another for a very long time and then curled up beside him and began a loud purring. Seconds later its body moved up and down regularly in sleep. Joe envied that. He wished he could fall asleep so promptly.

It was warm with the cat sleeping there. Its body was like a small furnace. He watched the fire grow less and less; he listened to the sound of the cat's rhythmic breathing and even thought he could discern the sound of the river and that it kept the same time as the cat's breath. He was only vaguely aware of himself dropping off the face of consciousness. He had not slept as well as that in years.

Joe took the train to Northumberland. He somehow couldn't rest until he saw the estate which he had loved. He didn't think anybody would begrudge him a look round, a few enquiries. He got off the train at Alnwick and found a taxi. It wasn't far, just a couple of minutes to the coast. He and Angela had often ridden the horses to the beach and walked them in the water.

He paid the driver at the entrance. The huge gates were closed, the gatehouse empty. So was the house. At the nearby village, which at one time had belonged to the family, there seemed to be nobody about.

He walked a little further. Memories rushed him. This had been his favourite place of all, the houses just above the beach, the little cobles in blue and white and black pulled up beyond the reach of the incoming tide, the tall spiky grass which held the sand dunes together. The tide was coming in now, its impact crashing up the sand, and it brought back a thousand happy times.

Joe banged on the door of a cottage in the middle of the village. He had tried to persuade himself that it would be all right here, but now he was afraid that his friend would not be there. He waited only moments before a man of about his own age opened the door.

'Tam!' Joe almost flung himself at the other man and then remembered that in the north you didn't – well, you didn't in most places – but he had worried that Tam was hurt, though he had heard nothing. To see him just as he had always been, tall and upright with bright ginger hair, took Joe aback.

Tam stood, transfixed for a few seconds, and then his face broke into the wide grin that Joe remembered so well.

'Ah, lad,' he said, 'you made it,' as though Joe had been away for just a few days.

He ushered Joe inside. He lived with his parents, at least he had, but the inside of the cottage seemed empty except for all the usual things which Joe remembered – the furniture and the fire and the smell of good cooking. As Joe wandered further inside he heard a noise and a tall pretty woman came forward carefully.

'This is my wife, Bet. Bet, this is Joe.'

Joe remembered her as a child of his age; he hadn't known her well, but she was from the village and had always been there. He was so glad to find something as he wanted it.

'My mam and dad gave us the cottage,' Tam said. 'They went off to Rothbury to live.' He said this as though it were a thousand miles away and not still in the same county. 'My mam was born there and my dad isn't too fit any more so they went to stay with her family.'

'Are you fishing?'

'What else would I be doing? I didn't know you were back.' Tam hesitated. 'We heard about your dad. Awful. And the house is up for sale.'

Joe nodded.

'We heard about Miss Toddington too.'

Joe didn't know what to say to that, but of course they would know everything. His father had loved this place best and it would be the biggest loss; people around would have been told what was happening. Joe wished the gossip had reached France. Somehow things never worked out.

Joe couldn't meet their eyes. He shook his head. 'Did you know she ran away?'

Tam didn't answer. Joe finally lifted his gaze to discover his friend had a questioning look on his face.

'Is that what you're doing here? You thought she might come to us? Ah, Joe, I'm so sorry. I wish she had. The folk around here consider themselves yours.'

It was one of the sweetest things anybody had ever said to him, and Joe had to look away once again.

Bet bustled off to make tea. Joe and Tam stepped outside. Joe was still blinking hard and considering Coquet Island, which gleamed off to the left, not far out to sea, as though he were counting every seagull.

'Stay here with us,' Tam said.

'After what I did?'

Tam snorted. Then he muttered something about 'bloody Londoners' which Joe didn't take personally.

'I can't believe the place is to be sold. Probably to some bugger who knows nowt about country ways,' Tam said. 'Howay, man, we'd love to have you.'

There were shells at Joe's feet. Angela had taken them home with her, to remind her, she had said, of the place she loved best. He picked up a handful and shoved them into his trouser pocket.

Joe went back to Durham, deciding that he would try to find out who Priscilla Lee had been. It gave him something to do; it took his mind off Angela now that he could think of nowhere she might be. Northumberland had been the last possibility.

He didn't know whether Miss Lee had been Catholic or Church of England. There was also Presbyterian around here, the Salvation Army and at least two branches of the Methodist Church. He went to the nearest church, St Nicholas's in the marketplace, but there were no records of her. He tried the Catholic church, St Godric's, slightly out of town, halfway up North Road, but there was nothing there either.

Each day Joe tackled a different church. He went to St Cuthbert's further up, in case she had preferred that one, the Methodist church in North Road and then the one in Old Elvet. He learned quite a bit about the old city and its workings as he scoured the churches and graveyards for any sign of this woman. He trod up narrow cobbled alleys leading to the cathedral or down on to the river. He walked the towpaths on either side and followed the little winding streets.

The walking itself made him feel a little better. He could concern himself in something which might have a good outcome, whereas his searchings for Angela were run through with the horrible idea that she could be dead.

He couldn't look further for her here and, although he often awoke in the night and wanted to run back to London, when the mornings came he told himself over and over that he had searched everywhere he could. Further investigating would not help because he was blind as to where to go. At least being out of London he did not see people walking around the house where he had been born and brought up, considering whether they would buy it. He knew that if anything happened Mr Barrington would contact him; he knew where he was staying.

And so the search for Miss Lee went on, although he still hadn't worked out what she had to do with him.

He went to the hospital in North Road and made enquiries amongst the doctors. The medical people were grudging, but Joe made himself charming and told a good story about how he thought she had been his aunt and left him such a wonderful house and he would be glad to know that she was sleeping peacefully. While this got him entry to a good many surgeries there was no information available.

After that he tried to talk to the people who lived nearby. Across the river were the big buildings belonging to the church and the university. Behind him up the steep slope the people who lived in the houses with long gardens were not Joe's near neighbours, but there was one terrace of poor people not far beyond his house. It was probably, Joe thought – having by now some idea of the city and where the poorest people lived – a series of terraces which went up sideways from the river bank, narrow dark alleys between the houses, the kind of thing he wouldn't want to go near on a dark night.

The nearest terrace to him, the only one where he could call the people his neighbours, was Rachel Lane. Starting with the far end, Joe banged on each door in turn, but found little positive response. At the first two houses nobody answered even though he had waited until when people may have returned from work. At the third house the large man on the doorstep told him to 'bugger off' and slammed the door. Joe worked his way along. One woman listened and then closed the door. A small child answered another and didn't understand what he was talking about. He had almost got to the end when he found a middle-aged, rather elegant lady smiling at him from beyond the step.

When he explained that he had moved into the tower house she said, 'Yes, indeed, do come in, Mr Hardy,' and then she called along for the other lady and Joe stepped inside.

Their dress was poor, the house itself was almost but not quite falling down and the furniture they had was very good, solid wood, shining with polish, which kept the smell of damp at bay. The two downstairs rooms were cluttered with books and ornaments. She guided him into the sitting room and then her sister appeared. They sat down and Joe told them he was searching for the woman who had owned the tower house before him. They looked slightly puzzled and glanced at one another.

'We haven't been here that long,' said Miss Slater, 'but I do remember her quite well. She had cats. Papa didn't care for cats, and we always had dogs, but the cats didn't seem to leave the area of the tower house. She was a very quiet woman; shy, I think. We did call and invite her to tea and though she was very polite she never came. And after that, well, one doesn't like to impose.'

Miss Slater went off to make tea for Joe. Miss Bethany furrowed her brow when Joe asked if they thought the woman might have gone to their church.

'I don't think she attended church,' Miss Bethany said softly, for this was not respectable. 'People did talk rather, but since nobody knew her and she went nowhere people assumed that she was not well. She looked very pale whenever she ventured out, which was not often. We didn't go that way to town and so we didn't bother very much, though I must say I did feel guilty. Papa always said one should care for one's neighbours and though it isn't always easy one must try.'

Miss Slater came back with the tea. Joe didn't really like tea much, but since it covered a great number of social pressures he accepted the white-and-pink-flowered cup and saucer and thanked them. When the tea was drunk and he had politely declined any more Miss Slater said she thought she should take him to see her neighbour, Mrs Formby, because Mrs Formby had lived in Durham all her life and would know if there was anything else about her.

She went next door with him and knocked. After a little while a diminutive woman came to the door. Joe had not seen real poverty close up before, but that didn't stop him from recognizing it now. She wore clothes so old that they had no colour. She was neatly dressed in her way, but her body was fleshless and her face had fallen in from lack of good food. Her hair was iron-grey, though Joe didn't think she could be more than forty. She didn't ask him in, but she came outside and stood against the door as though barring it. Yet she was helpful enough and seemed impressed with Joe.

Her eyes fairly shone on him and she called him 'bonny lad', which Joe very much appreciated. But she didn't know Miss Lee either, just that the woman didn't speak to anyone, didn't look at anyone for as long as Mrs Formby had lived here, which was several years. Before that she lived in Giles-gate, she told Joe, which was not that far away.

There were raised children's voices in the house as though there was some dispute and Mrs Formby had to go back inside. Then Miss Slater told him that Mr Formby was not a good man and Mrs Formby was kept very short of money.

Joe thanked them and went home.

He tried to settle into his new house as he would in any other, but he felt so far away from everything which was familiar. He had taken to carrying some of his father's letters around in his pockets. He knew it was silly, but it brought him comfort. He read the first two letters often and over until he knew them almost off by heart, and he was afraid to move on to the second, afraid that his father might have learned to despise him or even hate him and that he would rant at him and destroy all that the first letter had given him. But when he sat down by the fire and opened the third it was written from the time his father had been up to the house in Northumberland. It hurt Joe in a different way to hear how things were there.

I have just come back from our beloved Northumberland. It's too cold to stay and I think I must shut up the house. So many of the servants are doing war work and a lot of the young men can't wait to get away and join in what they see as fun. How can they know that so many of them will not come back?

I was glad to come to London, at least I am comfortable here. No howling draughts roaring along the halls. Although I do love our country home it cannot be said to be cosy at this time of the year. I worry about the many acres we hold there and how to keep the farm running. I am doing my best to recruit older men and women just to keep things ticking over. Some of the animals have had to be slaughtered. They are to keep and the meat is necessary. The horses have all been taken by the military. It grieves me. Such good bloodstock. I won't see any of them again. The war is ruining everybody's lives. If ever there was a mistaken pitiless adventure this is it.

All the German friends I had before the war I've lost. Men with brilliant minds. They've all gone. Do you remember Hegel? He loved London. We used to sit over the fire until the small hours and talk about governments and industry. How many of our sons must die before this is over? He has three. I suspect they are in the army now. You will no doubt be shooting one another soon.

It was when Joe had been there for two weeks that things were suddenly different. He awoke and did not see the reason for it. He was not thirsty, and he was too young for nature's call at that hour. He listened and waited.

He convinced himself that there was somebody downstairs. Yet he was not afraid of such things. There was nothing for anybody to take and if somebody needed shelter then where was the problem? He couldn't hear anything and he half told himself that maybe there was a cats' meeting in his hall. He still hadn't worked out how they got there, but he was generous enough to let it go.

In the end he got wearily out of bed and pulled a blanket around him to ward off the cold. He went noisily down the stairs, knowing that any cat would be long gone by the time he trod his way to the ground floor, but when he got there it was different.

There were lights, but not the lights he knew from the house. It didn't frighten him, but it was odd and strange, and somehow when you had been at war and knew there were no limits to anything, you worried. He went carefully from room to room and as he did so music played softly and faint images floated in front of him; he thought it was a mother and child

He heard a soft noise in the kitchen, ventured through there and it faded. By the door was a cat. It was the tortoiseshell. Small, not imposing, as though it expected nothing. It sat just inside the door like a visitor not sure of its welcome.

He went into the sitting room where it seemed the music was now coming from, but there was no person, no instrument, and by then he could barely hear it. Perhaps it was outside? He ventured there, the tortoiseshell cat following him, and as he stopped it sat down beside him as though it had discerned that he needed the company.

He could hear the music here too. He thought that it floated across the river, away from him. It could hardly be coming from the cathedral at that time of night. It wasn't church music anyway, as far as he knew. It certainly wasn't a hymn or a psalm; anybody with his schooling would have recognized if it had been.

He got down beside the cat and met its eyes.

'So, what do you think it is then, Kitty?' he said. He was quite surprised when all the cat did was purr and look comfortable, then as though it thought he needed reassurance, it rubbed around his legs before sitting down again.

He went inside and it followed him up the stairs, making itself comfortable on the bed as though it were taking shifts with the others. He could still hear the music when he fell asleep. It occurred to him that that was what lullabies were all about, but he didn't recognize it. When he awoke the cat had gone.

He should not have been surprised. When he had been in France, and even sometimes as he had been growing up, he'd had similar experiences, but it was unreliable, this extra sense. He had never told anybody about it and he had been irritated over the years because sometimes he had been in great need and it had not helped. He had come to the conclusion that it only happened when it was for someone else's sake, such as when he was fighting and one of his men was hurt.

This time he did not understand why this was happening. Nothing had come to his aid when he had come back from France and found that his father had died; he'd had no help when he had discovered that Angela had run away. Even when he slept he dreamt of her running and needing him and he was not there, or she was tired of waiting for him and had gone off with someone else – or they had married and it had not worked out. His dreams varied and each one hurt him when he awoke. Angela was so very real to him still.

The first thing he did that day was to go to the solicitors'. He hoped to make an appointment to see Mr Bainbridge later. He needed to talk to Edgar Bainbridge about the house and what he could do with it.

He encountered the man who ran the desk, Mr Clarence.

'Mr Bainbridge is in court all day,' he said, 'but Miss Charlton may be able to help. She's up here, sir, looking for some paperwork.'

Joe followed him up one set of stairs and then up another. The third-storey stairs had no carpet – and no heating either by the temperature of it.

He pushed open the door of an attic room, dark and badly lit, but he could see the young woman he remembered, sitting behind a makeshift desk. It was nothing more than a table with books and papers upon it. She glanced at the door at the noise, and he thought she looked like an Impressionist painting, one where the woman has gorgeous waving red hair and striking looks. She was slender and the cheekbones on her face were covered in freckles and cream skin, her lips pale but perfectly formed and her eyes intelligent and sludge-green and soft. Joe remembered that he ought to say something.

'Miss Charlton. It's good of you to see me.'

'Mr Hardy. A pleasure.'

Joe sat down. He wasn't convinced the flimsy-looking chair would hold him, but he sat carefully. Though it wobbled, it didn't tip him to the floor.

'You may remember,' he said, 'that I have recently acquired a property which was left to me by a woman called Priscilla Lee. I know nothing about her, whether she was a friend of my parents – though that seems unlikely – or whether she was some kind of relative. I don't understand what's going on, you see, or why she should leave me a house. I have no family here, I've never been here before in my life and I thought that if I could see the will it might help.'

She looked baffled but rather pleased. He couldn't quite work out why until she saw his expression, smiled just a little and said, 'It's like a mystery, isn't it?'

'I suppose it is,' Joe said. 'It must have a simple explanation, but I can't see it, and I would like some form of clue.'

'Yes, of course,' she said, 'I'm sure that I can find out if you will give me a little time. Could I have a day or two?'

She smiled suddenly and it was as if a sunbeam had come to rest in the room. 'I know your house. What a wonderful building it is.'

'It is a wonderful building,' he said, acknowledging it for the first time. 'How do you know about it?'

She laughed and shook her head, and it seemed to him that the world was suddenly a decent place to be. There was something about her which might make men feel uneasy, he conceded. She was not beautiful; her nose was sharp and her eyes had a no-nonsense look which could have discouraged the most eager of suitors. Her height was against her also in that way, but he could see how it might be useful in this business. She was formidable, even at such a young age, but it was her enthusiasm which held him; it lit her face.

She kept his attention as Angela had when they had first met. He had been in a ballroom and she had been wearing a white dress, with pearls around her neck. Her skin had been so creamy and her hair so shiny; everything about her was so perfect, yet now he felt the same in a small way about this girl he saw across the desk, and it confused him. He had been resigned to feeling nothing ever again and it made him very uncomfortable. He was obviously not to be trusted. He could transfer a slight degree of affection to someone else. My God!

'I live in Rachel Lane with two ladies, the Misses Slaters,' she said. 'Sometimes if the day has been hard I walk by the river and last night I saw your lights from there. The windows are all cream and it is such a lovely building – in a city of exquisite buildings, especially the competition you have from across the river, that is amazing.'

He couldn't believe that he was the person who said, 'I met the Misses Slaters. I didn't know you lived so near. If you like you could bring the key and the will and we could have tea.'

'That would be lovely,' she said.

Joe called himself names all the way home. He cared for no one but Angela. Yet this young woman had breached the huge defences that he had put up. Why was that? He was not ready for such things, he felt that he never would be. He had invited her into his home – if it was his home, such a strange, odd place. He remembered what he had said, offering up his problem for her help. Joe shuddered at the memory. He was obviously so desperate for company that he had invited a young woman into his new house. But he liked the way that she so obviously wanted to help people; there was something special about that.

Dear Joe,

Angela came to see me today. I am so glad that you are to be married. She is a lovely girl – so light, so kind and so in love with you. I want to live to see you together, to dance at your wedding.

Nothing is too much for her. There is no wildness or wilfulness about her. She has been raised in London ways. She likes to please. She reads to me in the afternoons sometimes while I doze over the fire. I keep late nights when I should not. I cannot bear the evenings somehow. When the light fades so do I and I want the company that I should not wish for, people given to excess. It doesn't feel that like that after a time. It becomes normal. I never sleep without something to help me and when I do I dream of you and your mother and what it was like when you were small, not necessarily together but bits and pieces. The best bits, I think, though sometimes you are running away from me and I cannot reach you.

I live for your return.

NINE

There was a banging on the door. Joe sat up. He had fallen asleep, mid-afternoon. He had been out, trying to find work; he had for several days now and found nothing. Toddy had been right, he was qualified for very little. He had no idea what to do, but he must make a living of some kind. He didn't have much money left and although he knew that in time he might have some from the sale of the properties, he couldn't rely on that, and anyway it wasn't of any use right now. He felt as though he needed to go forward.

He still had things he could sell – his guns, his father's half hunter watch and other things which were valuable – but he couldn't imagine who here would want such things or be able to afford them. It was not a prosperous city. He felt as though he must get on somehow, in spite of or possibly because of all that had gone wrong.

The only thing he was qualified for was the army, and he had had enough of that – and anyway, they weren't taking people on. There were so many men out of work. A lot of them had come back to the land that was supposed to be meant for heroes, but was nothing of the sort. There was no money and no job suitable that he could see.

He would make a good gamekeeper, he thought, but Durham City was hardly the place for such things. Other than that he had walked about the streets and couldn't imagine what he would do when he ran out of money. He must stay here a year before he could sell the place and in these times buyers for such a place would be scarce. He could be stuck here for a very long time. The thought didn't make him happy.

Yes, there it was again – not quite a banging, more a polite hammering. He debated whether to get up from his chair, and when the noise didn't stop he could feel the ire rising within him. He leapt up, ran into the hall and undid the bolts so that they shot back hard and almost caught him on the knuckles. He was just about to enquire of the intruder what the blazes he thought he was doing, when he became aware of the tall skinny outline of the woman from the solicitors'. Seeing her fear, he hastily swallowed his annoyance and managed, 'Miss Charlton. Hello.'

'I've brought you news and extra keys and the will.'

He ushered her inside and through into the sitting room, seeing it as she would – no fire, just the chair with blankets and a pillow, as though he had transported his father's chair straight from London. It brought him comfort, but his face went warm that anybody else should see it.

'I've been out. I haven't had time to see to the fire or anything,' he said.

He moved the ginger-and-white tom from the armchair as though that would help. The cat yawned, too indolent to complain, and merely sat on the rug by the dead fire and began to wash its paws.

'Please, sit down.' Joe only hoped the cat didn't decide that his ablutions must extend to his arse while the young woman was there. Cats didn't care about such things, in fact, he thought, they did it on purpose. 'On the other hand you had best not, unless you like cat hair on your clothes. We can go out and I will buy you tea.'

'There's no need. Such expense,' she said. 'I have brought cake.'

Joe was amazed. He hadn't felt that way in so long that he couldn't move for several moments. The cake was well wrapped and he tried not to ask her what kind it was, although he felt desperate to, it was a huge treat. It spoke to him of his nanny and the nursery fire and times past.

'I'll make some tea,' he said abruptly, and went off to the kitchen.

When he came back the cats were competing for the best place in front of the warmth because she had built up the fire. She was fending them off like a half-hearted tennis player, giving in when they persisted in wrapping their furry selves around her.

'They're selfish creatures,' he said in mitigation.

She looked at him and then she laughed. It made her face beautiful in the dim light. 'They're so bonny and I do like them.'

He had not heard genuine laughter in so long, but he listened to it now, like somebody playing Mozart on a good piano.

Miss Charlton had bought coffee cake from the Silver Street Café, she told him as she unwrapped his prize. She had been too busy to bake this weekend, she apologized. Joe didn't care where it came from, he was so pleased about it. She cut it up and put it onto plates. He poured tea and felt so comfortable with her. Sleet pounded the windows. It always did, he thought. Why on earth people lived here, he had thought – but that was why, because you needed bad weather so that you had an excuse to doze by the fire and listen to the comforting sound of the rain and wind from across the river, or lie in bed late and wait for it to clear, confident that it never would.

'Does any member of your family come from here, Mr Hardy?'

He shook his head. 'You can call me Joe. I don't know this area at all. I don't even know the woman who left me the house, just her name.' He laughed at that.

'It's a very common name here. Does it matter very much?'

'I don't know. It seems to somehow. I don't have any family. My mother died when I was small so I don't remember her. My father died recently, and I was an only child. My mother's parents died before I was born. I don't seem to have anybody and I don't see why someone I have no memory of should leave me such a house. It's so distinctive, so odd. I would very much like to find out why.'

'What do you mean?'

She was so easy to talk to that he found himself telling her things he didn't intend to.

He told her what it had been like to come back from war and find his father dead and everything left in a financial mess. How the banker was in touch with the solicitors' and they were trying to sell what he owned.

'I thought having the will might help, and it would give

124

me something to do – though I must find some work. I'm running out of money.'

Miss Charlton produced the will. They both read it in turn, but it didn't tell them anything they didn't know.

'There are ways to find out,' Miss Charlton said. 'You could start with her death. It sounds awful, but perhaps she went into hospital or there was a doctor who tended her.'

'I have been to the churches and the graveyards, the hospitals, everywhere I can think of.'

'Is there nothing in the house which gives you a clue?'

'No papers, no books that aren't ordinary novels and only a few of those, just there.' He hesitated and then he looked at her and said, 'This is going to sound ridiculous . . .' He hesitated; he had never told anybody this before and he couldn't understand why he was doing it now other than the fact that he couldn't stop himself. Was it the way that she looked at him? He didn't know . . . 'I'm starting to feel as though I was meant to come here.'

He hadn't known that until he said it and was as surprised as she obviously was, though she hid it under a veneer of politeness. 'I sometimes find that I get to places and then it was where I was meant to be.' He glanced at her. 'Do you think that's stupid?'

Miss Charlton was staring at him. 'Certainly not,' she said. 'Who knows what people are capable of.'

'They called me Lucky Joe when I was in France because I could judge things that . . . that I couldn't see, but it doesn't seem to work for me, only for other people and then not . . . not especially well.'

Miss Charlton gazed around the room. 'It's a sizeable house,' she said, 'there must be places you haven't looked.'

'I haven't looked anywhere much. Where else is there?'

She glanced at him in question, and Joe said to her, 'Help yourself,' so she went over to the desk and opened it.

It was empty. Above it were several novels by well-known authors – Dickens, Thackeray, Jane Austen. She pulled them out one by one and flicked through them, but there was nothing. Joe had wandered into the other rooms.

Lucy saw the garden surrounding the tower house and how it had spectacular views of the cathedral across the river. It had been built in the manner of a fortress, she was sure, though on the wrong side of the river. She didn't know whether Mr Hardy was right about his feeling that he was meant to be there, but there was something very special about it, like the knocker on the cathedral; it felt like a place of refuge, somewhere for people to run to when they needed safety.

She followed Mr Hardy upstairs, though it seemed a rather personal thing to do, so she left him behind on the first storey where through a door she could see a bed. It looked very impersonal and not slept in, as it was in the other rooms, all the doors being open. She took the stairs up again. This level had such a good atmosphere that she thought people living here must have been comforted. There wasn't much furniture – Mr Hardy obviously didn't use any of it, just the odd chair – but it was clean and what light existed at that hour from the city and the river and the sky poured in there like sweet oil.

She heard Joe take the stairs lightly. He appeared in the doorway.

'Anything?'

She hadn't really looked, she had been so taken with the views and the building itself, but really there was no place for anything to be secreted.

She went over to the window. 'It is such a beautiful place,' she said.

Joe went and stood beside her. The wind had got up and was blowing the water about, tossing little sprays of it in the air, like diamonds above the river. The window just along from them was banging in its frame, but the one in front of them was not because it was wedged with a piece of paper. Joe pulled it out to tear it in half because it was quite a big piece and would do for both windows but when he opened it he looked harder. It was a letter. It read:

Dear Cissie,

Why don't you come and see me – you know that I can't come there and it would mean a lot to me. Since you left I have had no word of you and we have all missed you so very much. You are good to tell me that you are back in the north. Please come – I have no one else of your family and even half a day would be a treasure to me.

Love, Uncle George

There was an address at the top right-hand side of the page from some place called Allendale. It was dated more than twenty years ago.

They both read it and then again. Lucy could feel excitement rise in her. She smiled at him.

'But I've no idea who she is,' Joe said.

'She must be the woman who owned the house, who left it to you. Perhaps she's a distant relative or was a friend of the family.'

'It doesn't explain anything,' Joe said.

'But you must want to find out. It could tell you all kinds of things that you don't know.'

Joe hesitated. He didn't want to go looking for some distant relative who had died and left him this ridiculous house. He wanted to go back to London and have everything as it should be with his father and Angela alive, his inheritance somehow intact. Short of that he didn't want to do anything; he felt as if life were dragging him along behind it and he wanted to run away. And then he thought, have I not run from London to here since I couldn't find Angela? I've already run away once.

'Allendale is not that far. Do you drive?' she said.

Miss Charlton was turning out to be something of a pain, Joe thought, urging people on, him in particular. Her eyes were lit with curiosity and excitement. It had him wanting to go back to the chair in the sitting room which he had adopted as his, pretending there was still something of his father around him. He wanted not to bother, not to be part of anything, but she was standing there, waiting for his response. If he refused it would be slapping her somehow. He thought of her in her cold scruffy office and saw the thin cheap clothes she wore.

'I'll hire a car and go there,' he announced, not knowing that he would and then, not knowing he was going to, he said, 'Would you be able to come with me?'

She hesitated but only for a second and then she nodded. 'I could do it on Saturday,' she said.

Joe had not known that it was quite a long way to Allendale and that the countryside altered. Once out of the city there were various little villages and after half an hour the road dropped sharply into Weardale. Then it wound through the valley in its narrow state and in another half hour or so it appeared quite different to anything he had seen before in England.

In fact in some ways it looked like the rural parts of France he had been in, with stone houses, lush fields and small villages which were so pretty that he could think of himself living there, the grey stone walls and farmhouses set against the sides of the valley or right on the tops. There were not many trees away from the river, and up on the tops sheep dotted the fields. The dale went on and on and then they were up beyond it where the land was scarred from lead mining, ruined wheels and rusted machinery, buildings open to the weather and water. They tumbled past it, all deserted now. If there had been any wealth from mining it had long since gone to other places, just as the coal wealth had. There was no evidence of it here.

They approached a large village green surrounded by shops, houses and hotels. Allendale. Joe parked the hired car to the side of the street and they made their way almost to the bottom of the hill nearby. It wound down to the River East Allen, to where the house lay in which Priscilla Lee's Uncle George lived. There stood an enormous house, so big that it took up most of Joe's vision. He hadn't seen such a large house in such a small place; it was as if somebody were trying to impose his importance on the rest of the area.

It stood in grounds which reached down to the river and then right up across the bankside and into the town. The garden was a series of steps which went up, on and on, reminding Joe of some fairy tale where the stairs wound in circles tight enough to make you dizzy. The house had many windows and stood tall to the sky. It even had a huge spire-like construction on one wing of it, the likes of which Joe had seen only in Scotland. It reminded him just a little of the tower house, as though the buildings were cousins. He liked this idea; it made him smile. The slate roof glinted in the cold sunshine.

It was a steep climb to the entrance. He banged on the doorknocker, but nothing happened. Joe had not been able to admit to himself that with his luck Uncle George would be dead and gone years ago. Somehow to him the house looked empty. There were thick curtains at the windows which let in little light, but it had that air about it – nobody at home. Joe banged on the front door again and then went around and into the yard and banged on the back door. In the end he gave up. They trudged onto the front street to find a woman watching them.

'He isn't here, love. They took him away ages since.'

'Where did they take him to?' Lucy asked.

'I don't know. But his son lives just outside Alston. Angus Firbank.'

She gave them directions and they motored over the hills to where Alston lay, a narrow winding cobbled street leading to the bottom of the hill. They turned off and climbed back up into a tiny lane through which the car could only just squeeze. At the end of it was another big house, very much the same as the other – Scottish-looking and with something forbidding about it, grey, tall and imposing. These people obviously had a great deal of money.

They got out of the car. Again Joe banged on the door and after a long wait a small, grubby maidservant opened it. Joe explained his business and after another lengthy wait they were ushered through the dark hall and into a darker drawing room, where a small fat man sat in an armchair. If Lucy had had to go there alone she thought she would have run away. There was something quelling about it; she didn't know what it was, but she moved nearer to Joe. Then she remembered she was supposed to be sensible and independent and moved away.

Joe took the letter from his pocket and explained that he had inherited the tower house in Durham from a woman he had never met and was eager to know more about the family. He said that he was looking for Priscilla's Uncle George, and at that the man got up from his chair with difficulty and said that he might be his father.

He asked them to sit down, but neither of them did. Joe stood in front of him while the man read the letter again. Lucy wandered about the room, though it was so cluttered with large ornate furniture of no consequence, that it wasn't easy to do.

The corners of the room were too black for shadows and there were a number of other rooms beyond; all the doors seemed to connect, leading on to Lucy was not sure what, but she didn't like it. There was something about the house which reminded her of circular towers, going round and round to confuse people and render them vulnerable. It was ridiculous, she told herself.

She could see windows but no views, nothing but gloom and cobwebs and tiny spots of light which seemed to land nowhere. She wanted to go back to Joe and tell him that they had to leave.

She breathed carefully and watched Joe standing so confidently in the middle of the room, watching the man in his turn. She saw how guarded Joe's eyes were, glittering like onyx. The man had had time to read the letter at least twice by now. When he looked up his face was not friendly but closed, forbidding.

'This means nothing to me. I don't know about this woman.'

'Is your father still alive?' Joe asked.

The man hesitated, obviously taken aback by the swift change of subject.

'He went mad. I had him put in an asylum. He was always a queer bugger. He doesn't talk much any more – he won't be able to tell you anything. There's no point in your going there. He saw things that didn't exist and worse.'

'What do you mean?'

The man shuddered. 'He knew when babies were going to die, when folk were going to be hurt, and he thought he could talk to those who had died. We're all good living people here, we don't hold with such things, and I couldn't work it out – we never had that kind of problem in our family. Somewhere somebody married wrongly.'

Joe nodded. All he said was, 'Where is he?'

The man looked worried. 'I said—'

'Yes, but you didn't say where.'

'I don't see that it's any of your business.'

Joe sighed. Lucy wanted to pull him out, grab his hand and urge him away, but he didn't seem bothered, nor even impatient. He stood as though the other man were the visitor and he were the owner, though why anyone would have cared to acknowledge such a thing she couldn't think.

The place was dirty, she realized; the floor crunched under her shoes, the fire smoked and she could smell thick dust everywhere. She thought she heard a rustling in the corner. It was a mouse or a rat. She deliberately didn't look that way, but she thought Mr Firbank could have done with a cat or two. Joe's cats would have sorted it out in moments.

'Where is he?' Joe said.

The man laughed uneasily and then he looked more keenly at Joe. Lucy saw the expression which dawned in his eyes, something worse than unease: fear.

'What do you mean by coming here and behaving like this? Who are you?' he said, his voice quivering.

'Where is he?' Joe said again. Something about the way that he said it made Lucy want to run outside and gulp at fresh air.

Mr Firbank's eyes were so wide with fear now that they might have stotted from his head like billiard balls.

Joe held his gaze and Lucy suddenly felt very uncomfortable. She had the feeling that the man couldn't move under Joe's eyes, that he was stuck there like a statue until Joe released him, which was nonsense, she knew. Was this soldiering? The man's face had gone so pale that she thought he might faint. He licked his lips and eventually he said, 'The place is in Gateshead, down by the river. By St Leonard's church.'

'There isn't a church down by the river called St Leonard's,' Joe said.

'It's something like that.' The man was nervous now.

'St Mary's perhaps?' Joe said softly.

'Who are you?'

They left. Lucy's first reaction was that she didn't want to go anywhere near Newcastle, but she could hardly say so. She reassured herself that Gateshead was across the river, that they were not going anywhere close to her family, but she worried that she would see her home yet would not be able to go there. She wasn't sure that she could stand it.

Joe didn't talk to her and she couldn't help saying, 'How did you know the name of the church?'

'I think it's St Mary Magdalene,' he said.

'You frightened that man,' Lucy said.

There was something else which worried her. The way that Joe had taken complete possession of the room.

They went through the middle of Gateshead, at least she thought it was, with shops selling shoes and pipes, and ironmongers and brush manufacturers. There was a splendid, grand-looking building, the Metropole Hotel. There were trams and a big shop called Snowball's, which was a drapers and house furnishers, it claimed.

If Lucy had lifted her eyes after they reached the riverside she would have seen the house where she had spent a happy childhood. Even so, she was in so much mental anguish that

Joe seemed to sense it and looked at her, enquiring whether she was unwell.

She shook her head.

'You can stay in the car if you want to,' he said.

She went with him, but averted her eyes to begin with. However, when it came to looking or not looking she chose to look, imagined Guy, Gemma and her parents in the garden, the day being bright. They would all be sitting down to eat and her name would never be mentioned. She didn't exist there any more.

That was strange to her. She had thought that somehow her life would always remain in Newcastle or that there would always be a part of her, like how buildings remained, but perhaps she had blown away, like the dandelion clock with a wind keening ever so gently and warmly that it did not know it was losing its life. And when the wonderful stems with their lovely heads were bare there was nothing left.

Gateshead was both beautiful and ugly. It was like a poor relation of Newcastle with narrow terraces running down to the river and big buildings erected from industry's past. Joe took her unerringly to the place he had spoken of and banged on the door. After a short time a woman answered it. She was a nun, wearing a black habit and a white whimple; when he explained his business she smiled slightly and allowed them in.

'Mr Firbank doesn't often have visitors. He will be pleased to see you,' she said.

It was nothing like Lucy had imagined places for mad people. The sun shone through the windows. It was quiet.

The nun led them through big doors and into the garden. There, under a tree and not far from the river, a man sat in a wheelchair. Joe spoke softly to him.

He looked up and smiled, but his eyes were vacant. 'Angus?' he said hopefully.

'No, it's Joe,' he said, putting warm fingers into the old man's hands.

Mr Firbank smiled from eyes that couldn't see much and then said, 'Do I know you?'

'I don't think we've ever met, but I have a house in Durham which I inherited from Miss Lee. I wanted to find out about her and so I found you. How are you?'

'I like being here. I like the river.'

'Yes, I like it too,' Joe said as Lucy sat down where a seat ran around the tree trunk most obligingly. 'I live on the river in Durham, in the house where Miss Lee lived.'

There was no response.

'Do you remember her?'

'Cissie was a bonnie bairn, the bonniest bairn in the world. And she could see.'

'What could she see?' Joe said, but the old man just looked at the river. 'Did she live on the Wear in Durham for a long time?'

The old man said nothing.

'Mr Firbank, I need to know about her. I don't know who she is yet she has left me the summer tower house. I'm confused. Please help me.'

Mr Firbank gazed out cross the Tyne. He sat for a long time like that and Joe waited, sitting himself beside Lucy.

Then he moved impatiently. 'Mr Firbank, I need to know. Mr Firbank . . .'

The old man still did not respond. Lucy thought he turned just a little further away as though Joe were a particularly tiresome wasp. She put a hand on Joe's arm. He glanced at her and didn't say anything. They waited and as they did so the old man fell asleep. Joe got up and walked away.

He stood with his head down. She went to him and again put a hand on his arm. Joe shrugged it off and made as if to go back. She spoke sharply.

'I think you should leave him alone,' she said.

Joe glared at her. 'I have come all this way. I want some answers.'

'Not from him,' she said, holding his gaze.

Joe stood still.

'He's old and tired and he can't answer your questions,' she said. 'Don't treat him like this.'

Joe hesitated and then let go of his breath in a sigh.

'You're right,' he said, and went back and sat down just as the old man jolted himself awake. Joe talked to him about the tower house and the river and the old man said that Cissie had been in Durham, that she had come home to the tower house where perhaps people always came when their lives were too much and they could stand no more.

Joe didn't ask him a single question. He talked about the flowers and herbs in the garden, how the cathedral looked at different times of the day and how he could hear the bells ringing for evensong in the middle of Sunday afternoons. He even conjured people coming from all parts of the town in winter. When it was Christmas they would gather for the carol services, and from across the river he could hear the sound of the organ playing late in the afternoons. It was so weighty, so majestic; Bach usually, mighty and wonderful.

Joe told him how when he was in France the German and British soldiers sang 'Silent Night' on Christmas Eve. He talked of how people went home to their houses in the dark days before Christmas after evensong at the cathedral, how they climbed the seven hills of Durham and made their way homeward in the failing light, and then they toasted crumpets over the fire and smothered them with good rich yellow butter and strawberry jam. He talked about how hot and sweet the tea was and the firelight reflecting round the room in shadows.

When Mr Firbank fell asleep again Joe and Lucy stole away. When they got back to the car she said, 'If you were never in Gateshead how did you know the name of the church? How did you know how to get there?'

He shrugged. 'I must have heard it somewhere.'

'Tell me what you're thinking.'

'I'm trying to decide whether she went mad like he did.'

'And?'

'That if I'm related to them somehow I'm going to go the same way too. I must be related or she wouldn't have left it to me.'

'There are other explanations. She could have been a friend of somebody you knew in the north, not necessarily here. Someone who had nobody to leave it to. Sometimes people do such things because of their memories.'

He looked at her. 'Do you think so? I see things, I hear things that other people don't.'

'We're all different. Mr Firbank is old now, he has for-gotten many things. That doesn't mean there's something wrong with it. He didn't seem mad to me.'

Joe hesitated and then said, 'In the house sometimes I see a woman with a small child. I hear music and she sings lullabies.'

'And who do you think it is?'

He hesitated again.

'Maybe it's me and my mother.'

'But you'd never before been there.'

'Perhaps it's what I want. Some place to belong, some family to belong to.'

It was almost six o'clock when Joe delivered the car back to Mr Palmer's Hire Cars. Mr Palmer was in the big building doing something similar to whatever he had been doing when Joe picked up the car.

'Nicely on time, lad,' he said.

'How much do I owe you?'

'Oh, give it to us next time.'

'I can't do that.'

'Won't you want it again?'

'I probably will.'

'Well then,' Mr Palmer said.

'I'd rather pay you now.'

'Do you know,' Mr Palmer said, smiling just a little, 'you are the first bloke I ever met who wanted to pay before he was asked. What were you during the war?'

'All kinds,' Joe said. 'What about you?'

'Organizing and digging tunnels,' Mr Palmer said. 'I was a

pitman first and we understood such things. Not much different than being down the pit really. But when I came back I thought I had learned a lot in France about vehicles and I was always interested in that kind of thing. So I thought I might start up a business. It doesn't make a lot of money, but I like doing it. Besides, I have no bairns and my missus doesn't care. Her mam left us the house and a bit of money, and I have this.'

'Have you got other cars?' Joe said.

'Bits of them,' Mr Palmer said with another smile.

There were all kinds of cars in pieces around the side and to the back and Mr Palmer talked to him about engines and bodies. Joe felt quite at home there. They went back to the office in the end and there it was a mess. Beyond it were all sorts of spare parts, most of which Joe recognized and the rest he thought he would if he got a chance to study them.

He was emboldened to say to Mr Palmer, 'You don't need any help, do you?'

Mr Palmer considered. 'I might do, but you've made me late for me dinner, you know.'

'I don't need much,' Joe said. 'I just want to learn about such things. I can drive anything. After the war I helped with tanks and different vehicles and learned about how they were put together and pulled apart because they kept breaking down. I know quite a bit about engines too. I'm interested in it; I have thought sometimes that I'd like to build a car.'

'I like putting them together and taking them apart and so on,' Mr Palmer said. 'I have ideas about what goes where.'

'And perhaps when it doesn't,' Joe said.

'Exactly,' Mr Palmer said, slapping his knee in his enthusiasm. 'Summat new would be good, summat ordinary folk – well, some of them – could have. Summat to take them wherever they wanted any time. They could go to the seaside on a whim or to see friends, or if they wanted to work in other places. They could do owt they chose – wouldn't that be grand?' Mr Palmer's face was lit like Oxford Street at Christmas. His vision was so real.

Joe felt a rush of dizzy excitement. In the end he went home with Mr Palmer and met his wife who sat down to tea with them. He and Mr Palmer talked until very late, even when Mrs Palmer gave up and went to bed.

Joe returned the following morning to help Mr Palmer with a number of vehicles he had in the garage and was mending, but they talked more about the ideas they had had themselves. Mr Palmer offered Joe work so that he could have an assistant and they could try to build something new.

Dear Joe,

I am losing my friends. They think this war was a good idea and are sacrificing their children to it like that bloody man in the Bible who had no more sense. I am being cold-shouldered and although I would have helped if I had been asked I think my views are becoming widely known. I wouldn't be surprised if they put me in one of those camps for conscientious objectors. My position has saved me so far. Perhaps I should find more easy company there.

Other than that I do help where I can because I feel so guilty over not doing so when all around me people are trying hard, but it does not give me any kind of satisfaction. I am teaching men to shoot. Boys! The stupid thing is that I'm not good at it myself but apparently I can teach. Glad to know I can do something. I spend a lot of time showing men what different kinds of guns are like, how they come apart, how they are put together, how some weapons are more effective than others so yes, I can be blamed for all those lads against us who are being shot. What a happy outcome. Angela has gone off into hospitals to be useful, as so many well-born young women do. Her father is still throwing other men at her, but luckily she doesn't like any of them – I don't think you have anything to worry about. I know they are very worried about Toddy – he is a changed man since war. Not like you. I don't think you ever change. You go forward as though it was meant to be your life. I can't think how, I just have to assume that it's right for you. When the nightmares come to me in the darkness I blot them out with brandy and I think of you and me in better times in better places.

TEN

Lucy was dreaming of home when she heard a noise. It was a lovely dream. She dreamed of home often, of her father tired and keeping out of the way in his study, of her mother shouting at her in the kitchen and of Gemma crying. But this was a comforting dream, they were all together, happy, and then she heard something. She examined it in her head, hoping that it might be part of what was going on there, but it wasn't. With a great reluctance she gave in to reality and allowed herself to wake fully in the little back room in the Misses Slaters' house.

The noise grew louder, people shrieking next door. Her first thought was that Mr Formby was wrecking his family life but no, it was much too late for that, she knew. As the noise went on she heard other sounds in the bedroom next to hers and then Miss Slater's voice joined by Miss Bethany's. She came out onto the landing, wearing what had been the sisters' mother's best thick dressing gown, and they too emerged with a lamp.

That was when Lucy smelled smoke. Miss Slater guided them downstairs and lit another lamp while Lucy took from her the first one. She went outside onto the towpath and saw the house next to them burning. She hadn't seen such a thing before; the smoke was thick and black.

There was nobody about. Lucy went straight back into the house and picked up the only scarf she possessed, soaked it in water and pushed it over her face, especially her mouth, tying it at the back of her head. She made her way into the building, holding her breath at first as the two small Formby children hurtled towards her, one of them sobbing and the other silent. She guided them outside and gave them into Miss Slater's care, then went back inside though Miss Slater told her not to.

She shouted Tilda's name, but heard no reply. She reached the stairs. She was beginning to cough horribly as she was forced to breathe in smoke. Clay was at the bottom of the stairs, Mrs Formby and Tilda behind him.

They went outside, coughing. A crowd had gathered by then and Miss Slater was soon there with big mugs of cold water. Lucy had never been so glad to taste it. She saw, amidst the lights of the sky, Joe large and looming and organizing people in some way.

He saw her and said, 'Is everybody out?'

'I don't think Mr Formby—'

'Dead drunk somewhere, likely,' somebody interrupted.

She caught hold of Tilda's hand. 'What about your dad?'

Tilda turned away, concerned about her mother and the children. By now there was a line of people with buckets, from the house to the towpath, and every minute they were pouring more water on the fire.

'Is Mr Formby still in there?' Joe said.

Behind her she could hear someone say, 'The bugger's

likely in some bar sleeping it off,' but she was not convinced and neither was Joe.

He went to Mrs Formby and asked about her husband. She was only just conscious because of the smoke and Tilda had gone to comfort the children. Without any more hesitating, Joe, with Lucy's wet scarf for his face and wrapped in a blanket he had upturned a bucket over, plunged back inside while people shrieked that he shouldn't.

She wanted to go in after him, and every second seemed like forever. After about five endless minutes she decided she had to go in, just as Miss Slater came and got hold of her by the arm.

'You aren't going to do something foolish, are you?' she said.

'I must—'

'No, you mustn't.'

Lucy wanted to say that it would be awful if anything should happen to Joe when Mr Formby likely wasn't there anyway – and even if he was he was a horrible man not worth saving – but she couldn't say anything of the kind. Instead she stood and waited as they went on throwing water at the house.

She saw policemen and firemen arguing about what they could do because the towpath wasn't wide enough for a vehicle.

It was some small eternity later when Joe emerged from the house with something large in his arms, staggering with the weight. People went to him and relieved him of it. He couldn't stand for the smoke and the fatigue.

Miss Bethany gave him water while other people saw to the huge weight Joe had pulled out. It was Mr Formby. Mrs Formby cried out when she saw him, and her daughter put an arm around her, but Lucy's attention was elsewhere. She got down onto the cold ground with a soaking wet flannel to put to Joe's face. His breathing eased and she wrapped the dressing gown around him. He smiled at her, coughing again and then breathing more freely.

Beyond the crowd she could hear Mrs Formby's voice, wailing, grieving. She left Joe and went over to where the Formby family stood grouped around Mr Formby. There was the doctor, saying how sorry he was. Although she had never liked Mr Formby she thought it must be a poor kind of person who was glad that somebody was dead.

She watched as the men lifted Mr Formby's body into the Misses Slaters' house, carrying him upstairs. She wanted to ask them not to put him in her room, but she couldn't really, because there were only two. She didn't like to think about the 50 per cent chance that Mr Formby was lying on her recently vacated bed.

She went back to Joe and watched as he recovered, giving him cold drinks of water when he could take them. He coughed and coughed, but eventually stopped, his breathing now easy as he thanked her.

The fire died down with so many people helping so that eventually there was little to do but watch. The doctor came across and insisted on examining Joe and then tried to force Lucy and Joe to hospital, but Lucy told him there was nothing the matter with her and Joe said the same. Lucy was pleased that the fire had not reached further, beyond the stones of the house, and so the Misses Slaters and the Formbys and she and Joe were able to go inside number three. Lucy started up the fire in the kitchen and they sat around in a state of shock over what had happened.

The two small children, wrapped in blankets which Lucy had taken from the beds, fell asleep as the fire began to warm the room. Tilda sat apart from them, staring beyond the window as though explanations would be found there. Just as Clay went to sit with her there came a knocking on the door. When Lucy opened it a large policeman was outside.

'I need to ask some questions,' he said.

'Won't it keep until later?' Lucy said, but he ignored her and pushed past inside. Lucy wished Constable Keane were there.

Everyone looked at him as he stood there, huge in the room.

'So, who started it?' he said.

Lucy stared and when there was silence she said, 'What on earth do you mean?'

'We found the petrol can round the back.'

Nobody spoke.

'Must have been one of you lot,' he said.

'Why would you think such a thing?' Lucy said.

Joe got up and went to him. 'Does this have to be now?' he said.

The policeman glowered at him. 'Look, lad,' he said, 'this fire was started deliberately and who else would do such a thing in the middle of the night, eh?'

'I would scarcely believe that any member of a family was going to start a fire with themselves inside the house, don't you think?'

'And Mr Formby was not an easy man. Maybe he owed money,' Lucy said. 'Maybe he had upset somebody.'

'Somebody who brought a petrol can and then left it?'

'It's no less likely than it was somebody here,' Joe said.

The policeman looked hard at him. 'Maybe it was you then. Do you live here with these ladies?'

'No—'

'And can you prove where you were?'

'He wasn't here,' Lucy said. 'He doesn't live here. He came to help when he saw the fire, like half the rest of the riverside. Now will you please stop throwing stupid accusations at us and go away. You have no right to come in here and do this. We are all in a state of shock. Constable Keane will sort it out.'

'Constable Keane is not on duty, miss,' the policeman said. 'We've got that petrol can and I'll be back. I shall want some answers then.'

'Edgar will deal with him,' Lucy said.

Joe went off to feed the cats and Lucy had to go to work, it being Monday.

It was later in the morning when Mr Clarence, the man who helped Lucy to man the front desk and dealt with a great deal of the paperwork, came upstairs to the little office where she sometimes worked. He told her that Mr Bainbridge was wanted down at the police station, to see a Mrs Formby.

Mr Bainbridge was in court that morning, but then Mr Clarence said that the message had been urgent. She didn't know what to think.

'But I shouldn't go.'

'I think one of us should and I'm not leaving the front desk. You know more about these things than I do, and what harm can it do? Besides, it's work we might get,' he said in a practical way.

So Lucy went, hurrying down Old Elvet towards the police station, her heart hammering inside her chest. When she got there she went up to the long counter which stretched across the entrance as though they were trying to repel boarders. The uniformed man behind the counter did not stop writing, but Lucy saw it was Constable Keane.

'I've come to see Mrs Formby,' she announced. 'She and the rest of us, we had nothing to do with it, you must believe it.'

'Don't worry, miss,' he said, 'I'm sure it'll sort. I thought it was Mr Bainbridge who was coming.'

'I work with him. I gather Mrs Formby asked for him, but he's in court so I had to come in his place. You will let me see her.'

'Of course, miss.' He opened the door beyond the counter which allowed access to the rest of the building and she followed him. The place was bigger than it looked. All the buildings in that area had been made with the idea of the law and how it worked in mind. Had she been alone she might have got lost, but they were soon down in the depths where it was not very light and there were cells on either side. She had the door unlocked and looked inside; a small slight woman sat on the bench there. She looked even smaller than she usually did and so pale that Lucy thought the poor woman would faint. The cell had a window high up, the bench, a bowl of water to wash, a pail for a toilet and a plate where crumbs of some meal were left.

Lucy stepped inside.

'Oh, Mrs Formby,' she said, as he locked the door behind her and she listened to his footsteps dying away.

'They said I could have somebody. I needed help and I remembered Miss Slater saying that you worked for the solicitor, Mr Bainbridge.' Mrs Formby's voice quivered and then broke. Lucy gave her time but she didn't say anything.

'What happened?' Lucy said eventually.

Mrs Formby shook her head. 'I'm sorry to bring you here, Miss Charlton, indeed I wouldn't have done it – but you're so kind and I don't know what to do. They said I killed him and I didn't. I did nothing of the sort. I really didn't.'

Lucy made comforting noises. 'Of course you didn't. How utterly ridiculous,' she said in a practical voice that she could see already helped, though still Mrs Formby wept and shook her head.

'The polis dragged me in here. Can they keep me here, Miss Charlton? Only I don't like leaving the bairns and Tilda has to go to work. The Misses Slaters will look after them but the little 'uns cried when the polis came and though Clay would have gone for Mr Hardy because we knew he would help, the little 'uns hung onto him after I was taken.'

Lucy reassured her, though she wasn't quite certain what she would do. 'Don't worry,' she said, 'Mr Bainbridge will sort this out. I know the constable who is on duty very often and he will try and help us – it will be all right.'

She went out and bought Mrs Formby a big rug and a pillow and some decent food and some sweets. She took her books, though she wasn't sure Mrs Formby wanted these, and a pen and paper in case she remembered anything else and wanted to write it down. Then she left, promising that Mr Bainbridge would come as soon as he came back from court.

She waited until Edgar Bainbridge came back into the office, then knocked on his door. When he told her to come in she hurriedly reported what she had done.

'I hope that was the right thing to do.'

'Of course it was. You didn't claim to be anything you weren't and since Mrs Formby had asked for you, you went as a friend. I will go and see her this afternoon. Perhaps you would like to come with me?'

And so that afternoon Lucy went with Edgar when Mrs Formby was due to be questioned by the police. Two very large policemen sat looking important at the table. One of them had a notebook and a pencil in front of him and the other one had already made notes, Lucy could see.

One of the first things they asked was had Mrs Formby bought some petrol.

She looked sceptically at them. 'Aye,' she said, 'for my big shiny motor car.'

The policeman looked at her. 'This isn't funny, Mrs Formby.'

'You would think so if you'd spent any time at all in those cells. I need to get laughs where I can.'

Lucy hadn't realized that Mrs Formby could be so fierce, but she soon understood why.

'You took me away from my four bairns without any . . .' Mrs Formby paused and then found the right word, '. . . any evidence and did anybody care what happened to them? No, they didn't. Dragged me out of Miss Slater's lovely little house – after all she's done for us – you did, for no good reason. They will vouch for me and Miss Charlton here too that I never did owt like that, I wouldn't – I was brought up proper as a good-living woman. I didn't buy no petrol and I didn't kill my man if that's your next question. Even though he was a bugger there was a time when I loved him and I put up with him when he wasn't. He didn't have any work, we couldn't get any help, but we were a family.'

Lucy was very impressed at this long speech, but then she thought about Mrs Formby having several hours in that wretched cell to work out what she was going to say, fired up by the fact that she and her four children were now home-less and the man she had once loved was dead.

'Mr Ronald Palmer of Esh Garage on the edge of the town has told us that he sold petrol to a woman who resembled you. We had men out early at all the garages in the place,' the policeman said proudly.

'Does he now. Who told him to say that, you?' was her reply. 'And where did he think I'd got a petrol can from?' Lucy thought Mrs Formby didn't really need anybody there, all she needed was an audience. 'And who on earth would think any mother would put her bairns at risk by setting her own house on fire? She would have to be a queer sort.'

'Did Mr Palmer give a description?' Edgar asked.

'He said she was poor and small and badly dressed with a shawl over her head and dark clothes.'

'That description fits half the women of Durham,' Edgar said. 'If she had a shawl on how did he get a good look at her face?'

The policeman said nothing to that.

'Do you have other questions?'

'Where were you, Mrs Formby, earlier that evening?'

'I was at home with my bairns, like any decent mother would be. I didn't go and buy no petrol and I didn't have no money either, so I couldn't have, could I?'

'That fire was started deliberately the Fire Chief says and it's common knowledge that Mr Formby treated his family, especially his wife, badly. Miss Charlton herself came into the police station and said so.'

'All I said was that it would be helpful if a policeman might take his beat past their house,' Lucy said.

'Because he was knocking his wife about.'

'If you had done something about this and kept a decent watch on Rachel Lane you would have frightened off the kind of people who do such things and you wouldn't be blaming innocent people now.'

Lucy apologized to Edgar later, but he only said, 'You judged it well. You and Mrs Formby had the tone just right, even though it shouldn't have come to that.'

Lucy and Edgar spent most of the rest of the day at the police station, while Mr Palmer was asked to come and identify the woman he had sold the petrol to. The police brought several shabbily dressed women in from the street for a line-up.

Lucy was worried, even though to her the women all looked exactly alike – Edgar was right, they were poor and shabby and Lucy was ashamed that she lived in such a place. Somewhere apparently rich from its empire but let its people remain so poor that they lived these desperate lives.

Mr Palmer, when he saw the line-up, shook his head and

said it could have been any of them, that he hadn't taken much notice. One of the policeman said sarcastically that it couldn't be something that happened every day, selling a can of petrol to any woman, never mind one as poor as this. Mr Palmer said he wasn't given to asking people what they wanted a can of petrol for and that he had never said who the woman was, he had never seen her before in his life, he didn't know what she looked like and he couldn't understand what all the fuss was about, bringing him here like this.

The policeman asked Mr Palmer what on earth he thought the woman wanted the petrol for, but Mr Palmer had clearly had enough by then, saying his wife had had his dinner ready for the past two hours. He didn't go asking questions of people as long as they paid for the petrol, he considered it was none of his damned business. The policeman said there was no need for him to swear, they were just doing their duty, and that was when Edgar said in a very loud but polite voice that he thought they had no need to keep Mrs Formby now, for they had no evidence to link her with the burning down of the house.

They were able to take Mrs Formby home – well, next door – and the children clustered around her, all but Tilda. When they had settled down Mrs Formby went outside and cried in the cold rain. Lucy went after her and took the woman into her arms.

'They thought I could do such a thing, even though he was such a bugger! I'm sorry to swear,' she said and then broke away. 'Thank you, Miss Charlton, I won't forget what you did.'

'They had no case against you. They're just not very clever and they don't understand.' She wanted to say that they didn't care about women and that thousands of wives suffered at their husbands' hands every day, but she couldn't. 'They had to find somebody who'd done it after they discovered the petrol can.'

'What if somebody does it again?'

'They won't,' Lucy said, much more confidently than she felt. 'Your husband must have been the target, it couldn't have been you. Maybe he had behaved badly to someone else – one of his friends at the pub or such.'

'I never wished him dead, you know, Miss Charlton, but I did sometimes think that if he'd just gone away that would have done. Maybe me wishing him away like that caused it.'

'It couldn't have,' Lucy said flatly. 'Don't you ever feel guilty. You did nothing wrong, you tried to do everything you could; you worked hard, gave him children, looked after him and them and you didn't blame him, not once. Don't spoil the rest of your life with it.'

Eleven

Joe wrote to Toddy. He didn't want to, but he knew it was the right thing to do. He apologized for his behaviour. He didn't feel sorry for what he had done, but Toddy would never help him unless they came to some reasonable kind of understanding. Joe became more and more convinced that Angela would go back there, Toddy being in London, and he needed Toddy on his side when she came home.

Where else would she go? She didn't know where he was, she could not come looking for him, and in spite of the fact that she knew her father did not want her there, if she was alive, with or without the baby, then she would go home. If not, she would at least contact Toddy if she needed money – which surely she must.

He put inside the letter to Toddy an envelope containing a letter to Angela, one he'd spent a good deal of time composing late at night. He felt nearer to her then, as though they were speaking to one another. He told her how sorry he was and how much he loved and missed her. He told her about the tower house in an almost humorous way. He told her about the cats, for Angela loved cats. Once he had started writing to her he couldn't stop. He told her all the day-to-day things, about how he had started work, about the search he was going to continue for Priscilla Lee and how he would do anything to have her back, he'd go anywhere. He missed her, needed her, wanted her, loved her more than ever.

Joe only sent the one letter inside Toddy's envelope. He didn't think Toddy would open a letter which was not addressed to him – Toddy was too much the gentleman for that –but there was no point in sending all the letters to Angela Joe wrote night after night when he couldn't sleep.

He kept them and reread them and imagined Angela sending letters back to him, but most of all he thought of her coming home and being forgiven by her family. For then Toddy would let her know where he was and they would be reunited.

He half expected that Toddy would not reply and indeed nothing happened for about three weeks. Then he got a letter.

Dear Joe,

I didn't know what to do about your communication at first. I didn't want anyone to know that you had been in touch. Sarah and my father are both angry with you so I confided in my mother. She advised me to write back to you and to say that if I ever do have any word from Angela I will contact you.

I think I would have done that anyway. Now that I can see this thing so much more clearly, now that I have put the war

and all that it meant behind me, I can see why you did what
you did. If it had been Sarah and me I would have done the
same. I'm not saying it was right, but you and I are not of my
father's generation.

I think he was wrong to tell you that your father killed
himself because of what you had done. It's nonsense. Your
father had his own demons to deal with and he would never
have blamed you for what happened.

I will put in motion what I can to see if she can be found,
though what more is to be done I can't tell.

Joe was glad to be forgiven, he needed Toddy there. He
wanted to go haring back to London, but there didn't seem
to be any point. Toddy was well known and liked, and his
circle of friends and acquaintances was huge. Joe knew that
he could not have asked anyone better, Toddy having always
loved his sister, to help him now.

Toddy also told Joe that he and Sarah were expecting their
first child. Joe was jealous – they were respectable, they were
married, they could enjoy the idea and then hopefully the
child.

Dear Joe,

Went to my club and there was Felix Toddington, going on
about the empire and the war and how brave his son is and
how wonderful we are. Several other chaps were there whose
sons are dead or have come back badly injured. What is the
matter with such people? The trouble is that the bastard, like
a lot of others, has never been to war and has no idea of the

reality of it. He tried to stop Angela from becoming involved, but I think Barbara stuck her oar in there so at least Angela continues working at one of the hospitals and seems the happier for it. I think she would like to be in France, hopefully somewhere close to you. She speaks so softly of you every time I see her. I wish your mother had been such a biddable pleasant creature, yet there is a core of steel which runs through her. I hope she learns to cultivate that. She gets it from her mother. Barbara was always an awkward moo. One of the reasons I never asked her to marry me.

Her parents badly wanted a proper title for her. The woman is enormous these days. She looks like a ship in the mid-Atlantic and has a backside like a frying pan. Your mother was so beautiful in every way. I wish I had been a better husband to her. That haunts me late at night. I didn't understand her and although I tell myself I was too young I think I was just too arrogant, too aware of my position to be better to her. We had nothing in common – all I could see was her extravagant and rather wild beauty. Men love to take beauty and have power over it. Some men even like to crush it because it frightens them. I think I was afraid of who she was. How awful to think that.

Joe didn't tell Lucy when he went back to Gateshead to see Mr Firbank. He began to motor up there every few days and after the first time Mr Firbank recognized him and was glad. Knowing that no one ever went to see him Joe felt the responsibility for the old man. If it was fine they would sit outside and if it was not they would sit by the window and watch the swiftly moving water that was the Tyne. Mr Firbank had lucid times and as he became comfortable with Joe's presence began to talk to him about Cissie.

'I lodged with them when I was nobbut a lad, I was sixteen then and they weren't much more themselves. They wanted to go places and do things. He was never there, he always had these schemes, and he would go off and leave us a lot and never send her any money. I would keep us instead. I didn't have much of a job those days, but Susie didn't care for such things. And when she had the little 'un it was such joy. I didn't know much about bairns before that, but right from the start the little lass was precious to me. When she was about four or so he started to make money and by then I'd long since left the house; he'd thrown me out. So I didn't get to see Cissie as much as I wanted though sometimes her mam would bring her to me. He was clever, like a chemist, you know, and he got silver out of the mines in a way in which made it easy. He made enough money in the end to go south and pretend he was a gentleman. He was no gentleman. He would do a man down for a ha'penny and he didn't look after her or the bairn. He wanted to be summat he wasn't.'

Shortly after this Mr Firbank fell asleep.

The following day Joe made his way back up to Allendale and went to the church and the vicarage. He talked to people, but it was a long time ago, and many had left the area for all sorts of reasons, mostly because the lead had long since become uneconomical to bring out of the ground. Joe wondered if Mr Firbank had got things wrong. Nobody called Lee had gone off to London with a fortune in silver. The whole thing sounded so unlikely to Joe that he felt he had come to a dead end.

TWELVE

Mrs Formby needed a new house. Lucy tried to talk to Edgar about her not wanting to go far. He looked frustrated.

'But it's an awful place,' he said.

'Well, it might be to you, but to some of us it's home, I mean, yes, the houses are falling down and the landlord doesn't seem to care too much, but surely he has another house the Formbys could live in, somewhere not too far away from the rest of us.'

Luckily it was a Saturday when the landlord came to see the state that the house was in, bringing with him another man who looked to Lucy like a builder. She was able to go out and to talk to them.

The landlord, Mr Manson, told her that he was going to rebuild the house immediately because it would affect those on either side. Lucy asked if he had another house for the Formbys, and said that they would prefer a better house, one which was not damp. She went on to tell him that her house, number three, was also damp – which was when Mr Manson decided that he had other things to do. He walked rapidly away, but Lucy ran after him and pulled at his arm.

When he turned around to object she said, 'You have a duty of care to the people you house, not to leave them in such places.'

He looked at her and smiled. It was a horrid smile, Lucy decided, superior and slimy.

'I have no other house to offer them.'

'You cannot leave them on the street.'

'They can stay with the Misses Slaters.'

'They cannot, it isn't big enough, and you know very well it isn't. You must find them somewhere else.'

He didn't answer. He strode up the street at such a pace that Lucy was obliged to watch him and to tell herself that he would do no more. She walked back. The builder had gone too, clearly also unwilling to take the responsibility.

She found out where the landlord lived, so angry when she heard it was one of the pretty houses up at the top of Claypath. That evening, when she reasoned it was late enough for him to be home, she took the hill quickly with rapid strides and rang the bell so loudly that it sounded inside.

A youngish woman, she guessed Mrs Manson, answered the door – though Lucy reasoned they could easily have afforded help. The woman was very formally dressed for an evening as though she might be going somewhere.

'My name is Lucy Charlton. I would like to see Mr Manson please.'

'We're about to have our tea.'

'It will only take a minute,' Lucy said. As she stepped forward the woman automatically stepped back and suddenly she was inside.

Everything was new in there, sparkly as though Mr Manson were still proving to the world who he was. The woman went off into one of the big side rooms and Lucy could hear murmurs. Mr Manson came into the hall, frowning. In the smaller space of the hall he looked bigger than he had done in Rachel Lane.

'What do you want?' he said.

'I want you to find a decent house for Mrs Formby and her children. You cannot put them out onto the street. Presumably the house was insured, you will have money—'

'Young woman, this has nothing to do with you—'

'Indeed it has,' Lucy said. 'I live next door with the Misses Slaters. We have two small bedrooms. We cannot look after another five people—'

'Then you will have to make some other arrangement.'

'You will have to make some other arrangement,' Lucy said. 'They were your tenants, they paid their rent. You can't just put them on the street.'

'I am doing what I can.'

'No, you aren't,' Lucy said, holding the man's angry gaze with her own. 'Don't you care about the people in your houses? Doesn't it matter that many of those houses are badly maintained, that they are damp and insanitary and that they will fall down and when they do it will cost you a great deal more money than putting them right now would? You must have other houses, don't you?'

'I own a great deal of property,' Mr Manson said, puffing out his chest to make himself important.

Lucy waved a hand at the hall. 'This is a splendid house. Did you do this yourself?'

She had found the way through. He nodded.

'Yes,' he said, 'it was in very bad repair.'

'It's beautiful,' Lucy said, though she didn't admire his taste.

'It was a big job – it was on the verge of collapse.'

'There must be a great deal of satisfaction to putting things right as you do. And people are bound to notice whether you do or not.'

He stared at her. 'That sounds very much like a threat, and coming from a young woman—'

'Oh, I'm not that young,' she said smoothly, 'and I'm about to become a solicitor. I have friends who care about these things, as well as the police, and I understand that the local newspapers are all run by the same family, a family who are friends of my employer, Mr Bainbridge—'

The man had put up both hands, his face a mixture of resentment and amusement.

'I will see what I can do,' he allowed.

She wasn't convinced he would, though she had told more than one lie, but then Edgar did know someone who ran the newspapers, an Edward Fleming.

Back at the little house in Rachel Lane she said nothing to the Misses Slaters or to Mrs Formby, for she wasn't convinced that the landlord had any integrity or care for such people. The little house had never seemed smaller. The children would not leave Frederick alone – they kept stroking him and prodding him and dancing around him – and although Lucy told them politely twice not to poke the old spaniel, because he had begun to growl and she was not going to have him blamed for showing his teeth, in the end she put on the fire in the sitting room – which they could ill afford – and Frederick was left to snore peacefully by the kitchen fire.

The Misses Slaters were worried about the beds and the bedding – though they found all the blankets they had. They had a sofa yet they could still not accommodate all these people. In the end everybody slept where they could – the two small children and Mrs Formby had Lucy's bed and Lucy and Tilda took the sofa, while Clay lay on the hearthrug with an old cushion and a blanket.

Lucy found the sofa uncomfortable and she could tell that Tilda did too, although she did not move. The girl was unnaturally quiet and though neither of them tried to brush up against the other it was almost impossible not to.

Mr Manson did not get back to her and day after day the house seemed to get smaller. She had no intention of going to the newspapers. She thought there must be something she could do, but she couldn't think of it.

The following day she went to the store in her dinner break and asked Tilda how she was feeling. The shoe shop was empty, she had timed it well. The shop was dark, in spite of having big windows at the front, and filled with long boxes which held the shoes. Lucy disliked the smell of leather, she presumed it was that; to her it stank of dead cows. The shoes on display in the window were not the kind of things which any woman longed for – no dancing shoes, no party shoes, they were all as stout as though they would keep out the rain, and in black or brown, all laces and plainness, not a ribbon or a decoration anywhere in sight. The day was so rainy that she couldn't see into the shadows at the back of the shop.

'You seem so unhappy,' she said. 'Are you grieving for your father, despite what he was?'

'He was me dad, even so,' Tilda said. She even looked up.

'Do you remember being little and him being kind?'

'Aye, he was, sometimes. He used to read to me when I was our Jan's age. He learned me the clock. I used to sit on his knee – we had this wooden clock and he used to turn the pointers to show me.' She stopped.

'And then?'

Tilda didn't say anything as though she might have other things to do and didn't like being questioned. Eventually she said, 'He wasn't me dad when he drank.'

'He began to hit your mother?'

'She pretended it was all right, but it wasn't, and I started getting in the road. He thought I was her and he would hit me. And—'

'And—' Lucy could scarcely breathe. Tilda had not spoken freely like this to her before and she did not want anything to break the spell. Perhaps it was because they were alone.

'After he lost his job he couldn't get another. It made him drink and he worried about me mam and the bairns. He wasn't even pleased when I got a job at the store. He said it showed him up, that he couldn't provide for his bairns. When I gave me mam the money he took it off her and spent it all at the pub, so I . . . I hit him the next time he did it and I bettered him, Miss Charlton, because he was so drunk he couldn't stand. I got the money back and gave it to me mam so she could feed everybody.'

'And then?' Lucy could tell the story wasn't finished.

Tilda's head was down. Lucy was so glad there was nobody about or she was sure she would not have gone on.

'He came to the shop. I was so pleased with my job, you know. I'd actually done something that made us respectable, in spite of where we came from. I felt like I might make something of me life like me mam wanted me to. She was so proud of me. And they told me that I would be the manageress because Miss Thompson is old and has had enough, and she's all right, anyway. She lives with her mam and they have a bit put by and she was pleased for me to have it – she showed me how to do everything and she was kind with it, you know, and I felt so good. I thought mebbe I could keep us all, that was what I really wanted but . . .'

Lucy waited. The girl was silent now, head down, her body almost turned away from Lucy. She was in tears – Lucy could see the shine of them on her cheeks – and as a friend it hurt her to push, but as a would-be lawyer she couldn't stop now.

'And then?' Lucy hardly dared say it.

'Miss Thompson had gone home to her mother. She let me lock up. She knew I liked to, that it made me feel as if I were in charge, you know. I locked up and I didn't look round and when I did, because I thought I heard something, he grabbed me and started hitting me. He pulled me hair and he forced me up the side street, just round there,' she indicated with a gesture, 'and then he . . . and then he . . .' She stopped.

There was silence and not much to listen to outside, just the general day-to-day things, Lucy thought. She wished she

168

was in it, and tried hard to listen to the conversation which was going on, the sudden laughter just beyond the door, but it meant nothing. She knew now that she could never be a part of that without thinking about how to make things better, having decided to try to do more.

'Can you tell me about it?' she said.

'I don't know how to say it.' The girl shook her head and the water from her eyes overflowed, making fresh tiny marks upon her face. The tears ran faster and faster until her breathing was ragged. She sobbed, tiny sounds at first, but they caught up with one another until they were continuous, even though she began to speak again.

'He was me dad – how could he do that to me? I don't think he knew who I was. Or mebbe he was so jealous of me job and that I had done well and me mam was pleased – he couldn't bear her to like any of us, you see. He wanted to come first always and when you have four bairns I don't think it works like that. I don't think me dad had ever come first with anybody until he met me mam and she was so lovely to him. She is lovely, isn't she?'

Lucy made soothing noises and nodded her head.

'Me mam cared so much about him. She really did. It must have been all right until I was born and I think he blamed me that she didn't put him first any more, although she still seemed to. He got his dinner first, she did what he wanted, she asked for nowt from him, but when he couldn't keep us then it all went wrong. He was ashamed of himself.'

Lucy said nothing. She didn't move. She didn't want to change the mood and she prayed as she had not prayed in a long time that nobody would push open the shop door and

169

interrupt because she had the feeling they would never get this far again.

She waited and waited, her nerves beginning to shred into tiny pieces. Any moment now some stupid person would want slippers or everyday sensible shoes in which they could walk for miles and not care. She glanced around the shop, but it was no comfort, it didn't distract her. She would not have said a word if Tilda had stood there forever.

'I'm having his bairn, Miss Charlton. How in God's name can I ever tell me mam?'

Lucy didn't know what to say. She felt as though her stomach had plunged to the floor. She couldn't help Tilda by saying that she'd had the same experience because she hadn't, and although at the time it had seemed to her the very worst thing that could happen to a woman, it was obviously not so, not nearly. She could have laughed at herself for her naivety.

'Should I say some lad got me like this and that I let him – and me mam would think I was cheap and not worth her time – or that somebody in the dark did it and I didn't know him, or that me dad did it, with three other bairns and she being his wife. She cared for him. How could she live with that, how could she live knowing that she loved a man who could lose himself in such a way that he could do a thing like that to his own daughter?'

Lucy's experience did not take her to here. She had no idea what to say. Tilda was looking at her.

'I'm going to lose me job because I'm having a bairn and it will show, and me mam will be ashamed of me because I'll be a bad lass then. Everybody will stop talking to us and we will have no money, not even to run away to some place where nobody knows us. What will we do?'

Lucy surprised herself. 'We'll think of something,' she said. 'We'll sort something out, I promise.' And then she realized, she saw coldly as if through sleet, what had happened to this girl, how she had taken matters upon herself. She should never have had to do that had the police or anybody cared enough to have helped.

Lucy was so cold that she wanted to shiver. She couldn't move. She kept on looking at the girl, pitying her and yet shocked, trying to see the situation as real so that she could work something out to help, but she was unable to do so.

Tilda stood there, silent. She was quiet for a very long time and Lucy waited. A sudden thought occurred to her, so awful that her skin felt as if it were crawling.

Tilda looked at her. 'You know, don't you, what I did?'

'Tilda—'

'Right then. I killed me dad. I would have said so too if things had gone any further. I never thought they would take me mam like that. I shouldn't have done it, I know I'll go to hell, but I couldn't stand it no more. I found the can, it was like a chance – and I went to the garage and bought the petrol. I dressed up and held meself like an older woman. I knew I could get us out – I planned it, I was sure of it – and I got the bairns downstairs, saying it was a game. Our Clay understood and he wouldn't have cared anyroad, our Clay cares about me first, so all I had to do was rouse me mam once I'd set it alight. It was so easy I wished I'd done it sooner, but when it was over I knew it was a terrible sin and that I shouldn't have. I knew the minute you came back

171

into the house to help us that it was wrong and when Mr Hardy went back in for me dad – I just couldn't think any more, I thought you would both be killed and I would have done it.' She broke down then. 'God will never forgive me,' she said.

Lucy was so shocked that she didn't know what to say. She was also very soon amazed at herself that she hadn't realized, but then how could she have done so – she felt that she had not known Tilda at all until now. She found her voice and made it loud; she couldn't have this young girl blaming herself for the things life had thrust upon her.

'Of course he will,' she said, hearing herself being brisk and glad of it. 'There's no point in vicars saying that God is merciful if people don't believe such things. That's what he's there for,' Lucy said with a confidence she didn't feel.

Tilda wept and Lucy stayed with her. But when the long afternoon finally ended, and there were no customers because the day was dark and rain beat off the windows and the roof, Lucy didn't know what to do.

Tilda didn't want to leave the shop and Lucy could understand that. She was reluctant to go home and face her family. Lucy didn't know what to say, the only place she had to go was the Misses Slaters'. She thought Edgar might help, but he was so respectable – she had the feeling that he cared so much for the law, he understood it and was involved in it, that he would have to give Tilda up to the police. Because however you argued it she had killed her father.

Lucy tried to look at the problem from the other side as well, because she knew that a good lawyer would do so. She thought she might go back and talk to Edgar and see how she felt about what he said, but she wouldn't tell him directly what had happened.

Tilda had to stay until closing time. Lucy said she would come back for her in an hour when she locked up. When she arrived back at the office the door was opened, although Mr Clarence had gone home. She knocked on Edgar's door and heard his voice, and when she put her head around the door he smiled at her.

'Miss Charlton.'

'Actually, I've got a bit of a problem,' Lucy said, 'and I don't know what to do.'

'Come in,' he encouraged her, getting to his feet like the gentleman he was.

She hesitated.

'It's about the Formby family, Tilda in particular.'

'I thought it had all been sorted out,' Edgar said with a slight frown. 'Not really,' she said.

'They had no proof that Mrs Formby did any such thing and the charges were dropped,' Edgar said.

'It isn't as simple as that.'

Edgar looked at her. 'No?' he said. He hesitated before adding, 'You do have to be careful, you know, not to get too far in so that your judgement is at fault. '

'What do you mean?'

'Well, you can get on the wrong side of things so easily and then a solicitor is not in a good position to do the right thing. You ought to try and keep the family at a distance because you will work better for them that way. You have to be able to see clearly so that you can do your best for them.'

'They trust me,' she said.

'I'm sure they do.' He smiled at her.

'They are living with us now. So many of them.'

Edgar frowned, but said nothing.

'The house is tiny and although I have spoken to Mr Manson he has done nothing,' Lucy said.

'It's not been long – you have to give him a chance to find some place for them.'

'I don't think he intends to.'

Edgar sat back in his chair. 'The law is vague about such matters. I don't think there's much I can do. They will have to look for somewhere else – there must be a number of empty properties.'

He was right, Lucy thought. She went back and collected Tilda from the shop, but when they got home and she spoke to Mrs Formby about such a thing tears came into the woman's eyes.

'I know you mean well,' she said, 'but we've always lived here. We can't afford any more and anywhere we went would be dearer.'

Lucy took time that week to go to several properties and to the owners of them, but Mrs Formby was right – they were all dearer than the houses in Rachel Lane. It was the worst part of town. With only Tilda working they had been barely able to afford the house there. Now the situation was becoming even more difficult. The two Misses Slaters, while good people, were not used to such noise in their house. Lucy could see that Mrs Formby was becoming nervous, apologizing all the time for her boisterous family. Frederick had taken to hiding in dark corners and Lucy could hear her own voice becoming sharp and impatient.

She didn't know what to do. She started lying awake at night, worrying, thinking of how soon the baby would show and Tilda would be dismissed. Then what would happen? Things were already bad anyway – nobody should have to live like that. She didn't think like Mr Bainbridge did. She was involved with the Formbys; she couldn't leave Tilda to try and sort this out by herself.

She began to collect Tilda from the shop in the early evenings because she was so upset for the girl. She had to reassure her, because she did not want Tilda to go home with guilt written so large upon her face. Lucy herself also needed time to gain some kind of perspective.

THIRTEEN

Joe had a letter from Mr Barrington with regard to the sale of his property, wanting him to go immediately to London. He would see Toddy and Mr Barrington. He felt nearer to Angela as soon as he stepped off the train. He had told Toddy that he was coming though he had accepted an invitation to stay with the Barringtons. He didn't think Toddy's parents would want him anywhere near their house. He and Toddy met for lunch at Toddy's club, which had once been Joe's club too. It was also the club where Joe's father had met Toddy's father. Joe felt his father's presence there.

The letter he had read on the train was one his father's rants.

Angela seems worried. Her father is pushing her towards Foxman. Do you remember him, Joe? His father was a bloody foreigner with some ridiculous title. The poor bugger has come back from the war blind, but Felix seems to think she would be better off with him. His father of course made a lot of money in India. God knows how many people he killed over it. They're all mad in that family. Interbreeding or something, and yet he is welcomed in their house, falling over the sodding furniture

and talking about his fine house in Paris. Paris, for God's sake!
As though nothing else was happening in France.

Joe felt strange going into the club after so long. He wasn't hungry and he didn't want to be there. Several people looked over but didn't approach. Joe tried to ignore it.

Toddy had no news of Angela, but he said he was doing everything he could to find her. He had talked to his business acquaintances and anyone he knew who was at all influential. He did not doubt that in the end she would be found. They didn't discuss whether she was still alive. Joe couldn't eat very much, the anxiety making him feel sick.

'There is something else as well,' Toddy said awkwardly as the cheese was brought to the table. 'I would like you to be godfather to my child.'

Joe was so taken aback that he didn't know what to say.

'What about Sarah?'

'She will choose the godmother. We have talked about this and we are agreed. You were best man at our wedding and I think we should all try to redeem ourselves here.'

'Thank you, Toddy, that means a great deal to me,' Joe said, and he took more interest in the cheese than he had in the four courses which had preceded it.

Mr Barrington greeted Joe with an open face.

'So the sales went well?' Joe said, smiling.

'My dear boy, though I say it myself, I don't think anyone could have improved on my performance in this matter and though I know the whole thing is a grief to you at least it's cleared up and out of the way.'

'And now I own nothing but an old tower house in Durham. Well, I suppose that's better than nothing.'

'The good news is that there is a considerable amount of money left over. Three thousand pounds.'

Mr Barrington paused to let this sink in and then said, 'I will invest it for you if you wish, but it's a decent sum – you may wish to come back to London and buy a house and do all sorts of things. Or perhaps you have a venture which you would like to use it for—'

Encouraged, Joe told him all about the car which he and Mr Palmer were designing. Mr Barrington got very interested and said he thought it was an excellent idea and that he did know one or two men in the car industry. He would be glad to send letters as references or to help in any way.

It was only then that Joe realized he had no intention of coming back to London to live, at least not at the moment, and it had nothing to do with the sale of the tower house. If he had wanted at this point to be in London he could have, but he didn't. Angela was not here; he would have known if she had been within a hundred miles, he thought – or perhaps that was just nonsense. In any case, Toddy would do all he could and keep Joe informed.

He felt so very far away from his father. The only way to ease this was to continue reading the letters which his father had sent. He read the same ones over and over while keeping some unread, so that he would have something to hang onto in the days when he could face nothing.

In his father's letters there were descriptions of pheasants, neck-deep in grass in June in Northumberland. He told how the rhododendrons were out, great splodges of pink and purple and orange. His father still went there and would ride every day, asking the local dignitaries and the vicar and the old ladies of the area to dinner. His father was kind to almost everyone. Joe remembered how his father would never change for dinner if he had an unexpected guest who had nothing to change into.

He was even kind to foxes and hated hunting. No wonder people didn't like him when he wouldn't let them hunt across his land. Joe thought it was more to do with them breaking gates and fences, but he had not forgotten the time the hunt poured into his father's formal garden and ripped up the lawns, trying to kill a fox outside his drawing room window. He had gone out there with a shotgun and threatened, 'I'll mow you down, you bastards!'

He wouldn't have formal pheasant shoots on his land. He regarded this as slaughter, but he would go up on the moors with his Labradors, bag one pheasant and come home, the dogs worn out from their day, their eyes torn about with brambles. When they had eaten their fill they would fall asleep by the huge log fire in the hall.

Joe longed for his father and Northumberland. He wanted to go fishing. His father's favourite sport was trout fishing in the wide, deep rivers. Joe thought it was the peace it brought to his troubled soul, the river tumbling on its way. All you had to do was stand there, thigh deep in water, and wait with the fly you had made yourself to imitate whatever was hovering above the river that day. His father said to catch a fish you had to think like a fish.

Joe thought back to the fishing he preferred when he and Tam had taken Tam's father's coble out. Once when they were a couple of miles out the fog had come down very suddenly and Joe had been afraid for one of the first times in his life. All he could see was the oily dark water immediately around them and then nothing. He had never been as thankful until he went to war to be with a man who knew what he was doing. Tam guided the coble safely back to the shore and it was only after they had dragged it beyond the waterline that he confessed to Joe that he too had been afraid. Sometimes the fog lasted for days and you could die out there.

It didn't stop them, however. They loved being beyond anyone else's reach and Joe also loved the feeling of the tug on the line and the sight of the codling beneath the boat as he drew it nearer and nearer.

Sometimes his father took him salmon fishing in Scotland or they'd go over to the west to the silver sands where they would fish at night for pollack. By moonlight the fish flashed white in the clear water beneath the boat.

The letter from his father which he opened then read:

I fear I am going to have to sell more paintings to pay the debts and more furniture, some of which is dear to me and belonged to my grandparents. I seem to use up such a lot of money. It somehow runs through my fingers like fine sand from a Northumbrian beach. I have so many faults and they are closing in on me now, showing me the way home. I need more and more of everything while my life gives me less of things which would keep me here. It's as if I want not to be here any longer, things being as they are. I can't abide people wittering on about their tiny lives. My life feels so tiny it is almost gone. The only times I feel alive now are when I'm drunk, which I am almost every day, when I'm dozing by the fire and congratulating myself about having got through yet another day. You and Angela were the only reality and she seems so busy these days, as young people are. Whatever will the women do when all the young men are dead? Dear God, I hope you come back to her. I miss her visits and I miss you more than I thought I could live through.

FOURTEEN

It was four days before Tilda broke down in tears and did not want to go home. She would not let Lucy comfort her, and Lucy could see the terrible strain that she was under, having to pretend there was nothing the matter when in fact everything was wrong.

Lucy thought hard for several minutes and then decided what to do. She would take Tilda out to tea, at least she told her that, so that the girl gathered up her few belongings and followed almost gladly – she would not have to face her mother for the next hour or so.

There was a boy in the street whom Lucy recognized from their row. She asked him if he would mind taking a message to Tilda's mam. She wrote a quick note to Mrs Formby and said that Tilda had been invited to tea at this friend of Lucy's and she hoped Mrs Formby wouldn't mind.

Lucy paid for one of Paddy's Cabs to take them to Joe's house. Tilda was so white and tired-looking and she worried – what if Joe wasn't home, what if he had gone to Mr Palmer's house for his tea as he sometimes did, what if he had had stayed late at the garage which she thought he often did. By the time she ran out of 'what if's' they had arrived.

She banged on the door. Joe opened the door and was so friendly that Lucy wanted to burst into tears herself. He was tall and solid and shabby and rather grubby because he hadn't been back from the garage for very long. He smiled at her.

'I've brought Miss Formby with me. You don't mind?' she said.

'Of course not,' Joe said in his decidedly well-mannered way. Lucy was so grateful that Joe had been properly brought up. How lovely to know that he would always say and do what you needed him to do and say. It was a rare talent to understand so much about people and to care equally as much.

He led them into the sitting room and made tea. The black-and-white long-haired cat sat at Tilda's feet, as though she could help, head on one side and eyes searching.

Tilda had looked so pale in the shop, but her colour was returning. After a while she smiled just a little and said, 'What is the cat looking at?'

'She likes you,' Joe said. 'And she's very particular, you know. She doesn't like everybody. She thinks you're special.'

A tear made its way down the girl's cheek and she sniffed.

'You aren't afraid of cats, then?' Joe said, and Tilda shook her head. 'That's good because if you give her any encouragement she'll be up on your lap, purring and sleeping there.'

Tilda seemed entranced. She reached down and the cat leapt at her right away and landed, with grace and without weight. Tilda sat there and laughed. Lucy hadn't heard her laugh before.

Joe told her to sit on the sofa because the cat liked that best, and Tilda did so, gathering the cat into her arms. He covered her over with a rug and gave her a cushion for under her head. The black-and-white cat curled up into a ball beside her and purred. After a little while Tilda went to sleep.

Joe asked nothing. Lucy admired it so much that she smiled at him. 'Thank you,' she said.

Joe looked blankly at her. 'If you think she'll sleep a while we could go and sit in the garden, unless you're worried about leaving her.'

They went outside; it was not as cold as she had thought it might be and she didn't care anyway. It was coming in dark by then and she had learned to be grateful for the darkness, for it hid so many things, faces and places. Even shadows that might haunt you faded into black. Joe gave her a big thick blanket and an old chair which fitted perfectly to her body. He was much too large for the chair he sat in – it looked as if it might break under his weight – but Joe didn't notice things like that, she thought, he just sat in silence and watched the river and the cathedral beyond. It was as though he had all the time in the world, that he could stay there for days and days while the slight breeze came off the river and the night fell down around them.

'What else have you done about Miss Lee?' she said.

Joe told her about going to see Mr Firbank and she was pleased about that. He also told her what Mr Firbank had said about knowing Cissie when she was a very little girl, and how her father had struck it rich with silver and gone off to London.

'But when I asked about it people had nothing to say.'

'Yes, but you're a southerner. In places like that they aren't going to open up to you. Here, if somebody lives four miles away they are almost foreign – just think what you seem like. I'm so glad you went to see the old gentleman. He was obviously pleased to see you or he wouldn't have told you such things.'

'I learned that from you,' Joe said.

'I would have gone with you.'

'I think you've had enough on your plate and besides, I needed to see him on my own. He's a lovely old man. I like him very much. I'm going to go and see him a lot.'

He also told her about Toddy – how they were now reconciled, and how much better he felt about it – and about going to see Mr Barrington, and the money.

Her face filled with excitement. 'Joe, that's wonderful. That's a lot of money. If you and Mr Palmer can get the car right you could do all kinds of good things with it.'

They walked slowly over to the river and sat down there on the low stone wall which separated Joe's house from the towpath. Nobody said anything for a considerable time and Lucy was glad just to watch the river and listen to it industriously chugging its way to Sunderland.

'Do you want to tell me what's bothering you?' he said.

She shook her head.

'I think you ought to.'

He waited.

'I told Mr Bainbridge part of the difficulty and even then he couldn't help, yet that was the easiest bit and he has . . . he has influence, and he and I—'

'Why don't you tell me the easiest bit and then we'll consider the rest,' he suggested.

Lucy nodded. She didn't look at him, she didn't look at anything. All she could manage was the way that the house was crowded and even then she couldn't get it out of herself without stopping a good deal, so she began to talk of Frederick and how he was lying in the shadows, hoping to be left alone. In truth he had ceased to be a novelty now and the children barely noticed him, but he had lost his chair by the fire, because it was too expensive to keep more than one fire burning for any length of time, as well as the attention of the Misses Slaters.

'So you see,' Lucy said stupidly, 'his life is hardly worth living.'

Joe smiled just a little. She could not see him but she could hear how he let go of his breath in amusement. It was quite dark out there now and it was easier to talk when you couldn't see. She had not known that the night brought comfort to such things.

'Frederick could come and live with me,' Joe said gently, and it made her laugh.

She found a handkerchief up her sleeve and mopped her face as a stray tear escaped. She knew he meant only to make her smile.

'I don't think Kitty would take to him,' she said. 'And Mrs Formby doesn't want to leave Rachel Lane and Mr Manson is just horrible and doesn't care and Edgar doesn't understand. Rachel Lane is all the Formbys have. I threatened Mr Manson with the newspapers and all sorts of things, but I just can't think what to do that might really help to make a difference.'

'All right,' Joe said, 'then why don't we ask the two old ladies if they want to come and live here?'

Lucy stared at him. 'Oh, Joe, I can't do that,' she said. 'I can't be foisting old ladies onto you.'

'Why not? If you could persuade Mrs Formby to come here with the children we could do that, but it doesn't sound as if she would manage it. Whereas the Misses Slaters are the sort of people who have lived in different circumstances. They might like it here.'

'They wouldn't come, they wouldn't impose,' she said.

'Are you telling me I can't charm two old ladies into moving into a spacious house like this? I think you should go back and suggest it to them and when they are done protesting that they can't I will come and transport them and all their belongings. That will ease the situation some.' He went inside to check on Tilda and came back – she was still sleeping. He asked Lucy if she wanted to go back inside, but she said she didn't.

'So what's really the matter?' he said.

Lucy couldn't tell him. 'There's nothing anybody can do about the situation,' she said. 'I know there isn't.'

'You could just tell me – sometimes that helps.'

'It's very personal and it isn't about me – I don't want to betray a confidence.'

'Talk very softly and nobody will hear.'

And so she managed to tell him all about Tilda, leaving nothing out. She felt the burden lifting from her. The words tumbled from her lips and somehow from her mind.

Much later, when she couldn't think of a single thing to say and Joe had been silent for quite a long time, he said, softly, so that the words barely reached her, 'You must wait and she must have care—'

'But what happens when the baby shows? It's not the sort of thing you can pretend isn't happening. I'm scared.' It was the first time she had admitted such a thing to anybody.

'When you don't know what to do, the best thing to do is nothing,' Joe said.

'She feels guilty about what she did—'

'It's just like war though, isn't it?'

'What do you mean?'

'She took on her father when he attempted to destroy her, and she won.'

'Oh God, Joe, that's awful. The law doesn't see it like that—'

'No, of course not. When your government says you can kill that's seen as moral; when you take it upon yourself then it's murder,' Joe said. 'She chose, she took the decision—'

'And the law would say that she must pay the price.'

'Hasn't she already done that? Hasn't her family too?'

'She wanted to look up to her father and now—' Lucy stopped. 'Why is it like this?'

Joe, who had good instincts about such things, she thought, waited. He let her talk and then he sat forward and watched her, his eyes sympathetic.

'I think you shouldn't tell Mr Bainbridge anything,' Joe said, 'because he would be obliged by law to act – it's his job, he couldn't not do it. You don't want Mrs Formby to have her child hang.'

Lucy shuddered. 'Tilda has to work, she's their only source of income.'

'We'll help her. Try not to worry. We'll think of something.'

She nodded. She was just about to suggest that they should go back inside so that she could take Tilda home when Joe said, 'And you must come and live here, of course.'

That had not occurred to her. She was glad of the darkness because her face and even her neck burned at the whole idea.

'I couldn't do that.'

'Well, what are you going to do? You don't really want to stay with the Formbys, and if you think I'm going to cook for two old ladies you can think again.'

'But it's not respectable.'

'Oh, for God's sake,' Joe said in a sigh. 'I'm not asking you to sleep with me.'

'Joe!'

'Well, try not to be such a prude. You and the two old ladies can sleep on the top floor. I don't. It's quite private up there. You could get the odd cat visiting you in the night, but that's all.'

She couldn't believe he had solved so many of her problems. The thought of living here in this lovely place and having the two old ladies with her, and of the Formbys having the Misses Slaters' house, which was slightly bigger and better than their own, was such a help. She didn't know what to say or how to thank him.

There was a long silence during which the moon came out and lit the cloudless sky. Lucy's mind went over and over the things that Joe had said and she felt relieved, eased, and then the ginger tom leaped onto her lap and yawned as though they had been talking for too long. For some reason it made her laugh and then Joe laughed too. The cat got down and sat between them, lifted its leg and began washing its bottom.

'Sorry,' Joe said, pulling a face. Lucy couldn't help finding it funny. 'That's what they do when they can't think of anything else. Perhaps we should do the same.'

'You do and I'm going home,' she said.

'I can't reach anyway,' Joe said, and then she laughed so much that she felt better.

Fifteen

Lucy talked to the Misses Slaters and Mrs Formby all together, to see what their reaction would be. She put it to them that they could decide among themselves who was going to stay and who to go, but she and Joe had been right. Mrs Formby said immediately that indeed it was very kind of Mr Hardy and they were very grateful to him for all his help and everything with the fire, but she really didn't want to leave this place. On the other hand she didn't want the Misses Slaters to go. This was their house, their home. Lucy watched the two sisters glance at one another. They didn't need to say anything, but it was typical of them that they held back.

Eventually Miss Slater said, 'It really is up to Mr Hardy. After all, he is a young man – I don't suppose he wants older ladies living with him.'

Lucy couldn't quite say that Joe was enthusiastic about the idea, it didn't sound right, but she did say, 'He lives alone there with three cats. The place is very big. He wouldn't say that he wanted you there if he didn't.'

'Cats?' Miss Bethany said doubtfully, and she glanced over at where Frederick slept in the corner.

'The dog could stay here,' Mrs Formby suggested.

The two small children were very keen on this idea, but Lucy said, 'No, Frederick is going with the Misses Slaters to stay with Mr Hardy.'

The children protested loudly, but Lucy was firm. Frederick was going and that was that.

The following Saturday Joe came to the house with a cart because, he reasoned, they couldn't get anything bigger anywhere near the tower house. The small house on Rachel Lane got bigger and bigger as Joe and the man who owned the cart carried all the furniture out of it. It was vicarage furniture, some of it quite enormous now Lucy saw it on the street; no wonder there had been no space in that house.

The trouble was that when the furniture had been completely decanted there was very little left. The house was empty. Lucy requested an afternoon off work, much to Edgar's annoyance when she told him what she was doing. She asked very politely if she might have a few hours so that she and Mrs Formby could go to the auction rooms. He said nothing, but she could see he was unhappy she had not taken his advice to keep her distance from people, though she didn't acknowledge his frustration.

Mrs Formby had a tiny amount of money and Lucy didn't have much, but she hadn't spent any of her wages other than the food which she bought, and she had become adept at housekeeping on little. So although Mrs Formby protested and said it wasn't fair to Miss Charlton, Lucy was brisk.

They bought new furniture, much to Mrs Formby's excitement, and arranged to have it delivered late on the Saturday afternoon. There were several rather old but serviceable chairs for the sitting room, a table and chairs for the kitchen and three beds with new mattresses and pillows.

The Misses Slaters donated bed linen of which they had an ample supply, and several rather decorative tablecloths which Lucy promptly sold, after she had asked their permission. She got a good price for them at a second-hand shop since they were trimmed with lace and rather gorgeous. It was not the time to be frivolous, she knew. They bought some newish clothes from the market for the whole family. Joe donated a large box of chocolates for Mrs Formby and sweets for the children, and a pretty bracelet in blue glass for Tilda, also from the market.

Lucy left Joe and the old ladies, Frederick being locked into the sitting room, since the cats were all waiting by the outside door when Frederick arrived. Joe told her later and they were not inclined to welcome him and variously spat, hissed and walked away. Lucy felt guilty about this, for they had been there first, but Joe told her that she was not to worry. They would come back.

She stayed with Mrs Formby and saw the new furniture into the house as Clay helped to carry, while the two small children ran about, delighted. Mrs Formby glowed, looking lovingly at her furniture. It was late in the evening by the time Lucy went to her new home. If she had felt self-conscious living in a tiny house with two single ladies, living at the tower house with a young man of her own age was quite another thing entirely.

She thought she would hear, 'Oh, Mr Hardy, how very kind,' for the rest of her days.

'Do you want to see your room? I think we've put all your things in there – bags and such. You can go up,' Joe said.

She nodded. There, upstairs, the room with the door ajar was hers. Joe had opened the window and laid the fire to be lit. It was the room which looked out across the river, straight at the cathedral – the nicest room of all, she was sure. She felt almost as though she were at home. She had longed to be in a room once more which beheld the river so that she could listen to it until she slept. She couldn't believe how perfect it was.

There was the neat little writing desk which at Rachel Lane had been shoved into a corner and covered in lots of other things, and a lovely bed which she did not recognize, with white linen and an embroidered quilt. At the window was a little dressing table, rather too small and very dainty, like nothing she'd ever had before. She was still looking around when she saw the two ladies watching her from the door.

'Do you like it?' Miss Bethany asked.

She laughed and went to embrace them both. 'You did this for me?'

'You have done so much for us,' Miss Bethany said.

The sisters had a room each, such luxury, and they had wardrobes and tiny bookcases full of what she was certain were precious books. They offered to let her read and she took the invitation up gladly. She hadn't read a book which wasn't to do with the law for years.

When she got back downstairs again Joe was about to take Frederick for a walk. Frederick had not done anything as energetic as that in years. He merely raised his head when

Joe called to him and then got carefully to his paws, reluctantly following Joe out of the door.

For some reason Lucy said, 'Can I come?'

Joe looked surprised. 'Are you sure? I don't think Frederick is a great walker.'

It was late by then. She'd had nothing to eat and she didn't think Joe had either, but she was suddenly so very happy. Frederick stopped and sniffed every few yards at first. But after a while he seemed to realize that they were actually going for a walk, and he began to get the hang of it. He was soon trundling along quite happily, catching up when they got ahead.

She wondered how old the dog was; the walk didn't seem to tire him. They met another dog, a scruffy little object with a man way behind. Frederick went over and the other dog sniffed at him. They smelled one another and danced a little and then Frederick came back.

'Are you hungry?' Joe said when they got to the bridge.

'Haven't you eaten?' Lucy ventured.

'I turned down a sandwich hours ago. Why don't we go into the town and have fish and chips?'

She thought it was the best idea anybody had ever had. They walked up the steps when they came to Framwellgate Bridge and then up North Road, where she could smell the salt and vinegar. They got the fish and chips wrapped up in newspaper and went back to the river. They found a bench and sat down and opened the parcels. It was heavenly. Joe had bought Frederick his own chips.

'We can't let him sit there while we eat,' he said as Lucy protested, 'and besides I don't think the poor chap has ever seen a chip. His whole life has revolved around sandwiches.'

She got the giggles at this. Frederick demolished his portion (plus scraps) with surprise and delight. Then he sat, waiting to be given more, so they could not help giving him fish, which Joe said was very good for him. He even got a few extra chips, which Joe said he begrudged.

On the way back Frederick seemed to have shed five years. He rushed up and down the towpath, and when they returned to the tower house he dashed inside. He stopped suddenly. The three cats were sitting in the kitchen. Joe had brought fish back for them and he put Frederick into the other room while they ate. When they were full the cats sat down by the dying fire.

Lucy wasn't sure about letting Frederick in, but Joe said they would try it. Frederick saw the cats sitting by the fire and very carefully went across and sat down behind them, thereby cutting off the draught. Lucy thought they might get up and stalk out, but they didn't.

As they woke up Frederick began to lick their heads. Lucy had never seen such a thing. She thought they would object, but Frederick was licking the back of their heads, the part they couldn't reach. He moved on to each cat in turn and they closed their eyes and let him continue. In the end the fur on their heads stood up, so slick with Frederick's spit, but they merely shook their heads to get rid of the excess, lay down between his paws and went back to sleep.

Lucy went up to the luxury of her own room and stood there for a long time in the darkness, being thankful for it and wondering how far she had pushed Joe into this. Then she climbed between sheets which smelled of lavender, and stretched out, something she'd not been able to do since she left home, her university bed having been so short and the sofa with Tilda so uncomfortable. She listened to the river and fell asleep, full of fish and chips and hope for the future. And then she opened her eyes and thought of Tilda and how she had said nothing that day, not even when she'd come home and seen all the new furniture. She tried to put the girl from her mind.

Edgar said on the Monday morning that he would like to have a word with her. Lucy followed him into his office. He closed the door, something he rarely did, and he didn't ask her to sit down.

'I don't think I quite understood when you were talking about the Misses Slaters moving and Mrs Formby not,' he said. 'Have I got this right?'

'Yes, Mrs Formby and her family have moved into the Misses Slaters' house, which they rent from Mr Manson. They needed somewhere to go and I went and asked the landlord twice if he would do something, but I couldn't get him to change his mind. Then Mr Hardy offered the two old ladies a home and he has lots of room, you know. It seemed a good solution so that was what we did over the weekend.'

Edgar paused as though he wanted to say something but wasn't sure whether he was right.

'And you?'

'What?'

'Well, are you staying with Mrs Formby and her family? Is there enough space, sufficient beds? I think I ought to put up your wages. You can't go on living there, and you could find a room somewhere if I helped.'

Lucy's face began to burn. She told herself that there was no reason why it should, but she couldn't help it. She looked all around the room before finally turning back to him.

Edgar went on, 'I feel as though I should have offered sooner, but I have had so much on my mind lately, though that's no excuse. It isn't correct for you to live with the Formbys without the two Misses Slaters.'

'I'm not,' she said, 'I've gone with the Misses Slaters. We have the whole of the third storey at Mr Hardy's house.'

Edgar stared at her. 'I didn't think you would do that.'

'He did ask me.'

'Yes, but—'

She cut in. 'It's perfectly respectable, surely, with the Misses Slaters there.'

'I'm not sure a lot of people would think so. Joe is a stranger and a southerner – and he's also quite different.'

'He can't help that.'

'I'm not saying he should, but he comes from a class of people who behave in ways that we don't.'

'I don't understand what you mean.'

'His family name is very old and he is titled. I don't think upper-class people think like we do and he certainly doesn't. They've been so privileged they don't understand. He lost everything—'

'That's not his fault either,' Lucy said. But she was cross with herself for defending Joe. He didn't need it.

Edgar said nothing else.

'He didn't have to offer his house to anybody,' Lucy said, wishing she would shut up. 'He solved the problem. I didn't know what to do.'

'This is what I mean about becoming involved. You cannot rescue everybody.'

Lucy looked hard at him.

'Isn't that what we try to do – rescue people, help them? I know that's what my father's always done.' It hurt even to speak about him, but also brought her a little closer to what she had lost. She didn't often admit to herself how much she missed him, how she longed for him, dreamt about him.

'Yes, but not in a personal way.'

'It is personal to me. I live with the two old ladies. They are my business and as for Mrs Formby – did you think I was going to let her be on the street—'

'It wouldn't have come to that.'

'It did come to that,' Lucy argued, angry now. 'All they have is what Tilda makes and—' She was about to say that Tilda wouldn't be able to do that for long, that they would soon have nothing, but she managed to stop herself.

Edgar was silent for several moments while Lucy went back and back over everything she had said. She was already reprimanding herself.

'We obviously don't agree on this matter,' Edgar said levelly. 'If you are going to allow your personal feelings into your life when you become a solicitor you will not survive. Do you understand what I mean? You will put at risk the very reason for your being there because your emotions will conflict with the law. Then what will you do?'

She was too angry to speak. She understood what he meant and the only defence she could think of was that she was not a solicitor yet, which was hardly the point.

'Perhaps this is why women should not become solicitors,' he said. 'They let their emotions cloud the issue. If you are going to go home and take all these pressures with you, your whole life will become a burden.'

Lucy didn't reply. She was seething. She went back to her draughty office and began work.

SIXTEEN

The car which they had decided to try to build became a bigger and bigger project to Joe and Mr Palmer. They went on with repairs as they must to make money, but they spent many hours in the little office at the back of the premises, talking about what they wanted, getting the ideas down on paper and then trying to make them real. Joe had questioned his reasons for doing this. It was a huge commitment and as such would take up a great deal of time and money. If it didn't succeed he would take the whole thing personally. It would change their lives. He wasn't sure whether Mr Palmer had taken in what it meant to them, whether he could see that far ahead, but then they thought of the project quite differently.

To Mr Palmer it was fun, it was something new and different to do. Joe knew it did not occur to him that they might be breaking new ground in the motor industry in England. Yet Joe thought more and more about what he was attempting. And it was quite new, the idea that the motor car would become the domain of every man and woman. It would change not only people's individual lives but how they saw themselves and one another. He was so scared at what he might do that images came to him in the night of chaos and black roads and lack of privacy and how speed might kill.

In daylight he laughed at himself for such ridiculous fears. The ideas would come to nothing or someone would beat them to it and build a car for the common man, someone else would end up taking responsibility for something which could become more important than trains, a place where man would feel invincible when he was nothing of the kind. It made Joe shudder at night, but during the day all he felt was excitement.

On paper the design was nothing more than a square box with wheels. It was the equivalent of a terraced house, Joe thought, hopefully ordinary, buyable. It was within the reach of those people who'd never thought they would have a form of transport so easy and so reliable and that they might take to the world without thought, without conscience. They would take control as they could never do with a train. Driving was something Joe had thought of as for necessity only, but it would do a great deal more than that if someone came up with the ideas.

He and Mr Palmer spent exciting evenings when the day's work was done and Mrs Palmer had filled them full of egg and chips. They would go back to the workshop and pore over their ideas. Joe liked it best when it was dark and he could hear the rain pounding the roof. They would sit there, Frederick under the desk, listening to the rain and feeling the heat coming from the old pot-bellied stove. He was happier there than he had been since he'd come back from France and before everything had gone so wrong.

The square box with wheels would be tiny compared with any other car, yet there must be room for luggage. It was so modest that Joe didn't think any of the car designers would accept it. Modesty was not something the car industry adhered to. Cars were all about speed on tracks, about competition – or they were the rich man's toy, the devotee's place. Joe and Mr Palmer imagined the little car outside a front door – so that you could get up in the morning, pack a picnic into a basket and take to the roads, going anywhere you wanted until you came to the sea.

As a concept Joe loved it, but the practicalities worried him. They took up many hours of thought. There was something which nagged at him too, the idea that every time you went forward and created something new, something which people might take to in a big way, you created a monster. Once you put that monster at people's disposal there was always a downside. But Joe had thankfully not allowed himself to imagine what this might be. So they went on, ignoring the 'what might happen'. They toiled night after night at the little square shape and what it must enclose. It would be the first car for the working man and his wife and his family, and after that Joe couldn't think. He determined not to.

First they built the car in wood, just to see where everything fitted. It had to take four people in it and not make them feel squashed. It had to have a boot which would take two big square boxes, Joe had decided, for whatever people chose to put in it. The car must be neat but not too small, it must be square so that it would stand in a street and allow traffic both ways, it must go down a fairly narrow side road and it must be robust so that it could be taken down an unmade back street and not clatter itself to pieces.

It must be tight so that water did not pour in at the doors or roof or sills. Everything must fit perfectly.

The engine was the most important thing of all.

They tried everything they could to get the parts in the right place and in the right order, but began to despair that they could not make it happen.

Joe wanted it to go in the front. Mr Palmer was prepared to turn the whole thing around and have the engine at the back. Joe's sense of what was neat and proper refused to allow this, but he had to keep the possibility in mind if it was the only thing they ended up being able to do. Also costs must be kept to a minimum if the car were to be made in quantity, and he thought that was the least expensive way of doing it. The whole point was for the car to be made as cheaply as possible so that it was available to as many people as possible.

Once the wooden chassis was built and things went where they should and Mr Palmer and Joe could even sit in the back seats, though Mr Palmer said he wouldn't have wanted to go any further than Whitley Bay like that, not with his aches and pains, they moved on. The engine didn't fit, and it didn't matter how they moved things around.

He began rearranging the engine in his sleep, having black dreams where he fell into it and drowned in oil. Every time they moved even just a small part the whole thing refused to work and they had to dismantle it again. It was like the world's biggest jigsaw being thrown up into the air and landing all over the garage.

Joe came to hate the big corrugated shed which was all the garage really was. In fine weather it was stifling. In the winter Joe mistook heavy sleet for bullets at first and threw himself onto the cracked concrete floor. The windows blew in and out with wind and rain and were spattered with dirt. If either one of them felt the call of nature they would have to rush up the back street into Mr Palmer's backyard and outside lavatory. Luckily it was not far.

In cold weather they found excuses to huddle by the stove in the tiny office. The snow blew in around the big doors at the front.

From the wooden prototype with the engine finally fitting, they moved on to building the car. It brought a whole new set of problems with materials. The real thing, Joe decided, was nothing like the prototype. He wanted to use cheap metal for the body, but it wasn't sturdy enough; too thick and the car was weighed down. The metal bulged or the doors wouldn't shut, the roof and the boot poured in water. Every time they solved one difficulty they created another. Mr Palmer would swear at nobody in particular and go home to warm up by his kitchen fire, boring his wife by telling her the same things over and over again, while Joe despaired and would walk Frederick right around the river.

Frederick, being a springer spaniel, didn't care about what the weather held or the time of day or night. Walking was joy to him, and while he sniffed at every bush and tree Joe had the time and space to think. Joe would sometimes solve a problem even before he and Frederick made their way back to the tower house, hoping that Lucy was at home. Otherwise it would be the inevitable ham sanwiches.

SEVENTEEN

Emily Bainbridge, Edgar's sister, invited Lucy and Joe to dinner. Lucy didn't understand why. But Emily came to the office to ask.

'We rarely have dinner parties somehow,' Emily said, sitting down across the desk from her. 'Edgar is socially stupid – he talks about his work all the time.'

That made Lucy smile.

'No, he is,' Emily said. 'He works and he comes home. He doesn't think about me, stuck all day with nothing to do but help Norah or to read and sit by the fire or do horrid things like afternoon calls as though I were ninety. And now . . .' her voice dropped just a bit and wavered a little, but Lucy had grown used to listening for such things and heard it, '. . . Norah is going to get married and we have to find somebody new and . . . it's all very hard,' she threw a smile, rather forced, across the desk, 'so you must come to dinner. I understand from gossip that you know a very interesting young man, Mr Joseph Hardy, and I wondered if you would like me to invite him.'

Lucy was about to disclaim and then thought that would look really bad since they lived in the same house, so she merely said, 'That would be nice. I don't think Joe is invited anywhere.'

'I don't know anything about him,' Emily said, 'except that from gossip I understand he's tall, rather handsome and an aristocrat.'

There again Lucy was about to protest and didn't. She didn't want Joe to think she was talking about him.

'He's very kind,' she said, and left it at that.

Lucy wasn't sure that she wanted to go to a dinner party at Edgar's home. Would there be other people? Would she be obliged to make conversation she wasn't used to? She had nothing to wear and could not afford a new dress. Somehow it seemed important not to be shabby, but all her money had gone to the Formbys.

That evening she looked through her meagre wardrobe and wished she had not said that she would go. While she was there Miss Bethany came in, and she said, guardedly, 'We thought you would perhaps care to have this?' She showed Lucy a dress, dark and formal.

It was red, almost violet, in crushed velvet, quite ornate and possibly not of this time.

'It was our mother's,' Miss Bethany said, as Lucy looked at it, 'so not what you would want perhaps,' but Lucy assured her that it was very fine.

'Our mother was tall like you and very slender, but you mustn't wear it if you think it inappropriate,' Miss Bethany said. She left the dress with Lucy.

Lucy put it on. It was the right fit and she thought it rather pretty. It clashed so beautifully with her hair that it made her look just a trifle wild. She wasn't sure that it would be right for a dinner party, but if she felt foolish, how would she cope? She could have done with a nice string of pearls and then laughed at herself. She had no jewellery.

She didn't want to go, she felt so inadequate. She remembered those nights when she had stood at the back of the hotel or place of the dinner dance or ball and how she had never danced.

She duly dressed up and walked downstairs. There stood Joe in evening dress, looking so different and so elegant that she couldn't speak.

'You look lovely,' he said.

She disregarded this and said to him, 'Where did you get that suit?'

'It's rather old, I know,' he said, 'but I brought it with me from London.'

Lucy wanted to laugh – as though people in Durham were abreast of such things and as though men's fashions changed so fast. The suit was perfectly tailored and must have cost a fortune. It made him look – she didn't like to think – like a box of very expensive chocolates.

She recovered and said, 'As you would, knowing that you would need such things in Durham.'

Joe looked at himself as though surprised. He had suggested they call a cab, but it was a fine night and Lucy thought of the expense. Besides, it was not that far, just down the towpath to the bridge and up the other side. The house stood apart and down a drive, alone. The weeping willows that lined the driveway were wet and dragged at the ground. Lights at the front door led her and Joe to find it, and they knocked on the door and were shown into the hall.

Several people were gathered. The men wore evening dress, though they didn't look as good as Joe, Lucy thought, and then she realized how stupid that was. Did it matter? The women wore gorgeous dresses and she felt drab and old-fashioned and tall – all the things that she had felt every time she had gone out with her parents and Gemma in Newcastle. She wished very much that she had stayed at home.

Emily came and introduced them to various people who were so obviously not interested in her but only in him, talking to him and smiling at him. She tried to see him as they would. Joe in evening dress, clean-shaven, tall and spare, with perfect hair that shimmered black and silver under the glow of the lamps, lovely dark eyes and lean face. He stood out.

A snobbish person would have said that he was the only gentleman in the room with his sweet southern voice, softly modulated, and that there was something clean and cultured about the way that he moved – she didn't know what it was, maybe it was that ghastly thing called 'breeding', as if Joe were a racehorse.

Lucy hadn't realized before now that Joe didn't have an accent. His present company was well beneath his touch, but like a real gentleman he spoke to everyone. He shook hands and held their eyes and he made every woman in the room watch him, though he was quite unaware of this.

His slender fingers were holding a glass of sherry, and Lucy noticed with some affection that his hands were no longer those of a gentleman. Joe's work at Mr Palmer's seemed to consist of both of them spending a lot of time leaning over engines, heads under car bonnets, underneath cars themselves and turning engines on and off. They fitted bits and took them off again and put in new bits and took those out again, arguing and discussing and then getting no further, so Joe's hands, unlike the rest of the men in the room, showed the kind of work he did. He had banged his fingers on something a couple of days ago and there was a bruise on the back of his hand, and there was something else on the little bit of his right wrist where she thought he said he had burned himself on an engine block.

And as she stood there watching him she thought that those four years of war had broken something about him. It wasn't obvious to everyone, but she knew him well by now and he hid his problems beneath a layer of dry wit and cool manners. He was so elegant, so tall, as if evening dress were his natural skin. The women tried not to stare, suddenly talking as though anything that was being said might be of vital importance.

Joe was caught up by Edgar and introduced to other men.

One of the women of about her own age looked at Lucy and said, 'My dear, that dress. What an amazing colour and how brave of you to wear purple with your hair. I remember my grandmother wearing something similar, though it was dark and rather more subtle, and she had hair as black as a raven's wing.'

Edgar introduced Lucy as 'the lady who helps in my office', which Lucy thought made her sound as if she went in to wash the floors.

'I'm learning to be a solicitor,' she said, 'and in time I hope to practise.'

They stared at her as though she had said something rude. The women glanced at one another and pulled faces.

Lucy was so cross that she said, 'Is there something wrong with that?'

It was directed at the two women across from her and they looked startled. One of them said, 'An unusual ambition for a woman.'

'Really?' Lucy said. 'And how do you suppose women will ever have justice if it is left to men?'

'Miss Charlton,' Edgar prompted her, 'we do care for the women whom we know. We protect them as much as we do men from wrongdoing.'

'Care? Protect? Should we not be in a position where we can care for ourselves? We are, after all, not children. Care is not enough; it never has been and never will be. We need laws which enable us to live our lives independently – we need to have our own ambitions and our own money so that we do not marry because we have to.'

There was a huge silence and then Joe emerged from the mass of people before her. He smiled and stood by her. She had to stop herself from putting her hand through his arm possessively, which she had no right to do, but she badly wanted to claim him for hers when the women had been so hostile to her. They moved into the sitting room and were offered more sweet sherry before dinner. Lucy didn't like it, but it seemed rude to refuse.

'Don't you like that?' Joe said, and then in a quiet voice to Norah, 'Is there a chance of two gin and tonics, please?'

Norah smiled at him and nodded. She came back with bigger glasses which sparkled.

'Try that,' Joe said.

Lucy gazed at it.

'Go on. See if you like it. If you don't, leave it on the side.'

It was heaven. It was the kind of drink which would lull you into sleep on a quiet summer's afternoon in a garden which smelled sweetly of thyme.

'What's it like?' he said.

Lucy laughed. 'I could see myself by the river with this on a lovely day.'

As she was going in they got separated and Emily came to her.

'I think your London friend is absolutely gorgeous. He has fabulous eyes, almost black, and he is so tall and aristocratic,' she said softly.

Joe was sitting next to Emily and as far away as possible from Lucy. Since the table was long she had no chance to talk to him.

The woman across the table from her was the one who had made the remark about her dress and the men on either side of her were older than Lucy and ignored her. Worse still, Joe was his usual self and made Emily laugh a great deal over dinner. It came to Lucy that she had been invited there only because of him. She could hear Edgar's voice as he talked about his work. Did the man never think about anything else?

She could hear Emily talking to Joe about art, at least she thought it was, and she wished that somebody would entertain her. She ached to hear what they were saying. At her side of the table the men talked business and the women talked of house furnishings. One woman asked another about her children and after that they bored on.

Another looked across the table, caught Joe's attention and asked him which school he had attended. Joe's eyes didn't even register what a rude personal remark it was.

'I only ask because we are unsure whether to put our dear Clive's name down for a school in the south.'

Joe evaded the issue beautifully, Lucy thought.

'I don't suppose it matters,' he said, 'they all equip one similarly for the kind of society that we have.'

Lucy understood, but she was the only person in the room who did – anybody would hate such a system which divorced its children from their parents at such a young age. It was diabolical. Why would you have children and then send them away from you for most of their young lives? Joe offered no further advice and luckily the dessert was brought in and nothing more was said.

Emily told them all how good Norah was, and that she had done all the cooking, as well as the waiting on, along with her younger cousin. Lucy was not surprised that they wished Norah was not leaving to get married. They would find it difficult to replace her.

The ladies left the gentlemen to their port.

Joe refused the port and asked if he might have some brandy. Edgar came and sat next to Joe and said, 'I understand that Miss Charlton is living at your house.'

'Yes,' Joe said ruefully, 'along with her two old ladies and an extremely smelly spaniel. I can't think how I was talked into it. Washing day is the worst. Miss Slater made me put up a line in the back garden so that it makes a triangle, and she sings hymns while she hangs out the washing. You can't imagine how awful that is first thing on Monday mornings – "Onward Christian soldiers,".'

Lucy was so bored that she couldn't wait for the tea to be brought in and for the gentlemen to appear. They brought a general smell of cigars and warmth. Joe came to her.

'How was the port?' she asked.

'I never drink port,' he said, as though the very idea were offensive.

'Why not?'

He leaned nearer as though he were telling her a secret and gazed into her eyes. His eyes were lit with fun.

'My dear girl – brandy, yes; port, no.'

The way that he said it made her want to giggle.

'You could have been kind to that woman and told her that you went to school in the country.'

'But I didn't,' Joe said.

'I thought you rarely saw your father.'

'It wasn't a geographical distance, he just didn't care for Slough,' Joe said.

She and Joe walked back together, just as she thought they would, but she was uneasy. She could not help saying to him, 'Don't you think Emily Bainbridge is beautiful?'

'Ravishing,' Joe said, which didn't help.

'And did you like her?'

'Very much.'

Lucy wasn't happy about this, though by the morning she felt much more sensible and upbraided herself for having felt such negative things, despite not being able to put from her mind Joe and Emily with their heads close together.

Lucy had been jealous of Guy before because of how close he was to her sister, but she had never felt like this for a man, and it made her want to scrub herself raw in a deep bath. She didn't want Joe, but apparently she didn't want anybody else to have him either. There was nothing wrong with Emily Bainbridge. She was not a woman Lucy could make a friend of, and that too she felt was a loss, but Emily and Joe together was not a concept she could keep positively in her head. She went off to work and felt like slamming doors all the way along the streets.

She had manners enough to compliment Edgar about the dinner, only to discover that he too had not enjoyed his evening.

'I didn't know that Emily had invited Joe Hardy. I don't want him near my sister. She can do a great deal better than him.'

Lucy was a little surprised to find that Edgar didn't want Joe close to his sister, and she couldn't help being pleased. She spent the rest of the morning berating herself for such feelings and trying to concentrate on work. But she was not very successful.

At the end of the day she hurried home to find if Joe was there, or if he was at the garage. She thought he might be pursuing Emily – she imagined them going out walking together – and she did not pretend to herself that Edgar's not wanting his sister with Joe would stop Emily, and it might even encourage her. But Joe appeared to go on as normal – he came home late from the garage, he left early, he was always where he was supposed to be. Lucy didn't understand it.

Eighteen

Dear Joe,

I miss your mother more since you've been gone. I don't know why. I thought I missed her as much as I could before you went away. Our marriage was a mess, I can admit it now. I was to blame. I have never forgiven myself. I feel like the kind of person who puts a linnet into a cage and expects it to sing.

And by God I expected your mother to become an opera singer in that sense. I was young. Is that an excuse? I thought she should have felt privileged to marry me. Her family was nobody from nowhere, for all the fuss and pretence there was that they were landowners. My God, they were vulgar. We used to laugh about it. That all seems so foolish now. You know what they say about people who care for their ancestry, don't you, Joe? That they are like root vegetables, most of their importance lies underground, but I was brought up to be proud and arrogant and very aware of who I was.

She didn't understand. She was a wild creature from a wild land. I didn't see it. Her family lived in London by that time and seemed respectable. I wanted what I couldn't have because at first she wouldn't have me, and then I was determined to have her. But after I won her I didn't want what she

216

really was. I was cruel to her. I thought she would endure, as
thousands of women did, but your mother was made of better
stuff. She put herself from me and left me wondering who the
hell I thought I was, but it was too late.

She had gone. I have regretted so much how I treated her.
I cared for things that didn't matter. I drank and stayed out
and went with other women. All I wanted from her was a
response, but I got nothing. It was what I deserved.

Joe was not so late that evening. The Misses Slaters had gone
to some event at St Nicholas's Church and were not due
home yet. Lucy was sitting over the fire with a book she
had been reading for a week. She seemed to get no further.

Joe sat down at the other side of the fire and he said,
abruptly, 'I need to go to London. Will you come with me?'

She was astonished. She thought he might have had something to say about Mr Palmer's business or that he might
have some kind of new idea, but not this.

'London?'

'Yes, you know, that big place at the end of the railway
line. It's something really difficult that I have to do and I
rather hoped you would come with me.'

'Is it something I can help with? A legal matter?'

'I've dealt with the legal bits of it, I just need the support. It's only overnight and one of my friends – Charles
Toddington – will put us up, I've already asked him. So it's
perfectly respectable. I've been thinking a lot about Miss Lee
and I think there may be a connection in London. Will you
consider it?'

'Are you sure you want me to go with you?'

217

Joe frowned. 'Why?'

'Well,' she trembled, 'what about Emily?'

'Emily?'

'Yes. I think she likes you.'

Joe's frown deepened. 'Emily likes me?'

'Didn't you think so, at the dinner the other night?'

'Not really. Did you?'

'She went on about you quite a bit – and you seemed to like her.'

Joe sat back in his chair.

'You were being very charming to her,' Lucy said.

'I'm just the same with everybody, aren't I?'

'I don't know.'

'I see. Well, firstly I don't think she does, and secondly it wouldn't do her good anyway because the only woman I have ever cared for is Angela Toddington, and she's lost to me now.'

That silenced Lucy.

'She died?' she asked eventually.

Joe pushed his hands through his hair and sighed as though his mind weighed a ton.

'I hope not. I don't think so, but I don't know. I suppose I should tell you before we go to London, if you'll come with me. I was betrothed to a lovely young woman. I left her here when I went off to France to fight and we planned to be married. Stupidly we spent a weekend together when I was on leave. I came back and she'd disappeared.'

'What do you mean, "disappeared"?'

Joe wasn't looking at her now, or at anything very much.

'She found that she was expecting a child. I had nothing

218

by then but a worthless title and her parents were horrified. They tried to send her away to one of those dreadful places where young women go to give up their children while their parents pretend it never happened. So she ran away.' Joe got up. 'So you see it isn't very likely that I would be interested in Emily or in anyone else. I've made a complete mess of everything and the girl I love has gone.'

Joe walked out of the house. Lucy was so shocked that she didn't move until the Misses Slaters came home, chatting about their evening. She put the kettle on and made tea for them. Joe didn't come back until very late. When she heard him she got up from where she had been sitting by the fire.

She went into the kitchen and said, 'I'll come with you on Friday, Joe, if you still want me to.'

Nobody spoke before they got on the train that morning. Joe insisted on buying her lunch once they got beyond York, but he stared from the window and didn't make conversation.

Finally Lucy's curiosity got the better of her.

'Are you going to tell me why we're going to London or am I meant to guess?' she said.

Joe went on staring out of the window, at the drops running down it, the scene beyond the window smudged with rain.

'I'm having my mother's body exhumed,' Joe said.

Lucy choked over her tea and clattered her cup and saucer on the table.

'You're what?'

'I'm having my mother's coffin opened,' Joe said. 'Tonight.'

Lucy was so shocked that she laughed. She put her hand over her mouth to stop herself.

He finally turned and looked at her. His eyes were bleak.

'I used to go to the graveyard and talk to her. My father is next to her and there's room for me. It's a sort of private graveyard, if you know what I mean, next to the house where we used to live.'

'But why?'

'Because I'm not convinced about what I've been led to believe.'

'You think your mother isn't there?' Lucy was horrified.

'I know. It sounds stupid, especially since I remember her funeral.'

Lucy thought if there was a sensible remark to be made she couldn't think of it and sat silent for the rest of the journey.

At King's Cross, to Lucy's astonishment, they were met by a chauffeur who carried the bags and led them to a huge silver car which stood against the kerb. He put the luggage into the boot and opened the back door for her and then the other one for Joe. Joe stood about as though he couldn't help it; she realized that it was only what he had been used to in the days before the war.

The house in Belgravia was the biggest house she had ever seen. It had a massive entrance hall and a staircase which swept high and disappeared around a corner. She tried not to gaze about her. There were servants, somebody to take her coat, and the luggage didn't come anywhere near her. They were ushered into an enormous highly decorated Georgian room where a man of about Joe's own age beamed his welcome at her.

'Joe,' was his acknowledgement.

'Miss Charlton, this is Mr Toddington. Toddy, this is my friend, Lucy Charlton. I'm very grateful you've offered to put us up.'

'I think you've lost your mind over this,' Toddy said immediately. Lucy was inclined to think this was correct.

'Very likely. Why would I not have?'

'I don't know why the authorities agreed.'

'Because I asked them,' Joe said and he walked around the room as if it were a garden he hadn't seen before. It was certainly big enough, she thought.

Chairs and tables were all over the place, grouped together as though a dozen people were expected. At the windows hung huge curtains which would not only keep out the draughts but the daylight too if necessary. She tried not to stare.

'Well of course, you being who you are, in spite of everything,' Toddy said. 'Your lineage is so perfect.'

'Oh, for God's sake,' Joe said.

Lucy was relieved when the door opened and the tea tray was brought in, silver, china and lovely little cakes, all pink and white. Lucy couldn't have swallowed a mouthful if she had been going to die without. She sat down and when the tea was poured she accepted a delicate cup and saucer, so thin she could see her fingers through it. Her hands shook.

When the maidservant had gone she wished more than anything she had wished in a very long time that she had not been so foolish as to agree to come here with Joe. She thought it was a kind of betrayal that he had not told her his mission, though she knew why not. Who would want to do such a thing alone? She had a horrible feeling this was going to make things worse – if Joe's life could be any worse than all these awful things which had happened here.

Lucy hadn't realized that there would be visitors for dinner. She got halfway back down the stairs after changing into her only decent dress and paused. She could hear voices coming from some big room nearby, a woman's voice among them. They were raised voices too; it was not a happy gathering.

She couldn't retreat, dinner would be served soon so she breathed carefully and went on into the room. It was a big sitting room of some kind and in the early evening the doors were open to the garden. An older couple were standing before the doors with drinks in their hands and along with the two young men they made a kind of disparate circle.

They stopped talking as she entered, and Mr Toddington came to her in a kindly way. He introduced his parents to her and Joe said that she was his solicitor. She thought they were very stiff and starchy. If this was what London society was about then she was better out of it. Perhaps Joe was too since he was standing there with a gin and tonic clutched in each hand. He was white-faced and his mouth was tight. He handed her a glass.

'I didn't want you to know anything about this,' he was saying to the older couple. 'Toddy should not have told you. I can't think why you wanted to meet me when I'm so aware of how you think of me.'

'Your mother was my dearest friend,' Lady Toddington said in a voice kept steady in spite of the fact that she was clearly angry and almost in tears. 'I cannot think why you have chosen to come back here to do such a dreadful thing, and after the appalling way that you have behaved to us and to Angela. Why couldn't you just have stayed in whatever place you went to?'

Lucy took a good slurp of her drink, wishing she was back in Durham, anywhere but here. Mr Toddington's parents obviously thought she was some bit of fluff that Joe had picked up in the north and were studiedly ignoring her. An unmarried woman who travelled with an unmarried man on such a mission could hardly be respectable.

It was a clear night with a moon, just right for lifting bodies out of graveyards. There was nobody about, though why should there be? Sensible people were at home in bed. Besides, Joe had been right, it was some kind of private place with railings about it, the family plot or whatever these people called it.

Mr Toddington had chosen to come with Lucy and Joe. There were also various other men, four to dig, who kept taking it in turns, and two others, who stood about, looking official and rather uncomfortable, she thought, from the way that they didn't stand still but sauntered around. Joe stood over the grave and didn't move.

Nobody said anything. What could you possibly say on such an occasion? She imagined it in a book of etiquette. Conversation for graveyards during exhumation. She felt sick. She stood between Mr Toddington and Joe because she could feel the antipathy between them.

There was very little sound, just the efforts of the men digging, sighing and groaning because it was hard work, especially at their swift pace, the spades going in and then the soil being lifted and thrown until it began to heap up at the sides of the grave. It took a very long time.

She wanted to stand behind Joe as she finally heard the spade touch more than soil. It made a flinty sound. Lanterns caught the glimmer of brass or whatever it was, but it was only the glinting to one side. She could see that the coffin itself had disintegrated. That was a surprise; she hadn't thought about how a coffin would not last more than so many years. But who thought of such things?

The biggest surprise of all was that she could see what had been buried inside the coffin, and it was not bones or anything which resembled the remains of a person. It was nothing but stones. She wished she could have stood there with her eyes closed, but somehow it was as if they were glued open during the whole procedure.

'God Almighty,' Mr Toddington said, and then, 'Christ,' in surprise and some exasperation.

Joe didn't move, and he didn't speak. The men around him mumbled and muttered to one another, but Joe was rooted. Lucy wanted to go home to Durham and get into her bed and have nothing whatsoever to do with this or with any scheme of Joe's ever again. She began to wish they had never met.

Lucy went to bed and lay there for a long while, but she couldn't rest and she got up and put on a dressing gown. There was a door between the two rooms with the key on her side. She turned the key in the lock and opened the door very softly. She could see Joe.

He was standing beyond the windows, on the balcony,

looking at home here as he had never looked in Durham. The windows were the kind that ran from floor to ceiling and opened with double doors. This room was even bigger than hers and had a quantity of furniture in it such as you would never see in a normal-sized house – chairs and tables and some kind of ornate sofa covered in silk material.

He had his back to her, still dressed for dinner, as though they had had a polite evening, for God's sake. He had a balloon-shaped glass in one slender hand, with some kind of dark liquid in it. There was something about the set of his shoulders which encouraged her to walk into the room. She pulled the dressing gown tightly around her. Not that she thought Joe would have noticed has she been naked.

'Joe?'

When he didn't answer she turned as if to go back into her room and he said, 'Please don't leave.'

When she stopped he added, 'I'm sorry. I had no right to ask you to come here with me or to burden you with any of my stupid concerns. Will you have a drink with me?'

And since it gave him something to do and put a few seconds between them she accepted.

'Are you going to stay here and see what happened?'

'No.' Joe was decisive, almost as though he had known this would be a fool's errand before he came. 'I knew she wasn't here, I just needed to make sure. She went to Durham, I know she did, and I'm going to go back there and find out what happened to her. I couldn't help thinking over and over again that maybe my father had killed her, but I just can't see it somehow and it's such a relief to believe it.'

Lucy thought about this for a moment. 'If she was a north-country lass maybe she missed home,' she said. 'Maybe London society wasn't for her. I don't think I would like such a thing. We don't all want a titled husband and to talk of vacuous things all day.'

'Vacuous, eh?' Joe said with a touch of humour.

That was when Lucy relaxed and she said, 'Wasn't your father an important man? His wife would need to be a society lady, a political hostess. And even though some women are bred for such things, they don't always want them. Think about Florence Nightingale.'

'I do often,' Joe said, and his eyes twinkled just a little.

Lucy sat back. She took a sip of brandy and pulled a face.

'This is awful,' she said, 'it's like cough mixture.'

Joe laughed. He hadn't touched his drink, though she had the feeling that left alone he might have drunk a considerable amount of it. Wasn't that what drink was for? To blot out the things you couldn't bear?

'Why did my mother leave me there?' Joe said.

This, Lucy thought, was the whole point.

'She mustn't have had any choice. No woman leaves her child if she can help it. You must know that.'

'I don't.'

'That's because you're a man. A woman has to be in a very bad way before she leaves a child. Women adore their children. Look at Mrs Formby and how brave she was. Your mother left you because she felt it was better than what she could provide, but she must have grieved over you her whole life afterwards. Giving birth, excuse me for being blunt, is the biggest bond anyone can ever have – it must be, that's how biology works. You cannot carry a child, give birth and nurture it, and, short of your own insanity, want anything but the very best for it that you can do. She must have thought you would be better off in London with your father.'

'Or that he prevented her from taking me,' Joe said.

She hadn't liked to put that into words.

'What if I'm wrong? What if he did kill her and hid her body?' Joe said.

'Is your instinct telling you that?'

Joe said nothing. He looked down into his brandy.

'Maybe he thought he could do better than she could,' Lucy said. 'He wanted an heir presumably – men do, I imagine – or maybe they just didn't get on.'

Joe would have protested, but she added, 'In his own way, did he not care for you?'

Joe smiled at the memory. 'He took me out of school as soon as he could. He took me to France and Italy and Spain and I learned the languages. We had such wonderful times.'

'Well then,' Lucy said. 'Does that sound like a man who didn't adore his child?'

'But they weren't together and they were my parents.'

'What a myth marriage can be,' Lucy said, and it made him smile. 'It doesn't mean because she isn't there beside him that he murdered her. That's very dramatic, you know. Men don't have to murder women to get rid of them. Perhaps he did want her there. He was a very important man. If she ran away surely his pride would ensure he did his best to pretend that she had not left him. Don't you think?'

'I loved him,' Joe said. 'He wasn't a fiend, he wasn't aggressive. He loved me and he talked well of her. Maybe he did make up her death.'

'Maybe he was downhearted because she didn't want him. Maybe she had left you with him because of that – because it was what she could give him?'

Lucy was doing all she could so that Joe wouldn't be upset further. She didn't like to think that his father might have killed his mother or even that their marriage had been so awful that he had hidden her death and then buried her, saying that she had been ill. How hard that would have been. Just as bad that she had left him because he treated her cruelly.

Joe didn't say anything. Lucy felt as though she should go back to her own room, but she wasn't happy about leaving him there.

'It was good of you to come with me and put up with this,' he said. He picked up her hand and kissed the back of it and that was when Lucy remembered Guy. It wasn't the kiss, which was, she reasoned, just a gesture – Joe was so well-mannered – it was the fact of him so close. It made a dozen birds fly up into her stomach. She tried to stop the horrible images from flashing one by one across her mind, but it was too hard.

She drew back so quickly that Joe looked surprised. But he went on. 'There was no reason for you to do so, and I'm sorry I deceived you over it, but I didn't know how to manage on my own.'

Lucy got to her feet. She was shaking. She tried to remember to breathe, but she could taste Guy's mouth and feel his body pressing on her and the hurt. She was back there in Newcastle, her heart thudding, and she wanted to turn and run.

'Lucy?'

'I . . . I have to go. To go back to my own room.'

'All right. Thank you.'

She couldn't move. She didn't know why, but she couldn't. Joe got up as though he was coming with her and she clasped a hand to her mouth so that she wouldn't scream. He was looking carefully at her now.

'Goodnight.'

Lucy nodded and then she turned and ran. She slammed the door and stood against it, her heart knocking so hard that she thought it would burst out of her. She couldn't stand. She slid down the door and then silenced the sobs that would have made a huge noise. The tears flooded down her face.

She sat there and waited and let the silence go on and on. She had the feeling that Joe was about to burst into her room, and she was so scared, but the minutes ticked on and on and nothing happened. After a while even the line of light around the door went out and the only lamps were from her bedroom.

When she could, she stood up and made her way over to the bed. She got into it and covered herself up and remembered how she had got herself into bed that night, the last night she had spent at home. She went over and over it, blaming herself and blaming him and blaming her family and hating and loving them and hating him so much for what he had done to them.

He had ruined their lives. He had taken not just the past but this very night and had made her afraid of a decent man like Joe. She wondered what on earth Joe thought and

229

then she remembered how upset he was. He had not meant anything; he was not thinking about what she did, how she reacted. He was remembering the emptiness of his mother's grave and the confusion which followed.

NINETEEN

Mrs Formby came to the office. Lucy had waited for this to happen; she had worried about it so often that she could hardly present a decent face.

'I'm sorry to come bothering you here, Miss Charlton,' she said, 'but I didn't know what else to do. I'm that bothered about our Tilda. She's not eating and I think she keeps reliving the night that the house went on fire. I think she feels responsible and that she should have rescued her dad and it sits on her conscience that she didn't manage it.'

'But he was drunk, wasn't he? She couldn't rouse him and you couldn't – isn't that what you said?'

'We did our best, at least I think we did. I keep thinking back and wondering how hard I tried.'

'Your house was full of smoke. Smoke kills people before fire gets to them and it doesn't take long. You had to get your children out of there. Isn't that so?'

'We did that.'

'Well then.'

'I don't know, Miss Charlton, I'm not happy about any of it. I suppose I'll get used to it, but I'm not sure our Tilda will.'

'I think you're wrong,' Lucy said. She could hear the crisp

note in her voice and thought that just for once Mrs Formby needed somebody else to take over here. 'You are lucky that you did not all die. You must stop thinking of yourself as less than you are. You are a fine mother to your children and you must go forward and try to come to terms with what happened. I tell you what – I will ask around and see if I can find Clay some kind of part-time work so that he can help the family income. How would that be?'

Lucy had already promised herself that she would do this so they could live a little better. She felt now that she should have acted sooner.

Mrs Formby brightened at that and soon left the office.

Joe woke up. He could hear something. He thought at first it was Priscilla Lee or his guilt about Angela, but then something dragged him back to consciousness. It was nothing like the lullaby which was by now familiar to him, but one of the most horrible noises he had ever heard.

He listened for just a few seconds as it went on and then he got up and ran to the front door. There was the long-haired black-and-white cat, standing still at the edge of the river on the towpath at full stretch, as though she could hear and see something he could not. She was howling in a high and ghastly way as though she were injured, but she was not. The cat's fur stood up on end in spikes.

He followed her gaze. Further along he heard a splash and a shriek and then another and then more. When the moon came out of the high clouds, he thought he saw something moving in the water. He heard cries and struggling then. He ran along the riverbank to the nearest place he thought the person was and plunged in. The water was so cold that his body went rigid with shock. Luckily he had not far to go.

The person couldn't swim and must have gone under more than once. They had stopped moving or making any noise and were about to go under again. Joe had the feeling that it would be the final time, but he reached for the body and pulled the face up above the water. The water made the person light and it was a calm night, there had been no rain, so there was not much pull to the river, not enough to kick against very hard. It didn't cause him any trouble.

Within minutes he reached the bank. He was able to push the body out of the water enough so that he could let go and climb out. It was a struggle and there was nobody about to help, but it was somebody light, a small woman he thought or a half-grown child. It was difficult to drag himself free while making sure she didn't slip back in. Above him he was aware of the black-and-white cat, sitting forward, eyes anxious as though desperate to help.

Joe had strength. He got the person up onto dry land and it took some doing. The cat moved back and then sat by the body like a nurse, head down, eyes intent. Joe flattened his palms on the top ground beyond the river and pulled himself up and free. He was breathing hard, but he was much more concerned for the other person.

He began to shiver; he hadn't thought it so cold. The other person moaned and that was a relief. He sat her up and she coughed and spluttered and the water came out of her mouth. When he was sure that she wasn't going to choke or pass out he gathered her into his arms and carried her towards the house. The little black-and-white cat followed him, as though in escort.

He put the person down on the rug in front of the fire and then saw the dark hair and young face.

'Oh God, Tilda!'

He made certain that she was still breathing, then he ran up the two flights of stairs and shook Lucy in her bed.

'Lucy! You have to wake up. Lucy!'

'What on earth are you doing?' she said hoarsely as she sat up. There was no light – Joe hadn't stopped for that.

'Tilda almost drowned. Come downstairs and help me.'

He went off and seconds later she followed. Joe went back up to change into dry clothes and find something to wrap the girl in, while Lucy peeled off her clothes. She wrapped Tilda up in her underwear in a huge blanket, which Joe brought down with him, and gave her a pillow. Then Lucy made up the fire, which had almost died.

He thought Tilda was going to be all right, and she seemed calm, as Lucy reassured her, but then the girl screamed and clutched at her belly. The screaming went on and on and she doubled up, holding herself close.

'She needs to go to hospital,' Joe said.

'You go ahead. I'll dress and come after you.'

Joe picked Tilda up and ran – along the towpath and up the steep steps to the end of Framwellgate Bridge and then up the cobbles of North Road. Eventually his breath gave out. He couldn't see a cab anywhere, but he couldn't run any further. He stopped until his breathing steadied.

In the distance he spied one of Paddy's Cabs. He was so

pleased because he knew that the man would get him there. He beckoned and the driver saw him, and came to him.

Joe said, 'The hospital,' and the driver merely nodded.

In the cab, Joe gathered Tilda very close in his arms as she cried from pain. When they got as far as the County Hospital the cabbie stopped right outside the door and Joe took the girl in his arms and ran in. She was heavy, had stopped crying and he was so afraid that she would die.

Lucy had only just put on her clothes when she heard a banging on the front door. She ran down the stairs and hauled open the door. Mrs Formby stood there, crying.

'My Tilda's gone, Miss Charlton. She didn't come home and I'm that worried for her. What if something happened? I sat there and waited and waited. I'm so frightened. Where can she be?'

There was no point in trying to tell her what had happened, Lucy knew. She said all the right things. She walked Mrs Formby back to her house and told her she would get Joe up and they would go and look for Tilda. She said that Mrs Formby must not worry because they would find her and everything would be all right.

Lucy ran all the way to the hospital. She didn't cry, for it wouldn't help her to run any faster, but her heart felt as if it had jumped into her throat and lodged like a football.

She asked for Joe and Tilda when she got there and was given directions. She went up and along the corridor and recognized the figure in the distance. Joe was unmistakable in the morning light. His head was down and his whole look was one of defeat.

'Joe?' Instantly he altered his face, but it was still pale and thin. 'Tilda?' she said. 'Is she going to be all right?'

'They don't know yet.' His voice was hoarse as though he hadn't spoken in a long while. He didn't meet her eyes and so she knew there was more to it – that he was upset and worried.

'What happened?'

'She fell into the river.'

Lucy waited. He stood there with his head down and then he brought it up, though even then he averted his face.

'She fell.'

Lucy knew what that meant. She sat down beside him and they waited. She had never before been in a hospital corridor while somebody she cared about was being taken care of, beyond sight and sound. It was so quiet, as though nothing were happening.

It made her want to beat upon doors and demand to know what was going on, but she didn't, she couldn't, and she was calmed by Joe's patience. Time was different here, not like in other places. She was relieved that he was here, that she didn't have to handle this by herself.

Lucy and Joe saw the day through and into early evening, listening to the few noises which came through the hospital walls. Lucy was not even tired – she didn't think she had ever felt so wide awake. She half expected every moment that Mrs Formby would come shrieking down the corridor, demanding to know what was going on, but nothing happened until a man whom she assumed to be a doctor appeared.

She and Joe both got up as the doctor said, 'Are you here with Tilda Formby?'

Lucy nodded.

He spoke softly to them though there was no one to over-hear anything.

'Her baby did not survive. I'm so sorry.'

Lucy didn't know what to say and Joe was silent.

'Do you think she might be all right?'

'We think so, yes.' He smiled just a little. 'She's asleep. I should go home if I were you.'

'I want to be here when she wakes,' Lucy said.

'Of course you do,' he said. He went off back into the hospital gloom where secrets unknown to the rest of the community were commonplace, Lucy thought.

She turned to Joe, about to say to him that she was happy to stay there alone, when she realized that actually she wasn't – but that he was not going to leave in any case. He sat down promptly and she did the same.

'We can't tell her mother about the baby,' she said, 'but what are we going to say and how do we make sure that the staff here don't mention it in front of her?'

'If we don't go to her then Mrs Formby will soon come here looking,' Joe said. 'You go. You know her very well. Just say that Tilda was so upset about her dad and that she had gone a long way and got lost and fell down and hurt herself. Say that it's nothing important other than a few nasty bruises, and that she will be coming home later. Don't let her come here – it's the last thing Tilda needs.'

Lucy worried all the way back to Rachel Lane about how she would convince Tilda's mother not to go to the hospital.

If Mrs Formby found out what had really happened every-thing would be gone. She steeled herself, hesitating before she went into the house.

Mrs Formby and Clay were sitting over the fire. The two smaller children had been put to bed and Lucy thought that if she ever got to be a solicitor she would never have to put a more difficult case to a more discerning audience. Mrs Formby cried to discover that her child was alive, then she wanted to go to her. Lucy had to persuade her that Tilda was well but exhausted and asleep, and it would do no good for her to be disturbed now. That Mrs Formby was much better staying here with the rest of her children.

Lucy offered to go back to the hospital, to wait until Tilda was awake and they said she could have visitors, then she would come back and bring Tilda's mother to her. She had no intention of doing anything of the kind, she just hoped the girl would be well enough to go home before her mother insisted on being there.

When Lucy got back Joe looked up and smiled just a little.

'They've said you can go in.'

Tilda lay, very neat in a hospital bed, in a tiny white room on her own. It was nothing like Lucy had expected, but she thought the people here might have guessed what could have happened and had given her this room on purpose. Tilda's eyes were glassy with tears.

'I lost it,' she said and wept.

Lucy took the girl into her arms. She was so warm and young and alive that Lucy wished things differently.

'I didn't mean to do what I did. I didn't mean to do it to

the baby, just to me. I couldn't stand to see the look on me mam's face and have to lie and say I had done it. She would have hated me, Miss Charlton, and I couldn't stand it. I love me mam so much – she means everything in the world to me.'

'The baby was too small. The doctor said that it was just one of these things that happens to thousands of women. It wasn't the water – how could it have been?'

Lucy thought to herself that she had turned into a fluent liar – she didn't know whether or not the water had affected anything, but she wasn't going to have Tilda think it had. The baby could have died anyway. She was bound to make a good lawyer with such lying, but also she was not telling Tilda anything which she did not believe. How could that be wrong? There was a possibility of course that she would have drowned and taken the baby with her, but Lucy did not let herself think about this. What was the point?

'I slipped and fell. I changed me mind – I was going to go home and tell me mam – only it was too late and I couldn't stay up and I couldn't breathe. Now I've got another chance. Now I have to.'

'No, you don't,' Lucy said, without thinking.

She was astonished at herself, but not dismayed. She didn't care beyond what Tilda would do now. There was no way that she was going to let this girl pay over and over for what had not been her fault in the first place – it was all too difficult, she acknowledged now.

She didn't care that men like Edgar would take a different view because they thought the law expected it and they must bow down to it. Women didn't have time to let the law catch up with them – they had to outwit it right now, and possibly a very long way into the future – and that was what made her decision.

The two women drew away from one another and Lucy looked hard at Tilda.

'One of the things about being an adult is that you don't hurt other people unnecessarily. Your mam doesn't ever need to know what has happened to you. All I told her was that you had been hurt and not badly and that you would be fine – and that's what you will do. You go home and get on with your life. You're young. You will go on and do other things, big, exciting things. You will have your job as manager and in time you might go on and run the whole co-operative in the area – just think of that. There's no reason for any of you to take on any more burdens. You're going to have the good life that you are entitled to – as a person and a woman.'

Lucy was amazed at this long speech, but it had the right effect, for Tilda's face cleared and then she glanced at the door.

'Is Mr Hardy outside?' she asked.

'He's waiting in the corridor.'

'Can I see him?'

Lucy went and beckoned Joe in. He came and sat down on the bed, and Tilda kissed his cheek and thanked him, though Joe disclaimed that he had done anything at all. He looked generally embarrassed, but said that he was so glad to see her better now.

That week Lucy went to see Miss Thompson at the shoe shop. She'd been told that Tilda had merely had a fall and hurt herself. She told Lucy she was looking forward to Tilda being back in the shop because she had taught the girl all she could and she was ready to give up the place.

'I've been here a good long time, Miss Charlton,' she said, 'and Tilda is perfectly capable of running the shop – she has exceptional ability, way beyond her years. Mr Bradley – who manages the grocery and is in charge overall – thinks well of her, you know.'

'That was why I came,' Lucy said. 'I was wondering if you could introduce me to Mr Bradley and whether there might be room to take on Clay, Tilda's brother, as a Saturday boy. He's very reliable and good at school; his mother has kept him there in spite of everything and they could certainly make use of the money.'

Miss Thompson said that she didn't know what the circumstances were, but that she would introduce Lucy to Mr Bradley. Since it was Wednesday and the store closed at twelve, she took Lucy around to the main shop. Though Mr Bradley said that he already had a Saturday boy, he thought that the hardware department needed help.

That Saturday morning Lucy took Clay to the shop and he began filling shelves with hammers and chisels and kitchenware. He propped up wheelbarrows and other things for the garden and swept up in the back premises, tidying around and washing the floor when the shop closed. He confided to Lucy that Mr Bradley had mentioned he was getting a bicycle and that he would need somebody to deliver the groceries in the area. He'd said that as soon as the bicycle was delivered, in a few weeks, Clay would be promoted. Mrs Formby was very happy about this, for two of her children were in work.

TWENTY

That Sunday Joe wished he could go into work, but even Mr Palmer didn't work on Sundays. Joe went for a walk around the river. He had to get out to think about the car and to brush off the idea that he felt so threatened by whatever it was that haunted him in the night. He had to sneak out otherwise the little long-haired black-and-white cat would always follow him and he was too afraid for the cat's safety. It was almost teatime. Frederick soft-pawed out after him and together they picked up some pace. It was a lovely afternoon and all kinds of people were pic-nicking on the river. It did Joe good to see them enjoying themselves.

Since he had been to London Joe kept thinking of the letter in which his father was still pretending his wife was buried there – Joe had not been able to read another or to think of forgiving his father for what he had done. Had his father wiped his mother completely from his memory? Was he deceiving himself about her death? How could you wipe things away as if they have never been? Joe wondered.

But his father had given him the best that he could in so many ways, and so while Joe found it easy to despise him it was impossible to hate him. There were many good memories amidst all of it, memories he'd held onto when things were at their worst in the trenches. Even now they brought him comfort, despite not knowing where his mother was or where Angela could be. The war had taught him to remember the good times, no matter what.

He thought about what tea had been like when he was a small child in the nursery. His nanny would toast crumpets over the fire with a long-handled fork and if he was careful she let him do the same. Melting butter and strawberry jam. He was within this thought, happy, when he suddenly came upon two people kissing in the shadows. He walked swiftly past so as not to intrude, but one of them turned. He recognized Emily Bainbridge. He merely waved in acknowledgement and went on with his walk.

When he reached home both the Misses Slaters were out and Lucy had gone to visit Mrs Formby. Sunday was the Misses Slaters' special day; they went to church twice and to visit people they knew. He was about to make something to eat when there was a loud banging on the door. He opened it, surprised by the figure who stood there.

'Miss Bainbridge.'

For a small person she looked like a storm cloud.

'May I come in?'

'Yes, of course, if you wish.' He held open the door.

She strode into the room and turned around so fast that Joe nearly had to take a step backwards.

'About earlier—'

'Whatever you're worried about is nothing to do with me. Other people's lives are their own business.'

She looked warily at him and then relief came over her face like a wave on a summer sea.

'You won't tell anyone?'

'Why would I do that?'

'Oh, thank God,' she said in a very unladylike fashion and sat down heavily in a chair. 'I thought you were all right when I met you.'

'What do you mean?'

'Well, for a start you didn't take all my clothes off with your eyes. You didn't spend any time at all looking at my bosom. In fact I began to wonder if I'd suddenly lost my looks. I usually make an instant impression. I thought that maybe you preferred men, as some do. I do like your house,' she said, getting back up again and going around the room as though she might buy it.

Then she sat down once more, sinking back into the chair. 'Have you got a cigarette?'

Joe provided the cigarette, lit it for her and sat down.

'My brother expects me to marry, you know. I have no money of my own and no education to speak of, no talents. It doesn't leave a lot.'

Joe sat back and looked at her. She seemed an entirely different person to the one he had met at the dinner party, when she had been playing the dutiful sister.

'My brother thought I was taken by you, which I'm sure he's very worried about.'

'So I gathered, at least something like that. A much-needed smokescreen in fact.'

She blew cigarette smoke into the air.

'Precisely,' she said. 'Not that I would have done it if I had thought you couldn't handle it.'

'If you don't like your life, why don't you change it?'

She laughed and then looked sad.

'What am I supposed to do? Go home and announce to my brother that I've fallen in love with our cook? She comes from a good Methodist family. Can you imagine how that would look at chapel meetings?'

Joe stared at her for a few moments.

'Oh, I see,' he said.

She stared back at him.

'I needn't have come here. You didn't realize.'

'I didn't look.'

'You still won't tell?'

He merely shook his head and smiled.

'Oh, Joe,' she said, getting up, coming over and kissing him right in the middle of his forehead. She wafted expensive perfume at him. 'You are such a gentleman.'

'You must be able to make the kind of life you want somehow.'

Her eyes glazed with tears.

'The trouble is that Norah is getting married. She can't possibly not, you see. She could never tell her family and she is so good and loyal that she would never see me afterwards. So now is all we have.'

She got up as if to go, waving her hand in confusion.

'Stay, if you have time,' Joe offered.

'I have nothing but time. Do you have any whisky?'

'Just the bottom third of a bottle I've had this age.'

'God bless you.'

The afternoon turned into evening.

'Do you really think I might do something, Joe?'

'Why not?'

'When Norah marries I ought to leave. Otherwise I shall spend my life looking for her on the street, seeing her putting her hand through her husband's arm, walking out with her children. Do you know what the worst thing is? I really like children, I wish that somehow I could have some. Why does everything have to be so difficult? I know you could say that I might make sacrifices and marry and then I can have children, but to be at some man's mercy all of the time, well, I don't think I would manage that, to say nothing of marital relations. If you think about it, it all seems faintly ridiculous, doesn't it? We are all so stupid and petty.'

'Why don't you run away together?'

'I have suggested it, but she can't do that to her family. We could never come back, you see, and while I think I could manage, she never could. Why should we give up everything?'

They were sitting on the floor, leaning back against the armchairs. She moved over and put her face against his shoulder. Joe put an arm around her and she moved closer and they sat there, watching the fire and drinking whisky.

Later, when the Misses Slaters came back, Joe walked her home.

Edgar was standing in the hall.

'Was that Joe Hardy I saw you with?'

Emily cast her eyes heavenward.

'He's just a friend,' she said.

'You asked him to the dinner party without consulting me, you talked almost exclusively to him the entire evening and now you meet up with him—'

'You wanted Lucy at the dinner party. She could hardly come by herself and seeing as they live in the same house I couldn't not ask him, it would have been rude. As for the rest, it was a coincidence.'

'I'm a lawyer,' Edgar said. 'I don't believe in coincidence.'

'It doesn't matter to me what you believe,' she said.

'The war broke Joe Hardy, you just have to glance at him to see it. His family were weak stupid people and I would rather you respected my wishes and didn't see him.'

Emily said nothing.

'What do you find attractive about him?'

'He's just a very nice person.'

Edgar almost snarled. 'Why do women say that of him when he's pathetic and worse?' He left the room.

TWENTY-ONE

Joe was by now going to Gateshead twice a week to see Mr Firbank. The old gentleman was going downhill fast and was no longer very coherent, but Joe felt the pull to see him as much as possible. It didn't have to be conversation, it was just sitting with him sometimes, even just watching him sleep. Joe didn't often stay long, but he always went. The nuns fussed over him politely and made tea, and Joe was told more than once that he was the only visitor Mr Firbank ever had. It made him want to be there more and more. He didn't know why it comforted him, but it did.

It made the Tyne almost as important to Joe as the Wear, or even the Thames which he had loved as a child.

The weather was almost always cool. Joe thought he would never get used to how it rained incessantly in the north. There were no seasons, every day it changed, but he had come to regard the weather as insignificant and was happy to sit there with Mr Firbank and tell him about what he was doing. He talked mostly about the venture with the cars because that made Mr Firbank's eyes light up.

Joe had no doubt the old gentleman slept when he had gone and perhaps he had sweeter dreams than he might otherwise have had. He had taken to patting Joe's hand when Joe left and thanking him somewhat incoherently for having been there.

'I'll be back in a day or two,' Joe would say, and he would watch Mr Firbank's eyes close as he left the room.

One Sunday that autumn he asked Lucy if she would go with him, though he knew she had sufficient to cope with keeping the two old ladies happy, as well as going back and forth to the Formby house to help with general problems. She enjoyed it, he knew, but they had not spent much time together lately. He thought they could go and see the old gentleman and go out to tea later.

She brightened at the idea and off they went, only to be met at the door by a sad-looking nun who told them that Mr Firbank had died.

'Peacefully in the night,' she said.

Joe didn't know what to do then, or where he wanted to be. No – he knew. He wanted to be sitting by the window where he had last left Mr Firbank and be talking of anything he could think of, while the old man listened to his voice, almost happy.

Joe hovered. The nun, having obviously dealt with things like this before, offered them tea, and Lucy accepted. They sat down in another room, thankfully different from the one that Joe was used to. But Joe couldn't rest. He didn't want tea; he wanted to go to Allendale and speak to Mr Firbank's son.

'You can't just barge in on his grief,' Lucy said.

'He didn't care,' Joe said savagely.

'You don't know that. He was Mr Firbank's son and just because you don't like him that doesn't make it right.'

'He never once came to see him.'

'Well perhaps he couldn't cope any more. People can't always, you've probably noticed by now.'

Joe was silenced by her, but only for a few seconds and then he got up and left the room. He went to ask about the funeral arrangements, but all the nun could tell him was that the undertaker had come from across country and taken Mr Firbank's body away once the doctor had certified him dead. Joe went back and told Lucy this.

'You see,' Lucy said. 'He has to do this and it's nothing to do with you. For goodness' sake, leave the man alone for a few days. All that really matters is that you were here for Mr Firbank and that he liked having you here and you were a friend to him. You got a lot from it and so did he, but now he's dead you can't do anything else.'

She poured out some more tea because it had gone cold, but Joe went into the room where he and Mr Firbank had spent so much time over the past months. He sank down in the chair where he used to sit, and looked out at the river. He hoped the old gentleman had gone straight to heaven, wherever that might be. He would miss him, this man who was his only link to Priscilla Lee. Now he was gone. Joe felt weary with loss. Was he never to have anyone he loved for any length of time?

The old gentleman had provided Joe with cover from the rest of his life; it was the only safe place he had away from the world where he was forever dodging bullets in one sense or another. Joe wanted to sit and weep from the frustration that he had not seen Mr Firbank when he was dying, that he had not been there to say something of comfort, that they had not taken leave of one another. He hated saying goodbye, but not saying it was so much worse. He felt as if there were a huge yawning chasm where the old man had been. Nothing would fill it. And, even worse somehow, he felt it would have been so lovely had they known one another for all of his life. It was not just the present and the future which were missing, but the past. Mr Firbank and Joe's mother were big empty blanks, gaping chasms that made Joe want to go around smashing things. He was shaking.

TWENTY-TWO

Joe was rather astonished to get the note that asked him to go to Edgar's office. It wasn't so much an invitation as a command and so he obeyed it round about midday on the Monday when he took a break from the garage. He didn't see any reason not to, and he was curious. He duly turned up and found that Edgar's face was stern.

'I understand you walked my sister home the other evening, Mr Hardy.'

Joe was not invited to sit down and stood there, looking across the room. He understood.

'Ah,' he said, 'you think I have evil intentions.'

'No, I think you're just like every other fellow in Durham, and Emily is lovely.'

'Edgar—'

'Don't use my first name. Don't pretend we are friends and don't see her again.'

All Joe said, to Edgar's surprise was, 'What is it you want her to do?'

It clearly seemed ridiculous to Edgar.

'I want her to marry well, to have a good life with a decent man and not some . . . some person like you.'

'Why must she marry well?' Joe could not help saying.

Edgar looked at him with hostile eyes. 'She deserves to be looked after – she is a lovely woman and I care for her. I want to give her to someone else who will feel the same and more so that she can have children and a future – so she can have some happiness.'

Joe nodded slowly. 'You want to give her to somebody. What is she, a Christmas present? You don't have to worry, Edgar.' He pronounced Edgar's name with a smile and emphasis. 'I have not been leading your sister up the garden path, as I think it's called. She would never marry me – she has more sense and I would never ask her. We are friends, just as I thought you and I were also. But it's your choice.' Joe got up and left the office.

Edgar half believed Joe. Over the next few days he watched Emily as she went about her daily life and discovered that she was unhappy. When he was with her, and she was among other young men at church or in the town, she was amiable to all of them, just as she had been with Joe. She smiled and talked of things they wished to talk of and most of them looked lasciviously at her in a way that made him want to push their faces into the trifle. He knew that many a man thought no one good enough for their sisters, he just didn't like the way that they surveyed her. He was honest with himself then and knew that Joe had not looked at Emily like that.

She wore her pretty clothes and sparkled for everyone, so that in the end Edgar became very confused. He asked her to come and see him in his office; he felt somehow as though he could not talk to her at home.

Lucy was sitting in her little office when she heard footsteps on the stairs and a tentative knocking on the door. Emily Bainbridge stood there.

'Do you mind? Only my brother is still in court and he asked me to come and see him. You don't know what it's about, do you?'

'I don't,' she said.

'Why couldn't he talk to me at home? After all we both live there.' She paused in the doorway, looked carefully at Lucy and said, 'Am I intruding?'

'Not at all. Come in and have a seat.'

'You don't have a cigarette? Edgar would be horrified if he knew that I smoked and I get so desperate.'

'Mr Clarence might have one.'

Emily wrinkled her nose. 'I'd better not ask him,' she said. 'How are things going for you? It's high time women got into these professions if you ask me. I think you'll be very good at it. I wish I wanted something like that.'

Lucy was just about to ask her what she did want when Mr Clarence called up the stairs. Emily said good morning and went down to greet her brother.

Emily sat down.

'So,' he said, 'what are you doing today?'

'You didn't really ask me here for that? I usually get to tell you over supper.'

He sighed. 'I'm worried about you,' he said.

Emily gazed at him in surprise. 'What do you mean?'

'I don't know exactly – all I know is that you aren't happy and I'm not helping you. I don't mean to go on at you, Em, but I worry about you.'

'Don't you have work to do?'

Edgar squirmed a little in his seat and said, 'I felt awful.'

'Well, don't. There's nothing the matter with me.'

'You don't seem to like anybody. You don't even seem to like me, though you used to. I'm older than you and I try to do the best I can, but it's as if you're acting out a role.'

'Aren't we all doing that?'

'Not to the extent that you are.'

She was looking at him as though she hadn't seen him in a long time and when she spoke to him again her voice was softer.

'What made you think about this?'

'Joe Hardy.'

'For goodness' sake. I have no interest in Mr Hardy except that I find him easy to talk to. I have no intention of running away with him even though I am inclined since you dislike him so intensely.'

'You could have any man you want. You have had half a dozen offers, two of them brilliant, from men who are wealthy and well born and have old names. Do you feel nothing for any of them?'

She didn't speak. She shook her head.

'Is there something you would rather do?' Edgar said. 'You don't have to get married if the whole thing makes you queasy. Would you like to run a dress shop or . . . or something like that? I would help you as much as I could.'

Emily heard the despair in his voice and she loved him so much that she couldn't say anything. If she told him what she felt he would never look at her that way again, as men did when their sisters were beautiful and difficult – how he admired her, how he would have done almost anything for her.

She could tell Joe how she really felt, but she couldn't hurt Edgar. She said nothing.

'Emily, if you don't tell me, there's nothing I can do.'

She lifted drenched eyes.

'I'm so sorry,' she said, 'I don't want to disappoint you, but I can't marry any man.'

'Why not?'

She shook her head and pulled a face at him.

'I'm going to be a nun,' she said, though even then he didn't laugh.

TWENTY-THREE

Lucy had gone to Edgar's house because he had left some important papers in one of the desk drawers in his study when he was working late the night before. He was due in court and so she must run and fetch them and deliver them to him.

Nobody answered. She rang the bell and nothing happened and then she hammered on the door. He had said that Norah would definitely be there, even if his sister was not, so in the end she went around to the back door which was actually at the side of the house. It was ajar.

Here she hesitated; she could hear the sound of laughter and she thought it was Emily. She had never heard Emily laugh like that, so openly giggling, but there was another voice too, lifted, light. From where she stood she could see through the window. She would have spoken, but she was so surprised by what she saw that she couldn't think of anything to say. She stood well back, not knowing what to do. They weren't aware of her at all, so concentrated were they on one another.

Norah and Emily were in the kitchen. Norah was obviously baking because the sweet smell of pastry and fruit hung in the air. They were flicking flour at one another. It reminded her at first of herself and Gemma when they were younger, but no, it was not the same. She didn't understand why.

The floor was covered in splodges of white and they began chasing one another, giggling even more. It was a game they had played before, because they kept changing direction, weaving in and out of the furniture, eventually coming face to face.

There were seconds together of hesitation and then they rushed at one another and the next moment they were kissing, long deliberate open-mouthed assaults, as though they were starving for touch and feel, as though they knew one another's bodies. They were crooning now, eager, lustful, cupping the other's face to get nearer.

She backed away, hoping that they had not seen her, that they wouldn't call out, but no other sound came to her from the kitchen other than noises she felt sure she was not supposed to hear. She ran away beyond the house and up the drive and didn't stop until she was quite out of breath. Then she deliberated. Edgar needed the papers.

She was shocked. She had never heard of such things. Was that true? Women who liked women and men who preferred men? It didn't seem right somehow, and then she thought of Emily's unhappiness. How could one love be worse than another, if the two people were adult and willing and free? The trouble was that Norah was not free, she was about to be married.

Lucy stood and waited. She felt guilty because Edgar was in court and she didn't know how long it would be before he needed the information. In the end she went slowly back down the drive and banged like merry hell on the front door. Nothing happened for a long while and so she banged again. Eventually Emily appeared at the door, out of breath, her hair in disarray and her clothes pulled on anyhow, Lucy thought.

She tried to be normal, to ask for what she wanted. Emily waved her into the study, told her to help herself and said she was busy. She disappeared into the shadows at the back of the house, banging the green baize door which led there.

Lucy found the papers in one of the drawers almost immediately. She ran all the way to Elvet, to the court.

She saw Edgar there in the courtroom.

'Where on earth have you been?' he whispered furiously.

'Sorry, I couldn't find them at first. They weren't where you said they were,' she said.

He seemed to accept this as reasonable and was so distracted with what he was trying to achieve that he took them from her without another word. She went back to the office and tried to work and found herself walking up and down. She understood so much now. She understood that she had been an idiot about Joe. No wonder he didn't understand her. But most of all she thought about Emily and of how Edgar had talked about not knowing what his sister wanted.

Lucy tried to dismiss Emily and Norah from her mind. She told herself it was nothing to do with her, especially as she didn't like Emily very much, but she knew that Emily was unhappy, as was Edgar about their home life. In the end she went to see Emily, one afternoon.

She couldn't go after work – she was too afraid that Edgar would come home or see her leave – so she lied to him and said she had some business in the town for him, which she had actually done the day before. She made her way back to his house, remembering what she'd found a few days before. She only hoped that Emily was there.

She was in luck. Emily answered the door. She looked tired and bored, as though she might have been dozing by the fire. She had a book in one hand and she frowned.

'Oh, it's you,' she said. 'He hasn't left some more wretched papers here, has he?'

'I just wanted to talk to you.'

'Me?' She looked surprised – why wouldn't she – but she opened the door wider and allowed Lucy into the sitting room where the fire burned small. Emily apologized.

'Norah usually sees to these things and she has gone off to her aunt's in Esh Winning. Her aunt is making her wedding dress. She's very excited about it – she didn't expect to go to her wedding in a white dress.' Emily tried to smile and didn't quite manage it.

'I did want to see you by yourself.'

'I can't even manage tea. You see how useless I am. At least you can have a seat. There's nothing wrong with Edgar, is there?' She looked concerned and Lucy saw that she really did care for her brother.

'He's worried about you.'

'Oh for goodness' sake. He didn't send you to talk to me?'

'I pretended I had somewhere to go.'

'How intriguing.' Emily sat down heavily in the armchair, across the fire from where Lucy sat.

'It's about you, really. And Norah.'

Emily looked hard at her. 'What do you mean?'

'Well, I don't know how to say it but – does she want to get married?'

Emily's face went blank. 'She must, or she wouldn't do it.'

'People don't always want to. There are other ways to live.'

Emily sighed. 'Not for her. She has a very good family, you know. They expect it and . . . she wants children. This is Durham. It's such a small city.'

'Emily—'

'Don't let's talk about it.'

'But—'

'There's nothing anyone can do or I would have done it, you see.'

The girl's eyes were bright with tears. There was a short silence and then she said into it, 'How did you guess?'

'I saw you together.'

Emily thought for a few moments and then nodded.

'Last week when you came to the house,' she said.

'I didn't mean to . . . to be there, and I didn't stay.'

Emily shook off the tears.

'And you cared enough to come here and see me?'

'I'm very good at interfering,' Lucy said. She got up.

'You won't say anything.'

'Certainly not.'

'Joe knows, but he's the only one besides you.' Emily hesitated. 'Especially not my brother.'

Lucy didn't know what to say. She knew that there was a great affection between the brother and sister, though whether it would survive such information she doubted. She looked straight at Emily and said, 'I wouldn't dream of such a thing. It would be a betrayal of both of you.'

She could see that Emily relaxed. The anxiety almost went from her face and the look of gratitude upon it made Lucy sorry for her.

Emily saw her to the door. 'I didn't think we were going to be friends,' she said.

'Well, we are. When you get tired of being alone come into town and we'll have tea together.'

Norah lived in Atherton Street, a terrace of houses just beyond the centre of the city which went down in a sweeping way. They lay south of the viaduct which carried the railway to Edinburgh in the north and London the other way.

It was early evening when Lucy knocked on the door. A middle-aged man opened it and she had her first sight of Norah's family. Her father was well dressed in a poor kind of way, in a suit of cheap dark material which was shiny with use. The hall smelled of polish. He seemed happy to see her when she explained who she was, and he ushered her inside. The stairs went up on the left, but on the right were two rooms. He saw her into the first and there were Norah, her mother and a young man.

Mrs Moody said how kind it was of Miss Charlton to call, and she offered her tea. Lucy despaired of being able to see Norah by herself. The young man was introduced as Norah's intended. He was short, skinny, sallow-faced and obviously wearing his best; he looked so uncomfortable in it, but he had hold of Norah's hand. Norah didn't look at Lucy once, giving Lucy the impression that Emily must have told her that Lucy knew of their feelings for one another. She hoped nobody noticed, but then why should they? She didn't stay long, but had a cup of tea with them and joined in the general talk.

Then Norah's mother said to her, 'You must come to the wedding. We know you are great friends of the Bainbridge family and that you work with Mr Bainbridge. They have always been so kind to Norah. She's been with them since she left school, when Mr and Mrs Bainbridge were still alive, and they are a wonderful family to work for.'

Lucy was so stunned to receive the invitation that she couldn't think of an excuse not to go. She found herself saying she would be delighted and Mrs Moody told her the wedding would be at the chapel in North Road.

Mr Moody took over the conversation then, saying that he was sorry to lose his only and lovely daughter, but glad that she was going to such a nice young man as Fred. Fred blushed. Mrs Moody explained that Fred had a job as a clerk on the railways and was doing well.

Lucy felt sad about the whole situation. These were lovely people, living a hard life, and perhaps it was wrong to criticize anything about them. Every minute seemed like ten until Lucy got to her feet, saying how kind they were and managed to get into the darkness of the hall. She could hear Norah stuttering that she would see Miss Charlton out. Lucy hauled open the door and took huge breaths of air. It was several seconds until she saw that Norah had closed the front door with herself outside it.

The street was mercifully empty. Norah came to her, straight-faced and empty-eyed.

'I understand what you're trying to do, Miss, and I'm

grateful for it, but this cannot be altered. I cannot give up my family for Emily.'

Lucy could think of nothing helpful to say.

'I'm the only bairn they have,' Norah said. 'My mam lost four of her five children. How could I disappoint them, hurt them so much?' She hesitated and then didn't say what Lucy was convinced she wanted to. Instead of saying goodnight and walking away, Lucy waited.

Norah dipped her head and then raised it. She was clear-eyed now and said, 'Emily would have got tired of me. She's that clever. We couldn't have lived here, and in places like London I would have let her down with the way I talk and my ideas. She knows about paintings and books and things like that. She goes to the kind of concerts where I know I would be really bored. This is what I know.'

'What about Fred?'

'He'll do all right and we'll have a nice house and maybe even bairns – and I do want bairns – and my mam and dad will be proud of me. They'll be grandparents, and they want that so much, Miss Charlton. And in time I'll forget how I felt about her, except as a lovely idea which I couldn't hold. She'll forget about me. She'll find somebody else.'

Norah turned and ran back into the house, closing the front door firmly behind her.

Lucy was about to cross the road when she saw a slight figure in the shadows. She stopped and moved towards it. It was Emily, sobbing very quietly. When Lucy reached out to her she turned in against the wall as though that were better than anything else she might do.

'I come here and watch them,' she said, 'it's as close as I

can get. I try not to, but it's become an addiction. I watch Fred White come and go from the house. I know he loves her, and it's not just the way that a lot of men marry because they want a woman – he cares about her. He's so poor. His suits are thin and his cuffs are threadbare. Why couldn't I be born a man?'

'Don't be silly,' Lucy said, mocking, 'they're nasty, smelly creatures.'

Emily laughed just a little bit.

'I hope you don't mean my brother,' she said. 'I'm devoted to him.'

TWENTY-FOUR

Lucy had so often envisaged the day that Gemma would walk into her office, but when her sister did arrive she had been obliged to keep her waiting an hour because she had no appointment and it was a busy morning. Lucy could concentrate on nothing despite trying hard to forget that the woman she had loved above all others was waiting for her just along the corridor.

Gemma looked objectively at Lucy's new office. Edgar had recognized her hard work and promoted her. Gemma saw the marble fireplace, the bulging files, the big square desk, the various chairs and the full bookcases at either side of the big window which looked out over the river.

Gemma also stared at Lucy herself. Lucy had bought herself a very stylish costume, black and fitted to her figure. It had cost her more money than she felt comfortable paying. She wore neat black shoes and had cut her hair very short so that her cheekbones, she felt, stood out to advantage. She had been having a very satisfying day until Mr Clarence told her that Mrs Brown was waiting for her. She'd said that she didn't mind how long she had to wait, but she must see Miss Charlton.

Lucy stared back at Gemma. She would not have picked out this woman as the beautiful sister she had known. She was thinner than Lucy had ever been, her cheeks blanched and her clothes so colourless and old they seemed to drag about her person. Her hair beneath her cheap hat was lustreless, her eyes dead.

'Please, sit down.' It was the first thing she said to everyone after greeting them, but she couldn't think of a greeting which would fit here so she just swept a hand in the air.

Gemma hovered like a moth afraid of a flame. She hesitated and then turned, as someone who was about to leave. She glanced at the door like a prisoner might, then looked all around the room. Finally she brought her gaze back to her sister and then it fell.

'Would you like some tea?' As soon as she said it Lucy wanted to clout herself for stupidity, but she couldn't think of anything sensible to say. 'How did you know where I was?'

Gemma gazed at her and it was frost.

'Mother asked around Father's acquaintances. We heard from Constable Keane that he'd seen you. You have to come back to Newcastle,' she said, obviously well-rehearsed. 'Father has lost his mind, Guy is dying and we have no money. Mother made me come here to ask you to help us.'

Lucy had a wild desire to laugh.

'Why should I do that?' she said.

'Because of how badly you behaved. You owe your family and Mother would consider forgiving you for what you did – for how you broke up the family and ruined my wedding day.'

'Why can't you work?'

'I have two small children.'

'I'm sure that Mother could look after them.'

'She is too busy looking after Guy and Father and the thing is—' Gemma faltered, 'we are pretending Father is well because the business must not go down. It's all we have. I knew you would have succeeded, that you could run it for us.'

'Actually it takes a lot longer than you think to become a solicitor. I had no money so I'm not one.'

Gemma glanced about the office.

'Then how did you get this?'

'Because I have a law degree and know more than most secretaries and Mr Bainbridge is the only solicitor here so I help him.'

'Father needs help. He can go to the office some days and the rest of the time you could run the place. He would still be seen as the solicitor and as himself – so many people believe in him, you see.'

There was silence and Lucy felt like a cock crowing, but that didn't feel good.

'My husband is dying,' her sister said. 'The cancer eats at his stomach.'

There was a horrid and wonderful part of Lucy which wanted to shout with glee, and yet she couldn't.

'I'm so sorry,' she said.

'He's in a lot of pain. He has to have morphine constantly. The doctor thinks he will live for just a few more weeks and then I will be widowed with two children, a father who cannot work and a mother who is grief-stricken.'

Lucy wanted to say that no matter how fast Guy was dying

she hoped he burned in hell, the evil bastard. She had told herself that nobody was evil, that people were a product of their upbringing and that everyone could be excused or understood for whatever they did, but she could not forget and could not forgive what Guy had done to her. Whatever his powerless background, and she didn't know whether it was right, he should not have treated her as he had done. Even if his mother had done something awful to him so that he had learned to hate women, to set one sister against another.

'Has your marriage been good?' she said.

Gemma frowned.

'He is the best of men,' she said. She stood so tall that Lucy was in no doubt that if she had been there for long enough she would have hit the ceiling with the top of her stupid head. 'You must help us. There is nobody else or I would not have come.'

'So you don't like me, you don't want me, but you want me to make money and save the family,' Lucy said.

'I have little choice. I have two children, an old man, an old woman and a dying husband. What kind of a woman are you?'

'I thought you knew. Graceless and lying and not your friend.'

Gemma stood and didn't say anything.

'I knew how it would be. Mother made me come. I didn't want to. You were always so difficult, you thought you were so clever.'

'I am,' Lucy said.

It was a comment she remembered afterwards, mentally

beating herself over the head for it. 'I don't have to come back to Newcastle. I can send you money.'

'It's not just money we need.'

'Really?' Lucy stared at her as she might a stranger.

'We need you to come home,' Gemma said.

She turned and walked out. Lucy was thrilled. She had finally bettered her family, she had avenged herself – she was glad, she didn't care. She looked around her office at the fire, at the sweetly red-and-orange flame in the grate, and she knew that her office here was what she had always wanted, was what she had really strived for. She could not claim that the loss had been so huge.

Lucy half thought that Gemma would come again to the office, but she didn't. Lucy tried hard to put from her mind the way her sister had come to her, knowing how much Gemma despised her – it must have been unbearably difficult – but she could not live with it.

Her family would not go from her mind. Night after night she dreamed of them loving and hating her, she dreamed of violence and blood and screaming and shouting and all the things that families were. She dreamed of comfort and laughter and her warm childhood.

She waited. She told herself that it didn't matter, she didn't care, that it was over, they had put her out. She made herself think of what it had been like when they did not want her any more, and for a day or two she held herself from them. Yet she thought of them so much that it was like a new grief.

She went to Edgar and he listened to her halting explanation. She so obviously didn't say what she meant and he frowned.

'I can't spare you,' he said.

'They're my family.'

'Your brother-in-law must have family and they must have means, surely.'

'Apparently not.'

Edgar hesitated and then he looked at her and said, 'I don't want to be without you, you have become so valuable to me. I was going to say to you that I would take you on properly so that in time you would be a solicitor. You have a great deal of ability and I must say a woman's touch is welcome here. You've boosted our client list. Mr Clarence respects you a great deal and so do I.'

Lucy felt excited, exhilarated that he should even think of her.

'So consider carefully. I'm sure your family is important to you, but so is this.'

Lucy thought her problem was solved. She went out of Edgar's office, worked hard all that day and discovered in the early evening as she walked back to the tower house that she was unhappy with her decision.

She stopped just before she reached it and realized how much this place had come to mean to her. Miss Slater was playing a hymn on the old piano they had insisted on bringing with them. The sitting-room windows would be open to the sunshine and she recognized the lovely Charles Wesley hymn, 'Love Divine All Loves Excelling', which people tended to play at weddings. The piano sounded tinny and yet she thought the whole thing was so beautiful. The idea

271

that she had to leave here and go back to Newcastle and give up the life she had made for herself was the last thing she wanted to do.

She had wanted her parents and Gemma to be wrong, she had wanted them to miss her, she had wanted to be asked back. But not in these circumstances.

When she reached the house, stepping over Frederick in the shade of the front garden, she found that Joe was not there, only the two Misses Slaters.

It was late when Joe came home from work that evening. She put a plate of food in front of him, but it was only afterwards when they were sitting drinking tea together at the table and she could hear the two Misses Slaters talking softly in the sitting room that she told him about her day. Joe sat back and regarded her attentively as he always did.

'And Edgar thinks I shouldn't go,' she finished.

'Do they have any source of income at all?' he said.

'I don't know what happened to Guy's business. He seemed so prosperous. But Edgar is going to offer me to be an articled clerk and after that a possible partnership. If I go to Newcastle he may not.'

Joe drank some more of his tea and then said, 'Can you stay in Durham and let your family eat grass from the back garden, while the brother-in-law you hate dies in a nasty way and your father gets worse?'

Lucy got up and walked about for five minutes or so until she could try to say something reasonable.

'I don't hate Guy,' she said.

'You loathe him,' Joe said softly.

'I don't want to go back there,' she said.

'Why not?'

'I just said.'

'No, you didn't. You've never explained what you were doing here and every time I've tried to talk to you about it you've sort of curled away.' He looked patiently at her. 'That day in Gateshead you hated being there because your parents' house was across the river. You never say anything about them or about why you left.'

'It's none of anybody else's business,' she said.

'No, of course it isn't, but you're making it my business,' Joe said. 'Do you hate him because he took your sister from you?'

She stared at him.

'Would that be a reason to hate anybody?'

'It might if you had been very close and were no longer.'

'If that had been all.' She hadn't realized she was gritting her teeth. She wanted to tell Joe what had happened, but she couldn't get the words out. Somehow she could not trust him because he was a man and he would fail to understand so she just kept still until he broke the silence.

'Why don't you go and then if things get too bad you can come back here?'

'Edgar says he won't keep my job for me.'

'Doesn't it ever occur to you that Edgar likes you, that he wants you there for more than because he thinks you'll make a good solicitor?'

She looked up, her threatening tears forgotten.

'Don't be silly,' she said.

'Why is that silly?' Joe was giving her such a straight look that she blushed.

'Because I'm not—' She couldn't go on. 'I don't want to go back there,' she managed, and then she cried.

Joe got up and went to her and put an arm around her, which made her cry more.

'You don't have to stay, just see how you can help. Then you can come back. It's only Newcastle, it isn't the far ends of the earth. Edgar's not going to give your job away. He'd have to employ another solicitor for the work you do. Give him a chance and give your family a chance, eh? With a bit of luck Guy will die tomorrow and he'll have left your sister a fortune – and you can come back to Durham.'

She thumped him and Joe moved away.

Lucy didn't want to tell Edgar that she was going back to Newcastle, but it had to be done. She stood in his office while Edgar wandered around like a farmer at a country fair.

He heard her story and then he stopped his meandering and said, 'I'm sorry to hear you say it.'

Edgar put his hands deep into his pockets and then took them back out.

'I understand that you feel you must go, but you must also understand that I need somebody to fill your role. I can't keep it open for you if you aren't here, and you won't become a solicitor without it.'

Lucy was shaking.

'They're all the family I have.'

He shot her a quick look, almost affectionate, and she remembered what Joe had said.

'Are they? What about Emily and me? What about the

Misses Slaters and Joe Hardy and your other . . .' Edgar smiled here, indulging her, '. . . adopted family, the Formbys?'

She wanted to cry then because he was making her face almost impossible choices.

Lucy left his office, but when she tried to get out of the front door she was so blinded by tears that she couldn't find the doorknob. Silently she called Edgar names, but it was only because she would have burst into tears if she didn't.

She hated telling the Misses Slaters that she was leaving; they looked so distressed.

'You have lots to do,' Lucy said lamely, as though that had any significance here.

'We do, now that the typewriting classes are going so well, like a proper business. And we have at least learned the elements of cooking through you, dear Lucy, and the concerts are a joy – but we don't want you to leave. You are the nearest to a daughter that we will ever have and we will miss you so much.'

'You have Mr Hardy and Mrs Formby and Tilda and Clay and—'

Lucy went to the Formby house to say goodbye, but she also went to the shop and hugged Tilda before she left. Over and over each of them said the same things and she wished she were the kind of person who could let her family shoulder the burdens which were none of her doing. But in the end she was not.

TWENTY-FIVE

Gemma answered the door. Lucy had thought when she came home that they might embrace, but all Gemma did was hold open the door. Lucy had an impression of herself as a budgerigar, going willingly into its cage because it couldn't think what else might save it. She almost heard the clanging of the cage door behind her.

Inside she could smell medication – the stink of hygiene, bleach and pills together – and, the desperate longing which women had to help men survive. It was like a hospital. She felt sorry for the house.

She did not know where to go. She had thought that Gemma and Guy had a house of their own, but it seemed that this was not so. Gemma moved in front of her and led the way into the kitchen. There her mother was busy as Lucy remembered her, at the table, kneading bread which she had always done when things were difficult. She didn't look up. Neither did her father who sat over the fire.

Gemma said awkwardly, 'Lucy's here, Mother.'

'Aye, I can see.'

Lucy wished that she had been courageous and could have challenged her mother, but she didn't even want to. Her father seemed unaware of her presence. She turned away in time to see two very small children behind her in the hall. Gemma had evidently left them to answer the door.

'This is your nephew, Lionel, and your niece, Phyllis. They're twins.'

Oh God, Lucy thought, what dreadful names. She had not met many small children and dismissed them as boring. They seemed so tiny and needy. She found out that night that they didn't seem to sleep, that they cried all the time. She was astonished at how much attention they had to have.

Gemma sent her up to see Guy then. She remembered it as her parents' bedroom. The bed was all she saw, Guy a shrivelled thing beneath the covers. His breathing was shallow and each breath seemed hard.

'He wasn't like this until the last few days,' Gemma said. 'He was fine earlier.' But her tone was uncertain.

Lucy sat down beside him on a chair near the bed and wished everything different. She could not keep from her mind the day that her father had dismissed her from his house because he believed a man rather than his daughter. She was also convinced that beneath the pain, Guy was somehow still laughing at her. He had bettered her, his eyes told her. She had not thought she could hate a dying man, but it seemed that she was capable of anything. Although the church might call her names for it she felt as though she needed that hate to get her through, so when his gaze held hers she looked straight back at him until he glanced away.

'You should come and have something to eat,' Gemma said. When she refused her sister said, 'You must or Mother will be offended.'

Lucy wanted to laugh, as though it mattered, but it seemed it did, even to her. She went downstairs.

The dining room was empty but for their mother and father. Her father did not seem to be eating.

When she came in he said, 'Who are you?'

Lucy stared at him. Her father's eyes were sunk in his head; he was nothing like the man who had dismissed her from his house. He was not her father, he was a stranger, and she was a stranger to him because he didn't know her. His limbs looked wasted, yet he had been so tall, so strong, the most important person in her life. She would have wept had there been anywhere to escape to and indulge her feelings.

The dinner was frugal, but Lucy couldn't eat. Her worst nightmare had become real. She saw now that she had been working so hard at Edgar's practice not just for herself. She had wanted to show her father what a good person she was, how she wanted to help people as he had wanted to, that he could not judge her by what another man had done to her. Now that was impossible.

Her mother did not acknowledge her. The meal had already been served so she did not have to look at Lucy or speak.

The small amount of food on Lucy's plate was like a mountain. Her throat filled and she could not take a bite. She managed one and the meal was cold.

'I'd like to go up to my room now,' was all she could say.

'That isn't yours any more,' Gemma said. 'The children need a bedroom and mother can't always sleep when father is there.'

Lucy couldn't understand why but she brought the luggage she had with her and Gemma took her up two flights of stairs. She could not help comparing the tiny airless attic room, filled only with a single bed, chair and washstand, with the lovely room she had at Joe's tower. She missed it and after that she missed him, and the Misses Slaters, and even the cats. She wanted to go home, for Durham was her home now, though she had not known until this second.

She longed for Joe's common sense and for his presence; she wanted to run back to him. She wondered if he was walking Frederick by the river right now, as he did every night. He said it helped him to think about the problems on the car, because they were huge and he didn't know how to solve them. She wondered if the Misses Slaters were managing with their cooking and whether they had reverted to sandwiches. She thought of Tilda in the shop and Mrs Formby managing her children and she wanted to be there so badly. She had made this life for herself. She felt as if it were all over.

She tried to think rationally about the situation, but all she could think was that Joe had said the right things and that Edgar had been unkind – but then what else could he say? He was trying to run a business and she did not know whether she would ever be able to go back to Durham. What future did she have either here or there? Somehow she must make money.

It was logical and right to be here, but she swore to herself that she would not become involved with people she had learned to despise. She had learned to hate them because it was the only way she could survive, considering the way they had treated her.

She remembered things which Edgar had said; they came back to her to her when she tried to sleep.

'How are they to live when your brother-in-law is dead? What about your father's business? He is a successful solicitor, after all.'

She didn't answer.

'Does Guy have any money – does he have anything to leave?'

'I haven't asked.'

'Perhaps you should,' Edgar had said.

The second evening when they were having a meal she said to Gemma, 'Does Guy have anything to leave you?'

Gemma glared at her for indelicacy and then got up and ran from the table. Their mother went on eating and didn't look up.

'Does Father have anything?'

Her father had sat back in his chair at the beginning of the meal while her mother fed him. Now he was asleep, snoring softly rather as Frederick did, and Lucy could not think of this thing as the man she had admired and adored; it seemed so cruel.

Her mother looked at her for the first time. She laughed mirthlessly and it was horrible.

'Do we look as if we do?'

'Didn't you prepare for old age?'

'We hoped we would have sons to keep us. You cannot imagine how disappointed we were when we had just two children and both were girls. I don't think your father ever forgave me for it.' Her mother stopped eating and got up, and although Lucy's meal was untouched she swept it away.

'What is wrong with him? He doesn't seem to know me.' Lucy spoke as though he were not in the room, and he didn't answer her, he didn't even look at her.

Her mother ignored her, but when Lucy was about to leave the room she said, 'You can take your father to the office tomorrow.'

When Lucy came downstairs the following day her father was all done up in a good suit.

'He's ready to go,' her mother said.

She ignored her father in the hall and went through into the kitchen.

'Why are you pretending?' Lucy said. 'He's no more use than a baby.'

Her mother drew in her breath and didn't answer and then Gemma came in.

'Take him to the office with you, please,' her sister said.

Lucy walked him to the office. He didn't object. He didn't speak. She wasn't sure whether he understood, whether he could be coherent at all. She pushed the wheelchair inside. The place was empty. She didn't know what she had expected. How long had her father been unable to go to his place of work? It was as unlike Edgar's premises as anything could be. It was dusty and neglected and there was an air about it of failure, of a business that used to be and had long since ceased to exist.

It was so different to the place Lucy had worshipped when she was younger. She went into the downstairs, down a steep and dark staircase, and found cupboards with polish and dusters. She collected coal and wood from the big shed at the back and poured water into the boiler beside the fire. Then she went around dusting and polishing the surfaces of the old and solid furniture. All it needed was a little attention.

He was awake and, although she was still convinced that he did not know her, he watched her and seemed to approve.

She washed the floors and polished the brass doorknobs. She went out and bought tea and milk and biscuits and then she went to the big office which had been her father's domain. He seemed happy to sit down there while she looked through the files and the paperwork. She took a typewriter from the desk beyond, where presumably his secretary had sat, and she began to type letters to all the clients whose addresses she had. There were many of them, but she could see herself making progress. Meanwhile he would sit there, saying nothing while she worked.

She stated that her father had been unwell but was much better. He would soon take up the business again and she was helping him. She said that the office was open and staffed during weekdays from nine until six and then she posted the letters and wondered what to do. It had taken her three days.

During that time she had to feed her father and take him to the toilet often. She was disgusted and embarrassed at first but then she realized it was just like teaching a child and he responded. She had never thought she might have to do such things, but if it gave him a little more dignity in his life she could forget having to help him.

She found a small café just across the road from the offices and she took him there. She deliberately pushed his wheelchair as near to the window as it would get and watched recognition flicker in his eyes.

'Would you like something to eat, Father?'

He looked at her. She had his attention now.

'Scones,' he said.

That made her smile. He had always liked the scones her mother baked.

'I don't think these will measure up, but you never know.'

They did.

'They're better than Mother's. Lighter.'

He managed a smile. She cut up his scone into small pieces and fed it to him covered in butter and strawberry jam.

She could see the office front door from where she sat in the window so that if anyone did come she would be there immediately.

Since her father seemed to like the place they began to make a habit of going there every day. Sometimes he would manage a scone by himself though he made a lot of crumbs.

Lucy dressed in her smart black costumes and her neat shoes. She tamed her hair with grips so that it was back from her face and away from her neck. When she looked at herself in the mirror, she thought, yes, I could do business with this woman.

On the third afternoon a man turned up and she greeted him gladly. He said to her father that he was glad to see him so much better and from somewhere her father found the normality to say, 'How good to see you,' and then he sat back and let Lucy conduct the business.

The man was not prosperous, but neither did he look poor. She waited and after a short time he told her what he needed. It was trivial. He wanted to alter his will because his children were not respectful of him. It made Lucy want to laugh, but she sat there gravely nodding and talking when he allowed.

As he was about to leave he looked at her with gratitude and said, 'Thank you, Miss Charlton, you were grand.' Then he went to her father and said, 'You have a sound lass there.'

And her father said, clearly for once, 'Yes, indeed.'

She saw the man out and then she went back inside.

'You do know who I am then,' she said to her father.

He smiled sunnily at her. 'You're my heir – you always have been.'

He did not remember what she had done, he thought he was still a man and she was still a child. She was pleasing him and he liked it as he had done so long ago.

'I'm glad you came back to us.'

It meant the whole world to her.

TWENTY-SIX

Joe got a note from Edgar's office to ask if he would come and see Edgar at half past five that Thursday. Joe was miserable. He missed Lucy so much. He didn't tell anybody or act as if he was – with two old ladies, three cats and a spaniel to sort out and a job to go to he didn't have much time for self-pity – but in the night he just wished Lucy were above, sleeping soundly within the safety of his tower house. He missed her more than he had missed anybody except Angela, and by now that was saying something.

Edgar didn't keep him waiting. He murmured a greeting and then Joe sat down.

'I've had a communication to tell me that Mr George Firbank has died and you are a beneficiary of his will,' Edgar said.

'I knew he had died,' Joe said – he couldn't help it – 'but I don't want anything.'

He was trying not to think about Mr Firbank too much but he missed the trips up to Gateshead. Lucy was right, the only thing that mattered was the time they had spent together, and he was aware of each minute. And strangely, there was some hope. If Mr Firbank's will included him then

285

it meant that he and Priscilla Lee both mattered to the old man.

'There's nothing I can do about whether you want it. Mr Firbank's will is his business and his only. Whatever he wants you to have you get it,' Edgar said.

'All right,' Joe sighed, 'I suppose as long as it isn't a tower house I can cope.'

Edgar went on looking at him in a comical sort of way so that stupidly they both laughed together for the first time.

'Oh hell,' Joe said.

It was obvious that Edgar was trying to keep his face sober.

'Where is it?' Joe said.

'I gather it's somewhere up at the top end of Weardale, which apparently was Mr Firbank's first home. Very cold and windy up there.'

'Oh lovely,' Joe said.

'You can't have it of course, not immediately, but I imagine you could go up there and see it if you were in the least bit curious. I can't imagine it being worth anything at all.'

'A liability then?'

'I would think so,' Edgar said. 'His son is his executor. If you get in touch with him I'm sure he'll be able to give you all the details.'

'Will you come with me?'

Joe had come to Newcastle to talk to Lucy. She was thrilled to see him and had to stop herself from asking all sorts of things – about the Misses Slaters and Frederick and the cats.

'You can't do anything until probate is through,' she said.

Joe had known she would say this, but he was losing patience. He had gone to the house in Sandhill where she had said her parents lived and her mother had been almost rude, but had redirected him. Now he was in this place where it was obvious she was doing very little business and by the smell of things her father was in a bad way.

'I just want to go and see,' Joe said.

'I can't just drop things like that, Joe, I have too much to do.'

'All I want is two or three hours.'

'Why don't you understand?'

Joe lost patience and walked out.

He was yards down the pavement when she caught up with him, clasping his arm so hard that he stopped.

'I'm sorry,' she said.

'No, I shouldn't have come. I can easily go on my own.'

'But I'd like to come with you.' Her face had lit up and she was smiling. 'I would dearly like to get away from here, even for half a day.'

Joe didn't answer at first. He looked away from her as though there were something fascinating going on in the street.

'I miss you,' he said.

No man had ever said such a thing to her and Lucy didn't know whether to be pleased or embarrassed.

'I miss you too,' she said, 'and most of all I miss Frederick.'

'He isn't as fat as he was,' Joe said.

Without thinking about it, Lucy put her arms around Joe and kissed him on the cheek. He didn't respond – he was obviously astounded, she thought, at least that was what she imagined. He stood stock-still as though he didn't know what to do.

'Yes, of course I'll come with you,' she said.

Angus Firbank's house had not changed. Lucy had expected it to have done somehow; she couldn't think why. He was no more welcoming than the last time they had seen him, though he took them through into the same enormous sitting room. Lucy looked for mice but could see nothing, although she wasn't so sure of the dusty corners. She moved a little closer to Joe.

'It's about your father's house. It has been left to me, because Priscilla Lee is dead,' Joe said.

'It's nothing to do with me.' Angus Firbank waved a hand like a magician about to conjure rabbits. 'It's a ruin in the middle of nowhere. Why would I want it?'

'It's very old and your family presumably has been here a long time. Did your ancestors live there?' Lucy guessed.

'A very long time ago, well before I was born. It's been there for centuries. We moved on to better houses, better lives, more money. I don't know what you're doing here. I've nothing to tell you. The will is quite straightforward, and since you are Priscilla Lee's sole heir you get it. Lucky you.'

'He left you nothing?' Lucy couldn't help asking.

Angus Firbank shook his head.

'He gave me everything of worth while he was still here. It was a very long time ago, when he suspected he was going to lose his mind. It's better so.'

'And you repaid him by putting him in that place?' Lucy said.

He glared at her.

'He didn't know where he was. He didn't know who he was and I couldn't manage any more. And besides, he liked being near rivers. When he was a child he spent his summers in Durham and that was not so very different, I think. I did the best that I could.'

'Why did he leave the place to Priscilla Lee?' Joe said. He hadn't spoken in a while, Lucy thought.

'Yes, well . . .' Mr Firbank shifted his stance, '. . . he had something to do with her.'

'What was that?' Joe said.

Angus Firbank shifted even further and walked about the room, finally coming to rest by the window though it was heavily curtained against the evening light.

'This is a very small place, you know, and little towns like this have traditions which go back a very long way. If you step outside of what is the norm you are no longer accepted. Nothing changes here. Cissie Lee's family ran things, they owned almost everything. They made a lot of money from lead and also from silver.'

'Silver?' Lucy said.

'It's a by-product of lead. It has to come in quantity and be worth extracting before it makes money, but there was quite a lot of it hereabouts. With the lead mining, well, up to the beginning of this century, it made some people rich. Like other industries here in the north-east, it wasn't the local people who benefited. They got by with small farms and they worked in lead mining. There were a lot of problems about how much they were paid and it was never enough for the awful work they did.

'Many of them went to other countries to do better – Canada and Australia. Eventually Cissie's family went to London because they had done so well and they were proud. They went there to rise in society. They could pretend they had never seen a place as poor as this. They never came back; they didn't even keep in touch. I don't know what rich people in London do, waste it presumably on big houses and gewgaws for their women. There's nothing left here now beyond the farming and the kind of respectability which people value when it's all they have.

'My father didn't even leave his family respectability. He lodged, when he was a young man, with the Lees. He had no family of his own, his parents had died and he had nothing, so he stayed with them. Cissie was his child. It was never spoken of. I think it was one reason they moved away. They had a great deal of money by then, but she was the only child and it had taken another man to father her.'

There was a long silence during which Lucy didn't want to look at Joe.

'Why didn't you tell us this before?' Joe said.

'It was none of your damned business. How could it be?'

'If it's none of my damned business then why did she leave the place to me?'

'I like to distance myself from such dreadful doings. A long time ago I decided I wanted nothing more to do with him or her.'

'How did you know about it?' Joe said.

'Everybody knew. She looked like him. It was unmistakable. That was why they moved away – they had had everything but a child – so when she was little they left and changed their names. He didn't see her again until she came back here, but she had known him long enough when she was a child to call him Uncle George.'

'So, she came back to her father?' Lucy said.

'She didn't know, as far as I'm aware, but he gave her the tower house for her home.'

'Did your mother know?'

'Silence is golden in places like this and if she did know she was wise enough not to speak of it.'

Joe got to his feet. 'Is the house far?'

'On the old road over the moor where the lead used to be carried from here to Allendale. The family wintered up here and summered by the river in Durham.'

Up on the moors it was bitterly cold. Joe banged the car across the ruts and the up and down and twisting turns of the road. When they got to what looked like some kind of settlement Joe stopped the car. Lucy tried to get out and the wind blew her almost off her feet. But she could see the winter tower. It was tall and grey and impressive, typical of the border lands. A fortress more than a home. It was bigger than the tower house in Durham and it stood there so proudly as though it were shielding people from harm, from marauders, those who would steal cattle and women. This was somewhere to be safe.

The animals lived downstairs, the people upstairs, and once you had drawn in the ladder nobody could get up there. The problem was you had no idea how long they would stay and they had no idea of your food and water supplies. It was a guessing game, a matter of survival and cunning.

The building had probably been there for seven hundred years, Lucy thought, as so many buildings like this had been. A lot of the dwellings around here were as old as Durham cathedral.

Joe wandered around like somebody at the fair on the town moor.

The windows were gone, the door was ajar and inside as she followed him every vestige of comfort was absent. The wind howled past her ears.

'Cosy,' Joe said. She came to him and slipped her hand through his arm in reassurance, but she liked it as she looked up and thought how safe it might have been when marauders came screaming across the land. She could almost hear and see and taste the fear of the times, the short lives most people lived. Things hadn't changed so very much, but the house was still here. The stones stood.

They went back outside. The moors had begun to take over the garden, but the stone walls held. Beside the house there were a few tall straggly trees and a tiny church which had lost its roof and most of its walls. What was left inside were two small rooms, their fireplaces, their outer walls and a lot of weeds which had grown thickly once the roof had gone. Beyond was a small graveyard. There were half a dozen graves. Several of the stones had fallen over but it was not difficult to make out the writing on one of the graves. It was the only one which was fairly new. It read: '*Margaret (Priscilla) Hardy. At rest.*'

Joe stood motionless for a long time while the wind howled around them. Lucy waited. She was glad now that she had gone with him; she wouldn't have wanted him to find his mother's grave by himself.

'All the time she was right here. Mr Firbank must have had her buried here and his son must have known, surely,' Joe said.

'He didn't remember – and his son was too ashamed of what his father had done.'

'This means that George Firbank was my grandfather.'

'Yes, and you got to meet him and spend time with him,' Lucy said.

'I wish I had known my mother better.' He choked then, and for the first time Lucy took a man willingly into her arms and held him there while Joe buried his face against her neck.

Joe tried not to hate his father, but his mind was full of the lies he had told him and the impact they had had on everything. They motored back to Newcastle and he went on to Durham and worked as though he would die without it. But the more he tried not to think about it the worse it got and he began to dream about his father every night. The dream was different every time. His father was moving away or out of sight, his mother came back and his father shouted at her and told her that he didn't want her and she cried. Joe could see her clearly perhaps for the first time. He thought her image had been lost to him and so he wished for more – it felt like all that he had left of a family.

How could his father have treated his mother so badly that she ran away? She and Angela had so much in common to his mind and he could not think of himself as being like his father, inadequate and stupid. The next letter was worse.

Dear Joe,

It had not occurred to me that I was the kind of person who found addiction pleasing. I didn't used to drink so very much. Now I cannot get beyond twelve noon before thinking of what brandy tastes like and therefore am inclined to while away the afternoons by the fire if the weather is cold, which it nearly always is. Also it means that I fall asleep and therefore am not fit company for anyone.

Was I ever?

I like to plan the day with nobody in it, just me and the dogs and the hours in front. Then I get bored by six and start drinking again, wishing that I would not, that I had made plans, that there were even people I wanted to see. But since you have gone and Angela has no time for me I get no further forward. When I wake up I wish I had not drunk so much but by lunchtime the need is gnawing away at me again. Often I succumb and am grateful for the sight of the sweet dark liquid which accompanies my food.

Lately though I have needed food less and brandy more, so that I cannot make any social arrangements for fear I will go to sleep or slur my words and offend people. Do they care? I think it pleases them to see others losing control. They never do. The stiff upper lip was invented for our class. Never a murmur, never a cry. Sometimes in the night I bury my face in the pillow and shout myself senseless.

In the evenings the brandy alters time. It can be seven o'clock one minute and then only half past seven and quarter of a

*bottle is missing. I pretend to myself that it isn't so because I
cannot bear the awful person I have become.*

*I have started going to different areas when I do go out in
the evenings. I dress to suit so that nobody will wonder who
I am and I can go most places in the darkness and join other
poor souls who sit at bars and little tables. I like being there
with them. They are men who have come back from the war
and had nothing. They are shabby and unkempt and often
cannot afford to drink. I pay for them so that I may have the
company and once I am there a great fuggy happiness per-
vades my whole being so that I forget my life. I even forget
about you and some days that is all that I want.*

In the weeks that followed, Joe made several visits to his
mother's grave. He liked the idea of her being there, although
he could not imagine it. Why had she left him the house?
He comforted himself. She had wanted him to be there for
some reason, or for more than one reason. She had brought
him to Durham, brought him to her after she died. Had
she thought there was a connection between life and death
which could be made between them? If so, it had been made,
and that pleased him. Somehow he could feel her there, feel
that she had loved him, that she had not lightly abandoned
him. She had loved him because of or in spite of his father.

He stood over her grave in a bitterly cold east wind which
cut into his face and howled around his body. He thought
she had loved it here, not just on the riverside but up on the
tops where the curlews cried and the lapwings dipped and
swooped to stop people from getting anywhere near their
nests. It was as wild as she had been, and he loved it and he

loved her for leaving him the tower houses and her heritage. This was it, twofold, this has been who she was as well as a big part of who he was. He was glad. He had gained so much from coming north even though he hadn't wanted to. This was her legacy.

He wished that she had revealed herself to him while she was still alive. He didn't understand why she had not – he had longed for his mother almost every day since he had been a small child – but he thought that perhaps she reasoned she would have destroyed the relationship he had with his father, and that had been as precious to him as his love for Angela. His mother had withheld herself from him, but not her love. He felt that here now. His mother had loved him very much.

He knew now that he had adored his father. The loss grieved him every day and yet it had not been an easy thing. He thought that where love was there was always discord and a desperate longing to be with that person when they were a parent and yet away. Instinct guided the young. His father knew that he had not been the future. For his father the loss of Angela had been the breaking point. She was meant to be his future and if she had been his father would have been happy to see them together. That was why he had longed for Joe to be at home, perhaps even to know that there might be a grandchild.

Joe's loss had broken his father, Joe could see that now, but his father too was somehow to blame because his mother had fled. She must have been too afraid all those years of what might happen if she had made herself known to the world.

He didn't know what to do with this place. Nobody would buy it, a ruin in the middle of nowhere, but the more time he spent there the less he wanted to sell it anyway. He didn't need to get rid of this place – he would have tried to hold it to him whatever had happened. He felt that his mother wanted him there in the tower houses, wanted him to make them home, to use them perhaps, to spend winters in Durham and summers here. He wasn't going to, her dream was not his, but he was glad that she had cared, that she had hoped and planned and made room for him even when she died.

He would have it repaired, he thought, and then he would make it available for people who wanted to be there, in the high hills in Weardale. It could be a stopping-over place for people, a rest for when they were weary. He could make it sound and put in order some kind of reception so that they could have a bed and facilities for making food. He imagined them sitting out on the hillside when the weather was fine or inside and snug amidst lots of blankets when it was bad. Then if people wanted to venture that high on foot they were welcome to stay, like the Young Men's Christian Association. He liked the idea. He thought his mother would have liked it too.

TWENTY-SEVEN

Gemma looked smaller each day. She had shrunk. She had never been tall, but now she was thin and white and so bowed that she looked like a much older person. She seemed to forget who Lucy was and she cried and told her what a good man Guy had been, how precious he was, how he had fathered her children and how she adored him. What would she do without him?

Lucy held her and comforted her and said nothing as she felt sure thousands of women had done before. The man that Gemma knew was nothing like the man Lucy knew and there was no point in making things worse. Her sister was grieving, she was losing the man she had made her life with.

They took turns in sitting with him. The doctor did not want to give him too much painkiller because he was not sure how much more Guy would need.

Then the day came when Guy's pain overcame the drugs and he cried out.

Lucy begged the doctor for more. Stupidly she could not bear to see her enemy in pain. It was not how she had ever wanted to win. Doctor Mackie looked confused and defensive, and shot her a straight glance.

'I can't do any more,' he said. 'I'm sorry.'

'You must be able to.'

'I will not take responsibility for killing him.'

'He's dying, for God's sake.'

'That is not the point. I am doing what I can.'

'Well then, can we have more of the pills you are giving him?'

'You cannot,' he said, and left.

Guy stirred, called out. She went back to the bed. He looked at her from pain-filled eyes.

'Gemma?'

'No, it's Lucy. Gemma is resting.'

He stared at her and then he closed his eyes. It hurt so much, she thought. His lips twisted, his face contorted and he lay back and squirmed against the bed. His head turned here and there upon the pillow.

'What are you doing here?' he said.

'I live here, you know I do.'

'No, I mean what are you doing by my bed?'

'The family is asleep. You have worn them out with your failure as a man, as a husband and as a father. There is nothing left, Guy, and a great deal of that is because of you.'

He closed his eyes for a few seconds; she wasn't sure whether that was because of the pain or while he considered what she had said.

'I thought I was marrying into money.'

Lucy gave a short laugh. 'That just shows how stupid you were.'

He managed a ghastly smile.

'Doesn't it?' he said. 'I never loved her – my parents made me do it.'

'What an excuse!'

'No, they did,' he said, then stopped as his face contorted again. 'I wanted to marry the vicar's daughter, but her father wouldn't have it and neither would mine. Isn't that pathetic? She was tall and skinny and plain like you. I loved her.'

'My heart is breaking for you,' Lucy said.

'I'm sorry,' he said.

'No, you aren't.'

'No,' Guy said, 'I didn't like you or your sister. I thought you were a couple of jumped-up little bitches.'

'Why?'

He didn't speak, and she wanted to shake him, but the sweat stood out on his face. While she watched in the lamplight it grew slicker and slicker as he fought the pain. Lucy had always thought she would want to watch him terrorised like this, for he had done something indescribably awful to her, but she wished she could have helped. Despite the doctor saying he could have no more painkillers, she went and got water and shook out twice as many tablets as was his dose. He was so hot, so uncomfortable, and gritting his teeth, as men did.

Finally she said to him, 'Oh, go on, yell – let it out if it helps,' but he didn't. The tears spilled down his face and the time ran on and on until she heard the nearest church clock striking the quarter, the half-hour, the three-quarters. He writhed and moaned softly and she wished she could give him more painkillers, but in that time what she had given him eventually took hold. He lay back on the pillows and she could see that the pain had eased. She had never thought she would be glad to see him out of pain, but she was.

If she had been his wife she would have given him every pill there was, she thought, even if it killed him; she couldn't watch anybody in such agony. In the end he went quiet and he slept and then she began to cry. She kept her hands up to her face so that no one would hear the noise. It was not for him that she cried, it was for everyone who died in such a way. Nobody deserved such a death, no matter what he had done. Where was God when people were in indescribable pain?

She cried herself to sleep. She was sitting on the floor by the bed, leaning forward, the blankets of some comfort to her face and arms. She dreamed that she was back in Durham with Joe and the Misses Slaters and she and Joe were walking Frederick by the river and everything was all right. And then she came to consciousness and her back was aching and her neck too because she had been in that leaning position for some time.

She pushed back and sat up. Light was filtering through the curtains and she couldn't move too far because Guy had hold of her hand. She hadn't known that, she thought – she would never have given him her hand to hold – but there it was, his fingers entwined with hers. They had slept like that. She should have been repulsed, but she remembered within seconds that he was not the man he had been, he was a creature in pain, and she had done what she could to help him.

His hand was cold and rigid somehow, and she moved

away carefully. He was so still. It was early morning. She heard the church clock striking five. The house was silent, nothing moved; her sister must be sleeping peacefully for once after all these weeks. Even the children who usually awoke around this time did not, so Lucy listened to the house and to her parents who made no noise. She sat back in her chair, closed her eyes and, since he was still sleeping because of all the drugs she had given him, she allowed herself to doze.

It was another hour before she realized that Guy was dead.

TWENTY-EIGHT

'When are you coming back to Durham?'

Edgar and Emily had turned up for Guy's funeral. So had Joe and the Misses Slaters and Mrs Formby. The Misses Slaters seemed to know so many people, but of course the church was like that. They introduced people to Joe and Mrs Formby, and though Lucy wanted to have her turn to talk to them, she didn't seem able to get that far.

'I don't know.' Lucy had been hoping he would not ask, but she knew that it was fair. She had been gone for almost three months. But she did not see how she could leave, and though she wanted to go back to Durham she saw her mother comforting Gemma at the graveside and her father wrapped in blankets a little way off, bowed in his wheelchair. He had slept through most of the funeral service. Privately Lucy did not think that he would live much longer; after that she didn't know what she would do.

'I can't leave here, Edgar. Look at how it is – who could go away and leave this?'

Edgar said nothing for a short while, and they stood about in the cemetery while the rain dripped through the dark trees.

'I haven't taken on anybody but a secretary, I really have to find somebody to help me. A partner, I think, somebody to buy his way in, to put money into the business.'

Lucy couldn't speak: it had been the only thing she wanted, to become a solicitor to help people.

'I'm sorry, Lucy. I wish I could keep things as they were, but the work has become too much and I can see how much you are needed here. The trouble is that when your father can no longer go to the office you won't be able to keep his practice open. It isn't legal. What will you do then?'

'He's not that bad.' She had lain awake the last two nights worrying about the future, about herself and her sister and her mother and the two children. She didn't know what would happen.

Edgar looked narrowly at her.

'The only thing to do is to come back to Durham and work. Then you will manage to make enough money to send to your family.'

'You're missing the point,' she said, 'they need me here.'

'You can't be in two places at once, and the way that you are trying to run your father's practice is ethically unsound, and you know it. It's no way for a junior solicitor to behave.'

Lucy pressed her lips together so that she would not argue with him.

'You can have a career that way and that way only,' he continued. 'You must come back and very soon. You aren't helping you, your family or my practice, and it can't go on. You're putting everything in jeopardy because you want to play nursemaid here, or sister and daughter. It isn't like that, and they should be aware of it as well as you.'

She knew that Edgar was right and she should be in Durham. Otherwise what future would any of them have? She could go back to the tower house and spend time with Joe. She wanted to be there in Durham so very much, but she doubted her mother could cope with her father, Gemma and the two children – and she should not have to at her age. There was also the knowledge that her father did know her for just a little time each day. Sometimes he said Lucy's name, occasionally he reached for her hand. She could not leave him now. How could she live with herself if he died and she was not there? And what about her mother and Gemma when that happened, for it could not be far off?

For the first few days after they buried Guy, Gemma would not come downstairs. Hour after hour she sat in his room; she didn't eat, she didn't want to see her children, she didn't want to move from there. Lucy stood it for two weeks, though she couldn't work the long hours that she intended because she could not leave her mother to do everything else.

The truth was that people were beginning to come back to the practice. She knew that her father made a very good smokescreen, he had been so much admired, and there was a trickle of work. If she could be there most of the time she could make things much better, though she was reminded every day that Edgar had said it was unethical. She knew that. She just hoped other people didn't or wouldn't think so. They assumed that she was qualified and she had to let them go on thinking it so that she could earn some money, even though it was not enough to keep them.

That evening she went upstairs to her sister.

'You're going to have to go out and get a job,' Lucy said.

Gemma was lying on the bed, and she sat up and looked at her sister as if she were somebody from another planet.

'I have two small children, a sick father, my husband has just died—'

'Yes, well, you aren't being any help and I can't manage. If you don't go out and get a job we can't afford to eat properly any more. It can't go on. They are looking for an assistant in the dress shop where you bought your wedding dress. I suggest you get washed, dressed and sorted out in the morning because if you don't your children will soon be living on bread and jam.'

Gemma stared at her. The tears were heavy in her eyes.

'Why don't you just leave me alone?' she said.

'Why don't you take your responsibilities?' Lucy slammed out of the room, though she called herself names for being so harsh with her sister.

Gemma stayed upstairs. Lucy didn't sleep. Half a dozen times she wanted to go to her sister, imagining that even from the attic she could hear Gemma pacing the floor.

Lucy was only glad when daylight finally broke. It had been such a long night. She had always imagined that as you got older and understood more, as life speeded up, you would get used to the darkness and it would seem less. Somehow it never did.

She was first downstairs for once and she lit the stove and set the kettle to boil and put out the butter and jam and bread. Then her mother appeared, bleary-eyed, as though she'd had no sleep either. The children tumbled after her.

Lucy made tea for her mother and saw to the children and asked after her father.

'He's still asleep, thank God,' her mother said.

Gemma did not appear, and Lucy, not wanting to seem impatient, washed and dressed the children and then she went upstairs. Her father had his own room now and he was awake. The room smelled of old age and worse.

She took hot water and soap and towels and she washed him from head to foot. He didn't object, he didn't even seem aware of Lucy but stared past her as though he could see a better land in the distance. She dressed him and then she helped him downstairs. Her mother flashed her a look of gratitude and fed him small sips of tea, and bread and jam cut into small squares such as you would for a child.

Lucy had made sure that her appointments did not start until mid-morning so she could see Gemma up and dressed. She even picked the dress for her – simple and old but expensive – and she put up her sister's hair.

Gemma went downstairs for the first time in two weeks. The children fell on her, crying, but Lucy made them be quiet with a few harsh words while she put toast and tea in front of her sister.

'Eat it,' she said, 'I don't want you passing out on me.'

'You bitch,' her sister said, regardless of the children. Before her mother objected, Lucy put up one hand and there was silence.

Gemma crammed the toast into her mouth, had two slurps of tea and then Lucy got her coat.

'It isn't black.'

It certainly wasn't, it was mid-blue, the first one Lucy had come to. Gemma objected, but she put it on and it made her look almost human, Lucy thought.

She walked her outside into the clean air and Gemma stood still for a few moments as though she had forgotten what being outside was like. Then she began to sob. Lucy gave her a handkerchief.

'I cannot work in a shop.'

'You damned well can.'

'I married respectably.'

'What happened to it?'

'The glassworks failed and it took everything with it. Guy and I moved back in with my parents when we lost our house.'

'What about his family?'

'They didn't want to know. They came to his funeral though; they drank my tea and ate my cake. Most of them didn't even speak to me, didn't send a card or offer to help in any way.' She sniffed hard. 'Do I look dreadful?'

Lucy smiled just a little.

'You always look beautiful,' she said. 'I don't know how you do it.' Somehow it was true. However deep her grief, her sister looked ethereal and as the sunshine poured onto the street it lit her hair as though it had taken fire. It was as if the fresh air had revived her as a drink of fresh cool water revived flowers, and Lucy could not help reflecting that Gemma had looked a lot better since her sister had come home. Lucy thought it was the relief of not having to cope alone.

Gemma wiped her face determinedly and they set off to walk into town. John Dobson's cream stone buildings were lovely in the light, Lucy thought, and when she and Gemma reached Northumberland Street and saw the dress shop and all the white dresses in the windows Gemma stopped.

'I cannot go in there.'

'I've made us an appointment. We are due in five minutes.'

Lucy was unsure whether it was an advantage that the woman in the shop seemed to remember her and her beautiful sister, but then she thought it was not often two red-haired women walked in like that together. She told the woman of Gemma's fate; she thought it might help and she didn't care that she was using the situation to her advantage. The woman smiled and told Gemma how sorry she was for her loss.

'Do you know what I was thinking?' Mrs Morpeth, the manageress, said. 'That you would make a beautiful mannequin for when we have our bridal evenings.'

Gemma protested that she was too old, she had two children, but Mrs Morpeth shook her head.

'I remember very well how you looked in a white dress, and every girl who comes into the shop will want to look like you. You'll be such an asset, my dear.'

'I don't know anything about selling,' Gemma said.

'That can be taught. What you look like is the first thing that people will see. You will model our dresses and every girl will crave a dress from our shop.'

Lucy went off to work feeling she had accomplished something.

But when she got back late in the day and went into the kitchen her mother, stirring broth on the stove, said, 'I never thought one of my lasses would be brought so low that she had to go and work in a shop. How will I ever hold up my head?'

'We'll eat,' Lucy said.

'You're a very hard woman,' her mother said.

'I can't think where I learned it,' Lucy said. She went into the other room and read stories to the children. Gemma was back upstairs.

'I hate it,' she said when Lucy walked in.

'You don't have to like it. You just have to like getting paid.'

'You're enjoying this, aren't you?' Gemma got up from the bed and glared at her. 'You never liked me. You were jealous. You wanted Guy and when he didn't want you, you told lies. He told me all about it.'

'It was nothing like that.'

'You went outside in your nightwear and offered yourself to my fiancé the night before our wedding.'

'I did nothing of the sort. I don't understand how you can still believe it.'

'Of course you did,' Gemma said.

'You'd better come and have something to eat. You have work to do tomorrow and your children are wondering where you are,' was all Lucy said as she went back down the stairs.

Twenty-nine

Clay had realized that Joe and Mr Palmer worked at the garage together, and any spare half hour he had he would go over. He was a good help and always looked so dismayed when he had to leave. One Friday evening, when Mr Palmer had gone home for his tea, Joe was explaining to Clay about the car they were building and that he had contacts in London, and somebody from the motor trade had expressed interest. Clay looked shocked.

'Does it mean you'll be going back there?'

'No, at least not at the moment, not as long as we can build cars here.'

Joe wasn't sure about this at all, but there was no point in discussing it with Clay. Mr Barrington had been working on Joe's behalf in London and seemed very excited about the whole thing. He had made contact with two top car men, one called Rogers and the other Eve, and was going to set up meetings with these people on Joe's behalf.

Joe liked Clay. He liked the loyalty which the boy had to his family, but Clay also showed signs of becoming a useful person to have around the garage. He was deft and could piece things together, he didn't have to be told anything twice. He would have stayed there all night if necessary and Joe could see that Clay was going to worry now about whether he might be left alone to cope with his mother, and Tilda and the children. Also Clay's father had been a disaster – much worse, Joe admitted to himself now, than his own father had ever been. Joe had had love and companionship, a decent upbringing and wide experience. All Clay had were memories of his father drunk and violent and treating his mother and his sister badly. He needed to see how other men went on, Joe thought.

'Why don't I ask Mr Palmer if you can come here and work properly, instead of at the store?' Joe said.

Clay's whole countenance shone like the midday sun.

'Could I really?' he said. 'I want to do summat new and cars are new and I like them. Every time I see one I think it's really exciting like, isn't it? I don't need much pay, honest, I just can't stand that shop any more. I don't want to let me mam down, after all she's put up with, but . . . do you think Mr Palmer might take me on?'

'I think he might,' Joe said.

One night – it was a particularly cold Thursday and for once Joe was glad to go home from the garage and sit with Frederick by the fire – he was awoken by an idea of an intrusion of some type. He lay awake for ages and listened. He told himself to stay in bed, but since it was so unexpected he made his way softly downstairs.

There in front of him in the hall a lovely young woman was cradling a baby. The image was fully formed and he knew that it was nothing to do with the house. He had the feeling that if it had been, Frederick and the cats would have woken up – but they didn't. He even went into the kitchen and there they were all curled up together in front of the dead fire, breathing evenly, content, tired out from their day. Frederick's legs shook a bit. Perhaps he thought he was chasing rabbits or just that he was out with Joe, as he was most days, walking around the river, stopping at every lovely smell, not caring what the weather was.

Joe didn't know what to make of it. It couldn't be anything to do with his mother and himself as he had first thought. The only other thing was that Angela was still alive and that she had their child.

Even after the image had faded he could remember the little golden-haired girl who looked just like Angela. He couldn't be wrong, she must still be alive, he decided, and while that was wonderful it was also frustrating. Why had she not been in touch? Why at least had she not contacted her brother? What was she doing? Had the child survived? Was she poor? Joe couldn't stop the various images from coming into his mind and yet he had no idea what to do. He opened a letter of his father's, hoping perhaps to find some clue, or some comfort.

Angela comes to see me more these days. She seems worried about me and I have to say that I becoming very tired of myself hiding from everyone and everything, drinking myself stupid every day. I am so glad that you are to be married. She is a lovely girl, so light, so kind and so much in love with you. I want to live to see you together, to be at your wedding. She is the girl for you. Nothing is too much for her. She is everything your mother was not, she's suitable. I don't say any of this detrimentally, but just that there is no wildness about Angela, no wilfulness. She loves to please. She has been raised in London ways. She reads to me sometimes in the afternoons. If it is fine we sit in the garden. She comes every day now however busy she is, as though I was an invalid and I am nothing of the kind. I live for your return.

This made Joe feel worse. He wanted to throw it away, yet it was all he had left of his father, so he folded it up and put it back into the pile from where it had come.

THIRTY

Edgar told himself that he missed Lucy in the office because she had been there for some time, but he knew also that she worked well and now he had everything to do himself. Having threatened her with a partner he found himself unable to do anything of the kind. The house was as empty as the business premises and yet somehow he and Emily kept falling over each other in an awkward kind of way.

They had a new maid, Liza Goodall, Norah's cousin; she used to help Norah so she was used to them. She cooked and cleaned and changed the beds and saw that the washing and ironing was sent out and she would leave sandwiches if he was late at the office.

Emily was becoming more and more quiet. When Edgar was at home he kept going through into the drawing room and finding her staring from the window. She got up at one point and dashed across as though she could see someone in the distance.

'Who is it?' he asked.

'Nobody,' she said.

Day after day, no matter what time he got back, she was sitting over the fire with a book in her lap or when it was fine she would lie in a hammock in the garden. She was always reading the same book. He suspected it was the same page.

One day when he found her asleep on a rug in the garden beneath the apple tree he sat down beside her and she opened her eyes.

'Is this how you're going to live the rest of your life?'

'Do let me know if there's something you'd like me to do,' she said.

'You're thirty.'

'One.'

'What?'

'I'm thirty-one. And you are almost thirty-seven. Can you see us in twenty years' time still living like this?'

Edgar didn't like to hear it and he squirmed a little.

'Like those dreadful old brothers and sisters who look so alike nobody can tell which is which.'

'Didn't you ever think you would marry?' Emily said.

'Yes, once or twice, but it never came to anything.'

'Who were they?'

'Well, one of them was the Lord Lieutenant's daughter and she was so far up the social ladder I didn't even merit a glance. The other was a French girl during the war.'

'You never told me,' Emily sat up.

'No, well, her husband came home.'

Emily lay down again and then she said suddenly, 'Have you thought about Lucy?'

He laughed just a little.

'I have. Isn't that silly?'

'Why is it silly?'

'Because I think of it in practical terms.'

'She is very practical,' Emily said, and then she added, 'I miss her.'

They didn't talk about it any further, but the first day that he was free Edgar went up to Newcastle. Summer was over and a cool wind rippled the Tyne. He wanted to catch Lucy in her office before she went home. She looked up impatiently when he came in. Her father was there, but he was asleep in his wheelchair, his head having fallen to one side.

'Are you almost finished?' he asked her.

'Completely finished,' she said.

'What about if we go back to your house and tell your mother I'm taking you out to dinner?'

Lucy looked surprised then and so relieved.

'Oh, that would be lovely,' she said, and that was what they did.

She pushed her father home and Edgar walked beside her. All he wanted was to have her to himself. He was taken with the house. It had not occurred to him that her home would be such a lovely place, with its curving black-and-white walls and big fires. Mrs Charlton greeted him with obvious pleasure and Lucy went up to get changed. Mrs Charlton gave Edgar tea.

Mr Charlton slobbered tea all down his front even when Mrs Charlton helped him. Edgar ignored it. The children were very boisterous and made a lot of noise. Shortly afterwards to his guilty relief they were taken to bed. He knew nothing of children and the elder daughter, Gemma, was not there; she was staying late at work. Her mother was so proud of her for going out to work so soon after her husband had died.

She had started work for one shop, Mrs Charlton said, and now was asked for everywhere. Mrs Morpeth, the manageress, was making a lot of money because she was hiring Gemma to other shops to display the lovely dresses and she'd had to find someone new to do the selling. Gemma even showed clothes in the big shops for top customers and it paid very well.

Mrs Charlton flushed and said, 'I know it isn't polite to talk about money, but these things are very pressing for us at present, Mr Bainbridge. You must excuse my manners.'

Edgar said he understood completely and that she was a lucky woman to have two such daughters. She said that she had not known it until now. Lucy was doing such a good job and Edgar said that he was sure she was, she always did a good job with everything she turned her hand to. Mrs Charlton's face glowed with pleasure.

Edgar took Lucy to a good hotel and was pleased that he had done so. Soft music was provided and the place was not so exclusive that it was dull, it was better than that – it was so expensive that it was almost relaxed.

They had gin and tonic and then they sat down at a table by the window and they had fish – fresh that morning, the waiter assured him – and then pork with juniper berries. Lucy didn't want dessert, but they had Northumbrian cheese and small glasses of port, and afterwards they sat in the lounge and had coffee.

It was only then that he said to her, 'Emily is unhappy. I wish I knew what was wrong. I thought that perhaps she might have confided in you.'

Lucy concentrated on her coffee and said nothing.

'She has no ambition and although the two don't have to be exclusive I thought marriage would be good for her. She always liked children. I cannot accept her as an old maid – that's for women who are plain and penniless and have to go out to work.'

'That's awful,' Lucy said, stung. 'Don't you know how bad that sounds?'

He looked blankly at her as though he had never thought to associate her with such people, but she felt for every woman who was outcast because of such ridiculous ideas.

'She ought to marry. It's what respectable middle-class women do. I don't know what she wants, do you?'

Lucy floundered and didn't look at him.

'Marriage isn't for everyone,' was the best she could manage.

'It is for women; it's what God intended them for.'

Lucy eyed him. 'Are we sinking as low as biology?' she said.

'I don't understand you.'

'Yes, you do. Women's reproductive organs are larger than their brains, is that it? And those who don't marry are wanting in some respect. Or could it be that nobody asked them because, what is it . . . they were not tiny and beautiful and submissive?'

Edgar blushed dark scarlet and it was not all embarrassment. He hid his anger well she thought, but he needed to.

'What else would they do?' he said.

Lucy was furious.

'If they were allowed they would do everything men do and earn income and have choices.'

'Children cannot be a choice,' Edgar said.

'If men had to have children they would have adapted such things to suit them by now,' Lucy said, 'but they don't want it—'

'That isn't true,' he got up but then stopped and the colour faded from his face. 'Some men want children as dearly as women do. In the end how else can we go forward but through our children?' And he looked at her so earnestly and said, 'I wish things were different. I wish you were still in Durham.'

Lucy was so surprised at his vehemence that she got up, took his hands in her own and smiled at him.

'You're a good man really,' she said.

Edgar laughed just a little while he recovered himself.

'Nothing of the kind,' he said.

He walked her home and when they got to her door he kissed her, very swiftly and rather sweetly on the mouth. She was so astonished she didn't react until it was too late. He hadn't intended doing it, she could see.

'I'm sorry,' he said, head down so that he wouldn't have to look at her, 'I thought I would get through the evening without being so obvious.'

She smiled.

'No, it . . . it was me,' she said.

The following day he took her out for lunch. The day was fine and they found a tiny café which had a garden. They sat out there under the trees and drank tea, and while they watched the river go by Edgar said to her, 'I've been thinking about your situation here with the business and I wondered if you would let me help.'

'There's no reason why you should,' she said.

'There are several excellent reasons,' he said. 'I need you in my business and I thought that if we got together businesswise you could become a solicitor. In time you would become a partner.'

Lucy stared at him. It was exactly what Joe had said to her.

'Oh,' she said, 'that would be wonderful.'

'Which brings me to the second part of what I want to say. Will you marry me?'

She almost let out a little cry.

'Oh my goodness,' she said, softly.

'Will you?'

She wanted to say that she would, that it was what she had wanted for so long, but she couldn't.

'I . . . I will have to think about it,' she said.

'Well, think about it now,' he said.

But she couldn't. There was a part of her which panicked, that made her want to get up and run, and yet she remembered what her ambition had been. If she married Edgar she could become a solicitor, even a partner; she could have everything she had wanted since being a little girl and finally she would make her father and her family proud of her.

Then she thought of Joe and how alike they were and how much he made her laugh and that he was unconventional, but then Joe had not asked her to marry him and he would ask no one to marry him because he was still in love with the girl who bore him a child.

Lucy thought he always would be and that eventually he would find her and they would be married. If she did not marry Edgar she would be left alone and she would struggle always, having to work for her mother and her sister and her sister's children with no offer of marriage then, nothing to help, nobody to get her through the days or nights, and she was afraid of the abyss she looked into.

Edgar was offering her a great deal. She would never have another offer like this. If she married him she freed her family, and she wanted so much to do the right thing. If she could have considered just herself then it might have been different, but no, she decided, it would not have been. She wanted to be a solicitor and this was the only way she would manage it.

He was waiting. He sat there across the table and she urged herself on so that in the end she nodded and agreed to marry him.

'Emily will be so pleased,' Edgar said.

Lucy was not hiding in her office, at least she told herself that she was not that week. The work was beginning to come in now. She was not making a good or a reasonable living, but it was a start, what with Gemma's wage and hers, and they could eat and keep the children warm. Her mother had stopped complaining now that Lucy was marrying Edgar. As far as her mother was concerned all their problems had been solved.

Lucy had given up taking her father to work. He no longer

spoke or recognized anybody. He slept for much of the time and she had stopped the pretence that he was useful there. She didn't need to pretend any more, but she did feel that she still needed the man he had been – she needed his approval and the presence of him as he had been when she was young and he had loved and admired her.

The pleasure in her life included being here in the office, and she was ashamed that she only hoped she and Edgar were married before her father died. Edgar did say to her when he came to visit that it would be so much easier when she lived in Durham and they could give up her father's practice.

Lucy thought she had misheard.

'Give it up?'

'Why yes, of course. We cannot run two offices unless we employ somebody else and I didn't think that was what you wanted. Bainbridge and Featherstone won't run to any more work and we cannot be forever going back and forth between the two. It isn't practical.'

Lucy had not understood up to that point that it would not be Bainbridge, Featherstone and Charlton, but of course it would not be because she would have Edgar's name.

'And you still aren't qualified, so when your father dies you will have to give up this practice. It isn't legal for you to do anything else.'

'But I've built up the client list again. I've worked so hard.'

'I know you have and it's laudable, but the circumstances have changed entirely. We'll both be living in Durham.'

'What about Gemma and the children and my mother?'

Edgar misunderstood, she could see.

323

'Do you want them to come and live with us?' he said, as though he didn't relish the idea.

Lucy stared at him.

'They cannot leave the Tyne,' she said and she knew how ridiculous it sounded, as if Edgar were asking them to go to Australia, but she was determined.

'That house has been in our family for hundreds of years. If I marry you I want to be a solicitor and run the Newcastle office myself and I want my family to be able to stay in our house because I will have to look after them financially. It couldn't possibly be any other way.'

She looked hard at him.

'And I want my name on the door, it's my family name, my father and my grandfather ran their business from it, it's very important to me, Edgar.'

He didn't speak for a few moments, and Lucy held her breath, worrying, but then he smiled and said,

'Very well, if that's how it has to be,' but she knew he wasn't happy about it.

When Edgar had gone back to Durham and told his sister what he had done he was surprised at her reaction.

She had looked wearily at him and said, 'I'm so very pleased for you – it was what you needed.'

That wasn't what Edgar wanted her to say. He sat over the fire when it was late and drank rather a lot of port, which he didn't usually do, as he tried to ponder over his sister. He wasn't happy, even now.

He thought of how it would be when Lucy was mistress of the house. Everything would be so brisk – no dust, no dirt, no late meals. All would be in order. Would he be in order? He had the feeling that he might be. But the more he thought about it the more he was happy. He would be coming home to a good dinner, in fact they both would, and if they had to stay in Newcastle some nights they could stay at a fancy hotel and drink wine and . . . He tried not to think any further than that.

'When is the engagement to be?' Emily asked, and he realized that he had not thought about it.

So that week he went back to Newcastle and told Lucy that he must buy her the most beautiful ring in the world.

He took her to an exclusive jeweller's on the corner of Northumberland Street and there they looked at diamonds.

'I think rubies would be better,' he said, but when Lucy faltered he added, 'You are so beautiful, and you may have diamonds if you choose, but any of the other stones would suit you, in particular rubies and emeralds. Choose what you most like.'

She chose an oval ruby with tiny diamonds around it and he said that it was perfect for her. They went back to her house and told her mother and Gemma and the twins that they were now formally betrothed and he would be taking the family out to eat.

They went out to tea because of the children and after that he took Lucy out by herself. He had never been so happy.

It was late when Lucy got home and everyone was in bed. She didn't remember that having happened and then she saw a shadow in the corner. Her mother had waited up for her and she suddenly felt such a warm affection for this woman who had always seemed to put Gemma first.

Her mother came to her and kissed her and said, 'I'm so pleased that you are happy, and what a lovely man he is.'

'Yes, he's very nice.'

'Nice? He's everything that you might want. To think that your father and I thought you would never marry and here you are with your cleverness and with a man like that who wants you.'

Lucy went upstairs into the attic to bed, but she could hear soft crying from below. She worried that it might be the children at first, but it wasn't. It was Gemma, sobbing into her pillow as though she did not want to disturb the children.

Lucy listened and waited for her sister to cry herself to sleep, but she didn't. Even though the sobs grew very faint she knew that Gemma was awake.

She tiptoed down the stairs and hovered in the doorway of the room where she and Gemma had slept together as children. She said her sister's name ever so softly. Gemma stilled and then said, in a throaty voice, 'Come in.'

Lucy did so. There was a big candle still lit. She closed the door and sat down on the bed. Gemma didn't look at her, but neither did she turn away as Lucy had thought she might.

'I'm so sorry about what happened to Guy,' Lucy said. 'To have your husband die so young of such an awful thing must be really hard for you.'

'It isn't that.'

'What is it then?'

Her sister swallowed the rest of the sobs and then she moved away. Lucy could see by the candlelight her sister's wan face and the tear streaks down it. She put her arms around herself for comfort.

'You were right,' she said, looking at nothing, 'I should never have married him. Our wedding night was . . . I think it was just like what you experienced with him. It was so awful and I couldn't go home and I couldn't tell anybody. On the second night I tried to get away and he hit me, he pushed me down, and I was so sore and he didn't care. He wouldn't let me go out anywhere, he wouldn't let me see my friends, he didn't want anybody anywhere near me.

'The house we lived in, he didn't own it, he had lied to me. Nobody had told me and the business he said was his family's, the glassworks, was in a very bad way. They went bankrupt.

His parents were just glad that he had married a respectable woman; they needed to get rid of him. They thought I would change him but nobody could have changed him, Lucy, and I wished I could have told you but I was so ashamed of myself. I couldn't tell my parents that I had been wrong and after what had happened to you . . .' She broke down and sobbed audibly. 'I was glad that he was so ill. I was even glad when he died because he put me through hell. Nobody knew and I wanted to come to Durham and talk to you and tell you and say how awful I felt about what I'd done to you and how you'd suffered, but I couldn't admit it to myself. Now I've got his children and nothing else.'

'You couldn't have known any of these things,' Lucy said. She tried to bring logic and sense to the situation, but she couldn't see it clearly, she was so near. She had put up with the loss of her family because of Guy. Her sister cried and she wished she could do the same.

Gemma lay down, exhausted. 'I think I've only told you now that you have Edgar and a chance to be happy,' she said. 'I can't tell you how pleased I am for you and how much I like him. He's a sensible, decent man and God knows there can't be many of them about.'

She went to sleep then. Lucy lay down with her and thought about how in some ways it had not altered, that they were there for one another as they had been as children, and she felt comforted.

THIRTY-ONE

Lucy didn't want to go back to Durham and tell the Formbys and the Misses Slaters and Joe that she was going to get married. She didn't know why she was finding it hard; she wanted to marry Edgar and she knew they would be glad for her, but it would alter their friendship. It had not occurred to her that she would never come back to the tower house to live and that jarred on her.

It was late one Saturday afternoon when she finally went back to Durham.

She went to the Formbys' house first. Tilda, who was just home from the shop, hugged her shyly. Clay hung back but she thought it was probably his age. The younger children she gave sweets to and they were happy with these. Mrs Formby hugged her and kissed her, and when she announced that she and Mr Bainbridge were getting married, Mrs Formby cried and said how proud she was. Lucy and Tilda and Mrs Formby talked about what they would wear and Mrs Formby said she would make a lovely bride.

Mrs Formby made some tea and she told Clay that he must wear a suit. He went pale. Then Lucy said that she expected him to give her away, at which Clay looked at her in a very studied way and said, 'Yes, very likely, Miss Lucy. Don't take the mick,' and they all laughed.

It was therefore much later than she had intended when she reached the tower house. It was for once a mild evening. She thought she heard voices in the garden and when she got there the two sisters were sitting under the trees, enjoying the evening light.

She told them her news and they were so overjoyed that she would be coming back to live in Durham and that they would see her so much more often (she assured them they would). They were delighted that she would be married in the cathedral in Newcastle. When there was finally a lull in conversation she asked after Joe and was told that he rarely came home until it was late, he was so busy.

When she left she debated whether to just go back to Newcastle, but she didn't think it was polite not to tell Joe so she walked to the garage. Lights were on and the big doors at the front of the building were open. There was no noise, nothing seemed to be happening and when she got inside the lights were centred in the small office. Joe sat with a lamp close by him, working at the table. In front of him were all kinds of sketches. He didn't hear her come in. She thought he looked thinner than he had been; perhaps the Misses Slaters were back to feeding him sandwiches.

Frederick lay under the desk. He was asleep. Mr Palmer was not there. She said Joe's name softly, and he started and then he saw her. He smiled and got up and came over. He kissed her on the cheek and asked her how she was. She asked what was he doing and he said that they were ready to sell the car to the public, but that they had to find out how to do this and that he would be going to London to try to get the big car men interested.

'We've let the stove go out so I can't offer you tea,' he said.

Lucy said she'd had several cups of tea since she had got here at about four and couldn't face any more. He asked after her family and she said all the right things.

Then she said, 'I've got something to tell you. I'm getting married.'

Joe looked at her as though he didn't believe her, and then he did and drew back.

She said, 'I'm marrying Edgar.'

'Oh,' he said and his face went blank.

She sat back. 'I want you to give me away.'

Joe looked at her, his eyes dark.

Lucy felt awful. She wanted to run.

'I can't expect Clay to,' she said, trying to lighten the moment, 'though I did ask him. You will do it?'

'Me?' he said, as though he thought she had meant some-body else.

'Please.'

Joe's breathing seemed to be all over the place.

'Edgar?' he said finally.

Lucy didn't know what to say. She wished Joe would leave this alone. It had nothing to do with him and yet she had known his reaction would not be positive.

'Why?' Joe said, staring so straight at her that she didn't know where to look.

'What you do mean "why"?'

'Just that. You and Edgar?'

'We have a great deal in common.'

'You have nothing in common.'

'Don't be silly, Joe, we have the two practices. I'm going to be a solicitor and I'll be a partner and we'll run the whole thing.'

'That isn't what I meant. You don't think the same way. If you marry Edgar you'll always feel that he is the main person in the marriage, that's what you'll do. You won't have the independence you need. How on earth will you cope with the kind of life which Edgar is offering you?'

Lucy regarded him levelly and could feel her temper rising. She had not let loose her temper against her father and she had not done it with Guy, but she was in great danger of letting go of all control here and he didn't seem aware of it.

'I have thought about that but there are other things to consider.'

'Like keeping your mother and Gemma and the twins.'

'That's one thing.'

'It's not a good enough reason to marry anyone.'

'I don't think you're in any position to give people marital advice, considering what you did.'

She wished she hadn't said it the moment it was out. Joe glanced away, towards the table where he had been working as though he wished he were still there.

He walked back and threw down the pencil he was still holding, then he picked it up again and snapped it in half. He threw down both halves onto the paper where he had been working on figures and then turned to her.

'I understand why you're doing it. Your father is ill and you have nothing; I can see that. Edgar has money and influence and position and a beautiful house and he's respected and . . . If it's money you need—'

'That isn't why I'm marrying him.' Lucy was stung by the inference. 'You really think I would marry for such a reason? That is a horrible thing to say to me, Joe. You made such a complete mess of it that Angela ran away rather than face the future with you.'

'You love Edgar?'

'Is that so impossible to believe?'

'You'll make the poor bastard's life hell,' Joe said.

'I will what?'

'You'll drive him completely up the bloody wall.'

Lucy, who had never hit anybody in her life, cracked Joe so hard over the face that he banged into the table behind him in shock.

'You are still in love with a woman who hasn't even bothered to get in touch with you,' she accused him.

'She could be dead.'

'Rubbish. You would have heard something by now if she had been, it's just that you don't like to face the truth. She doesn't want you, Joe, because of what you did to her. No man of any worth would do such a thing. She has disappeared so completely that you can't find her, no matter how many times you go to London or write to her brother or think you are searching for her. You aren't searching any more because in your heart you know she doesn't want you.'

Lucy walked out of the room.

THIRTY-TWO

Emily came downstairs. Edgar was in the office at home. He liked that room; it had been his office for a good many years now, though he thought of how he would have better things to do in the evenings when he was married. He was so pleased about it that he could not help but smile even though he was alone.

He was not by himself for long. His sister put her head round the door.

'Can I talk to you?' she said.

Every night they sat and talked about what it would be like when he married Lucy and how happy they would be and how there might be children and she would be Aunt Emily, which she said she had always hoped to be. In the anticipation of such joys he encouraged her into the room and she sat down and he sat with her. He was so pleased with it all that he smiled at her as the evening half-light poured into the room.

'I know you're planning your marriage—'

'Yes, we thought December. It's a nice idea to be married at Christmas – it could even snow.'

'That's lovely, I'm so glad. The thing is . . .' She stopped and then she began again, 'I might go away – after the wedding of course.'

Edgar was stunned.

'I don't know what you mean. I thought you were happy for me.'

'I'm very happy for you, but you must know that it's quite difficult to be in a house with a newly married couple.'

'You mean you might like to go on holiday. I can see that. Where were you thinking of going?'

'London. You wouldn't mind though?'

'Well, no, but when would you really be coming back? A month, six weeks?'

'I wouldn't ever be coming back,' Emily said. 'Joe has said he will help me—'

Edgar shot up from his chair.

'God damn Joe Hardy – everything I try to do he gets in the bloody way.'

Emily stared at him.

'He knows people in London—'

'Of course he does. He's so bloody important.'

There Edgar stopped. He knew how he sounded, that he was ranting about Joe, but Joe was irritating and thought about things so differently.

'His world in London is full of rich idle people. Are those really the kind of people you want to spend your time with?'

'I just want to get away.'

'From me? From people who know you and care for you? What could you get in London that you can't have here?'

'Freer thinking for one thing,' she said, and then regretted it because Edgar looked perplexed. 'It's a big place. London is a melting-pot. It doesn't matter who you are or what you do, you can find somewhere to fit.'

'You don't fit here?'

'Did you think I did?'

Edgar stood for a few moments and then slowly shook his head.

'No,' he said, 'no, I didn't, and it worries me. I don't want you to go.'

'You're going to be married. Lucy will run the house—'

'Is that the point – you're leaving because of my marriage?'

'It will change everything. You won't need me here.'

'I'll always need you here,' Edgar said with a slight tremor in his voice.

'That's lovely to know, but I need more than I have. I can't live out my life being . . . being decorative and just your sister, sidelined in society because I don't marry. I have no place here. Joe has offered to help, that's all.'

'I don't understand you,' Edgar said, 'I really don't.'

Edgar asked Lucy to talk to her. Lucy didn't agree. They were in her office and here she was in charge.

'If she's made up her mind—'

'She's only done it since I said we were going to get married.'

'It would be strange if she wanted to stay with us when our lives are moving forward so very quickly and hers apparently not at all. Don't you think?'

She said this softly. Edgar frowned.

'You mean she might have particular plans?'

'Possibly. Why shouldn't she? Durham is a very small city and if she goes to a big one she might find it better.'

'She doesn't know anybody there.'

'I'm sure Joe knows plenty of people.'

'I'm sure he does too, I'm just not sure they're the kind of people I want my sister to be associating with.'

'She's a woman, Edgar, not a child. Let her choose for herself.' Lucy looked hard at him.

'I worry,' he said.

'The way that you feel about it isn't the point,' Lucy said. 'It will be good for her to go somewhere else, at least for a while.'

It had not seemed to Emily that things could be any harder than they were. For a long time she had been able to lie in the garden, learn not to think and let the days drift on, but then she wanted to see Joe, to talk to him, just for the change. She tried to put off the day but the longer she left it the more the desire increased. In the end she walked into town.

It was strange to be there. It was a Saturday and there were lots of visitors, strangers, people gawping at the buildings, walking by the river, crowding into the shops and little cafés, and then she saw Norah, though Norah didn't see her. She was walking up Silver Street bank with her husband. They were holding hands.

Emily thought she could discern a slight bump beneath the dress Norah wore. Emily ducked into a shop before they could see her and she stood for a long time afterwards, showing apparent interest in a dull blue dress so that the assistant came across and asked whether she would like to try it on. Emily smiled and shook her head and moved on to other dresses. The assistant followed her, desperate for a sale, so Emily came outside and hurried down the bank and across the bridge and ran for home.

After that she knew that her instincts had been right and she had to get away. It was as though every avenue had closed for her. Edgar and Lucy's marriage would make her single-ness seem even worse. Lucy would understand, she knew, but she could not tell Edgar. She thought how he would have Lucy – he would not want his sister there like an unhappy shadow. She did not think she could stand their happiness; it would be like slowly starving to death while the people around you were given the best food and lots of it.

Emily went to see Joe and he'd said that he did have friends in London. He would be happy to write to them so that they would help her when she got there.

'I will probably be going to London myself. There are two car companies there and I want to get them interested in the car that Mr Palmer and I are working on. I could go with you and introduce you to the people I'm staying with. I'm sure they would help you.'

That was such a relief that it made Emily feel better about it all. She told him that she had seen Norah and she thought that Norah was going to have her first child.

'I can't bear it,' she said. 'I think she's happy,' and she started to laugh and then stopped. 'She was right, there was not going to be a future for us. She went to bed with a man.'

'Ugh,' Joe said, which made her laugh more.

'It's all right for you,' she said.

'It isn't all right for me. I don't have anybody to go to bed with. I'm just stricken you don't want me, you're so mind-numbingly beautiful.'

'Stop making me laugh. It isn't funny.'

'It bloody well isn't,' Joe said.

Mr Palmer worried about the new car and was fiddling about with it, Joe thought. He wanted to get on, and to both of them this was a huge thing, but Mr Palmer was finding it difficult to cross the line and announce to the world that they had done something new.

Joe stood it for a while until Mr Barrington had got him interviews with men from two big car companies. Mr Palmer didn't want to go with him. He said he felt that his background might impede him and more to the point his apparent lack of confidence would get in the way. But Joe could tell that it was worse than reluctance. He had got cold feet about the whole project. He was afraid of succeeding or perhaps that his ideas would be so badly rejected that he would never be able to think of building a car again. It had become so precious.

Mr Palmer had been so sure all the way along, not doubting himself even when Joe did, but now he hesitated and wouldn't agree that it was finished, that the plans and drawings were enough so that Joe could take them to London and show them to these men, to try to persuade at least one of them to come north with him to see the car itself.

'I think we should just wait,' Mr Palmer said that morning when they were drinking tea and sitting about over the stove. It was a cold wet day and a howling gale burst under the doors of the building.

'For what?'

Mr Palmer didn't answer that at first but when he did he looked clearly at Joe. 'What if it doesn't work?'

'It will work – it's just a question of finding somebody who really knows about these things to get us in, to help us.'

'I'm a miner from nowhere,' Mr Palmer said.

'Miners from nowhere have always done new things, have gone forward, have always been there. Think of what the miners did during the war, how hard they tried, how much they achieved and what you did. Do you think this is going to more difficult than fighting a war?'

He won from Mr Palmer a slight smile and a shake of the head.

'You have nothing to lose,' Joe said.

'I'm quite happy with my life here. I feel comfortable and so does my missus. I don't think she wants jewellery and a big house and stuff like that.'

Joe laughed. Mr Palmer really believed that they were going to get rich. He was the first man Joe had met who didn't think it would be so good. In that, he thought, Mr Palmer showed rare wisdom. So many men had thought everything could be bought.

'It probably isn't going to work out anyway,' Joe said, 'it's a very dubious thing to do. There are lots of people out there in little garages like ours all over the country doing the same thing, so at the moment it doesn't matter. We don't have to make any decisions. All we are doing is trying to contact the people who can help and if it doesn't work out it doesn't matter.'

Mr Palmer looked at him.

'It does matter though,' he said.

He was right too – it was a race to find the first car of its kind: small, neat, utilitarian. The men who did it would make a fortune, but they all had different ideas, Joe suspected, and people were drawn to big shiny motor cars which moved quickly. This was an entirely different machine. He thought in the future the two would come together but for now the car's usefulness would be its main selling point. Also he was thinking not as the Americans had done, that a man would buy a car and keep it for life, but that there was a whole industry ready for turnover, for cars to last so many years and then be superseded by something just that little bit better, with that little piece more interesting. Different gadgets and different paint jobs until the look of it became so involved with the machine that the two were as one. That was when everybody would want a car and he was determined that it would be his.

When Mr Palmer went out to look at some car over in Hexham, Mrs Palmer, who usually went with him on these occasions, came to the office.

'Don't take any heed of him, lad,' she said. 'He wants this just as much as you do but he's scared.'

'He's come through a lot worse.'

'You an' all,' she said, 'but sometimes that can be off-putting. You get yourself to London and do what's necessary and I'll take care of him.'

'He didn't think you wanted it.'

'He's right, I don't care about things like that, but I know him. He's going to be very disappointed if this doesn't come off so do what you can,' she said.

*

341

Joe asked Emily to go to London with him. They would stay with Toddy. He wasn't sure whether it was a wise decision but he offered and Emily accepted. Joe was going there for three days, two nights – perhaps that would be enough for her. London was so unlike Durham and she hadn't been there since she was a small child, she'd told him, so perhaps the way that it was faster and less caring and less intimate would make her wish she was back in Durham with Edgar and the prospect of his and Lucy's marriage.

Joe had tried not to think too much about it since Lucy had smacked his face and run away. She was right, he acknowledged now, and that was hard. As time went on he thought more and more that the girl he loved so very vitally was no longer there for him in any way. He just wished he could have had some news of her which would be positive. Anything would do rather than worrying about whether she was dead or admitting that if she were alive she would have got in contact long before now. Why wouldn't she?

The visit to London was nothing like he had thought it might be. That was typical. He was trying to convey to Emily that London was vast and impersonal, whereas in reality it was a set of villages, just like most other big cities.

Mr Barrington was having a party the first night they got there and it was champagne and canapés all the way, the attendees people in politics and the arts. There was no sign of his brood of children who had no doubt been taken early to bed by a nanny and the atmosphere in his large and gorgeous house was so jolly. Emily looked about her admiringly.

Mr Barrington was the perfect host and introduced Emily to a great many people. Joe felt guilty for Edgar but he could not help being glad that Emily was laughing and talking, though she always did that, but he thought he saw something in her eyes to show that she was having the evening she wanted to have above all others.

The following day Joe had two meetings with men from different car companies, Mr Rogers and Mr Eve. Both had their headquarters in north London and their factories in less expensive parts of the area, in the south. Both were eager to see what his design was like and both showed him around their factories. He was very impressed with them; they were so organized and their factories made Joe's heart beat a little faster. He could see his car there, his and Mr Palmer's design being built, but he had to be shrewd too and not give them everything or they might run off with his ideas and build their own.

Mr Eve also had a factory in Birmingham and he said he was going up there soon and that he would come to Durham and look in on Joe and Mr Palmer. Joe was slightly concerned that the premises they had were tiny and he had nothing with which to impress Mr Eve except the car itself. He worried that he had overestimated their invention.

He worried more when Mr Rogers said that he had been approached by several other people, all with what he said was the same idea. He told him that the car he decided to back would have to be exactly the right one so he could promise Joe nothing.

Joe offered to put Mr Eve up at the County Hotel while he was in Durham but Mr Eve smiled and said he would be happy at Joe's house. Joe thought that Mr Eve was keen to see how he lived. Considering it was a tower house with two old ladies, three cats and a dog, he didn't think Mr Eve was going to like it, but he couldn't think of any way in which to refuse without being rude when Mr Eve showed such enthusiasm.

That evening he took Emily to have dinner with the Toddingtons and everyone was very polite.

'Miss Bainbridge is hoping to spend some time in London and get to know people here. I thought that you might be kind enough to help her since she knows no one and you know just about everyone.'

'My only brother is marrying and I want to do something for myself,' Emily said.

'So you should, my dear.' Lady Toddington nodded approvingly at Emily. Joe could see that the older woman had taken to the younger one and he didn't have to work at this any longer.

They went home the following day but Emily's expression was so much lighter. She said that Lady Toddington had invited her to stay with them, and had said she would launch her into London society if that was what she wanted. Joe interpreted this liberally since Lady Toddington knew a great many people in the arts world who would accept Emily for who she really was. It would no doubt set her off on the route she wanted to follow. Joe was grateful to Lady Toddington because he knew how the family felt about him, but no doubt she could see what a lovely woman Emily was.

Thirty-three

Edgar watched the children. They were sitting on the grass in the backyard and Gemma was hanging out the washing. He was surprised that she looked so well when her husband had been dead for such a short time. She was singing. He knew that she liked her work now that she had got used to it, that she was pleased to bring money into the house. There was something about her which was a puzzle. He wasn't sure quite what it was. He had said to Lucy that he thought they should wait a year out of respect for Guy's death, but she said that the chances were that her father would die then and they would feel obliged to wait for another year. Didn't he think they should do something joyful?

It seemed a reasonable answer and the truth was that he didn't want to wait. He was tired of sleeping by himself in a big house. He had spent a great many nights wishing that Lucy was there; he wanted her so badly, but the first time that he took her into his arms and kissed her properly she pushed against him until he let her go. He gazed at her. There was a wild look in her eyes which went in an instant, but he saw it. She said she was tired, but Edgar had been a solicitor for too long not to be concerned about what went on in people's faces. Each time he tried to put the worry from his mind it came back.

Now, seeing her sister reaching up to hang out the clothes to dry in the midday pale sunshine with a cold wind behind it, he was not sure what he felt. He had come to Newcastle on impulse; they had not said they would get together that day, but all Gemma knew was that her sister had gone out early and not said where she was going.

He thought she was probably at her father's office. She liked going there and it was not necessarily to work – she just liked being there. But that day he didn't want to pursue her. If she had gone there it was because she wanted to be alone.

He didn't mind very much. Mrs Charlton had made individual steak pies and he consumed several of these with beef tea poured over them and carrots, turnips and potatoes. The family sat at the table, the children too, and although they made a bit of a mess nobody took any notice. Since they were hungry they ate everything.

He thought they were lovely children. He hadn't known Guy at all, but the children both looked exactly like Gemma, with startling red hair and huge green eyes and creamy skins. They had blushed cheeks and dimpled hands and they talked all the time. He couldn't understand most of what they said, but it didn't really matter. He thought it was charming.

After the meal Gemma made them sit down for a while and she asked Edgar to read to them. He was rather taken with the idea, and they sat at either side of him, watching the picture book carefully and taking in every word he said so attentively. Edgar, who had never been listened to like that except professionally, enjoyed it.

Later Gemma said she was taking them to the park, so he went with them. It was a fine, bright, bitterly cold day. The twins were too little to do much except run about which took all their concentration. They had to be helped; they kept plumping down on the ground and crying from frustration when they couldn't get up or wanted help.

Edgar had never pictured himself in such a role. He began to think that when he and Lucy had children he might turn out to be reasonably good at this. A girl and a boy, twins, having to go through such a thing only once perhaps, but then some people had a dozen children – not something, he thought, which he could look at with any degree of equanimity. It would cost a fortune to bring up so many.

Lucy didn't come home, even after Mrs Charlton had asked him to stay for tea and he had thought he should go, for he didn't want to impose. But she said in what had become a jolly way that he was about to be a member of the family shortly, so there was no point in him standing on ceremony.

She too seemed reasonably happy considering how ill Mr Charlton was but she talked to her husband as though he took in every word. Mr Charlton slept a lot, so that Edgar thought Lucy must have been right and her father would not last much longer. That would be sad, but he sensed that it would also be a kind of release for this family; they had been through such a lot lately. Lucy was right about this too – there was no reason why they should not be married.

Mrs Charlton and Gemma talked a good deal about the wedding. That bored him; he wasn't interested in times and

347

cakes and flowers but he sensed that it was the thing which gave them most pleasure at the moment. He stayed for tea and was glad he had done so when his hostess delivered a huge portion of ham, two eggs and a hill of thick fat chips onto his plate. She told him to dig into the bread and butter, pouring him huge cups of tea thick with sugar and rich with milk.

He waited on into the evening. He didn't want to stay when Lucy wasn't there but somehow he didn't want to go home either. It was as though Emily had already left and even if she was there he felt as though he was counting the days. He would have given a great deal for her not to go. The house felt so empty.

'Where were you on Saturday?' Gemma asked her sister. 'Were you avoiding us? Have you told Edgar what Guy did?'

Lucy shook her head. She didn't want to look at her sister. They were alone, that was rare, and she had hoped they would not have this conversation, but somehow it had happened. They had hung out the washing in the back garden, slight and cool though the day was. It was not yet time for the midday meal and the children were with their grandmother.

She had hidden that day, she didn't quite know why, only that she could not go back to the house, that she didn't want any of the complications. So she had taken herself off and for once ignored her responsibilities. She'd been glad of it.

'Don't you think you should?'

'What if I tell him and he doesn't want me because of it?'

'I think he's too decent for that.'

Lucy had told herself the same thing over and over again, but somehow she didn't believe it. She had stayed at the office.

'But what if he isn't?' she said.

'Better now than to find out on your wedding night. You have thought about your wedding night?'

Lucy sighed.

'I try not to. At the moment every time he comes near me I jump. What if I can't do it?'

'It won't be like that.'

'How do you know? It has to be like that to some extent, doesn't it, and it is a horrible thing for a man to do to a woman. I have nightmares about it. Do you think you would ever marry again?'

'Not unless I was financially destitute,' Gemma said. 'Would you still marry Edgar if he wasn't prosperous and well respected and going to let you join the firm?'

'I've asked myself that and the answer is that I don't know, the one is so near to the other. He has a beautiful detached house with big gardens and help to do everything and he would make Father's business right even if he dies—'

'When he dies,' her sister corrected her.

Lucy could only think about the inevitability of her father's death alongside the idea that when she married Edgar the Newcastle business would go on.

'I'll be able to ensure that none of us needs ever worry about money again and whatever I went through with Guy, you went through so much more.'

'I got the twins out of it.'

'They don't look anything like him,' Lucy said. It made them both smile.

'You have to tell him about Guy,' Gemma said.

'Why?'

'Because he will know.'

'How?'

Gemma's face was like raspberries.

'Because it's different after the first time. You don't bleed, you react differently. It just is.'

'Maybe he doesn't know. If he doesn't have much experience—'

'Men of his class always know these things. They've had other women.'

'I can't believe Edgar has.'

'You should believe it because if he hasn't and you have that's even worse,' her sister said. 'He will have had. Men always do.'

Lucy stared at her.

'He isn't like that,' she said.

Gemma looked hard at her.

'You are so innocent, in spite of Guy being awful to you. They are middle-class men, they have money, they can afford prostitutes.'

'He hasn't!' Lucy declared, ready to burst into tears.

'What makes you think such a thing?' her sister said tiredly.

Lucy shook her head.

'He's too nice, too respectable.'

Gemma laughed.

'Men aren't governed by such things. All they care for is their own bodily satisfaction and if you don't tell him he will be disgusted with you when he finds out that you aren't a virgin.'

'But that's not right, not fair,' she said.

'It's right and fair for them,' Gemma said. 'But maybe . . . maybe you could pretend to be a virgin. You could simulate the first time. There must be a way.'

'How on earth could I do such a thing, Gemma? I love him.'

'I loved Guy and look what happened to us. What woman can trust her feelings? We know so little, we try to save ourselves for them with what consequences – why should any woman?'

'I can't even imagine being in the same bedroom as him,' Lucy said softly, honest at last.

'It will be all right. Just tell him,' Gemma said.

Lucy tried to choose her time to tell Edgar about Guy, but it didn't happen. She excused herself over and over, that she was busy, that he was in Durham, that it was late, that it was early, that he was at lunch. Over the next few weeks she became exhausted, trying to get right something which she felt would never be. She could not envisage a future without the man who had helped her so much.

He was always there in the background as a saviour. He would make her a solicitor and they would have a home such as few people had. They would have children, and things would go on and on through the years, fires in the winter, the garden full of daffodils and tulips and crocuses white and purple and yellow in the spring, children tripping and laughing down the paths towards the grassy places and summers where he might suggest they went to the seaside for two weeks. They would stay in a hotel which looked out at the waves and build sandcastles, and when the children were asleep they would sit on the balcony and think how good the sunshine was.

Then there would be autumn with the apple and plum trees giving up their fruit for pies and crumbles. In the winter she could see a huge tree in the hall that would greet visitors when they arrived, and she and Edgar would have parties, for themselves and their friends and the children's friends. She would carry on her father's practice in Newcastle and she would be able to help Gemma and the children and her mother.

She woke up happy in the mornings whether she was at the office in Newcastle or was going to Durham, though Edgar mostly managed Durham and she mostly managed Newcastle. She could have skipped to work, sung. She could see the strain go from her mother's face and from Gemma's.

Thirty-four

Joe found Lucy at her father's office. She was so busy that she didn't look up and when she did she found herself bridling.

'What do you want?' she said. 'I'm very busy – I don't have time for you.'

'I thought you wanted me to give you away.'

'Strangely enough, Joe, I changed my mind after you were so awful to me about my marriage. I'm not even going to send you an invitation.' She turned her back to him and pretended she needed something out of the filing cabinet.

'You weren't very nice to me either.'

'I didn't feel like being very nice to me after you told me that I wasn't good enough for Edgar.'

'I didn't do anything of the kind.'

'You said, I remember it distinctly, that I would make his life hell. You were very rude.'

'You hit me.'

'I wish I had done it twice.'

Lucy threw down the file she had extracted from the cabinet. She had no idea what it was.

'I don't know how you dare come here at all, wanting something.'

353

'I don't want anything.'

'You are a liar, Joe Hardy, you only ever come to me when you need my help. It's not enough that you've insulted me when all I wanted you to do was support me on my wedding day because my father is confined to a wheelchair and has lost his mind. You couldn't even do that for me.'

'I'm sorry.'

'No, you aren't,' Lucy said. She opened the file and pretended to read it. 'Please just go back to Durham. I don't need giving away. I certainly don't need you there doing it. It's a horrid idea anyway, I'm not a parcel. I'm trying to do the right thing here and you are not helping.'

'I was just shocked, that's all. It didn't occur to me that you would ever marry Edgar.'

'Why not?'

'Well, because . . .' Joe stopped. 'I just didn't think you would.'

'That's pathetic, Joe.'

'I did say that I could help you financially—'

'You're insulting me again. I'm sorry I was nasty to you about Angela. I know how much she means to you.'

'I've got this man coming up from London to see the car that Mr Palmer and I have built. I need to make a good impression.'

She said nothing. She didn't even look up.

'He wants to stay with me.'

Lucy wasn't seeing the page at all any more. She had a vision of the man staying at the tower house with the Misses Slaters and Frederick and the cats, and she started to laugh.

She couldn't help it. 'You are so stupid,' she said. 'You could have sent him to the County.'

'I tried to.'

'Oh dear.'

'I need a woman—'

'There are lots on the streets.'

'So that I can take him out to dinner.'

'Why don't you ask Emily? She's so respectable and speaks a bit like you do.'

'Please.'

'No.'

'I'll give you away.'

'You will not. You can take him out to dinner by yourself.'

'He'll think I don't have anybody.'

'You haven't.'

'Lucy—'

'I am not going to play games to suit you,' she said.

'It could be a very lucrative game if I win. I would help your business. You could deal with all the legal stuff and it would be huge, if I get that far. There is a very small chance that I will. Isn't it worth a dinner? You could stay at the County.'

'I'm not staying at the County on my own. People will think I'm a prostitute.'

'I don't think many of them stay there.'

'I suppose you would know.'

'Mrs Formby would put you up for the night. The children would love it.'

'And how exactly am I meant to tell Edgar that I'm having dinner with you?'

'It's business. Edgar is a very shrewd businessman. He's not going to mind when you explain it to him.'

Lucy was inclined to tell Joe that he could explain to Edgar himself, but she didn't. She thought it was enough that Edgar didn't like Joe and he would never agree to it.

'Did you say you would?' Edgar said when she talked to him about it.

'Certainly not.'

'There's a lot of talk you know, about this motor which Joe has built. If he pulls it off and has a factory here it may create a lot of jobs, and it would make him financially. I have no objection to being in on the ground floor.'

'What if it turns out to be nothing?'

Edgar shrugged.

'Then it doesn't matter – but if he has got something then Joe has the manner and the wit to bring it off, if you see what I mean. There's a lot of competition in the motor industry and it's building right now. It's going to hit a new level where many people can afford a car, it just needs somebody to build it, and Joe could be that man.'

'It's just another car.'

'Well, it's new in England Christopher Eve is coming up from London especially to see it, I would say it has a fair chance. I don't know much about these things but if Joe has designed something clever then his timing is exactly right. More and more people want motor cars and they need them cheap and well-built, and there isn't one so far. If this works and Joe puts business our way it could be very good for us. If it doesn't work then what have we lost?'

'You know this man, Eve?'

'I know of him. He is one of the leading lights in the industry so I wouldn't write him off. Besides, it would be nice for you to visit the Misses Slaters and stay with Mrs Formby. You're always saying you don't see enough of them. It's only a couple of hours and then you can go.'

'I shall need a new dress and you will have to pay for it.'

'You can have half a dozen new dresses and everything to match,' Edgar said.

It was typical, Lucy thought, of a man to change his tune when it suited his pocket. She would have liked Edgar to be just a little jealous. Perhaps Christopher Eve was gorgeous. He probably wasn't of course, he was probably middle-aged, fat and boring and very short, with terrible dress sense and no manners.

Worse still he would be staying at the tower house; he'd be covered in cat hair and offered sandwiches. Mischievously, Lucy was pleased about this.

Joe worried what Mr Eve would think of their shabby premises but when he opened the doors wide the sunshine poured in upon their creation. In Joe's mind he had made it so much less than it was now in reality. He looked at the little black car covered in sunlight and was proud, yet also worried.

He watched Christopher Eve make his way slowly around the outside. Then he opened the driver's door and looked inside, and the passenger side door and looked again. He opened the boot and after it the bonnet, and he spent what seemed like an eternity eyeing the engine and all the different bits and pieces. Then he put down the bonnet and walked around the car again. Joe thought he would die if Mr Eve didn't say something soon. His visitor straightened up.

'Why,' Mr Eve said, with the enthusiasm that only a devotee could have mustered, 'it's perfect, Mr Hardy.'

Joe would have disclaimed, but he checked himself. Instead he stood and tried not to let his face change while his mind soared.

'Let's take it for a spin, eh?' Mr Eve said.

Joe had wanted to show off and take Mr Eve somewhere special for lunch, but he didn't. Mrs Palmer was nervous to have such a man in her house, but since Mr Palmer had not volunteered even to meet the visitor Joe had said they would go there for lunch. He wasn't certain it was the best idea but he thought Mr Palmer would be a lot happier meeting Mr Eve under his own roof.

My God, Mrs Palmer had cleaned. She had clearly never heard of the word 'lunch'. Dinner was what you had at midday and Mr Eve was treated to a proper beef dinner with Yorkshire puddings first, covered in white pepper. She had made gooseberry crumble and custard and there was plenty of tea for afterwards.

Mr Eve, Joe suspected, came from a fine New England family, but within half an hour he looked like a man who had spent all his life in a backstreet house such as this one. He sat there smoking and drinking tea and chatting, smiling beguilingly at his audience. He had, Joe thought, perfect manners.

Mr Palmer took to Christopher Eve from the start. Joe was so relieved. They had of course their obsession in common and they talked and talked about the industry right from the beginning. Mr Palmer relaxed and Joe was soon glad he had decided to do this. He followed Mrs Palmer into the pantry for a second when she was clearing the plates and thanked her softly for all she had done and told her it could not have been better.

That afternoon they took him to Sunderland, to see how fine the port was, how good the rail links, to assess the cost of setting up a factory there. There was plenty of space, and hundreds of men out of work, many skilled, dozens more who could be taught.

They stayed there, walking around prospective sites and driving all about the area. On the way back they talked about the costs, the size of site they would need, the number of men they must employ from the beginning. When they returned to Durham they were exhausted.

Mr Palmer went home a happy man and Joe could see by then that Mr Eve had had enough business talk. It was time to take Mr Eve home to the tower house and introduce him to the Misses Slaters. Mr Eve took to Frederick instantly, rubbing the dog's ears so that Frederick, ecstatic, leaned up against his knees. Mr Eve cuddled the cats, and they let him. By the time Lucy arrived in the early evening everybody was ready to go out and party.

Joe had said they could meet at the County if she preferred, but Lucy wasn't going to stand around there alone so she duly turned up at the tower house just before six. She had thought Joe might have farmed out Frederick or banned the cats but everything was just the same. When she walked in and called out she heard laughter from the sitting room and an unmistakably American voice. She had not counted on Mr Eve being a Yankee.

They were sitting around drinking gin and tonic and Mr Eve, well mannered, got up and came straight to her, saying that he loved everything about England but Durham best of all – what a cathedral, what a beautiful place, this building was so amazing and he loved animals. He shook her hand and beamed at her, and Lucy thought immediately that Mr Eve was a lost cause.

Apparently he loved northern accents; he was ready to adopt the entire area, she could tell. He was effusive and kind, and when he asked about what she did and Joe had said she was a solicitor, he told her he was very impressed. He said she should come to the States where women had been lawyers almost since time began.

Lucy laughed at this and disclaimed. The trouble was, she thought, that she was already having a very enjoyable evening. Mr Eve was charming. He was tall and slender and handsome and well dressed and made sure everyone was at ease.

The Misses Slaters were also coming to the County. She thought this was a nice touch, but then Joe really didn't need her there; he had lied, he wanted her there, though she wasn't quite sure why. She was wearing the most beautiful green dress, which Edgar must have choked over when he got the bill, and the Misses Slaters were done up in their best finery.

Nobody said anything about business and Lucy wasn't sure whether she should talk about it, but in the end she couldn't help it. Besides, she didn't want Christopher Eve to think she was Joe's piece of fluff, pretending to be something better, so she asked him what he thought of the car.

He glanced at Joe and then he smiled and said, 'We're going to have a contract drawn up and Mr Hardy, Mr Palmer and I are going into business together. He assures me that the law firm you work for is the best in the area, Miss Charlton, so we are expecting great things of you.'

THIRTY-FIVE

Lucy sat in front of the mirror in her bedroom on her wedding day and looked at her reflection. She wondered what it must be like for a virgin to be married and was it fair considering that she was almost certain he was? What was it like when only one of you knew what to do – was that an advantage or did it put the woman into a position where she was obliged to be submissive? If he did know what to do then where had the knowledge come from and what were the circumstances of the women who had supplied it? And why should they and how clean was he and how faithful – how many times had he satisfied his baser instincts?

She felt that it was only through money and desperation on the part of women that they would do such things. She could imagine no woman doing it for any other reason. Did men really think that women enjoyed having their bodies invaded for money? Did many of them enjoy having their bodies invaded when they had married because they must?

Edgar had told himself that his desire to marry Lucy was based on a number of sensible reasons. He had even ticked them off to himself. He couldn't manage at the office without her, she would make a good solicitor and a fine partner in the firm, she was organized and would look after his house as well and they could have children. He didn't intend to keep on the Newcastle office and he was convinced she was aware of it. She would look after her family at a distance and everything would be fine.

Lucy was attractive. She was not beautiful like her sister; Gemma was stunning. He thought of her hanging out the clothes in the sunlit backyard, even then she was amazing, but when he saw Lucy outside the office he saw things which he liked about her so very much. Since he had asked her to marry him the worry had gone from her eyes; she was excited about marrying him, he was sure, pleased that they would work together, grateful that she would be able to keep her family.

After the first time of trying to kiss her when she had avoided his mouth he contented himself with talking, holding her hand and sometimes just a brush of lips to her neck, but as the days went on he thought of them in bed. He wanted her so badly that when they were together he couldn't concentrate on anything else.

He watched the lines of her body – she was too thin – and he wondered how her breath would come and go when they had sex and what her breasts would feel like beneath his hands. Would he be able to feel her ribs under the smoothness of her skin or would he be so grateful to have her close that he wouldn't care?

He thought her hair smelled of lavender and noticed how her eyes danced. They were darker than her sister's eyes but no less attractive.

They would be married before the year's end and he would be able to have her as much as he wanted, but also it seemed to him that he should have been allowed to kiss her without her backing off. He understood that in young women inexperience made them shy, but he didn't think she was shy, he knew her too well for that.

One afternoon that autumn when they were alone by the fire, her mother and sister having taken the children out, he got down on the hearthrug beside her, put an arm around her and kissed her.

She hesitated and then she kissed him back, but only very briefly. She stopped and made an excuse, then got up and went into the kitchen. He was left sitting by the fire wondering what he had done.

Lucy hadn't slept the night before her wedding. She panicked and wondered what she was doing and she was up before anyone else. She waited in fits of impatience for the rest of the house to rouse itself and was finally grateful when she heard the children shouting.

She went down to breakfast although her mother fussed and said that she had been about to bring a cup of tea up for her – but Lucy wanted to sit there. She couldn't eat. Her mother tutted over her lack of appetite. Lucy swallowed the tea and felt sick. She could not stop thinking about Gemma's wedding day and what Guy had done. She thought she was going to pass out, she felt so ill.

Emily had stayed the night in the other attic room, but somehow it seemed to make things worse. Lucy wanted to run away. She went and hid in her room and as the time drew nearer she stood in front of her mirror in a white velvet dress and a long veil, shivering. Emily and Gemma hovered in the hall. Their mother had gone off with their father and the grandchildren, to be at the church ahead of the time. St Nicholas's Cathedral was not far away but at this moment she felt as though it were right on her doorstep.

Joe said, 'I thought she was ready.'

Gemma went upstairs, but came back down again and said nothing, so Joe went up next and knocked briefly on the door. He thought he heard her voice and went in to find her seated at a tiny dressing table. It was nothing like the way that he had thought she lived in Newcastle – it was an attic room with scarcely enough space for a single bed and a chest of drawers, the kind of thing servants slept in. There was no fireplace and it was bloody freezing, despite the pale sunlight which ventured through the window.

She looked as though she were in a white mist. Really, Joe thought, did women want to envelop themselves like that when they were married – or was it tradition, was it something to do with a man unwrapping his prize? He didn't like to think too much about it.

'The motor's here.'

She didn't move. She was facing the dressing table. He could see the top of her head through the mirror. She was wearing some ridiculous ornament like a tiara, the kind of thing he had seen other women wearing at parties in London when he was young, with silver and diamonds all done up like a bow. It was awful, and the veil that went with it looked like huge curtains around her.

'Are you coming?'

She shook her head.

Joe went over. She looked up. Brides always thought they looked beautiful. She looked scared, so pale, her eyes darker than they should have been on such a happy day. She looked like a child dressed up as though she was going to disappear in among all that white.

'Nerves?' Joe ventured.

She got up, taking deep breaths. The dress and its apparently endless veil got up with her, and Joe wasn't quite sure he could get her out of such a tiny room without half the outfit left this side of the door. In the end he called down the stairs and Gemma came up and rearranged the damned dress with all the bits that went with it. She got her through the door.

It took time to get Lucy down two flights of narrow stairs but they managed it eventually and then there was another palaver to get her into the car. The car with the bridesmaids went off and Joe got in beside Lucy. He was only thankful to leave the house.

It was not far to the church but it felt like a long way. He was glad when they finally pulled up outside, though it was raining – not quite sleet, but very cold. Joe got out. Emily was standing in the porch but she ran down the path to him.

'He isn't here yet,' she said.

'But it's twenty-five to.' The wedding was set for half past eleven.

'Just ask the driver to go away for ten minutes and then come back.'

Joe got back into the car and made up a story, that Edgar and his best man, Joe couldn't remember his name, had got stuck somewhere and would be there in a minute or two. Lucy's face grew even whiter than her dress. She looked out of the window as Joe gave instructions to the driver. They set off again.

The minutes crawled by. The driver went down to the river and then back through the city, up a couple of side streets, past some pretty terraced Georgian houses and then round again. By then, Joe thought thankfully, it would be all right, so they made their way back to the church.

Emily was still outside, her face grim. Joe got out again.

'Where can he be?' Emily said.

'It's ten to twelve,' Joe said.

Lucy, somehow unaided, was now out of the car, scrunching up her skirts with white clenched fingers just as her sister reached the path.

'Where on earth is he?' Gemma said to Emily. 'You should get back in the car, Lucy. Your dress will be spoiled.'

The rain was coming down harder now, turning to sleet.

'I don't want to get back in the car. I came here to be married.'

Nobody knew what to say.

'Why don't we all sit in the car,' Joe said, 'and just wait? Something has happened. Everything will be all right.'

The two women did so but Lucy stood there.

'What if he's had an accident?' she said.

'There's no point in supposing anything bad. Just get back in or you'll be soaked.'

She didn't move. She didn't even look at him. The sleet was heavy and turned the streets to darkness. There was nothing to do, he thought, but stand there with her as the dress began to show spots of grey where the sleet hit it. The bottom of the dress was gathering dirt from the wet pavement so that it already had a grimy edge and the church was beginning to blot out behind the weather.

Nobody came out of the church, nobody came into view. No cars stopped. Joe looked up and down the road so many times that his neck was weary. It must have been at least another half-hour before a black car drew up at the pavement. Joe was so relieved he could have cried out. He watched for Edgar and the best man, but only one figure emerged.

He came slowly across and looked at the bride. She was now wet through. Her veil had sopped onto her back and her skirts had gone limp. The best man cleared his throat, tried to say something and didn't manage it.

'Where is he, for God's sake?' Joe couldn't stop himself from asking.

'He isn't coming.' The man didn't look at him, but off to the side. His voice was only just audible.

Gemma stood beside her sister, but Emily came to Joe.

'What's happened, Peter?' she demanded.

'He went home.' Peter didn't look at her either.

She stared for a few seconds and then said, 'He what? Do you mean you let him go?'

'I couldn't stop him.' Peter did look at her then, as though somebody was about to blame him. His words came all in a rush. 'I did everything I could, I told him she was waiting, I told him about the guests and the vicar and the . . . the food. I said everything I could, but he wouldn't take any notice.'

'What did he say?'

'Nothing. Just that he couldn't do it.'

'Dear God,' Emily said and turned away.

They stood about for a few more seconds and then Gemma said, 'Somebody ought to go in and—'

'I'll go,' Joe said.

Lucy turned and began to get back into the car, pulling at her clothes which by now resembled seaweed, thick and unwieldy as though they were covered in sand.

Joe was glad he had to go back into the church, even though everybody turned around and stared into the silence and he heard his shoes so sharp on the bare floor. It stopped him from running back to Durham and knocking seven kinds of shit out of Edgar. He argued with himself.

It wouldn't have helped, he would have looked stupid and none of it made any difference. He couldn't stop thinking about how she had looked in that awful little attic bedroom, as though only the voluminous whatever of her outfit stopped her from running down the stairs and out into the street and wherever the hell she could get to away from here. Mentally he cursed Edgar again as he went to the front of the church and whispered to Mrs Charlton that there was a problem and he thought she and her husband ought to come outside. He wheeled Mr Charlton out. Mrs Charlton went straight to Lucy and demanded to know what was going on.

Joe went back inside and he told everybody as briefly as he could that there would be no wedding and gave them his apologies.

He stood at the front as they moved awkwardly out of the pews and down the aisle towards the door, all in their wedding finery, disappointed and somewhat gleeful that they had witnessed such a display, though they weren't sure whether it was the bride or the groom. He knew that by the time they got outside the car would have taken Lucy and Emily and Gemma back to the house. Lucy's parents and the second car had gone too.

He was last to leave, and he thanked the vicar or whoever he was. Joe had long since stopped thinking about churches or the men concerned with them, for war had somehow knocked all faith out of him, it seemed such a useless thing to him. He strolled back up the aisle and out into the sunshine and wasn't that just typical, he thought, the bloody sun coming out now.

The churchyard was full of gossiping people. They looked let down because there would be no wedding feast and that was always the best bit. He was sorry he had written a speech, not something that came naturally to him, and as the area gradually emptied and the guests went back to their homes Joe went on to the hotel and cancelled everything. He had half thought he might urge them to go there and eat and make merry – since it was all paid for – but it didn't seem right. He was only glad that Edgar was paying for it, the bastard.

He didn't understand what the hell Edgar was doing. He certainly loved her; he had done everything he could to help her. It wasn't like Edgar not to go through with such a thing, for he was so much the gentleman, he would not let her down at the last minute, he would have worked out long before that this was not a good idea and stopped before it got this far. And yet he hadn't.

Joe went back to Durham, still in his wedding finery, taking the two Misses Slaters and Mrs Formby and Tilda and Clay. He thought he could do no good returning to Lucy's house, he wouldn't be wanted there. On the way back it occurred to him that he was glad they hadn't married. It had always been a stupid idea and unless he was a complete idiot Lucy didn't want Edgar at all. Perhaps she liked him very much – she admired him and was grateful for everything he had done for her and for her family – but he didn't think Lucy had an ounce of lust in her for Edgar Bainbridge. She had none for any man; she was too scared. He didn't know what or who had scared her, and she'd never said anything, but at least Edgar had had the sense to save them from a bigger disaster. Maybe when she calmed down she would be able to see it.

He would help her now if she would let him.

Nobody spoke all the way back to Durham. The Misses Slaters went home and changed and made sandwiches. Joe went to the garage because he couldn't rest and then on to Mr Palmer's house because he knew that Mrs Palmer would give him tea and cake no matter what time he went. They were both there, and Joe sat down and told them the whole story. They were horrified.

'Oh, that poor girl,' said Mrs Palmer, and Mr Palmer shook his head.

'The poor bugger must've been terrified,' he said. Joe didn't think he meant Lucy.

*

It was far too late for visitors, Edgar knew, so why was the hammering on his front door going on and on? He thought at first that it was his sister but it was too heavy even for Emily in a rage. He hadn't expected her back, was counting on it.

In the end he went and hauled it open and there stood Joe, still wearing morning dress, and the rain was pouring down again. He looked so stupid, Edgar thought, as though he had been through a storm – his clothes were wet and creased and crumpled. Edgar left the door open and went back inside to the comfort of his drawing room. Joe followed.

'Have some whisky,' Edgar said largely, gesturing with his glass. Since he had drunk so much he didn't want anyone there who was sober.

Joe went across and poured a large quantity of it into a squat glass. He joined Edgar at the fire.

'Nasty night,' he said.

'I don't know what the hell you're doing here,' Edgar complained. 'I thought that Peter might have had the decency, but I don't want you bloody telling me what to do.'

'I haven't told anybody what to do since I came back from France,' Joe said, as he settled himself into an armchair by the fire and regarded the whisky with some respect before putting the glass to his lips.

'Does Lucy know you're here?'

'She would probably have instructed me to pull your head off.'

'Feel free,' Edgar said.

'I'm not sure I could twist your neck properly any more. You lose the skills you don't keep up with.' Joe lowered himself further into the armchair, shivered and sipped at his drink.

Edgar sat down too and gazed into the fire.

'What the hell are you doing in Durham anyway?'

'I live here, idiot.'

Edgar ignored him and took another slurp.

'I tried to talk to her. She was so pleased with the idea of the practice and the house and she had even got as far as rearranging the furniture, but she wouldn't say anything. She wanted security for her family and to be a solicitor. I think the rest of it got lost somehow.'

'And you?'

The question was so soft that Edgar almost didn't hear it.

'I wanted her,' he said. 'I hadn't been in love since 1916 and it was more than that, so much more. I thought we would have children and see her family from time to time, we'd go to the park on Sundays and have big dinners, you know, with her mother. I thought that Emily might not go off to London so that we could be a family. It was going to be so perfect. Lucy's become so very beautiful, and I was afraid that someone would steal her away.'

'She got her dress all wet and dirty,' Joe said. 'She'll never be able to wear it again.'

The fire crackled and fell apart. Edgar wasn't surprised. It had become a huge effort to put coal on it. He was exhausted.

'Why does it always rain?'

'So that we can blame it. If that happened on a nice sunny day with the park all full of roses it would seem like an insult.'

373

Edgar glanced at the dark window; with a wind behind it the rain was ceaseless.

'I should go and see her.'

'I wouldn't if I were you.' Joe looked at him, then shook his head slowly. 'I would leave it a while. Like a year.'

Edgar got up and fetched the whisky bottle. He poured generously for them both, being very careful since he wasn't that steady. He didn't spill a drop, and he was quite proud of this. He staggered to his chair with the bottle in one hand and his glass in the other, hoping Joe hadn't noticed.

'So why didn't you turn up?' Joe said, at length.

'Because she doesn't want me.' Edgar waved his glass in the air. 'I knew it weeks ago and I kept telling myself that she would come round, that a lot of women are scared, but it wasn't like that, it was something more. She wouldn't tell me what it was and in the end I couldn't ask any further. She wouldn't even let me touch her. I don't understand. How could you marry somebody when their touch is repulsive to you?'

'She was afraid.'

Edgar looked at him.

'What, of me?'

'No, of any man, I think.'

'Oh, for God's sake.' Edgar got up and walked about the room in agitation and then wished he hadn't and sat back down again. 'But why? I wasn't going to hurt her.'

'I have a feeling the damage was already done.'

Edgar looked sharply at him.

'What gave you that impression?'

'I don't know, just instinct somehow. She shies away.'

Edgar frowned.

'God, you could be right. That I never thought about.'

'Maybe she was worried you would be upset.'

'I would be upset?' Edgar stared at him.

'Well, wouldn't you?'

'I don't think so. I mean if a woman's been widowed it doesn't stop another man marrying her.'

'That's different though, isn't it?'

'I had a woman in France until her husband came back. I thought perhaps . . . I hoped that he'd died. To be fair I think she did too, but I couldn't go so far as to bring her back here when she was somebody else's wife. So I came home without her.'

'Exactly,' Joe said. 'In your kind of business these things matter.'

'Only if people know.'

'And if you knew?'

'Maybe some bad experience when Lucy was a student?' Edgar frowned. 'Yes,' he said finally, 'yes, I would care. And she was going to let me go ahead and find out on our wedding night? I don't like that.'

'Sometimes people have to take a chance.'

'Women shouldn't take chances with such things.'

'And that is the point,' Joe said.

'She should have told me.'

'What a huge risk and so much to lose.'

'Well, it's all gone now,' Edgar said. He emptied his glass and stared into it.

'Maybe you don't love her that much.'

'I don't think I could love any woman that much,' Edgar said. 'Wouldn't it matter to you?'

'Not after what I did.'

'What did you do?'

So Joe told him.

'You were a bloody idiot, but it's perfectly understandable.'

'Not for a woman though, eh?'

'I wonder why she didn't marry him. And if she gave herself to a married man then I wouldn't want anything to do with her,' Edgar said.

'And if it wasn't like that?'

'What, she got it wrong? Misjudgement?'

'Worse?'

'I'm not sure there is worse,' Edgar said.

'That's because you can't face what you've done and you're drunk,' Joe said.

'There's another bottle in the court cupboard. See if you can find it,' Edgar said.

It was difficult getting the dress off. Gemma had to peel the soaked material away from Lucy's skin. Lucy would have dragged it off had she been able but it took time and patience which neither of them had, Gemma thought. She just helped until her sister stood there, shivering in her underwear. Gemma handed her a thick dressing gown.

Emily was downstairs, trying to talk to their mother. Gemma couldn't hear her but she was certain it was not an easy conversation. Their mother had gone from the chance of security and prosperity to poverty in two hours and it was not an easy thing to face. Lucy was white, almost translucent. Emily also had the children with her and their father needed looking after too. Gemma would have gone downstairs to help except that she didn't like to leave her sister. Lucy hadn't spoken.

'I'm sorry,' she said now. 'I can't stop thinking about the church and all those people and my friends, Miss Slater and Miss Bethany and Mrs Formby – they all came from Durham to see me married. I'm so ashamed, I behaved so badly. What must they think?'

Gemma's heart pulled.

'You didn't do anything. This isn't your fault.'

'Yes, it is.' Lucy's voice broke.

'It's Edgar's fault.'

'No.' Lucy shook her head wildly. 'He's a perfectly nice man and he loves me and the only reason he didn't come to the wedding is because I treated him so badly.' She sat down on the bed, sobbing.

Gemma sat down with her. The bed creaked as though it couldn't withstand two people's weight.

'You did everything you could. You worked with him and you were nice to his sister and—'

'I couldn't let him near me. I just couldn't do it. And I couldn't tell him about Guy, but all I could think about was what Guy did to me.'

Gemma took her sister into her arms while Lucy cried.

'I'm never going to want a man anywhere near me again and I don't think you are either. I feel like he stole everything away.'

'Guy seemed so genuine,' Gemma said, and she smiled against herself. 'I needed to marry decently because I was so worried about Father. I didn't see Guy for what he was.'

'How could you know such things?' Lucy sniffed and moved back and for the first time Gemma saw a hint that she was getting better.

'I feel guilty about what I did to you.'

Lucy looked at her. 'I don't think that's fair to any of us and besides here we are together, with not a man in sight. Mother was counting on this.'

'Well, she's going to have to learn not to count on things, like the rest of us have had to.'

'It would have been so nice.' Lucy sat back and then said in a more determined voice, 'Go and ask Emily to come up, will you? She must feel awful and it's nothing to do with her.'

Gemma nodded and she went off downstairs. Emily looked so uncomfortable in the kitchen and relieved when told she could go upstairs. She was still wearing the sky-blue dress which looked so pretty on her.

She trudged up two flights with a cup and saucer in her hand.

Emily opened the door and put down the tea on the dressing table.

'Is this heaven? It's certainly far enough.' she said.

Lucy smiled and got up and hugged her. 'I'm so sorry.'

'You're sorry? What about my brother?'

'It's nothing to do with him. I wish I hadn't put him through it.'

Emily stared. 'You don't love him?'

Lucy squirmed. 'I thought I did. I think it all got ravelled up, how I wanted to be a solicitor and mistress of your lovely house and how well Edgar is connected. You know.'

Emily looked at her. 'I don't, but then I do. What is it? What happened?'

The tears began to run down Lucy's face but she couldn't say anything. It was only when the sobs bettered her that she allowed the other girl to come to her.

'Oh, God,' Emily said.

Lucy had not realized that she could cry so hard and so much without feeling sick, without feeling that she should draw back from whoever was comforting her, but Emily held her tight as though she knew. She said nothing, even when Lucy couldn't cry any more, even when the day was long gone and the evening had wrapped its cruel arms around everything and urged them to move on.

'I just couldn't,' Lucy said. 'Your brother is so nice, but I can't marry him.'

Emily looked into Lucy's face and then she said, defiantly, 'I was almost persuaded once or twice myself by various nice men. I know it isn't the same thing but I did so want children.'

Lucy shook her head. 'What about you? What will you do now?'

'Oh, I'll be all right. I'm going to London,' Emily said.

The following day, when Emily reached home, the house appeared deserted. She let herself in with her key and walked through the hall. It was empty and echoed somehow, her footsteps making a huge sound.

She went into the drawing room and there her brother lay upon the sofa, asleep. He did not wake up, he didn't hear her, so she sat down and waited. When he did not stir after a few minutes she went upstairs. Her cases were packed, her room looked unoccupied, as though she had already left. In her mind and heart she had.

Lady Toddington had written to her twice and offered to help and she had written back enthusiastically. She had been eager to make a new life there; she thought she could run from this. Somehow it seemed pointless now.

When she made her way downstairs he was on his feet. He looked sheepishly at her.

'My fault,' he said. 'Please do what you planned. I'll be fine.'

'I'm not going anywhere,' she said.

She could see that he tried to disguise the look of relief which came over his face. She went to him. They were not a demonstrative family but for once she held him close to her.

'Let's have a drink,' she said, embarrassed for having got that near.

He coughed and moved away but she felt better and he looked better. She remembered how they had been as children, so close, telling secrets and sledging down the banks of the river. He had been her big brother and she had adored him; even as a young man he was good at sorting problems, all she had to do was tell him. No wonder Lucy had wanted to marry him. Now he needed her.

Later, when they had made their way down the whisky bottle and beyond, he wound his way to bed and she climbed the stairs. In her room she unpacked her cases. It might be a kind of prison, she thought, but it was also a refuge, and she did not have the courage to leave now that Lucy was not coming to take over her role. There was some stupid satisfaction in that.

She liked Lucy very much but she loved her brother. He might in time find someone else he wished to marry and she might think again of going south and having new adventures. She started to decant her clothes back into the wardrobes and drawers and thought she could hear the sound of the trains going south. She did not mind so very much.

Thirty-six

Spring can be pitiless, and this one was. Every day it rained and as the weeks went by it got no better. Emily was reminded of that old northern joke: the only way to tell the difference between the seasons is that the rain is warmer in summer. Emily had never seen anything like it. She sat by the window and watched it day after day. She longed for winter. How could you hide when the tulips were drowning in their beds? Emily sat outside, wishing it were winter when it was dark at five o'clock.

In her world now it was always too late for tea and too early for whisky. Edgar would not be home until at least seven – often it was eight or even nine. Some evenings he came home only when she was in bed and she would hear him creep in so as not to disturb her. She knew why he was hiding at the office. He could not forgive himself for having jilted Lucy and though his sister had not reproached him, he seemed to think that Emily blamed him for what had happened. She needed to talk to him, to tell him that they could at the very least have dinner together and talk. It was all that was left.

Even when the days lengthened and the evenings should have become lighter they didn't because the rain was incessant and the days full of heavy cloud.

She didn't even know what day of the week it was, just that the air should have been softer and dry and she should have been sitting under the shade of the apple tree drinking iced tea and contemplating gin and tonic for later. She was, however, outside. The rain had ceased for once and she was huddled there, thinking that she should go inside as it was about to start once again. Liza, who had taken on Norah's role of housekeeper, opened the door of the conservatory.

'You have a visitor.'

'Who is it?'

'Mr Fred White.'

Norah's husband. What on earth was he doing here? Emily wondered.

'Send him out.'

Liza hesitated, then closed the door. Emily wished she had said that she was not at home; she couldn't imagine Fred White had anything to say to her that she wanted to hear.

It was only a minute or so later that Fred stepped into the garden, carefully as though he feared he might slip on the wet stones, and turning up his collar against the rain.

'Miss Bainbridge.' He hesitated. 'It's good of you to see me here in the garden and in such grand weather.'

That almost made her laugh. Fred put just the right intonation into his voice, as if she were slightly mad but he was prepared to put up with it. She was surprised; she had not taken Fred for a wit, she had thought he was an ignominious gnome.

'Would you like a cigarette?' she offered.

'Aye, thanks, I wouldn't mind,' Fred said, and they went back into the shelter of the porch above part of the patio.

They both puffed away, the cigarettes making comforting little swirls of blue smoke against the dark day.

'Norah said I was to come and tell you that we have a little lass.'

'That's very nice for you – I'm so pleased,' Emily said, though every word scorched her.

Fred hesitated again. Emily waited, regarding him critically. Fred seemed to have grown; he looked a lot more substantial than he had been before the wedding. He was taller – or was he just standing taller, as though he was more confident now that he was a husband and a father? She thought with a pang that was what happiness did for you – security, a home, a loving family and a fireside. What more could anybody need?

'The thing is,' he said, 'Norah and me, we would deem it a big favour, Miss Bainbridge, if you would be godmother to our little lass.'

Emily didn't know what to say, she was so taken aback, and to her surprise so pleased. She liked Fred. Oh God!

'Is Norah all right?' she said.

Fred hesitated as though not certain he should speak on so delicate a subject.

'She is now. The bairn was early you see. I don't think it was easy for her. We were lucky it lived. I was that worried about her.' Fred stopped there – men weren't supposed to talk about such things – but Emily could not help being impressed with his attitude.

'I'm not a Methodist,' she said.

'It doesn't matter. We'd really like it if you would. Norah says to tell you that we are naming the bairn after you.'

Emily stared at him. The rain stopped and suddenly the light in the garden was the colour of lemon. It accentuated Fred's neat head and dark hair. Emily thought she could see a rainbow just above them.

'Norah would like you to come and see her when you have time. She would like to show you the bairn. She's a bonny little lass. We . . . we sort of hoped that you might take to her and mebbe spend some time with us when you aren't too busy, like.'

She wanted to cry and to laugh and to say that she had nothing but time, she had nothing to fill it, and she was desperate to see Norah, to be with her – but not the Norah he had married, not the woman who had borne his child, but the lovely giggling girl. That Norah was gone. He looked so honestly at her that Emily said she would go.

She tried putting it off. In some ways it was just like putting off the packing and in other ways it was not. Norah was living as Emily could never have lived and then she tried to look at her own situation. She thought Norah had been braver than she was and more honest and looked at things in a realistic light, and that was when she made her way down the street to where Norah and Fred had set up home. She banged on the front door and Norah's mother answered. She beamed at Emily.

'Why, Miss Bainbridge,' she said, 'come in.' She held the door wide and Emily went into the hall, knocking the rain from her umbrella before she did so.

Norah's mother ushered her into the front room.

'We would have lit the fire if we had known,' she said.

Emily disclaimed, but she could smell the cold air. Shortly afterwards her hostess came back, looking flustered.

'Our Norah says will you come into the kitchen, Miss Bainbridge. I don't think it's right but with the weather being so awful Norah said you wouldn't mind. I'm away home. Give my best to your brother.'

She shrugged into her outdoor things in the hall and Emily made her way as slowly as she could into the kitchen. There a small figure sat by the fire with a baby in her arms. Emily could hardly breathe, it hurt so much to see that not only had Fred mattered more than she did, but this child mattered in a different way. She knew that Norah would have died to protect this infant, just from the way she held it, cradled it, and Emily was ashamed of herself for wanting to matter more and being jealous not just of a man but of a tiny child. She hurt from knowing that her life was wanting in so many ways.

Norah smiled, but tentatively. Everything was different now. She was very thin and there were big dark smudges under her eyes.

'Are you all right?' was the only thing Emily could venture. She wanted to touch Norah but somehow the child in Norah's arms made it impossible, so she could only gesture and give a forced smile and sit down.

'I would get up and make tea but—'

'I could make it.'

Norah laughed. 'I've tasted your tea before,' she said and Emily joined in. She remembered the time she had tried to make tea for them and she had forgotten to boil the kettle so that the leaves floated on the surface of the cold water. 'I thought you would have gone from here.'

There was something about the rhythm of what Norah said, of the very way she spoke, that fulfilled all of Emily's dreams. Norah understood what she was going through, even now when she had other concerns, when their lives had changed so much.

Had there really been a time when she had hoped she and Norah could go away somewhere and live together and be happy? Even the lilt of her voice was heaven so that Emily had always willed her to say more. But Norah was careful with language, somehow aware of how much it might mean and that once a thing was said you couldn't take it back.

There was something criminal about not being able to hear Norah's voice. Emily longed for the sound of it in the darkness when she lay in bed beneath her brother's roof. How could they both have had such bad luck? How could they both be single? Perhaps it would always be so. How would they bear it? How would they stand the lonely nights, the never being touched, the way that she would have to pretend that there was nothing wrong?

'I tried to leave, but somehow I can't,' was all she managed.

Norah nodded and the baby slept on. The child was tiny – round face, eyes shut, quite a lot of dark hair – and she couldn't make out whether it looked like Fred or Norah. But did it matter now? Everything that Emily had wanted was lost.

'How is your brother?' Norah managed into the silence.

'I think he's broken-hearted.' Emily said it with a modicum

of lightness, but the words held in the air like smoke. Two broken hearts. The weight should have sent their house crashing down if there had been any acknowledgement in nature, but there wasn't, the days went on and on. She got up in the mornings and was amazed how nothing was in sympathy. But why should it be? Day and night, night and day, on and on, regardless of people in pain or dying. She had learned to be grateful for it.

'I didn't think that Mr Bainbridge and Miss Charlton would work out,' Norah said.

'Unlike Fred and you.'

Emily wished she had not said it. Norah's face went so dark and hot and she looked into the fire.

'I'm so sorry,' she said, and Emily was ashamed.

'May I hold her?' she suggested.

Norah looked surprised and then pleased. She handed the sleeping child to Emily. It didn't feel wrong, that was the hard part; she liked holding a child in her arms.

'Will you stand as her godmother?' Norah said.

'Didn't Fred say?'

'He wasn't sure. We talked about it and I thought mebbe you would hate it so much. But you've meant more to me than anyone and I want my bairn with your name. Will you come?'

'Yes, of course,' Emily said. As she looked down the infant opened its eyes.

'Do you think your brother would stand as godfather?' Norah asked.

'I think he would be delighted,' Emily said.

THIRTY-SEVEN

Lucy spent every day at the office. She didn't know what else to do and at least it gave her a purpose. As long as her father went with her she could maintain the charade that he was still a fine solicitor.

It was Friday, and she had just put her father into the wheelchair to push him home when he murmured something to her. She got down by his chair and smiled into his face. He smiled at her and half lifted a hand and then the hand fell and the light went from his eyes. Lucy waited for it to come back and when it didn't she panicked. She got up and spoke to him again and again, saying anything she could think of and imploring him to be better.

He moved, his eyelids flickered, and she began to hope, and then she cried and she talked to him while his eyes lit once more and recognized her. She willed him to be all right, to be better, not to leave yet – she had not done what she had promised herself she would do so that he would be proud of her, and she wanted it so badly, just as much as she ever had, despite all that had happened. Her father could not die and leave her in such a state. It was selfish of her, she knew.

In the end she got him home as quickly as she could, crying all the way back. She thought she would never have wrinkles, she had so many reasons for these blessed tears. Her mother and Gemma both ran into the hall when she shouted. By the time they reached her the water was falling down her face like rain.

Gemma ran for the doctor and her mother talked endlessly to her father. Lucy knew that for your husband to die, no matter what age he was, no matter what the circumstances, was one of the worst things that could ever happen. Who would you talk to in bed at night? Who would you discuss your children with? Who would save you from the dark demons at four in the morning? Who would argue past events with you and be there for you in old age so that you could sit back and sigh and think about the past and perhaps envisage some kind of future twilight and a gentle death?

It seemed to Lucy a very long time before her sister came back with the doctor. He was the man they had always consulted, Dr Mackie. He had brought Gemma and Lucy into the world, her mother was always saying. They relied on him completely. Lucy did not think he had been good with Guy. Guy had suffered too much. She wanted to make sure her father did not. The illness was different of course, but she did not want him to treat it the same.

She was in the bedroom with the doctor while he looked at her father. Her mother and Gemma had gone downstairs.

'Is there anything you can do for him?' she asked, impatient as the doctor pondered.

'My dear Lucy, your father is dying,' he said gently.

'There must be something—'

'I will do all I can to make him comfortable in his last hours. It is a blessing in some ways. He would only have gone further downhill and surely he has had all the humiliation he can bear. Let him go. His time has come.'

'It's too soon.' She sat down on the bed.

'It is always too soon unless the patient is in pain. Your father is not in pain.'

'He's not conscious either.'

'God willing,' Dr Mackie said and he left.

Lucy wanted to pummel him into some kind of magic but she knew it was useless and he was right.

A short time later her mother and Gemma came upstairs. The children had gone to bed unusually early and the three of them sat there. It was almost companionable. From time to time one or the other would offer to make tea, but nobody wanted it. The light seemed to go early and darkness fell. Lucy wanted to open the window to hear the river and she didn't know who suggested it but they did just that, and they watched the water tumble towards the sea through the open curtains.

From time to time her mother dozed. She was exhausted, Lucy thought. She'd had so many months of this as well as all the other problems which her two daughters had imposed. Lucy felt guilty and then she thought, it was how families were – awful and wonderful and somehow all there was.

She and Gemma didn't sleep. They wandered over to the window as though the river was reassuring and it was; it kept going on and on when nothing else did.

Eventually even Gemma dropped off for a few minutes in the chair, but Lucy couldn't sleep. She couldn't reconcile this dying man with the father she had loved so much. The man who had put her out of his house because he thought she had done wrong.

She sat there watching the reassuring way his chest went up and down. She could hear the cathedral clock striking the quarter, the half, the three-quarters and the hour. She heard it reach four and she was the only person awake.

Her father opened his eyes and looked mistily at her.

'Lucy?'

'Daddy.'

'I thought you had gone.'

'No, I'm right here.'

'I'm so glad you are. I missed you,' he said. He reached for her hand, closed his eyes and went on breathing.

A few seconds later his breaths seemed to cease and then they began again. Just when she was thinking that he would go on living he took a great last breath which resounded in his chest and then he lay still.

He was a huge loss. There seemed so little to occupy them, the house empty without his great wheelchair. Luckily he had made provision some time since to pay for his funeral. Her mother did not have need to be ashamed that they could not afford to bury him in proper style.

His friends and business acquaintances and a lot of other people came to his funeral – some out of respect and many out of love. Lucy remembered as the service went on the lawyer her father had been when she and Gemma were small children. How he had helped people, even so far as to give them money as well as his skills free of charge, which was exactly what she would now be able to carry on. She determined to do it, no matter what.

She knew now that that had made her want to be a lawyer so that she could try to find some kind of justice for people. There was a very long way to go, especially for women. She thought the law treated them badly and she must help, attempt to change things for them and their children. She remembered how kind her father had always been to everyone; he wanted no one to have to face the law alone because he knew that it was inadequate, and always would be, though it tried.

She stood and listened and sang, and watched her mother's white face and Gemma's grey one. It was never just the present that a wife lost, she thought, it was all the memories of your life and the future you might have had if your husband had been in his right mind and lived a little longer. It was thieving of a kind because for the past few years her mother had not had a husband but only an invalid.

Lucy doubted that her mother had forgotten the lovely years when her children were small and the sweet times when they would go to the seaside in the summer. She would take her children to church in new outfits for Easter and when the days were dark they would sit over the fire.

A good many people came back to the house and she was glad to see Joe and the two Misses Slaters. She spoke to them briefly. The Misses Slaters were at home on such occasions. Funerals had always been part of their lives and they were invaluable, going around and talking to people, those they knew and those they might have known and even those they had never met before. Mrs Formby was there too with Tilda.

She was so glad to see them, so grateful they had come, even though Tilda was very white-faced and Mrs Formby looked tired.

Later, when most of the people had left and Mrs Formby and Tilda were about to leave, Lucy took Mrs Formby aside in the hall.

'If everything all right?' she asked.

Mrs Formby looked bravely at her.

'Of course it is, lass. And isn't it typical of you to go worrying about other people on the day you bury your father.' Mrs Formby had a habit of touching Lucy's face, which Lucy missed, and she did it now. The tears welled in Lucy's eyes. And then Mrs Formby kissed her.

'We do miss you, you're such a grand lass. Come and see us some time when things are easier and if there's anything at all that we can do to help we will.' She nodded towards Tilda. 'She's got herself a lad. She was bound to in time.' Mrs Formby smiled into Lucy's eyes.

Mrs Formby went to Lucy's mother then and to Gemma and to the children. Lucy was sure, even though she couldn't hear it, that Mrs Formby said all the right things because her mother smiled just a little and the children looked up at her while she slipped them sweets she had brought. She kissed Gemma and touched her cheek too and Lucy could not help being just a little bit jealous. Mrs Formby was her friend. She wished she wouldn't go; the house would be darker without her.

Joe merely pressed Lucy's hand before he left with the Misses Slaters, and neither of them could think of anything to say.

THIRTY-EIGHT

Lucy had been in Durham, trying to talk to Emily. She still thought that Emily should leave, that if she didn't she would end up as some kind of aunt to Norah's child, and though she was certain that would suit Norah's family it was not nearly enough for Emily. She should go south. Joe had set up connections there and Lucy was sure Lady Toddington would do everything she could to help even though Emily had hesitated so far. When Emily finally agreed Lucy was quite pleased with her efforts.

Lucy didn't want to go back to Newcastle; there was nothing but problems at home. She had no idea what she could possibly do next except go on looking for work of any kind. She tried to comfort herself with the idea that something good must happen in the end, it just must, but she didn't know how she could go forward.

The nearer to home she got the more she wished she could have stayed in Durham. She stepped down from the train in Newcastle and began to make her way through the early evening crowds. People were going home, some of them from work. She envied each of them.

She thought she saw someone she knew. She wasn't sure but she stopped and watched. The woman was taller than most and there was something about her stance, her height, her hat which looked familiar to Lucy. At first she didn't know who it was, certainly nobody she knew well, but they had met before, she was certain of it. She began to push through the crowds, back towards the train, though she wasn't quite sure why, and then she paused. She had lost sight of the woman. She stopped. No, there was no one of that look in sight. Lucy didn't know why it had seemed to matter.

Steam rose in front of her as she got nearer to the train, but it was no good, the woman had gone. Lucy was not even sure now that it was someone she knew, then in a kind of flash of recognition she remembered and she knew now why. The woman was Lady Toddington. How strange, and how unlikely.

Lucy searched the station. She looked at every train. She ran over the footbridge. She ran up and down again and again trying to find her, to see what she was doing here in Newcastle, but the woman was not there.

She ran out of the station and into the traffic, but if Lady Toddington had been heading out here she was long gone. Lucy was so frustrated. She walked home, her problems forgotten. She didn't think any more about the poverty which awaited them if they didn't do something soon.

Once home she was caught up in putting the twins to bed, Gemma was at work, then she went and sat by the fire. Her mother always went to bed early now, as though she had grown old since her husband had died and all her hope was gone. She was quieter than she had ever been.

Lucy didn't mention the woman she had thought she saw. She lay awake all night and in the morning, though she could not explain her extravagance, she went out on the pretence of looking for work with a particular company and took the train back to Durham.

It was a Thursday morning and Joe and Mr Palmer were hard at work. To her delight Clay was there too. Joe didn't ask her what she wanted, but he immediately offered to take her out for some breakfast since it was still early and she was glad of that. She didn't eat much at home, she left most of it for the children and for her mother. Gemma did the same. Joe took her to the Silver Street café and when she said she would have tea and toast he ordered a full English breakfast for her. Lucy protested.

'I'm not hungry. I had breakfast before I came.'

'That's why you're so fat,' Joe said.

The smell of the food made her even hungrier. The waitress brought tea. Joe told her all about Mr Eve and how he was going to help finance the car production.

'And I went to Darling's bank and they gave me a loan – because Mr Eve is backing us and he's so well-known and reputable.'

Lucy was glad for him. She hadn't seen Joe happy like this before. She debated with herself as to whether she should tell him about Lady Toddington, but there was no way round it. The food arrived but Lucy didn't feel hungry any more, remembering what she wanted to say to him and dreading it.

'I came here for a reason,' she said. 'I thought I saw Lady Toddington on Newcastle station.'

Joe stared at her.

'You only met once,' he said.

'She's not the kind of woman you miss. What would she be doing here?'

'She wouldn't be here,' Joe said. 'I don't think the woman's ever been further north than Regent's Park.'

'Joe, I'm sure it was her.'

'So what was she doing?' Joe threw her a sceptical glance and then picked up his knife and fork. He cut a fried egg in half as viciously as though it had done something to him so that the yolk cascaded over everything else on his plate. 'Did you see her get on a train?'

'Well, no, but—'

'Did you see her get off?'

'I didn't see anything. She disappeared.'

'Eat your breakfast before it gets cold,' Joe advised, pointing at her plate with his knife.

'Why don't you believe me?'

'Because it's a ridiculous idea.'

'So you won't come to London with me then, to find out about it?' she said, not knowing she was going to say anything quite that odd.

Joe stared.

'You don't mean it?' he said.

'I may be many things but I am not an idiot.'

'You haven't got enough money to get you as far as York,' Joe said.

'You can pay for it. You're obviously about to either make a lot of money or lose your shirt. I'd better have it before you get involved.'

'I wouldn't dream of it. It's completely stupid.'

'Stupid?' Lucy glared at him. 'I am trying to help you.'

'I appreciate it.'

'No, you don't! You think I don't know what I see.'

'I just think you're mistaken,' Joe said patiently and set about eating his breakfast.

'You could come with me. You know them very well.'

'I'm not doing anything of the kind,' he said.

'Well then I shall go by myself.'

'Not if I have to pay for it.'

'I shall pawn my father's pocket watch.'

Joe went on eating. Lucy got up and walked out. She had reached as far as the pavement by the time he caught up with her.

'Will you wait?'

'No, I will not. You are very rude and since you don't believe me we have nothing more to discuss.'

'It's a wild goose chase – and for what?'

'Is it? Is that really what you think?' She did stop then. Joe, who was half a pace ahead of her, wheeled round.

'I do understand what you're trying to do,' he said simply, 'but really there is nothing to be gained. I know that my mother is dead, I've seen her grave, and I've learned to accept that I have lost Angela. I am just beginning to put my life back together. I would like a little peace to be able to do it. I can't raise my hopes again. I just can't do it. If it was Toddy's mother then maybe she has a friend here or she was on the way to somewhere. There will be a perfectly sensible reason for her being here if it really was her. Leave it alone, Lucy, please.'

She set off walking again and this time he let her.

When Joe got back that night he went upstairs and took out one of the unread letters – there were only a few left. He didn't want to think about Angela at all any more but somehow his life kept getting dragged back that way.

Dear Joe,

I cannot think how things got as bad as this. For several weeks now Angela has not been to see me. I thought she was too busy at first but when I went to the house to enquire I was not admitted. I could not think why. I know my behaviour has become abhorrent to my friends but all I did was ask how she was, if she was well and what she was doing. Later in the day Toddy came to me and told me that Felix had decided that she was better out of London. I could not find out what had happened. Toddy didn't like lying to me, I could see, but no matter how I urged him I could get nothing more out of him.

He said that his father did not want me to try and contact her. I made a joke of it – what else could I do? I don't understand what is happening. Why would they send her away? Why would she go without coming and telling me? It's so unlike her. I have nobody to turn to, I don't know what to do. I only wish that I knew how to get in touch so that I could be reassured. I wish I could talk to you, just for five minutes.

Lucy thought a lot about the trip to London. She could see why Joe wouldn't want to go, that he had been through enough and that he did not want to find out that the girl he loved was dead. At least if he didn't know he could hold on to the illusion. She thought about how much he had done for her and for the Misses Slaters and the Formbys and she decided that she would go to London. If she got no further then it didn't matter and he wouldn't know and if she did then she would think about what to do next.

That evening she and Gemma sat over the fire until late and she told Gemma about the proposed visit. Gemma didn't say very much until Lucy had finished telling her all about it.

'You could be opening a can of worms,' she said.

'Yes, but he doesn't have to know.'

'You really care about this, don't you? Do you love Joe?'

Lucy shook her head.

'Every time I see him we fight about something, but when I don't see him I want to be there, and I wonder what he's doing. I don't know, I was never in love – I never got that far.'

'Neither did I,' Gemma admitted. 'I thought I liked Guy very much before I knew him, but with what we've gone through maybe neither of us will ever love anyone again. I would like a father for my children but he would have to be very good and quite rich – the possibility isn't great. Who would take me on?'

'Any good man would,' Lucy said, putting an arm around her. 'I do miss Joe.'

She didn't like to say to her sister that she longed to go back to the tower house on the river and spend time with Joe and be a part of his life. If that was love, if wanting to be with somebody so much was really love, then yes, she did love him. But she didn't think Joe would ever love anyone again.

If Angela was alive then was it possible that Joe and Angela could be together? Would she be sorry that she had brought them back together? She didn't think Angela was still in love with Joe, that if a woman was so much in love that she would give herself to a man like that, she would have found him by now – unless she was dead of course. And yes, she would be jealous, yes, she did want Joe to herself, but she wasn't sure that was love. But she had to do the right thing; it was her job as a solicitor. She would not fail in that, first and always.

When she mentioned selling her father's pocket watch to finance a trip to London, Gemma agreed it was the only way Lucy could raise some money. She suggested she should approach their mother the following morning. Lucy was still a little bit scared of her mother; their relationship had never been like her mother's with Gemma. She was worried about what would happen.

She hadn't noticed until now how much weight her mother had lost since her father had died. She was bent over the kitchen range. Her mother had always been quite a big woman but now she was slender, and her hair was thin, it had lost all its colour. Lucy didn't know whether to ask her or not. She hesitated.

'If you've got something to say I'd like to hear it,' her mother said as she turned around.

'I don't know whether I should.'

Her mother looked levelly at her.

'I know now that there are a lot of things my lasses don't tell me – you keep secrets from me because you don't want me to be more hurt – but you know, Lucy, you're a good lass. Since you came back to us you've been so good with your dad and with the bairns and in all sorts of other ways. I thought at one time I would never say it to you, but I am now. You're a good lass and it isn't your fault that things didn't work out. You did what you thought was best for your family and not necessarily for you, and don't think I wasn't aware of it.'

The tears sprang into Lucy's eyes. Her mother had never said such a thing to her.

'Whatever it is, tell me,' her mother urged.

'It's just that I'm trying to help somebody. I need some money to go away for a couple of days. I have nothing and it's important. I know it seems awful but I wondered if I could pawn my dad's watch – or do you think that's a dreadful thing to do?'

Her mother smiled just a little.

'He's dead, what does the watch matter? It's upstairs in my jewellery box, and there's a jade brooch he gave me when we first met. I don't think it's worth a lot, but take that too. We have more important things to think about now than such trivia.'

Lucy kissed her mother quickly.

'Oh, get away with you,' her mother said, and flapped a tea towel at this show of emotion.

Lucy ran upstairs before she could change her own mind and took the watch and the jade brooch. She left the house swiftly so that she wouldn't have to see Gemma or the children. She took the jewellery to the pawnbroker's and borrowed against them. She swore to try to retrieve them. There was enough money to get her to London so that she could stay overnight and come back the following day.

THIRTY-NINE

Edgar decided that he would go and see Lucy on the Saturday morning; it was the first day he didn't have appointments. He had grown to hate days off and most Saturdays he went to the office anyhow. Mr Clarence began making appointments on what was meant to be their day off, and took to going in on Saturdays too.

Edgar paid him and handsomely because Mr Clarence had a wife and also because he couldn't have managed without him. Edgar saw how their life together was disrupted because of his own life and it didn't sit well with him. When he announced that he was not taking any appointments that Saturday Mr Clarence looked relieved. Edgar told him to enjoy his weekend, though he did not think he was going to enjoy it himself.

He had the feeling that the door would be slammed shut in his face when he got to Sandhill, but there was no putting it off. He couldn't wait until Lucy and her family were on the street before he offered to help. He walked swiftly to the house and banged on the door, his heart pounding.

It was a lovely day in Newcastle, cloudless blue sky, though there was a wind coming off the river. Mrs Charlton opened the door herself. That had been Edgar's first concern. Lucy or even her sister would not be as bad as their mother. He reminded himself that he had been too much of a coward to come to Mr Charlton's funeral and he felt ashamed.

'Good morning,' he said, 'I'm sorry to bother you but I wanted to see Lucy.'

Mrs Charlton said, 'She's not here.'

'Is she at the office?'

Mrs Charlton looked patiently at him.

'She doesn't go to the office any more. Now that she has no father she cannot. We are trying to sell the premises.'

'I'm so sorry,' he said.

'Come another day,' she said.

She went to close the door as Edgar said, 'When will she be back?'

He heard a younger voice in the hall and Gemma appeared. She looked stiffly at him.

'Mr Bainbridge, what can we do for you?'

'I was wanting to see Lucy.'

'She's gone away overnight,' Gemma said.

'May I come tomorrow?'

Gemma hesitated.

'It is important,' he said.

Mrs Charlton muttered something under her breath and went back down the hall.

'Gemma, I'm so sorry, I really am. I came here with the intention of offering your sister work. I know it won't make up for the awful things I've done, but I want her to become a solicitor. She worked so hard and I'm sure we could reach

405

an agreement. Would you at least let her know that I came here and what it was about?'

He was going to leave, he even turned around to go, when Gemma stepped back and said, 'Do come in.'

Edgar would have given a lot to get away but she stood back to let him inside. Not wanting to appear rude, against all his instincts he went in.

It was not a poor house, and in many ways it was beautiful. It had been well looked after and was still. There was the smell of lavender polish in the hall and the old furniture added grace and dignity. At least none of this had been sold. He couldn't imagine having to sell his house, or even the business premises which had been his father's and his father before him, but he thought that it would come to this for them if somebody didn't help.

There was the smell of baking. When he got into the kitchen Mrs Charlton had taken a batch of scones from the oven. The children sat at the table and she was halving and buttering them. Edgar watched the butter run golden across the top of the halved scones, and he longed for one.

'If you sit at the table,' Mrs Charlton said, all good manners and sour face, 'I'll pour you some tea.'

He demolished three cups of tea and three scones thick with butter and homemade raspberry jam before he remembered his manners. The twins made a mess, with raspberry jam all over their faces and hands, but nobody took any notice and they were enjoying themselves.

'Mr Bainbridge has come to offer Lucy her job back,' Gemma told her mother. Mrs Charlton's face filled with relief and her eyes with tears so that she looked down as though her scone held something more fascinating than melting butter.

When they had finished eating Gemma got the twins down from the table. She said she was sorry to be inhospitable but she had promised to take the twins to the park. She told him she was sure that if Mr Charlton came at the beginning of the week Lucy would be here to talk to him.

'She'll be home late tomorrow,' Gemma said.

Edgar thanked Mrs Charlton for the scones and tea and made to say his goodbyes. The twins didn't want to put on their coats and since Gemma was struggling with them in the hall, her mother still in the kitchen, he ended up helping her. The idea of leaving and going back to his empty Saturday in Durham made him feel desperate.

Outside, both children in their coats and leaping about, he saw how tired Gemma looked, the lines on her face that shouldn't be there at her age. She was weary. He guessed that often Lucy was there to help.

'Perhaps I could come with you to the park,' he said.

He remembered the day he'd spent with them in the park, before he and Lucy had been due to marry, and she didn't say no so they set off. The children skipped along, excited. Since it was uphill they did not wander because it was steep and hard work for them.

It was a very good park, with a boating lake and lots of swings and roundabouts. There were other children playing as well as dogs chasing balls and running about.

Edgar and Gemma each pushed a child on a swing. He thought that perhaps she couldn't have managed without him, and that made him feel good.

They tried to imitate Gemma and called him, 'Mr Bainby,' and it became a chant whenever he stopped pushing the swing.

They screamed and cried then because they both wanted him to push their swing. It made Gemma smile and he thought she was so beautiful – she looked ten years younger when she smiled.

On the way back the little girl fell asleep so he carried her. It was a strange feeling. He immediately wanted to protect her. She smelled young and good and she huddled in against his shoulder and the little boy cried because he wanted Edgar to lift him up too.

Gemma said Mr Bainbridge could only carry one child at once and she couldn't carry him at all so he would have to walk. So he did and he stopped crying when Edgar clutched his hand. At least it was downhill all the way.

Edgar would have left at that point, but Mrs Charlton opened the door and ushered him inside and told him that he couldn't go all the way back to Durham with nothing in his stomach. She made it sound as though his journey was as far as Edinburgh, but Edgar didn't mind since the table was laid for tea.

There were sandwiches and cakes, pink and white and chocolate, light and delicious. The family ate together, the twins too. It was fun.

Afterwards Gemma offered to read, but the little boy took the book to Edgar and ordered him to read it. Like the time before when he had read to them, they believed every word, looking hard at each picture and holding their breath as the pages were turned. Edgar read three picture books to them before they were tired and Gemma announced that they must go to bed.

They didn't want to, but she insisted, telling them they must bid Mr Bainbridge goodnight. They were only used to people they knew well, he thought, because each of them came and put their arms around him and kissed his cheek before they went off upstairs. He said goodnight to them and goodbye to Gemma and after that he thanked Mrs Charlton for his lovely day.

'Children are such a blessing when everything goes wrong,' she said.

'You will tell Lucy that I will come back on Monday and that it would be good to see her back in Durham at her desk?'

Mrs Charlton didn't seem too impressed with this and merely nodded and saw him out.

All the way home on the train Edgar thought that he had truly had a lovely day, he was not just being polite with Mrs Charlton. He was the lonelier for it when he trudged down the hill from the station and made his way home.

Joe tried not to think about what Lucy proposed to do. He couldn't put it out of his mind and made so many mistakes that afternoon that Mr Palmer asked him if he felt all right. When he said he wasn't sure Mr Palmer told him to go home and get some rest, he had been doing far too much for far too long. For once Joe took his advice.

The Misses Slaters were out somewhere and he and Frederick sat in the garden because the sun was out. He picked out a letter from his father to read. There were only two left.

Reading the letters always made his hands shake and this one was no different.

Dear Joe,

When I woke up this morning I didn't recognize where I was or myself. It was dark and I was lying on the pavement. I was filthy. People coming past stepped onto the road to avoid me. I just hoped that no one recognized me.

I had no money on me – I think I must have got rid of it all, unless somebody robbed me – and I was so tired that I could hardly get up so I shuffled to where the stone wall would hold me. There I sat as people went by, many of them avoiding even looking in my direction. I fell asleep more than once and the day got through until the light was fading and then a gentleman passing tossed a few coins in my direction. He obviously thought I was a vagrant. I was so ashamed of myself but it enabled me to get into a cab. I had to pay more than I should have in order to persuade the cabbie to take me. It was everything I had but I didn't care.

He looked hard at me when he put me down and watched me go in at my own front door. I have never been so horrified at my own behaviour. I don't remember the last time I had a coherent thought. My best times now are when I'm out of my mind in some way – it's the only way I know to cope.

The house is empty but for a few sticks of furniture, my chair which I always loved so much and my bed – but mostly I don't even stagger up there. I only go out because I have no drink and nothing else which I need daily. I have played cards and lost and won. I don't do that any more – I don't retain sufficient of my mind to do so. Now I go to see friends, make merry and they give me money. I tell myself I won't do it and then I do or I take anything I can find to the pawnbrokers – even things which belonged to others which I purloined under guise of friendship. I have so few friends left now. Who can blame them?

I have found friends in what other people would call opium dens. Can I sink lower? It helps me to forget who I am, who I have been and all the wrong things that I have done. It makes me think that your mother did not leave me, that I did not make her go, that we were a family. We never were. She saw me for what I was and it was not pretty and so she left as people do. It doesn't matter how they leave, once they are gone you are lost and all that you can do is to pretend. I can convince myself of anything when I am lying there and the Orientals have supplied my needs. I feel no shame, I feel no urgency. All I am is here. It doesn't matter what I did or what I might do or even how I am now. I am right, I am wonderful, I am the best.

Your loving father,
John.

FORTY

By the time Lucy got to London it was afternoon and she was nervous. She couldn't bear to think that Lady Toddington would not be there. She knew people like that went to various things in the year, boating and musical venues and to stay at their friends' houses in the country and she just prayed that Lady Toddington would be at home. That was all she wanted, that and a short audience with the woman.

She made herself not run, though she was anxious. She hurried along the wide London street until she came to the imposing house where sir Felix and Lady Toddington had their home. She could feel, almost hear, her heart thudding after she rapped on the knocker with gloved hands and waited a lifetime until the door opened.

She expected a man but it was in fact a small, very young maid. Lucy gave her name and enquired and the girl asked her to step into the hall. There she was left, not seeing anything, worrying that the woman was not at home or would say that she was not at home to such people. Why would she see Lucy? Why would she bother?

Eventually the girl came back, smiling and ushering her forward into the sitting room. Lady Toddington came to

Lucy with a swish of expensive skirts and a small degree of curiosity in her eyes.

'Why, Miss Charlton. Whatever are you doing in London? Do come in and sit down. Would you like some tea?'

Ten minutes ago Lucy had been desperate for tea. Now she couldn't have swallowed anything.

'It's very good of you to receive me,' she said in a rush. 'I thought you might not be at home or you might be busy or . . .'

Lady Toddington sent the small maid for tea and cake. She was so normal that Lucy felt relieved. She was not going to be thrown out straight away.

Lady Toddington said to her, 'If I can help I would like to very much, but I can't imagine what you're doing here.' Her smile was polite but her eyes were dismissive, Lucy thought.

'It's quite simple,' Lucy said, trying to look straight at her and finding it difficult. 'I saw you the other day at the station in Newcastle.' She stopped there; she thought it was her lawyer's training.

Lady Toddington tried to alter her expression but Lucy saw the surprise, the horror, the telltale signs that she had been right. Lucy's heart did plummeting things inside her.

'It was you,' Lucy said, before her quarry could recover. 'You are unmistakable. Please don't deny it.'

Lady Toddington bowed her head. She sat in silence for so long that Lucy willed her to speak.

'You're right,' she said, 'of course. And this made you come to London?'

'I think you went there with a specific purpose, and I think that purpose was something to do with Joe Hardy.'

She watched the other woman's expression harden.

'I was there visiting friends and it had nothing whatsoever to do with that man,' she said.

'Your daughter loved him.'

'That was a very long time ago.'

'He doesn't think so. He has spent a great deal of time looking for her and ever since grieving over what he did. Do you want it to ruin the rest of his life?'

'I don't care,' Lady Toddington said. 'He is no concern of mine or my husband's. I would like you to leave.'

'Joe loves her. He can never go forward with his life the way that things are and I think that if your daughter died then he deserves to know that if nothing else.'

There was silence. Lucy expected Lady Toddington to pull the bell and the little maid would come back and see her swiftly across the hall and out into the street. There would be nothing more and she would burst into tears of frustration and run back to Durham. But this didn't happen.

'He deserves to know if she is still alive, surely. You know, don't you?' Lucy prompted.

'He deserves nothing but what he can get. He treated my daughter as other men treat prostitutes.'

'There wouldn't be any prostitutes if men had not constructed society to suit themselves,' Lucy said, 'and anyway, I think you're wrong. Joe loves her. Yes, he behaved badly, but it was excusable, surely.'

'It was nothing of the kind,' Lady Toddington said.

'Did she play no part in it, is that what you're saying? Because I don't believe for a second that he had to force her into anything. Are you telling me she had no will?'

'She was very young.'

'And sheltered? Is that the excuse? That you treated her so that she wouldn't grow up and take responsibility for her actions.'

Lady Toddington eyed her.

'You are a very good lawyer, Miss Charlton, and a very rude woman.'

'And you, Lady Toddington, have sentenced a young man who fought long and hard for his country to a lifetime of regret because he loved a woman too much.'

'You care for him?' the other woman said.

'He's the most decent man I ever met.' Lucy sat forward and told Lady Toddington about how Joe had behaved when the Formby house was on fire. She said what he had done for Mrs Formby and Tilda and Clay and the Misses Slaters and how kind he had been to her.

Then she told her about finding Margaret Hardy's grave. That was when Lady Toddington broke down and began to cry. Lucy didn't know whether to be pleased or horrified at what she had done. She sat and waited until the tears stopped and her hostess dried her eyes. The maid had brought in tea long since and they had not touched it; Lady Toddington had listened so very carefully to Lucy.

'It all began a very long time ago,' Lady Toddington said, not looking at anything as far as Lucy could judge. 'Joe's mother was my best friend. She meant a great deal to me, but she was so unconventional that she was not accepted, and her not being accepted made her husband angry. She was such a northerner, you know, and she had a thick accent, at least to us and she . . . she saw things that other people did not so that she was called 'witch'. Though I knew the whole thing was ridiculous there was only so much I could do to help. She didn't care for parties or for any of the things which we were meant to do so she did not endear herself to other people. She was too strange. I loved her for that, she was so different, such a lovely woman and clever too. That wasn't looked on with favour either. She had a dry wit and she always made me laugh. We spent many happy afternoons at her home when the children were small. We used to hide in the tiny garden there where she grew roses. We would drink champagne in the sunshine and it was perfect – but her husband soon grew to dislike her.

'When Joe was born she wanted to spend her time with him but that isn't how London society operates. You don't take your children with you, you don't . . .' Lady Toddington blushed, '. . . nurture them yourself, and she wanted to and he wouldn't let her. It was so easy to see both points of view. I don't know why he married her except that she was very beautiful. Joe looks like her. She was dark and had flashing eyes. She was tall but with a gorgeous figure – all the men wanted her. They didn't care for her voice, but they wanted her body.'

Lady Toddington stumbled here and passed a hand across her eyes.

'Margaret was not of our kind – she was a wild creature of the north and he tried to tame her. I know it sounds ridiculous but he did. He wanted her so much but not as she was. Why do people capture other people and try to change them? I don't understand it.' Lady Toddington stopped there.

'So she ran away?' Lucy prompted.

'She couldn't bear it any more. She wanted to take her baby north and give it all up, but he wouldn't let her. He made her leave without the child. I thought it was cruel, and I didn't know how bad things were until she left without her boy. How could any woman not stay with her child? Though I think she would have died if she had stayed here.'

'So she went north and you helped her?'

'Nobody knew, not even my husband. He still doesn't. Joe's father told everyone that she had died. I could have killed him. Now that I'm older I understand better. He was a proud man with a long history and he couldn't be seen to be bettered by a woman, so I gave Margaret money and she went north to Durham. I used to go and see her quite often.

'Her father's family had owned the tower house for centuries and gave the place to her. I had fun setting it up for her. I kept her all that time – I had plenty of money. She hated that but there was nothing we could do about it, for she was so conspicuous – everywhere she went men looked at her. So she retired as though she had gone into a convent except that I used to go and we had some fun. My husband is very wealthy and he never asked me what I did with my money. I had my own money of course, he made certain of that, so we didn't stint ourselves. Sometimes we used to go other places and nobody ever knew – even abroad from time to time. She was happy to, so long as the cats were fed and I made sure someone was paid to do that. You can pay for almost anything you know. Money is the most useful commodity of all.

'In some ways she had such a difficult time there. She pined for her child; she wanted him so much. I used to tell her all about his life – well, the bits I thought she could stand. He was her only child and she knew he would grow up thinking she was dead, knowing nothing of her, but I couldn't do anything other than to shield her. I came to love the tower house. When you talk about it I'm taken back there. It didn't occur to me that she would leave the place to her son. Why would she? It was such a shock when she died and I knew that I could never go there again. I could not tell anyone about what had happened. I grieved for her alone, since her father had long since lost his wits and nobody else cared.'

'You knew him?'

'Yes, we spent time with him. They grew very fond of one another.'

Lucy told her about Mr Firbank – how Joe had gone to see him in Gateshead and how upset he was when the old man died.

'And your daughter?' Lucy asked.

Lady Toddington shook her head and brushed a few tears away.

'I hated Joe Hardy for what he did to my child. He destroyed her life.'

'Did he?' Lucy said, 'or did you in fact alter it?'

'I had to,' Lady Toddington said. 'Her father, like most men, blamed her. As though Joe Hardy had barely been there. My God, men! My husband treated her as I wouldn't have treated a dog or a horse so I got her out of there. I sent her to Margaret.'

'I thought as much,' Lucy said. 'Does she believe that Joe died in the war?'

'I wouldn't do such a thing to her. I didn't ever tell her any lies, but she had enough to cope with having his child without him.'

'So she knows he didn't die in the war?'

Lady Toddington said nothing more and in the end Lucy prompted her.

'She knew from the beginning, didn't she?'

'Yes, she knew.'

'And that didn't prompt her to go to him?'

'She didn't want him by then.'

'Even though she knew what he was going through? Doesn't that strike you as cruel?'

'It was not my decision to make.'

'There was another man?' Lucy said.

Lady Toddington hesitated, but she nodded in the end and took a particular interest in the embroidered skirt of her dress.

'She was rescued, if you like. She was lucky. She was most concerned about keeping her child and we couldn't see a way round it. Joe Hardy had disgraced them both and his father had impoverished him. He had nothing to offer her. I'm sorry if you think I was unjust, but my daughter and her child had to come first. I couldn't like Joe after what he did. The world would blame her and not him, but I always blamed him for what happened. He could have had so much and he threw it all away for a weekend.'

'Don't people do that in war?'

'Do they? I suppose if they have no courage, no principles then they would.'

'How long would you have gone on punishing him for it? He didn't give up, you see. I think he still envisages a life with Angela, he still thinks that she will come back to him.'

'I didn't care what happened to him. His behaviour can never be excused. He almost destroyed my daughter's life – something too many men have done to too many women.'

'So where is your daughter now?' Lucy's heart was thudding again.

Lady Toddington didn't reply.

'If you don't tell me I will go back and tell Joe what I know – that Angela is alive, that you and she have held him to account all this time. He will search for her around Newcastle and he will find her in the end. All this time she has been within a stone's throw of where Joe is and she never once gave him the chance to redeem himself.'

Lady Toddington said nothing.

'You must have made certain she was safe and that she had a good life, otherwise surely you would have helped her to get back to Joe. Is she married? Did you and Margaret and her friends in Northumberland introduce her to someone else whom the Firbanks knew, perhaps? You must have done. A woman alone with a child is not accepted anywhere unless she has very good connections.'

Lady Toddington still didn't reply.

'You took her out of Joe's life,' Lucy accused her. 'You put her beyond his reach. He did everything he could to find her. Surely you could stop blaming him?'

Lady Toddington considered this for several seconds, which seemed to Lucy like several weeks. Then she looked up and held Lucy's gaze.

'She lives between Newcastle and Hexham on a farm. She is married with two children,' Lady Toddington said.

The last letter from his father was the one which Joe didn't want to read. In the end he made himself.

Angela has gone. I don't understand what is happening. Her father came here and called me worse names than I can remember anyone ever having done before, as though her going was my fault. He wouldn't tell me why, only that it was because of you and that you would not be allowed to marry her. It's true that we never liked one another, but if he had even offered a crumb of comfort it might have helped. As it is there is nothing left. I have talked to Mr Barrington. If you ever come home he will help you to sort things out, but I can do no more, stand no more.

I'm so empty now, I can't see beyond the next few seconds. I haven't the energy to go out in search of something to take my mind beyond the horrors which enfold me. I don't even know if you're still alive. I know you should be, I hope you are, but so many men have died even since the war ended – over silly things, in awful ways.

I don't think that you and Angela will be married now. It was the only thing I hoped for. Forgive me, Joe, for not having been the father you must have hoped I would be. We did have some fun, didn't we? I'm afraid I wasn't a good husband or a good father. I wonder if any man ever thinks he is. I hope you live. I hope you come back some day and find what you are looking for in life. I hope that you get what you want.

Your loving father,
John

There was at the bottom of the pile another letter, but written in a different hand, on different paper. Joe couldn't stand any more. He put it back, let it wait for another time and another mood.

Lucy went back on the train the next day. As she watched the endless fields go past she wondered how on earth she would tell Joe that the love of his life was alive and well; that she was living close by and cared nothing for what he was going through and would go through in the future. Lucy didn't want to tell him, but there was no hope for him and it was better that he should know than to go on believing either that Angela was dead or that she somehow still cared for him.

It took her all afternoon to debate this with herself. In the end it was nothing to do with anything other than instinct which made her get off the train at Durham when she longed to go home to Newcastle. She made her weary way to Mr Palmer's garage. It was late, and she half thought she would have to go to the tower house and she didn't want to go there. She couldn't stand the idea of trying to explain herself away to the Misses Slaters and to be nice to Joe before getting him to herself – then what would she say?

So she was glad and worried when she saw the light on. She knew that it was Joe, that he was sitting at the back of the garage, in the little office, devising ways of bringing cars to people he thought might buy them.

She stood outside for a long time but eventually she made herself go in. He looked up and frowned in the lamplight.

'Lucy, what are you doing here?' Then he understood and said, 'What the hell are you doing?'

Lucy came forward.

'I went to London,' she said.

Joe shook his head. He looked back at the desk and then at her.

'What did you do that for?' he said.

'You know why I did it.'

'You had no right.'

'Yes, I did. You have been unhappy for as long as I have known you and even though you think this work will fill your life, it won't. Work never does. We pretend because perhaps it's all we have but we need people to fill our lives.'

'That's lovely,' Joe said, looking at her so straight that she wavered. 'So what did you discover?'

And that was when she lost her voice. She shook her head.

'Well, come on then – what was the result of your interference?'

He was not quite glaring at her, his dark eyes lit with anger but controlled, waiting. She wasn't afraid of him, that was the first thing. She thought she would have been, but Joe was patient, even like this. He could be trusted, though it was the first time she had put herself into a difficult situation with a man that she could not see the way out of. Even in London, in Joe's spacious bedroom, she had not felt as safe as she felt now and yet he was angrier than she had ever seen him. He was on his feet too now and he was a lot bigger than she was, but still she held her ground and didn't even feel like budging. This was too important to Joe's happiness for her to let it go. He had done too much for other people for her not to stand up for him even against himself now.

She looked him straight in the eyes.

'Angela is alive, living in the north here. She is married and has two children.'

Joe stood there for so long, without saying anything or moving, that Lucy worried. She didn't flinch, she didn't move back. She stood as if her feet were glued to the floor. She felt so bad. She wished she had not gone to London. She wished that they had never met.

'Go away,' he said finally in a very hoarse voice without looking at her.

'Joe—'

'Please, just go away.'

Lucy began to feel the tears fill her eyes and although she tried to ignore them they coursed down her cheeks so fast that they tickled her neck. She tried to breathe very carefully so that Joe wouldn't know – he wasn't looking at her so he might not have been aware of it – and then she turned and walked out of his office. She got herself along the street and to the end of it before she let go of the sobs that threatened to strangle her throat.

It was very late indeed when she got back to Newcastle but Gemma had waited up for her. Her sister, with a big blanket around her shoulders, was there in the hall to welcome Lucy when she more or less fell in at the door.

'I got it wrong. I shouldn't have gone there. I made his life worse than it was. The girl he loves is here and she has a husband and two children and I had no right to do this to him. What was I thinking? Am I so stupid, so vain, that I thought I could make things better?'

'No,' Gemma said, 'it's just love.'

Lucy wept in her sister's arms.

'He'll never forgive me. What a mess I have made. I wish I had never gone. I wish I had never met him.'

Gemma took her to bed and lay down with her. When Lucy had cried herself to sleep Gemma kept her arms around her in case something more should come out of the shadows and haunt her.

Halfway through Monday morning there was a knocking on the door. Lucy was expecting Edgar; Gemma had told her about his visit. She hadn't known what to think. She didn't want to go back to Durham to work – she didn't think her sister could manage the two children and her mother and everything else – but perhaps there was no alternative. She braced herself as she opened the door. She had expected to see a very penitent man, since they had not met after he had jilted her.

To Lucy's surprise Edgar smiled just a little and then said, 'I'm so very sorry. Will you ever forgive me?'

She let him in. She felt nothing for him. Nothing at all other than glad that he was apparently offering her a job.

She was intending to step out and for them to go to the office and talk there. She was not prepared for the two screaming banshees who ran shrieking down the hall towards Edgar, yelling, 'Mr Bainby! Mr Bainby!' in a way which amazed her. They grabbed him by the legs as though he was trying to get away and he lifted them both into his arms. They shrieked and grabbed him and Edgar laughed.

Lucy couldn't believe it. Gemma rescued him.

'They think they are going to the park because you are here,' she said.

'Are you going later? Could I come with you?' he said and she assured him that they would be going in the afternoon. He said he would be back long before then.

Gemma took the struggling twins from him and Lucy put on her coat. She and Edgar walked to the office.

'I didn't know you liked children,' she said.

'I never knew any before.'

'You went to the park?'

'Boys were sailing boats and the twins love the swings,' he said. 'It was fun.'

Lucy said nothing. As they went along he told her that he wanted her to take her job back and more, that he didn't want her to sell the premises here. When he said that in time it would be Bainbridge, Featherstone and Charlton, Lucy stopped and put both hands over her face.

'Oh dear,' Edgar said, 'I didn't think it was going to have that effect.'

'I'm sorry,' she said, standing back and taking her hands from her face. Her cheeks were so pale that Edgar thought she was going to pass out. 'I just didn't expect it and I'm rather tired. It's everything I ever wanted since I was a little girl.'

'Yes, I suspected it was,' he said dryly.

She managed to look at him.

'You think I wanted to marry you because of it.'

'No – I think we were muddled, both of us, but I ought to have done much better. I haven't stopped being sorry.'

'But not regretting not marrying me. I haven't regretted it either,' she said, 'it would have been quite wrong.'

426

As they walked the rest of the way to the office Lucy thought about her father. It occurred to her for the first time that he would be proud of her now. She couldn't wait for the day when the brass plaque outside his office read Bainbridge, Featherstone and Charlton.

Edgar waited for the visit to the park as impatiently as though he had been a child. The sun was shining as the children skipped and ran and kept coming back to their mother. Once they got there he was on duty on the swings. Gemma sat and laughed and watched. It was mid-afternoon by the time the children tired and were taken back for a little peace and quiet. They had run around so much that they fell asleep on the old sofa in the sitting room while the sun poured in at the windows.

Gemma got up to go and see what her mother was planning for tea but he stopped her with just a slight touch on her arm.

'Don't go just yet,' he said.

Surprised, she sat back down again.

'I am aware that your first marriage was not as happy as it ought to have been.'

Gemma shook her head.

'It isn't something I want to talk about.'

'No, I understand that. It's just that I . . . well, I wondered if it was something you might ever consider again.'

She was staring at him. She looked and sounded so like Lucy when she said baldly, 'You want to marry me?' as though the skies would fall first.

'I know.' Edgar smiled ruefully against himself. 'My record isn't very good and especially having left your sister at the altar – it might put you off just a little – but I feel as if I had the right idea with the wrong sister. I very much want to marry you. I adore you and I love your children. I can't live without you. I'm lonely and bored and I'm turning out to be incredibly selfish so if you want to end my suffering please at least think about it, will you?'

Gemma was still staring. He wasn't sure that she had heard a single word he had said.

'You want to take on the twins? Have you completely lost your mind?' Gemma laughed as though she couldn't take any of it in.

'Yes, I do.' Edgar pulled a face. 'And your mother of course if she wishes to live with us. I don't think Lucy would consider such a thing, at least I hope not.' He wished he would shut up with the silly banter, but he couldn't think of anything sensible to say and silence would be unendurable. 'It did occur to me that perhaps if you thought it a good idea I could come here and live with you and run the Newcastle office when we get that far and Lucy could run the Durham office. I'm getting ahead of myself – I don't want you to marry me for her sake or for the children or for your mother, especially your mother. I love you, Gemma. Will you marry me?'

At that moment the door opened and Lucy came in with teacups and saucers and plates on a tray. It was, Edgar thought, the most awful timing. Gemma got up to help – she went off to the kitchen to fetch cake and the teapot and other things – so he shot out of the room after her.

She heard him and turned around in the dimness of the hall.

'Will you? Please?' he said.

Gemma started to laugh. Even through the gloom of the hall he could see her beautiful eyes shining. She didn't say that she would straight away and Edgar didn't know how to breathe for so long that he thought he might expire.

'I think I had better,' she said after what seemed like several years. 'I'm sure my mother would prefer one of us to be married to you. She has been so very disappointed so far.' She came to him then and kissed him very lightly on the lips.

She got hold of his hand and raised her voice and said as they broke into the light of the kitchen, 'Mother, we've got something to tell you.'

Her mother looked up at her with a worried expression and more than suspiciously at Edgar. He had never felt quite so stupid as he tried to explain that he wanted to marry Gemma. Mrs Charlton studied him for a very long time, then she said, 'Eh, lad, make your mind up, will you?'

Forty-one

It was a week before Joe appeared at their door. It was Gemma who opened the door.

She looked him up and down as if he were a tradesman and said, 'What do you want?'

'To see Lucy. May I come in?'

'She doesn't want to see you.'

'I know she doesn't, and I don't really want to be here either – all I want is an address. Surely I can have that.'

Gemma saw him into the nearest room. It stank of damp. He couldn't think what to say and then he heard the footsteps and turned around. Lucy was even skinner than she had been and he thought, not for the first time, what it must have cost her to go to London to try to sort this out. She was so thin she was almost transparent. Her cheeks were sunken and her eyes were dull so that he could scarcely tell what colour they were.

'What is it?' she said.

'You know what it is. I want the address so that I can go and see Angela.'

She looked down.

'Of course you can have it,' she said.

'Lucy, I'm sorry. I got a shock. I didn't mean to speak to you that way. I know that you were right to go to London and make things clearer, but I found it so difficult. I don't think I wanted the truth because I long since suspected it – but you knew what was best for me, you knew better than I did. I just couldn't believe that she didn't want me. I thought that somehow after all this time I was going to get her back, and I know now that I was pretending to myself. My common sense should have told me that if she had died somebody would have informed me, somebody would know where she was – I should have understood that but I didn't. I didn't want to go forward; I didn't want to stop believing that I would get her back. I've always loved her so very much – I can't take in that she would do this to me, that she hates me so. I want to see her now and ask whether she'll forgive me for what I did.'

'She was there too. I won't have it that way.'

Joe didn't understand.

'What do you mean?'

Lucy couldn't think that she was saying this, but she had felt angry about it ever since she had begun to know what Lady Toddington and her daughter and even Joe's mother had kept from him.

'I mean that if women want to be independent and accepted by men as adults and their equals that they must stop blaming them, that they must accept their share of what is done. Angela and her mother had no reason to treat you like that. You didn't force her, you didn't compel her to go to wherever you went for the weekend. Presumably she went there of her own free will and gave herself to you as you did to her. So it's not right for her to have done this to you. I don't care who thinks what. I think her father was to blame for trying to get rid of the child, to pretend that nothing had happened, to sweep it all under the carpet, but for you to . . . to ruin your life over such a woman, well I don't think it's right.'

Joe was silenced.

Lucy said, 'She's living at a farm just this side of Hexham. It's called Castle Tower. Quite in keeping, don't you think, everything considered?'

Joe stood there for a very long time.

As Lucy turned to leave the room he said softly, 'Come with me, will you, please?'

'I don't—'

'I've got a car outside. You so obviously know so much more than I do and you've tried so hard to help me. Get your coat or your wrap or whatever you have.'

She went off into the depths of the house, though was not gone long. She brought back with her a thin wrap which would not have kept a child warm. The weather had turned grim and the rain was blowing sideways.

She got into the car and pulled the black scarf from her hair. It was only then that he remembered in the full light of the day how fiery her hair was, how pale her skin, how dark her eyes, how white her knuckles, how thin her body and how she sat forward as though even now she was willing to take on what would happen and he knew how brave that was.

He drove the car as if cattle were stampeding before it. He kept at the road as it twisted and turned, beyond the city, over the hills and into the wilds of Northumberland. He told himself that he couldn't stand any more, that after this he would go back to London. To hell with them all. Mr Eve had said things were better in the south. It was where he belonged, he knew that now.

He pushed the car forward and the roads narrowed. They came to a farmhouse, a lovely stone building with other neat stone buildings around it and long, wide Northumbrian fields.

There he halted the car and they got out. There was not a person to be seen, but as they watched the people inside must have heard the car, because the front door opened, there was a happy sound and children spilled out from it. It was almost an insult, Lucy thought, for Joe.

First of all a little boy, screaming and crying and falling, almost but not quite walking. Then a little girl, with blonde curls dancing up the path and looking back at her mother and laughing. She was such a beautiful child. Lucy knew in that instant that she was Joe's. She had his black eyes and his creamy northern skin. She would be a beautiful woman one day, as her grandmother had been.

The woman was tall and blonde and so lovely that Lucy drew in her breath. No wonder Joe had fallen in love with such a creature. She didn't come any closer, but she beckoned.

'Joe,' she said finally as though they had met just a day since. 'Would you like to come inside?'

Joe's gaze was riveted on the little girl, but Lucy's on the woman. She was heavily pregnant. It was so crudely cruel to Joe that Lucy wanted to grab his arm and run away. She didn't know how he was still breathing.

'What is she called?'

'This is Dinah. Dinah, this is Mr Joe Hardy.' She looked at Lucy.

'I'm Lucy Charlton.'

'And Miss Charlton. Say hello.'

The girl was not shy. She gazed up at them from Joe's almost black eyes and said, 'How do you do?'

Joe said the same and took her hand and spoke softly to the little girl. Then another woman called from the house and the little girl ran away with the boy close behind.

Lucy and Joe followed Angela into the house and there she ushered them into a comfortable sitting room. It was the kind of room Lucy loved. It had bookshelves full of books, some of them quite old. A big log fire burned in the grate; the room was shabby, untidy, very lived-in. The armchairs were old leather and there were little side-tables. Lucy could imagine the couple sitting there when the children were gone to bed. It was a happy house. A house that had been there for a very long time, as the tower house had been, and it held memories and the warmth of people and of grief. It held them all as houses did.

'My mother wrote to me. She told me that you, Miss Charlton, had been to see her and to expect a visit probably from both of you very soon – so I'm not surprised to see you.' Her smile was serene. Lucy had a great desire to hit her and knock it off her face. Angela looked at Joe.

'I'm sorry that I didn't help you or get in touch; it was out of respect for my husband. He took on your child. I can't see any other man who might have done it.'

'Is he here?' Joe said.

'Yes, he's in the barn, I think, and will come inside. He knows who you are. I kept nothing from him. I have a very good life here, one I prefer to anything I found in London. What a dreadful life it was, where people cared so much for things that didn't matter. Even my father wouldn't forgive me. I think you might say that your mother influenced me. She was a lovely woman, Joe, and so is my mother. They did their best. They didn't mean to deceive you, but they were afraid that people might know where I was and what had happened. It was best this way. I hope you understand.'

Joe said nothing. Lucy wanted to shout at her for what she had done to him but she couldn't. There was too much at stake here. Angela had Joe's child and but for her goodwill he might never see the little girl again.

At that moment the door opened and a tall dark man, much older than they were, came into the room. He came across and shook Joe's hand and Lucy's too. Angela introduced him as Erik Cuthbertson. It was a good northern name, Lucy thought. The man had clear eyes and a steady gaze and the lovely lilting burr of Northumberland in his voice.

'I'm sorry it has been such a long and difficult road for you, Mr Hardy,' he said. Lucy was amazed at his generosity and yet she hated him. 'We were afraid to do anything at first. I was so worried that Angela's family would find out, especially her father. I know how he treated her and you and until we were established here we didn't want to be found. I'm sorry it cost you so dearly. Since we heard from Angela's mother we have sat down here . . .' Mr Cuthbertson nodded towards the armchairs at either side of the fire, '. . . and talked about this and we would like you to be part of Dinah's life. She is your child and we want her to know you. You don't live so very far away. I don't know if we can be friends because this is a very difficult thing to sort out but as long as you accept that Angela is my wife I daresay we could let you see Dinah often.'

Joe had gone very pale. He said nothing. What would he have said? Lucy thought.

The little girl was brought in before she went to bed and though Joe hung back she was told that Mr Hardy was special to the family. Then, from the safety of her mother's arms, she smiled at him and Joe smiled back. They told her that she would see Joe often in the future and she went on beaming at him from her lovely, light young face.

The little girl went off and Lucy saw how Joe's gaze followed her. She wished things had been different for him. After that there was polite talk and then they left. Neither spoke all the way back to Newcastle. Lucy got out of the car without a word and went inside.

Joe was confused now. He didn't know what to do. His first instinct was to give up his dream of starting a motor factory here in Durham and leaving as soon as he could. He wanted never to see Angela again or her smug husband or her children, but his memory of the little girl kept dragging him back.

He told himself that it was of no consequence, that she would never miss him. She hadn't known him, she wouldn't remember him. Lots of men got by without their children, many of them ran away, so why shouldn't he? Angela's treatment of him made him smart; it was humiliating, as though he didn't matter.

Somehow Erik Cuthbertson's offer had made Joe want to punch him hard in the face. Angela was so beautiful, so fertile. Her small children and her swelling belly were like an insult to him. It made Joe want to burst with frustration that she had married a man so far beneath him, a farmer. Joe was ashamed of himself. She looked happy. He didn't think he could stand much more of that happiness.

Lucy wished in some ways that she had not discovered where Angela was. It had made things worse. Joe still loved this woman. She could tell by his face that he did. It didn't matter that she had betrayed him, cared nothing for him, made him take the blame for what had happened to them. No decent woman would do that, she thought, and yet so many of them did. They just didn't think they were to blame for such things, whereas in fact society looked at it the other way round, as though Angela herself were to blame. Angela had so obviously not thought like this. In its way it was admirable but her treatment of Joe was not.

Lucy didn't understand how Angela could marry a man so much older than she was. She understood why she had done it, but for Angela to look at him with love? He was a very nice man, Lucy thought, but he was not Joe. It was only at that moment that Lucy compared herself with Angela and knew that subconsciously she had done so from the moment they had met. With a sinking heart she realized that Joe would never love a woman such as she was.

She and Angela could not have been more different. Lucy knew that she was not beautiful, though she was in many ways attractive – but somebody like Angela could carry the whole world before her. She must have had many suitors when she lived in London. Joe had been lucky to gain her and then unlucky after that. Angela was spoiled. She thought she could have anything and anybody she wanted. Then she had learned otherwise and Joe had borne the brunt of it.

Lucy had thought when she went to London that in a way she was freeing Joe, but she could see now that it was not so. He might go on loving this woman, despite what she had done to him, for the rest of his life. Sometimes people didn't recover from such things and Joe had had so much to recover from. And the worst thing of all somehow was that Lucy knew now how much she loved him, how much she wanted to be with him and that it would not happen. She vowed never to bother him again.

Joe didn't know why he had left the letter he'd found, the letter in a different hand, until now. He could have read it at any time and yet he had carried it around with him as he had carried all the letters. Each time he read one he could feel it in his pocket and think of his father and all the trials of his life. By carrying the letters around with him, his father's unmistakable black flourishing hand stayed with him, and he remembered the content, most of it word for word. During the day, when he wasn't thinking of business, the words were there in his mind, in his father's voice, his very tones. Somehow they helped.

But he knew that the final letter was not written by him and he dreaded opening it because the hand was lighter. It was plain, the envelope so long and narrow, that it scared him. His life kept breaking open again and again, like an onion shedding its skin to the slippery one beneath. This letter felt to him like the very core, the last one, and he carried it around for days because he couldn't bear to open it.

At last, when the night was quiet and he had gone back to the tower house, as the Misses Slaters slept safely above and Frederick and the cats cuddled up by the fireside, he sat down and in the dim light he read.

Dear John,

I know we agreed that we would never get in touch, no matter what happened, but there are one or two things which I wish to say to you.

I did what you wanted me to do – I left in secret and did not make it known so that you could tell all those important influential people whom you care about so much that I was dead.

I think the problem is that we were never suited. We can look coldly back and say that I was so impressed with your lineage, your title, your way of life, that I didn't see you as the man you are, but rather the person I wished to be in love with. I feel so foolish now that I thought it so glamorous, but you were and it was, and I'm sure I'm not the first woman to believe in the fairy tale of Cinderella.

What you saw in me I cannot think. Yes, I am beautiful, but you were used to beautiful women. I was different – I didn't flatter you or agree with you or laugh at your pallid jokes – and you wanted what you could not tame in order to master it.

How stupid we both were. I feel such a failure. I had no notion that I would love our child as much as I love Joe. I love him so much that the only thing I can do is to stay out of his life and yours. I know that you love him. It seems to me that you will make a better parent without me. You don't need me. Any woman would do. If we ever did love one another it has been long since trampled into extinction by disappointed expectations and affection destroyed.

I know that you will do your best for Joe. He was the only good thing to come out of our alliance. I am reconciled to the fact that I will never see him again since you have made my life in London impossible and I have made you so very unhappy.

Try not to speak badly of me to him. We did the best that we could.

I know that a man in your position cannot have a wife who leaves him, so I am giving up both your name and mine. All I have left is the place that I long for beyond anything.

We failed so badly in our attempt at such a trusted institution. To be fair I think such a thing is doomed to fail most of the time. I'm sure that to the Church it seems such a fine idea, to couple people up and have them live narrowly because they see one another gloriously for a brief period. Dear God, how could anything be more unlikely? To enclose people together with their faults and their screaming offspring and different needs and wants.

It would be fine if one were not obliged to live with the other person when the reality has hit them both. This much at least we have achieved! Your life in London seems very shallow to me now. No doubt mine would be boring to you. I have nothing but the tower house and the river and the sounds of the cathedral bells and the snow falling softly against the windows.

Try to forgive me for not being someone you could go on loving and I will do the same for you. At least we made something good, and hopefully Joe will outlive us and go forward. Maybe he will make a better job of his life than we have – or does the next generation just make different mistakes?

I wish you could see what it's like up here when the wind whistles across the Weardale fells. The sheep lean in against the grey stone walls for shelter and folk sit over their fires together. I like to think that some of them want to be there such as we do not.

Maybe we'll be born again and learn how to live out our lives, to hold our child and have love to sustain us when all we had were empty rooms and cold disappointments.

The darkness is clean here where the curlew cries upon the tops at the winter tower house and ghosts flit across the shadows searching for their lost loves.

Perhaps we will meet again and this time we will be together and teach our child how the man and the woman and their baby can form a circle against the world if they have sufficient feeling for one another.

The tower house in Durham is my sanctuary now. I see the seasons. How the wild cherry blossoms cover the lawns in pink, the wild garlic festoons the woods in green and white, the summer when the riverbanks are filled with daisies and the *willowherb is tall and waves purple in the wind. In autumn the red and white currants glisten like jewels against the sinking sun and in winter I stand inside the open door, glad of my refuge and watch the ice breaking up as it flows on down from the hills and dales of the Wear on its way to the sea.*

I leave my child with you. It is my greatest grief but I know that you would have hunted us down had I left with him and he would have known no peace. Look after him, John. He holds my heart.

Perhaps next time we will be kinder to one another.

Margaret

FORTY-TWO

Gemma and Edgar were to be married soon. They were hoping for a fine day, though this being the north the season didn't make any difference. People picnicked on Boxing Day and huddled inside during August. Lucy had with some satisfaction and not a little jealousy watched her sister blossom. She watched also as Edgar lifted them so cleanly out of poverty that it might never have existed.

He was for once tactful, and since it seemed that Emily was definitely going to live in London, he decided to sell the house in Durham. If their mother didn't mind he would move in with them.

Mrs Charlton shed ten years and all possible bad moods in the process, and though Edgar said that they could have a bigger house she didn't want to move. Nobody cared for such trivialities, so they stayed where they were. Edgar put the Durham house on the market – Lucy felt a pang – and then he took on the bills and the repairs. There seemed to be a great deal of money for the general running of the household.

There was no betrothal ring, Gemma had insisted on that, but she had a great many gorgeous clothes, as did the children. Gemma tried to get Lucy through the doors of decent shops, though Lucy said she had not the time.

It was a very small wedding. There were no bridesmaids and no best man. Edgar's sole desire had been that Joe should be invited. Lucy had to stop herself from protesting. She was very often at the Durham office and had not failed to hear the rumours in the city that Joe had won a particularly lucrative deal from Mr Eve to do in England what Henry Ford had done in America. Lucy's opinion was that if Joe wanted to do such things he should go south to do it so that she didn't have to hear any more about it.

Rumour also persisted that Joe might be looking at some place just outside Sunderland for his car factory. If it were true, it would bring many jobs to the region. A lot of people were impressed with this, though Lucy couldn't see why he couldn't go at least as far south as Birmingham so that he couldn't cause any more chaos in her life. She would be happy to be left alone now that she was reaching her life's goal. She was a solicitor. Her name was on the door both in Newcastle and in Durham. She was grateful for that and would ask no more.

The wedding day dawned. It was warm and fair, much to everyone's astonishment. Mrs Charlton tried not to fuss about the meal – it was to be very modest – and they were going back to the house on the river where there would be champagne, courtesy of Edgar (a lot of it for a few people). Mrs Charlton had made a fruitcake and there was a whole salmon, a big piece of beef, some salad and some Jersey potatoes. Together with a chocolate pudding and a lemon pudding she said it must satisfy most people.

It was all set out for them coming back from the church. Gemma had not been happy at the idea of the cathedral, since she had been married there the first time and Lucy had been almost married there, but because it was near to their house and the bishop had been friends with their father they decided to do it anyway. Lucy thought of how the sunshine would fall softly on the stone through the stained-glass windows, blue and red, and they made themselves happy about it.

When they reached the church Joe was just arriving in a rather nice car, Lucy thought, though not knowing what it was, all black and gleaming silver. She could not help noticing how good Joe looked when he got out of it. His suit appeared so expensive that it could only have been made in London. She wasn't sure whether that meant he would be spending most of his time there, but she admired what he looked like. He greeted them affably, kissed the bride on the cheek and shook Edgar's hand.

He spoke to her mother and nodded at Lucy and merely looked at the children who were hiding beside Edgar. She liked the way that Edgar carried them into the church, one either side of him.

It was so casual, the way that they all went in together. The bishop was at the door to greet them and as he turned the choir began to sing. That was his surprise for them. The organ swelled and the children sang. They went inside and the sunshine cast its yellow glow upon the building.

The wedding service was brief and Joe left his car there, walking back with them to the house. There were to be no toasts, no speeches, nothing but champagne and food.

The children ran about outside while the adults took plates of food and sat either in the back garden or at the front where the river ran on regardless. Joe talked to Edgar about the new factory and Gemma was busy with the children. Lucy rearranged the food on the dining-room table and then went outside, beyond the garden down to the river, only to find that Joe followed her with a glass of champagne in either hand.

Lucy found that she must say something to Joe.

'Congratulations. I hear things are going well. You'll be heading back to London?'

'Not at the moment,' Joe said, paying particular interest to the far bank of the Tyne, 'I'm starting up a place in Sunderland. It's useful for transport, but I daresay in time we may move to London or at least have a factory there if things work out.'

'I'm sure they will. Have you see Angela?'

He didn't answer immediately and took so long that she thought he wasn't going to and her heart beat hard.

'Yes,' he said. 'It was more of a shock the second time, I think. A married woman with two children is not the girl I fell in love with. When I got there I couldn't believe I had spent all that time trying to find her when it should have been obvious that she hadn't wanted me right from the first when the situation became so difficult. I just wish she could have brought herself to tell me so that I hadn't gone

446

on believing something which wasn't true. She seems fifteen years older than me now and I don't love her one little bit, especially since she has given Erik Cuthbertson another son.'

'Have you seen Dinah?'

Joe acted as though she were talking to someone else for a few seconds and then he said, 'Yes.'

'And is she well?' Lucy persisted.

'I think she is much too small to understand the concept of her mother not being with her father and I don't want to confuse her or hurt her in any way – so I'm not going to see her any more. She needs two parents together and they have a very good marriage, so—'

He stopped there for a few moments.

'She will have a happy childhood. She's lucky. Perhaps when she's older Angela will tell her, but if she doesn't then – she'll judge it, I expect.'

'And you?'

'I shall be busy bringing motor cars to the masses. The car will change transport forever, I daresay. People will be able to get about and communicate and it will move things on.'

'You should be very pleased with it,' Lucy said.

'I'm still trying to persuade Mr Palmer to take charge of things here so that I can go and set it all up in London.'

'How is Mr Toddington?'

'They had a little boy. I am his godfather.'

'That's lovely, Joe.'

Joe looked straight at her possibly for the first time that day.

'I understand that it is Bainbridge, Featherstone and Charlton.'

Lucy nodded.

'So you have got what you wanted.'

'I'm going to be running the Durham office. Edgar is coming to live with Gemma and my mother and the twins, so he will run my father's office here.'

'Your father would have been very proud of your achievements,' Joe said.

'I do hope so.'

'Well, if you need somewhere to stay in Durham I daresay the Misses Slaters would be glad to have you at the tower house. I'm not really there much any more.'

'Who is walking Frederick then?'

Joe paused.

'Frederick died. He had a heart problem, bless him.'

Lucy stared at him.

'Frederick died?'

Somehow she couldn't believe it. Stupidly, it was just that bit too far. Frederick was always there and she and Joe were always at the tower house.

Lucy stared at him. Joe watched her in dismay.

'But he wasn't very old,' she said.

'No, well, sometimes these things just happen.'

'They shouldn't. Frederick was . . . he was lovely – even the cats liked him and he licked their ears.'

'It's very special when you can get somebody to lick your ears,' Joe said.

'Oh, shut up,' Lucy said. 'Did you have to tell me?'

'I'm sorry. Would you like a handkerchief?'

'No, I damned well wouldn't,' she said and she got up and moved nearer to the river for comfort.

When he followed her she avoided him altogether by turning to look at Gateshead.

'Why don't you just go away, back to your wonderful life and your cars and your brilliant future, and leave us alone? I don't know why you came here today. You didn't even have the decency to refuse.'

'I wanted to see you,' Joe said. 'I behaved so badly last time we met.'

'It was perfectly understandable,' Lucy managed and she found her own handkerchief, tucked in the short sleeve of the dreadful pink dress which Gemma had told her looked wonderful and didn't. 'Why couldn't Frederick be here? Why couldn't just one thing go right? The Misses Slaters must be really upset.'

'They're older than we are. They accept things.'

'Well, I don't. I'm never going to accept anything. Don't you go giving up on Dinah, Joe. You stay with it. She can do with more than one father, you know. I don't think there's a limit on parents. Don't cut her out of your life. She'll love knowing you and though Mr Cuthbertson is a very nice man he is a little bit countrified, you must feel, and she would benefit from the way that you live. You are her father. Don't let anybody stop you.'

'Do you think that next time I see her you might come with me?' Joe said. 'I would feel better about it if you were there.'

'Oh God, Joe. You're always asking me to go to places with you. You always say that and I don't think it makes a ha'porth of difference.'

'You're so wrong about that,' Joe said. 'I need you to be there. I don't seem to be able to do things without you. I give up when you aren't there, pushing me on and telling me what to do.'

'I do not tell you what to do.'

'You tell everybody what to do.'

Lucy thumped him as he moved just a little nearer.

'So will you come with me?' Joe said. 'I think if there were two of us Dinah would be a lot happier.'

'Is she a nice child?'

'No, she's just like all the other women I've ever known. She's impossible.'

'I'm so pleased,' Lucy said.

'Can I get a bit closer?'

'Why?'

'Because.' Joe put both hands around her waist then, very slowly and carefully, in case she didn't like it, she guessed. She was about to tell him not to, but then she didn't. She thought that in spite of Guy she wasn't afraid of Joe. She didn't think she had ever really been afraid of him and that was what made him so dear to her.

'Joe—'

'I do know.'

'You do?'

'I think so. It was Guy, wasn't it?'

'You—'

'It's never going to be like that. Not ever.'

'You shouldn't say such things.'

'I have to now. You see I want to win you, Lucy.'

She laughed just a little but Joe didn't. He looked serious.

'I'm trying to get my promises right. They haven't been too good up to now.'

'I've witnessed a great many of your promises and they aren't that bad,' she said.

'If I promise to be good to you and stay in Durham and live at the tower house, will you marry me?'

Lucy shook her head, but she moved in close and buried her face in his shoulder as she had thought she would not manage to do. She felt safe, though to her own surprise she didn't stay there. She lifted her face and kissed Joe and he kissed her back – but it was very carefully, very gently.

'Where did you get that suit?' she said.

Joe lifted her chin with gentle fingers and cradled her face and smiled at her.

'Don't you approve of my tailoring?'

'Savile Row, already? If you want me around I must tell you now that I have no intention of living in London. I have a job to do here and I've waited a very long time for it.'

'All right,' Joe said. And then he kissed her again and this time she put her arms around his neck and leaned in against him.

Author's Notes

I don't suppose Paddy's taxis were operating in Durham City just after the First World War, but I like to think that they have always been there – the best cabs in town.

There is a church in Gateshead near the river called St Mary's, but the one in this story is my creation.

I want to thank the librarians at Durham Clayport Library. I go there all the time, in search of chat and for the brilliant atmosphere they create and sustain. It is a pleasure for people to visit – a social occasion.

I am proud to have been patron of Books on Wheels in County Durham for several years. This is a service run by Durham County Council where volunteers travel to the homes of people who are unable to get to the libraries. It provides large-print books and audio editions so that they can be enjoyed at home. Until recently, Andy Raine ran the service, along with his excellent team. Andy was one of the most wonderful people I ever met. He died when I was writing this book, only weeks away from his retirement.

Andy was the best of men – kind, dedicated, modest, brilliant and a family man. He is missed by everyone who knew him. We are all the poorer because Andy is gone from us and count ourselves lucky that we did know him and had him on our side, fighting government cuts, so that the people of County Durham could have their books and their libraries to entertain them and bring joy.

ACKNOWLEDGEMENTS

A big bouquet of thank-yous to my wonderful editor, Jo Dickinson, and all the team at Quercus. Also to my agent, Judith Murdoch, who assured me that people did not sit on the riverbanks in Durham outside tower houses drinking chilled Chardonnay in 1920, so I took that bit out. I'm sure she's correct, but we can all dream.

Question & Answer
Elizabeth Gill

Where were you born?
Newcastle upon Tyne

What's you comfort food?
Smelly cheese like Stinking Bishop

Dog or cat?
I'm a country girl. You name the animal I love it
and have probably kept it

What's your favourite holiday read?
Anything by Hilary Mantel or Peter Robinson

What would people be surprised to discover about you?
I can milk a goat

What is your favourite way to travel?
Orient Express

What are you currently listening to?
Bach, Beethoven, Brahms. I love opera. Favourites:
Madam Butterfly, Handle's *Julius Caesar*. Live music is so
inspiring and fills me up and makes me happy

What are you currently reading?
William Boyd, *Waiting for Sunrise* and various books
about women in medicine, especially the first women
doctors in America in the 1860s

If you enjoyed
The Fall and Rise of Lucy Charlton,
please try Elizabeth's other novels in ebook

THE SINGING WINDS

FAR FROM MY FATHER'S HOUSE

UNDER A CLOUD-SOFT SKY

THE ROAD TO BERRY EDGE

SNOW ANGELS

SHELTER FROM THE STORM

ALSO BY *Elizabeth Gill*

Miss Appleby's Academy

'Original and evocative – a born storyteller'
Trisha Ashley

'An enthralling and satisfying novel that will leave you
wanting to read more from this wonderful writer'
Catherine King

'Elizabeth Gill writes with a masterful grasp of conflicts
and passions hidden among men and women of the
wild North Country' Leah Fleming

www.elizabethgill.co.uk
www.quercusbooks.co.uk
@ElizabethRGill

AVAILABLE IN PRINT AND EBOOK